TRIALS OF THE BLOOD - BOOK FOUR

A Place to Change

Becca Lynn Mathis

First paperback edition September 2024

Edited by Christina Dickinson

Cover by Joolz & Jarling – Julie Nicholls & Uwe Jarling

ISBN 978-1-7331626-9-2 (ebook)

ISBN 979-8-9911225-0-4 (paperback)

ISBN 979-8-9911225-1-1 (hardcover)

www.BeccaLynnMathis.com

DEDICATION

Let's see if we can't keep this one short, eh?
To my positively fabulous fans who have been so very
supportive and kind while waiting for this book to make
its way into the world.
To Ben, who helped make this shine, and to Stina, who
made it dazzling.
To Andie and Trishinator, for reading it before it was
really ready to see the world.

To my amazing family, particularly my wonderfully
loving husbeast who makes it possible for me to keep
bringing these stories to life.

And, of course, to Amy Lynn, whose absolutely
invaluable patronage and support makes this author's
heart swell with joy.

In loving memory of Dante.
Fourteen years could have been forever and it still
wouldn't have been long enough.
I will forever miss you, my baby boy.

PROLOGUE

*** (PAIGE) ***

"COULD THIS THING RUN any slower?!"

Why is it that computers just seem to know when someone's in a hurry and turn on their defiant chip that makes them go at a snail's pace instead? Thank God Blair was at lunch and couldn't hear my frustration with this damn machine.

This was the last thing I needed today, even if it is what I get for procrastinating. I should have built these reports already; I'd had plenty of time, despite the office switch. And Blair was going to kill me, or at least give me an earful, if I didn't have them ready for today's meeting with the pack. It'd be the third time this week I delivered something late to her.

God, like learning about werewolves hadn't been weird enough, now we're tracking how people talk about them in online spaces so we can appropriately build a PR campaign for them? It was crazy, but I couldn't argue with the reasoning. Debunking the false information would be crucial to the campaign's success.

I'd traced some of the popular questions online myself, trying to learn what people were finding, which was nothing truly good. There was a lot of talk about mates and mate-bonding and how viciously protective packs were and honestly, a lot of it harkened back to the way we used to think of wild wolves, back before we understood that they were family units.

But I couldn't get lost in that research again. I had a report to rebuild.

"What do you mean 'the file is corrupt and cannot be opened?!' I just used it yesterday!" I clicked around on the computer, trying to think of another way to access the report template, but I'm not exactly the most tech-savvy person on the planet, and I kept running into the same error message. "Uuugh!"

A headache started to press at my temples as I stared blankly at the screen, my hands clasped behind my neck. The only thing to do now was completely rebuild the damn thing from scratch. Well, mostly from scratch. At least I had a copy of last week's reports to look at. With a deep breath, I took a sip of my coffee, opened a new file, and got to work. I had just forty five minutes to get well over an hour's worth of work done.

Dammit.

My phone rang, making my eyebrow twitch at its sudden sharpness.

Double dammit!

I picked up the handset and turned on my customer service voice. "Eclipse Media, this is Paige."

A male voice answered me. "Hi Paige, Eric asked me to run some diagnostics on the PCs connected to the pack's network. I'll need to remotely access your PC for a few minutes."

I didn't recognize this guy, but I knew Eric was the one who ran IT for Jessica's pack. I glanced at the clock. Forty-four minutes to get the report done.

"Seriously? Now?" I huffed. "I have a report to rebuild and nowhere near enough time to get it done!"

"I get that, but we need to make sure the network is secure. It'll only take a couple of minutes."

A couple of minutes? Nothing any tech guy ever did actually went as quick as a couple of minutes. I was going to lose nearly all of my time to this. I raked a hand through my hair, and then smoothed it back into place as I took a deep, slow breath. Murphy's law. Of course they'd need to do this when I have forty-three minutes left to get this report done.

"I don't have a couple of minutes."

"If I can't get your PC secured today," he said, "I'm going to have to lock you out of the pack's network until I can."

Triple dammit!

I needed on the pack's network, or I'd have to try to rebuild that report from memory. Another glance at the clock. Forty-two minutes.

"Fine," I said with another exasperated huff. "But you're gonna have to walk me through it. I know spreadsheets and presentations, not the technical stuff."

The guy on the phone chuckled. "No problem. It's super easy."

A few clicks through menus later, and the pointer on my screen took on a life of its own as Eric's assistant got to work. My screen flashed a couple of times before an installation progress bar popped up.

"What's it installing?" I asked, like I'd have any clue what the heck the answer would mean.

"It's just a new network support framework," he said. "It'll secure the firewall and ensure no intrusions on the network come from your PC."

"Oh, okay." Like I figured, technical mumbo-jumbo. Why the hell did I even ask?

The pointer moved around some more and a keyboard popped up on the screen. He typed out the word 'test' in the document I was working on.

"Perfect," he said. "You're all set. Thanks a bunch, Paige."

"Sure. Great. Have a nice day." I clicked the handset down a little harder than I meant to, not even waiting for a final reply from Eric's assistant.

Twenty-eight minutes left to rebuild this damn report.

Blair was gonna kill me.

ONE

*** (JESSICA) ***

IT HAD BEEN NEARLY two months since Sheppard went home with his newest pack member and all their newly-minted bureaucratic protections. Well... technically she was *my* pack member, at least on paper, but I wasn't about to try to make a wereleopard choose between a werewolf pack she barely knew and one she didn't know at all. Hell, I'd be shocked if she was even *capable* of pack-bonding.

Still, I had plans in motion, and Blair had been pestering me for over a month to find a face to this PR campaign already. We knew I wasn't the best choice—I was much more reactive than cool and collected.

But Sheppard was practically the opposite. And he owed me three favors now.

So, I called him up, and told him he should come

out to San Antonio while his pack figured out their next steps. I had a guest house they could stay in on my stretch of land, and they'd get out of a town they were done with.

At least, I was pretty sure they were done with Colorado Springs. Once they took down the major vamp nest in an area, his pack usually moved on. Sometimes they'd stick around to clean up the stragglers, but I was under the impression there weren't many of those left. I didn't know exactly how many brood destructions that made for them, but I knew it had to be more than four times what my pack had under their belt. Besides, with the military wolves right in his backyard, Sheppard and his pack could move on and let the Army pack clean up the scraps.

He seemed hesitant to leave, though.

"Come on, Sheppard. It's easier to sell a house if no one's living in it, and we have an international airport in our backyard with plenty more connections than Colorado Springs has."

He chuckled. "We don't exactly have a shortage of housing here, but you make a fair point about the airport. That said, Denver's only about an hour or so north of us."

"Sure," I said, pacing around my room for the fifth time this conversation. "But San Antonio International is only twenty minutes from my place, so it'd be more convenient than a bunch of road trips."

"And this has nothing to do with the favors I owe you, huh?"

I snorted as I stepped onto the cool tile of my bathroom and leaned a hip on the counter. "I'd be lying if I tried to tell you that wasn't at least part of my motive for the offer. I think I know something you can help me with."

"Oh?"

"Nothing you can't handle, of course." I grabbed the bottle of red nail polish on my vanity and shook it. The little metal ball bearing clinked rhythmically against the interior of the bottle. "We'll talk once you're all settled. Get out of the military's backyard and come be around people who actually understand your pack."

"I'll give it some thought."

"Lemme know when your flight arrives."

He laughed. "Talk to you soon, Jessica."

I ended the call and put the phone down next to the sink as I opened the bottle of nail polish. Crinkling my nose at its sharp scent, I got to work on my toenails.

He hadn't said no—at least, not right away.

That was something.

Getting him to agree to be the face that made the world aware of werewolves would be another thing altogether.

TWO

*** (SHEPPARD) ***

IT TOOK A LITTLE over a week to make sure we had everything settled, though we *did*, in fact, clean up the tail end of the vampires that had nested downtown. Those vamps had been Buckheim's problem before we came to the area, but as soon as we arrived, they became our problem, and I wasn't about to shirk that responsibility. Still, once Colorado Springs was as safe as we could possibly make it, there was no sense in us staying.

So, I decided to take Jessica up on her offer, and told the pack to prep for San Antonio. It felt like our only choice, really. If we didn't leave, we'd be in danger of setting down roots in the military's backyard, and that's the last place I'd want to do something like that. Comfort breeds complacency, so getting us moving so we could get to the *real* move was a far better choice than staying put.

We made it to San Antonio at the very tail end of August, which meant it was about as hot as Texas gets when we arrived. The heat and humidity was a stark contrast to the cooler mountain temperatures we'd known in Colorado.

The house Jessica had available for us was a little tight, but it did fit the whole pack under the same roof—with a master bedroom and a media room in the back corners of the ground floor, plus four more bedrooms and a loft on the upper floor. I took the master bedroom on the ground floor, of course, and all of the mates had private rooms upstairs. Kristos took up the loft, which was next door to Naiya and down the hall from Lynn and Jonathan. Jamie and Ian shared the media room on the ground floor, since there was more than enough couch and floor space for the two of them there.

Once everyone had staked their claim on rooms, I intended to send three pairs of them out to scout potential places for us to settle again. Kaylah decided she wanted to do more than just cook, clean, and do laundry, so I set her up with the task of keeping all the arrangements organized and keeping in touch with the traveling pack members.

Naiya, on the other hand, didn't take too kindly to the idea of us all splitting up as soon as we arrived in San Antonio.

"I thought you said you were staying together," she said, piling her long black hair up into a messy bun on top of her head as her piercing green eyes held my gaze.

It was disconcerting that she could comfortably do that for as long as she did, but it was yet another in a long list of reasons that made me unsure she would ever pack-bond with us. And I wasn't sure how that would affect the long-term stability of the pack.

"We are," I replied. "But we have to go *somewhere*, which means we need to find the right location."

"Don't you have contacts that can help with that?"

I nodded. "Sure, but there's only so much any

given pack knows about the goings-on outside of their territory."

"'N we don' wanna step on toes by tryin' to share territory," Kaylah added.

Naiya looked over her shoulder, through the window, at Jessica's main pack house. "So, that's *not* what we're doing here?"

I gave her a gentle smile as I shoved my hands into my pockets, hiding them as they clenched into fists. I did not appreciate such direct opposition, but I wasn't the 'giving orders' type, and Naiya was not quite pack. She wasn't quite *not* pack, but she didn't have the same instinctive need to lean on a leader, nor the instinct to trust in that leader's decisions.

She wasn't questioning my leadership. She simply didn't understand.

"I owe Jessica favors," I said, keeping my voice cool and level. "She's asked us to come here while we figure out our next steps so that we're close enough that she can call in those favors without too much trouble."

"Uh-huh." She crossed her arms with a sigh.

Ian placed a hand on her shoulder, drawing her attention. "*Sarcina eiusdem sanguinis*, Naiya. "

Ian had really taken that aphorism to heart. Despite his youth, he was unfailingly there for the pack, even when he had his own rather close-knit group of human friends from before he'd been turned.

Naiya raised an eyebrow at him. "What?"

"It's Latin," Kristos said as he sat down on the couch. He pointedly looked at the cushion next to him before looking back at her.

"It means 'the blood and the pack are one,'" I said as she sank to the couch next to Kristos.

At least someone could get her to do what they wanted her to.

"I suspect New Orleans might be a hotspot of vampire activity," I said. "The last I'd heard of a pack down that way was decades ago. Since Matt is our best fighter, sending him there makes the most sense. And since he's likely to be there for a week or more, sending his mate with him so he doesn't try to rampage across the city, or get himself killed—"

"Hey!" Matt surged forward in his seat.

Chastity put a hand on his shoulder. "He's not wrong, Matt."

With a sigh, Matt sat back in the chair.

I jerked my chin at him. "That's why sending Chastity with you makes sense. She keeps you level."

Naiya nodded along with the explanation, so at least that was something.

"Ian has been tracking the online news about the rifts," I continued, gesturing to him.

"There have been a *lot* of them in New York," he said.

I nodded. "So sending him there to check them out simply makes sense as well. With any luck, we can figure out what the hell is causing them."

"'S'not really our job, though, Shep," Kaylah said as she rearranged packages of meat in the freezer. She marked something down on a scrap of paper she had on the counter and then looked up at me as the freezer door closed.

"It's not," I agreed. "But the creatures those rifts occasionally spit out are just as dangerous to people as vampires are—maybe even moreso, since daylight seems to have no real effect on them."

Kaylah shrugged. "So who d'you wanna send to Montana?"

I surveyed who was left. Kristos said he didn't trust airplanes. Naiya was too new to know what kind of space we needed, as was Lynn. If I sent Kaylah, we'd mostly have grilled food—which would be a pain in the ass thanks to the heat—or takeout—in a town we were wholly unfamiliar with—until she got back. That left just Daniel and Jonathan, both of them mated. I could send Lynn and Jonathan, but Kristos would object to that unless he went too, which put me back at the problem of airplanes. Plus if Lynn and Kristos and Jonathan went, Naiya would likely end up going too, and that was just silly. I didn't need that many scouts in one place.

"Daniel and Jonathan, you guys up for some time out

and about?" I didn't like splitting up mates, but they were the only two that made any kind of sense.

"I've cleared my caseload for the next month," Daniel said. "So I'm happy to go where you need me to."

Jonathan squeezed Lynn's hand, and he kissed her temple. "Absence makes the heart grow fonder?"

Lynn placed the back of her wrist against her forehead as she leaned back in her chair. "How ever shall I live without you next to me every moment of every day?" She straightened with a laugh and elbowed him. "I'll be fine, my love."

He kissed her then, giving me a thumbs-up as he did.

I was so glad those two came together. They could not be more perfect mates for each other. The same was true for Kaylah and Daniel, and Matt and Chastity, of course, but I'd had more time to grow accustomed to their bonds. Unfortunately, all three mate-bonds were a stark contrast to the darkness that swirled around Naiya. Sending that guy across the rift had torn off a piece of her, and I wasn't sure how long it would take her to recover from that, if ever. Those two might as well have been mate-bonded, even if that wasn't necessarily how wereleopards and humans worked.

I looked over at Kaylah. "So, Daniel and Jonathan, then."

Kaylah clicked her tongue as she nodded. "Gotcha. Y'all'll have flights out by the end of the weekend."

"Thanks, Kaylah." I nodded at her before pacing back to the master bedroom to finish unpacking.

I hadn't forgotten Jessica already had something in mind for one of her favors. The sooner we got settled in, the sooner I could get that done.

THREE

*** (JESSICA) ***

MY MONTHLY KEYWORD-UPDATE MEETING with Blair had gone longer than I'd liked, but with the vampires pulling their online shenanigans, we had to figure out a way to get werewolves trending positively again. Normally, Blair would assign that to someone on her team but, since we were specifically keeping the circle of trust small until we knew we could safely widen it, Blair took on the task herself. She explained how she'd set up dummy social media accounts with computer-generated posts to help get people to question the motives of the ones releasing these fight videos online.

It was a good plan. And just another reason I was glad I'd hired her. We put the plan into the chat server for the pack, and set the wolves who were social media gurus on the task of helping her. It didn't take much nudging, but

Blair insisted on making sure to follow everyone that was going to be assisting with the task so she could be sure everyone was staying 'on brand.'

It was a little before lunchtime when I finally got back to the pack house. The scent of beef and chicken tamales was heavy in the air, and my mouth watered at the thought of biting into a fresh one. But Jay, our resident chef, wasn't in the kitchen when I came around the corner from the garage. Instead, I found him lying on one of the couches in the great room, his arms behind his head while a wind-up kitchen timer ticked away on his chest.

"Jay," I called. "You make enough for the visiting pack?"

"*Si, mami,*" he replied, not even opening his eyes. "And enough for the Howlers crew. Timer says three minutes." He held up his hand with three fingers extended.

"You didn't even look at it!"

"I've been counting the ticks!"

I plucked the ticking box from his chest. Sure enough, two minutes and fifty two seconds left to go.

"See?" He opened one of his eyes to look at me. "I know what I'm doing, *mami.*"

My phone buzzed from my back pocket. "You tell the rest of the pack yet?"

"*Porque no,*" he replied. "You wanna stampede on the house? Besides, they gotta set for ten to fifteen before you eat 'em. Figured I'd let you tell the pack once you claimed the ones you wanted."

I laughed as I pulled my phone from my pocket and turned back toward my master suite. "Thanks."

He waved a hand. "You better claim more than you think if you're hoping to have leftovers. I keep making bigger and bigger batches, but they still keep disappearing."

"What do you expect?" Imogen asked, coming around the corner of the kitchen with her hair wrapped in a towel. "Homemade tamales are the best!"

I stepped into my bedroom with its red walls and

black furnishings and sat on the leather chair in the corner to take off my boots before thumbing open my phone. It was a text from Sheppard.

> **Sheppard:**
> *I ran into one of yours running pack errands today.*

I huffed out a little laugh as I sat back in the chair and tapped out a reply.

> **Me:**
> *Color me surprised. You can't swing a dead cat in this town without hitting one. Who'd you run into?*

> **Sheppard:**
> *She had loose, dark hair and big eyes. Maybe about as tall as Naiya? She seemed a little jumpy. The barista called her Thalia. When you get a chance, you should probably let her know that a triple espresso isn't gonna do anything for her that a single wouldn't.*

Thalia was one of the wolves I had taking journalism and video editing classes so she could help my teams around the country with debunking the videos the vampires kept releasing. And I'd told her probably a dozen times already that a triple shot of espresso wasn't doing her any favors

Me:

lol – She knows, but she swears she can feel the difference. She was probably on her way to class. I've got a handful of wolves working on communications degrees at UTSA.

Did she clock you?

Sheppard:

I'm pretty sure she did. She kept her head down as she passed me, very clearly focusing on the ground in front of her. She knows she doesn't have to do that for an alpha, right?

There were a lot of things Thalia didn't have to do. But she'd grown up in a very conservative home, and her first pack was a church pack, though she cut ties with them as soon as she had her first 'disciplinary action' for daring to question why they'd captured a bloodsucker instead of just killing him. Turns out they were using the vamp to track the rest of the brood, but church packs don't take kindly to even a hint of insubordination. It'd been an uphill battle to get her to relax, and her breakup with Eric a handful of months ago didn't help any.

Me:

She does that to me too sometimes. I keep telling her, but she's pretty big on assumed protocol.

Sheppard:

Kaylah used to be like that too. She'll mellow out.

Me:

They always seem to, at least a little… excluding your pit fighter, of course.

The typing bubble came up and disappeared a few times before I finally got a reply.

Sheppard:

Matt?

Me:

You mean to tell me there are multiple members of your pack with faces all scarred to hell?

Sheppard:

No… and Matt has mellowed over the years.

Mellowed? Really? I didn't see it, but then again, he wasn't my pack. I just knew I didn't ever wanna be on his bad side.

Me:

He was a real force of nature back when the church got pushy.

Sheppard:

You were too, as I recall.

I couldn't help but smile at that. Sheppard had been

instrumental in putting the church in its place back then, though I'd only realized that in retrospect. Losing my own alpha to those fights while simultaneously turning away from the church had me stuck in a rut of just going through the motions. So it was nice to know that I hadn't been completely useless back then.

Me:

Thank you.

"Jess," Jay said quietly, standing in my doorframe. "Tamale time." He jerked his head back toward the kitchen.

I nodded as I stood. "Thanks, Jay."

I'd completely missed the ding of his timer. I furrowed my brow. No, I bet he stopped it from ringing so he wouldn't call in the wolves before he was ready for them.

I padded out to the kitchen and gathered a plate full of tamales.

"Put the ones for Sheppard's pack to the side," I said. "I'll take them over when I'm done eating."

"You got it, *mami*," Jay replied. "I found a nice big basket at the farmer's market when I got the corn husks and the stuff for the *masa*."

"Perfect," I said, sitting at the breakfast nook. It was built into the curve of the bay windows overlooking the backyard, across from our positively giant kitchen.

I had half my plate of tamales down before my phone buzzed again. I unwrapped the next one and licked some of the seasoning from my fingers before wiping them off on a napkin. Imogen, her blonde hair now blow-dried and straightened, plunked the bottle of hot sauce onto the table as she sat down across from me with her own plate full of tamales.

She jerked her chin toward my phone as she unwrapped the first few tamales on her plate. "Who's buzzin'?"

I thumbed open the screen. "Sheppard."

"Problems?"

I shook my head. "Nah, he's just chatty."

I started to type a reply, but deleted it as I thought about it. Did I want to show Sheppard the back roads? He had brought a motorcycle with him. I shoved another bite of tamale into my mouth before I realized Imogen was watching me.

She'd stopped with the hot sauce dripping onto her first tamale. "I never pegged him for the chatty type."

I met her gaze and glanced at the hot sauce puddle on top of her tamale. "Spent a lot of time with the Colorado Springs alpha, have you?"

She scoffed as she rolled the now-drenched tamale into and on top of one of the others on her plate before turning her fork sideways to cut off a bite of both at the same time. "That one's not my type." She speared the cut bits onto her fork. "I prefer my men more... malleable."

"It means she's into BDSM," Jay said.

"A lady doesn't kiss and tell," she replied.

Jay snickered. "The only lady I see here is sittin' across from you, *mija*."

Imogen just raised an eyebrow and stared him down as I thumbed open the screen of my phone again. I understood well the need to find a quiet place to just be away from the pack and think, so I didn't really want to keep one of the only alphas I was actually on good terms with hanging. What could it hurt to give him a tour of the dirt roads Google hadn't mapped?

I finished up my tamales, grabbed my boots from my room, and headed out to the garage. As the motor cranked the door up, I took stock of my bikes, glad I hadn't left one at the studio this week. They were all parked in a row next to my F-350: three Ducati's and my Indian Super Chief. Anthony's Ninja and Imogen's Yamaha were parked on the far side of the truck, along with space for Alayna and Tran's Ninjas as well. There was an open cubby on the near side of the garage, where shelves held a handful of helmets and a closet bar with our gear. It was hot enough that full leathers just didn't make any sense. We ran hot enough that their normal discomfort would be exacerbated into something just this side of heat exhaustion if we decided to suit up. Sure, it would hurt more if we crashed, but skipping the utter discomfort of cooking inside a suit of leather was worth the risk. I pulled on my armored vest, but left it open for now.

The bike Sheppard had brought with him was a sport bike, so I suspected he'd be more comfortable on one of those. My DesertX was more for off-roading and really just too much for what I had in mind. But my Ducati Supersport and Diavel would work beautifully. And it gave me another excuse to take my fave out on a ride.

I pulled a helmet off the shelf for Sheppard, along with one of the vests with thick polycarbonate plates in a row up the middle of the back as heavy footsteps hit the gravel of my drive.

"Do you intentionally get vehicles that match your hair?" Sheppard said as he came into view. "Or is red just your favorite color?" He'd taken my advice, and wore a pair of stonewash jeans with his white t-shirt. The sleeves of his shirt clung to his biceps, and his sandy blond hair was loose around his shoulders. He had a bit more scruff on his jawline than he had when he first arrived in town, and his golden eyes sparkled with mirth.

I gestured to the Supersport. "That's iconic Ducati red, thank you very much!"

He rumbled out a little chuckle.

Tucking the helmet under my arm, I held up my other hand with four fingers up. "Motorcycles come in four colors at best, Sheppard: Ducati red, Yamaha blue,

Kawasaki green, and then usually either black, white, or yellow."

"Sure," he said, the smile still in his voice as he nodded at my truck. "But Fords come in a lot more than that."

"I guess so, if you count brown and silver as 'a lot.'"

He put his hands up in surrender. "Alright, alright."

I eyed him, trying not to let my vision wander over his muscular frame. "But if you must know, yes, red *is* my favorite color."

His laugh was infectious then, and I couldn't help but join him as I tossed him the helmet from under my arm.

"I saw the bike you brought. It's a little smaller than I'd have pegged you for."

It was actually a lot smaller than I'd have pegged him for, since he practically towered a full foot or so taller than me.

He eyed the helmet in his hands. "It's Jamie's, actually."

I paused then. "Do you even know how to ride?"

He smiled. "Of course. It's been a while, but I still remember how it works."

I nodded and tossed him the vest. "Show me?"

He shifted the helmet to his left hand as he caught the vest. He eyed it for a moment before looking back at me.

"It's too hot for full leathers." I jerked my chin toward the vest. "But that'll keep you from severing your spine if you crash." I grabbed my helmet off the middle shelf and patted it. "And never skip the helmet."

He nodded as he pulled the vest on. He had to let out some of the space on the sides with the heavy duty velcro to get it to fit around his broad frame. "Who's this normally fit?"

"Anthony," I replied. "He's a newish kid. Wandered up this way from South Texas a handful of years back."

It took another round of adjustments before he could finally zip up the vest. "Not born, huh?"

I shook my head. "I don't see a lot of those these days, though I do have a handful in the pack."

"I'd say I'm surprised," he said, "but given the size of your pack, I'm glad to hear there's still some of us kicking around."

"Even got one of the next generation, actually," I said. I couldn't resist a little bit of bragging. My pack was freaking phenomenal, and Emma and Levi had worked their asses off to get Oliver into the world.

Sheppard was suitably impressed. "That's really great, Jessica. Congratulations."

"I'll pass that on to the parents."

"Oh," he said, his eyebrows trying to crawl up into his hairline. "It's not yours?"

I scoffed and shook my head. "Hell no! Why on Earth would you think that?"

He shrugged. "I just figured you'd be well off the market by now, snatched up by some lucky guy or another."

"Nope. Not really in the market, actually. My pack keeps me busy enough." And the last thing I needed was to get drawn into some moon-eyed wolf's concept of mates... or some human's idea of marriage. No thank you.

But, I had him come here to see what I do to get some room to think. So, I showed him how the comms worked in the helmets and tossed him the key to my Supersport.

"Lay it down or wreck it and you owe me a new one."

"Yes ma'am." He gave me a mock salute with two fingers and a click of his tongue before closing the visor of his borrowed helmet.

"Alright," I said, flipping down my own visor. "Follow me."

"Where are we off to?"

"You'll know it when we get there."

It took about seven minutes to get past the last of the houses in the area and out to the dirt roads and the scrub that followed along an old riverbed. The heat of summer and utter lack of recent rainfall left the ground cracked along our path, but the scrub here was tenacious, and it clearly refused to yield to the drought-like conditions. It certainly wasn't the prettiest view in the world, but it was among the quietest.

"Oh wow," Sheppard said. "Who would know there was this swath of space just outside a bustling city like San Antonio?"

"God and the cicadas," I replied, nodding. "*This* is how I get some privacy in a pack as large as mine."

He pulled alongside me as we reached a somewhat straight stretch of the riverbed and put a hand to his chest. "I'm honored to be included."

"Call it a perk of being alpha," I said. "Some days it feels like you can't go *anywhere* without running into one of my wolves. So, if you ever want an escape, just hit me up and we can take a ride."

"I'll keep that in mind." There was a smile in his voice, but it rang of politeness more than sincerity.

"I know that tone," I said. "You won't. But you'll wish you did."

We were far enough out now that the road was a mere suggestion and there was no telling which county or city had jurisdiction here. Which meant I'd never have to worry about human law enforcement harassing my peace. I looked over my shoulder and revved the Diavel.

"See if you can keep up, Alpha!" I shot off ahead of him and buzzed around scrub, keeping my wheels on the cracked riverbed.

Sheppard laughed into the comm, and he dropped a gear to gather the Supersport's power to catch up to me. He wasn't half bad for someone clearly out of practice with riding. He even caught up to me a few times before I darted ahead of him again. But then we hit my favorite stretch of the riverbed, where nothing but smooth cracked ground stretched in front of us and I could really open up the throttle. A glance at my speedometer told me I hit 115, and Sheppard was mostly keeping pace with me, but the Diavel had more power than the Supersport did, which meant he'd hit the top end of that bike well before I hit mine.

But the speed had him a little more wobbly than I'd have liked, and I slowed down till he was more stable again. I'd've liked to have raced him back to the house, but it wouldn't have been fair. We were on familiar ground for me, but he'd have to scent his way back if I left him out here. Not that he couldn't—it would just take him longer than seemed fair. Besides, the whole point of this was to show him where an Alpha can get some peace, not to rub his nose in my off-roading skills.

"I bet this place is just gorgeous at night," he said.

"Like diamonds scattered across blue velvet," I replied. "There's still a lot of light pollution from the city proper, but it's absolutely stunning."

"What kinds of creatures come out at night around here?"

"Mostly raccoons and coyotes, but the latter stay further out. They don't like the thought of competing with a bunch of werewolves. We get lots of possums and sometimes even some brush rabbits, but it's a little late in the summer for them to be hanging around."

"I'm surprised there aren't more reptiles," he said.

"We get plenty of snakes, but rattlers get a bad rap. Most of them just want to be left alone. There's plenty of mice and rats though for them to thrive, so you gotta keep your eye out. They won't hesitate to bite if you step on 'em."

"More the 'bite first, question later' type, huh?"

I shrugged. "If the bitten survive the bite, sure."

"How's it affect wolves?"

"It takes a little longer to heal, but it's not like when a human gets bit."

"Good to know. No reason to worry or rush to get antivenom."

I shook my head. "Nah. No need for it. Your system can handle it. Let's get back and cool off."

"Sounds like a plan."

I led him back to the house, and we pulled the bikes into the garage before dropping the kickstands. Taking my helmet off and setting it on the bike seat, I flipped my head upside down and shook out my hair. I gathered it all together as I stood up and used the hair tie around my wrist to pull it into a messy bun on the top of my head.

The simple warm scent that was Sheppard filled the air as he handed me his borrowed gear. His white shirt had gone nearly sheer with the amount of sweat in it, and his hair was now slicked back. He peeled off his shirt and just... well. Part of me wanted to touch the toned muscles along his stomach, but that part could just shut the hell up because his skin was absolutely soaked with sweat.

I turned to put the gear in the closet-cubby before the thirsty part of my brain could do anything stupid. The vests would dry on the rack. I'd take out the armor plates and toss 'em in the wash later on.

Sheppard shook out his shirt. "So what is it you're hoping I can help you with?"

I huffed out a little laugh as I shook my head. "That's gonna be a long conversation. It can wait a few more days." And then I remembered the tamales. "Ooh. Wait here and I'll walk you back."

He looked over his shoulder. "I didn't know it was dangerous to walk across the gravel drives."

I raised an eyebrow at him. "Dressed like that? You'd be lucky to make it without getting accosted."

A laugh rumbled through his chest. "What if I'm into that?"

I snorted. "Nah. You're not the type. Wait here."

I went inside, grateful for the cold blast of air conditioning. Half the pack was home now, judging by the level of noise in the house. There were too many scents to tell who specifically was here, but Jay's tamales would eventually bring everyone out. I ducked into my room and grabbed a fresh tank top and bra, draping my soaking wet ones over the edge of my black claw foot bathtub to dry out before I tossed 'em in the laundry. As I straightened my top, I went over to the kitchen, dodging around no less than four pack members who'd managed to crowd into the breakfast nook. Three more were dropping their husks into the garbage or helping themselves to seconds—or, more likely, thirds—in the kitchen. And beyond that, it was standing room only in the dining room. A contented sigh escaped me at the sight of so many gathered, and it took me a moment to stop basking in it so I could pick up the basket of tamales Jay had set aside for Sheppard's pack.

By the time I got back out to the garage, Sheppard had wandered around to the other bikes on the far side of my truck. Alayna and Tran had made it back from class, and their Ninjas had joined the other bikes over there.

He perked up as the door shut behind me. "These yours too?"

I shook my head. "Nah. Those belong to Anthony, Imogen, Alayna, and Tran." I pointed to each bike as I named its owner.

"You got your own little motorcycle gang going."

"You could say that. Lemme walk you back."

He fell into step beside me, but I still had to work to keep pace with his long legs.

"Whatcha got in the basket, little Red? It smells delicious."

The thirsty part of my brain surged to reply, but I shut it down.

"Tamales," I replied. "Homemade. Jay always makes enough to feed an army, but they still go quick. So I asked him to set some aside for you guys."

He opened the door to the guest house I'd loaned them, and the scents of his pack as well as raw meat and spices washed across me as the cold blast of air conditioning whisked away the summer heat.

I recognized Kaylah, in her sunny yellow shirt with her long blonde hair pulled back. She was in the kitchen, likely prepping the meat for whatever dinner they were gonna have, though she smiled and waved as we came in. I was a little surprised to see the grumpy-ass werebear sitting on the couch in the living room. He wore a black tank top with grey sweats, and his curly dark hair was pulled back with a strip of leather. He was wrapping a thin wire around a couple of thicker ones in his hand, setting a sparkling blue stone into place as he worked. Spread out in front of him, on the coffee table, was a black velvet cloth with a number of small hand tools, including a soldering iron and a spool of silver wire. It was interesting to see a man as thickly built as Kristos—and with such large hands—work on such a small scale.

"Whatcha got there, Jessica?" Kaylah asked, nodding at the basket in my hands. It must feel great for her to be back in an area where so many people had the same accent as hers.

I held the basket up. "Fresh homemade tamales. Beef and chicken."

Kaylah wiped her hands on a towel and came around the kitchen counter to take it from me. "Well 'at's mighty kind of ya! Thanks!"

"Sure," I replied. "Just remember, peel off the corn husk before you eat it. That's just there to hold it all together while it cooks and cools. They're pretty good cold too, like pizza."

"Well, good to know," she said. "Thank you!"

I jerked my chin toward Kristos as I turned to Sheppard—who was still shirtless, my thirsty brain reminded me. Like I could possibly forget. "You still keep interesting company. I must've missed him when you guys were moving in."

Sheppard smiled and leaned close to my ear, dropping his voice. "I could put in a good word for you."

Kaylah tsked at something in the kitchen.

"I don't need a wingman," Kristos said flatly, using needle nose pliers to curl the wire in his hand into lacelike shapes without so much as looking up at us.

"Hmm. Think I'll pass anyway," I said. "But thanks."

Sheppard nodded toward him. "He's a recent re-addition."

"Uh huh." I raised an eyebrow at my fellow alpha.

"He earned it this time," he said.

"Oh?"

"He helped heal the pack after a daywalking *consanguinea* vampire tore through us."

My eyes went wide. "Holy shit. I thought the daywalker rumors were just that." I gestured toward Kristos. "But how'd he help? He doesn't exactly look like the medical type."

Sheppard cocked his head to the side. "Ever been hurt by a *consanguinea*?"

I shook my head.

"They don't heal like normal," he said. "It takes longer. Not human long, mind you, but not werewolf short either."

My eyes widened even more. "Holy shit, he can bypass that?!"

Sheppard shrugged. "Apparently."

"No," Kristos said, still not looking up from his work as he grabbed the soldering iron and held the tip to the joint he held in his other hand. "But I can augment the healing through Lynn."

I turned to face him then, stepping into his field of view. "Through Lynn?"

"Yep." He gently blew on the freshly soldered joint to cool it down.

"He's got a connection with *consanguinea*," Sheppard said. "It predates anything us wolves can do."

I turned back to Sheppard, stepping away from the living room. "I didn't realize he was *that* old."

"Older than any living thing you've seen," Kristos said, wrapping another wire onto the piece.

I snorted. "Not likely." I was pretty sure Kaan was the oldest thing on the planet these days. But he had yet to show his face since the pack moved in.

Kristos raised an eyebrow and paused what he was doing to look up at me. "You know something that's two thousand years old?"

There was a note of...was that hopefulness in his voice?

"You mean aside from the vamp elders? Pretty sure I do, yeah." He narrowed his eyes at me, but I held his gaze. "I'm sure you'll run into him. He's a nice guy." I waved a hand dismissively. "You probably won't like him."

"Hmph." He turned back to the wire-wrapped gemstone.

"You stayin' for lunch, Jessica?" Kaylah's tone was full of that southern hospitality you couldn't help but smile at.

I pulled a couple of grapes off the bunch in the bowl on the counter. "Not this time. I've got some meetings to prep for. You guys enjoy the tamales though."

"Well you jus' come by anytime you want," Kaylah said. "We're more'n happy t' share."

"I will." I popped a grape in my mouth and turned to Sheppard, giving his ass a pat as I took a step toward the door. "Thanks for the ride. Hit me up when you're not still living out of your luggage."

I opened the door and stepped back into the blistering heat.

"Motorcycles," Sheppard said as the door shut behind me, his tone wry.

I heard Kaylah's 'uh-huh' even through the door. She must've given him a look.

I huffed out a laugh as I crossed my gravel drive.

FOUR

*** (SHEPPARD) ***

WATCHING THE DOOR, I listened for Jessica's footsteps on the gravel to be a safe distance away before turning to Kaylah.

"What was that about?"

Kaylah tossed me a water bottle from the fridge. "Whaddya mean?"

"Jessica," I said, holding the cold bottle to the back of my neck. "That wasn't your usual southern hospitality—you *wanted* her to stay." Sweat, or maybe condensation, dripped down my spine, and I swear I could feel the salt of it crystallizing on my scalp.

I needed a shower.

Kaylah put a fist on her hip. "I jus' think she'd be a good match for you."

A good ma—? I shook my head and blinked at her.

"What?"

She stepped around the kitchen counter, closing the distance between us. "I'm sayin' I think there's sum'n here," she poked my chest, "that here," she poked my forehead, "ain't cotton'd to yet." She made a face at my sweat on her finger and wiped it on her denim shorts.

I wiped at the sweat on my face, but my hand was just as sweaty, so I moved it around more than anything. "What could possibly make you think that?"

Kaylah took a deep breath. "When'd you meet Jessica? Two hun'red years ago?"

"Two hundred and fifty four." Back when we were fighting our own because the church wanted to oppress the native people of this land.

She raised an eyebrow at me. "Mmm-hmm."

"When we pushed out the church and signed the treaties," I explained.

"And how many alphas survived that?"

Jess wasn't an alpha then. I tried to do the math, but it had been quite some time. "Hers was among those lost. Only maybe twenty or so survived."

Kaylah smiled knowingly. "And which, of any of those wolves, did you ask for help when Lynn joined us?"

I shook my head as more sweat dripped down my back. "None. We had that handled." I opened the bottle of water.

"You called me," Kristos said as I gulped down half the bottle.

"And the Gen'ral," Kaylah said with a roll of her eyes.

"I—"

"'N who'd you call 'bout Naiya?"

I put my hand on my hip and pointed the mouth of the water bottle at her. "That's different. We were in her territory."

"Uh-huh." Kaylah leaned back against the bar-height counter that separated the kitchen from the dining room. "'N of th' wolves who survived all those years ago, how many you still got the phone number of?" She crossed her arms. "Off the top of your head, can you tell me where even *one* of the survivin' alphas is at?"

I think one of them ended up in California? Or was it Florida? I couldn't be sure. Which was definitely her point. I gave her a level look through my eyebrows.

Kristos snorted out a laugh.

Kaylah pointed a finger at me, waggling it up and down. "Right. So don' try an' tell me you dunno what I'm talkin' 'bout, 'cause there's a part a ya that does." She looked me up and down. "Maybe two parts."

Kristos' snicker turned to a full belly laugh as I downed the last of the water bottle.

"It's th' third 'at's gotta catch up." She made a shooing motion toward the hallway. "Go shower'n cool off. It's hotter'n hell out there."

I tossed her the empty water bottle. "You said it."

FIVE

*** (JESSICA) ***

I TURNED OFF THE water and bent over till my hair was practically touching my toes as I wrapped a thick black towel around my hair. My phone buzzed on the counter as I straightened and I grabbed a second towel to dry off my body. I tapped the screen to see who it was.

Sheppard. Of course.

I had a couple of notifications from the pack's chat server as well, but those were likely just updates on the wolves I had around the country.

And Sheppard could wait until I was dry and dressed.

I'd visited with my pack and had some more tamales after getting back from the ride along the riverbed. And then I'd taken a nice, long, barely room temperature bath to cool off. I was about as relaxed as I could possibly be without a session in the studio.

I took my time blow drying my hair. I put on some eyeliner and got dressed in my comfy shorts and sports bra, grabbed my phone, and sank my toes into my thick black carpet as I stepped over to the bed. I plopped onto the black satin sheets, once again glad I had gotten the extra soft mattress when I replaced my old one last year. My bedframe was an industrial canopy type, and I'd put up shimmery black chiffon curtains at the corners to soften the look of the edges. I crossed my legs as I settled into all of my pillows—most of which usually ended up on the ground at night—and thumbed open the screen.

Just as I expected, the notifications from the chat server were updates, though Blair also sent me numbers on how some of the social media posts were going as well. None of it was particularly pressing, so I tapped on the text message.

Sheppard:

I haven't forgotten I owe you dinner.

I narrowed my eyes and cocked my head. "What the hell?" I knew what the words meant, but intent always gets lost in text. Was this supposed to be his attempt to ask me to dinner? I methodically typed out a reply.

Me:

Good. The sky is blue today, and Texas summers are hot.

Honestly, I was making it hard on him on purpose, largely because a simple declaration like his didn't actually mean anything. And I wasn't above a little power play with a fellow alpha.

Judging by the typing bubble that kept appearing and disappearing, he was not entirely sure how to put his request together. So, I waited him out, a wry smirk pulling at my mouth the longer he took.

It was dark for a moment longer before his reply finally came.

Sheppard:

What?

Me:

If you're asking me to dinner, then ask me, Alpha.

But then I wasn't so sure I wanted him to ask me to dinner. What if he did? Would it be weird? Was he reading into our ride earlier? Why the hell was I reacting to him like a little damn schoolgirl?

The typing bubble did the same thing as it did before: popping up and disappearing without a message coming through a few times.

Yeah... he's gonna make it weird.

Sheppard:

How about we meet up for dinner tonight? Lady's choice, my treat.

I rolled my eyes. The least he could do is show some effort.

Me:

How about you do the work and tell me where we're going?

Sheppard:

It's your town, but sure.

While I waited for his reply, I switched over to looking at the replays of the latest news segments my remote pack members had appeared on. I was proud of them. For not having a lot of technical know-how or video editing experience, they sure made it sound convincing when they talked about how the vampires' videos were faked. It was a couple of minutes before my phone buzzed again.

'Meet you there?' He was right across the driveway, wasn't he? Well, I shouldn't assume that. He could be practically anywhere in the city. I looked at the time. I had a little more than forty-five minutes to get dressed and ready to go.

I kicked my legs over the side of the bed, leaving my phone on the blanket. I'd just agreed to go to dinner with the visiting alpha. I mean, sure, he owed me a dinner anyway, I suppose. But he knew that was just a flirty joke, right? I mean, the Brazilian steakhouse was nice, but it wasn't super fancy. Though it was perfect for a couple of werewolves who preferred meat to anything else in our diet.

A *couple* of werewolves? Was he hoping this would be a date? He wasn't even picking me up. He couldn't be hoping this is a date.

I eyed my display case full of dildos and vibrators and remembered something I'd heard a comedian say once: if you aren't sure you wanna sleep with the guy or gal you're gonna go have dinner with, masturbate before you go so you can make the decision without your thirsty brain getting in the way. That's probably not exactly how it went—comedians had that whole timing and phrasing thing down to an art. But the gist was the same.

So I queued up some of my favorite videos and took care of myself before getting dressed.

There. Now it's *definitely* not a date.

And just to be sure, I put on the tightest black jeans I owned, my lace-up boots with the blocky heels, my longline bra with its seven hooks in the back, and a flowy grey-blue tank top that I tucked into the front waistband of my jeans. I tied a wide black ribbon snugly around my neck as a choker, swiped on some red lipstick, and checked my reflection.

I mean, I looked good enough to eat for sure, and that longline bra was sexy as hell, but getting any of this off me with any kind of grace was gonna be a chore to say the least.

SIX

*** (SHEPPARD) ***

THE STEAKHOUSE HAD A very open seating space, but I still managed to get us a booth in a corner. I didn't really want to make it an intimate thing, but I also didn't need people overhearing if we ended up talking shop. Which was likely since we were two alphas having dinner.

Alphas. I ran a hand through my hair, smoothing it back out of my face. Jessica had fought fang and claw for every scrap of that title. It was wild to compare the confident and self-assured woman she was now to the shell-shocked and lost wolf I'd met all those years ago. She had really come into her own, and her pack... whew. It was something else. I hadn't tried to count all the wolves I'd seen around on the grounds, but I know there were a handful that must've made up her inner circle. Beyond those? I don't know that I'd ever seen the same wolf twice. I'd only been here a few days, but still. It made me wonder just how big her pack really was.

"More water?" The pretty young waitress held up a jug. She'd told me her name, but I'd promptly forgotten it.

I nodded. "Thanks."

She refilled it as I watched the door. I'd made it to the restaurant a few minutes early, just in case. I didn't know if Jessica had been at home or out in the city somewhere, and I didn't exactly know whether she was the punctual type.

A couple minutes past seven, I had my answer as she breezed in the door. She looked stunning, in her tight black jeans and her breezy shirt. The former accentuated her shapely hips, the latter just barely brushing the swell of breasts that were sizeable for her frame without off-balancing the delightful hourglass shape that was Jessica. I waved her over and the waitress came by again to take our drink orders and make sure we knew how a Brazilian steakhouse worked.

"And are we celebrating an anniversary tonight?" the waitress asked.

I furrowed my brow and looked at Jessica before blinking up at the hostess. "N—"

"We're just colleagues," Jessica said. "Business dinner."

The waitress' cheeks colored. "Oh! I'm so sorry! I just assumed... I shouldn't have—" She cleared her throat and collected herself in a breath. "My apologies, of course."

I shook my head and smiled at her. "Not a problem. No harm done."

She hurried off to gather our drinks, and the servers soon came by with a variety of meats, cutting pieces off for each of us. Once the commotion of it all had settled down I raised my glass.

"To your continued success," I said, smiling.

Jessica returned the smile and clinked her glass against mine. "And to yours."

"I have to thank you again for the space... and the getaway earlier."

"Don't thank me yet," she said. "You still don't know what I have in mind for you."

I chuckled. "I know you well enough to know it can't be all that bad."

She raised an eyebrow at me and something devilish touched her smile. "You sure about that?"

"You'd be hard pressed to shock me, Jessica."

She huffed out a laugh as she cut off a piece of her sirloin. "We'll see. Any chance you've gotten word out to the other alphas about checking their treaties?"

I shrugged. "I sent emails to some of the alphas I'm closer with. I can't tell you whether they took it seriously. It's hard to read tone in text."

"Yeah." She nodded. "Hard to trust it."

"Exactly." I took a bite of my lamb. "Where the heck did you get all our signatures from anyway to pull that paperwork together for Lynn and Kristos? The ones that put them officially under my pack's protection, I mean."

She side-eyed me. "You know the treaties have a lot of signatures on them, right? And that I had to sign one myself once I became alpha?"

"Sure," I said. "But you know that most of the wolves that signed the treaties with my pack back then aren't still around and kicking, right?"

She bobbed her head side to side. "I know that. But the church doesn't."

"They're gonna figure it out."

She huffed out a laugh. "Don't worry! I used yours and Matt's to cobble it together. Even if the church traces it all back, they'll find they're signed by wolves that were alive at the time."

I smiled. "Good."

The waitress was back. "Refills?"

Our drinks weren't particularly low, but she refilled them anyway.

As she hurried off, Jessica leaned over to me, the heavy lavender-and-cloves scent of her wafting toward me as she lowered her voice. "I think the waitress likes you."

I scoffed as I sat up. "She likes everyone. It helps with

the tips."

"I dunno, Shep. She keeps looking over here and then chatting with the other waitresses."

I shook my head. "They're probably just discussing their guesses for what we do for a living."

She snorted out a laugh as she took a sip of her water. "Sure. That's it." Her tone was sarcastic and dry.

"Wait... Jessica?" A younger Hispanic man in a black button down with grey slacks paused as he passed our booth. His hair was long, pulled back into a low ponytail with gel keeping his curls in check.

Jessica's cheeks colored and she tried not to make eye contact with the guy.

"Jessica!" He said, much more sure this time. "It's been a while! How come you never called?"

Never ca—? Wait. Was this one of her flings?

She pressed her lips together as the color on her cheeks deepened. She glanced at me and then up to him as she plastered a forced smile on her face. "Hey... uh... Miguel, right?"

"Yeah!" His face lit with a too-bright smile. "Good to see you! How you been?"

This was one of her flings. Someone she'd clearly scratched the itch with, so-to-speak. I tried to keep my amusement silent, but a quiet chuckle snuck out nonetheless.

She gave me a look that would have killed an ordinary man before plastering the fake smile back on. "Good, good. Just been keeping busy, you know?"

"Yeah, I hear that. Hey, we should catch up sometime. Maybe I can buy you lunch tomorrow?"

That was enough wriggling on the hook for her. I cleared my throat and Miguel suddenly noticed my presence. Except it was an act—something I hadn't been completely sure of until then.

He'd tried to make an ass of me.

"Oh shit." He pressed his palm to his forehead. "I didn't realize you were on a date like right right now!"

He was lying.

Jessica's voice dripped sarcastic sweetness. "I think

maybe you should move along, Miguel." She angled her head toward me once before straightening. "He's the territorial type."

Miguel met my eyes then. And immediately looked away again. I don't know what he saw, but I didn't much care either. Jessica didn't need to be harassed by someone who hadn't gotten the point however long ago when she didn't call him back.

"Sorry." He put up his hands in mock surrender. "I didn't mean to bother you."

Another lie.

"Yes, you did," she said. "But now you're done."

"Right." He nodded and eyed me before hurrying off. "Right."

She shook her hair back from her shoulders and turned back to me then. "Would you knock off that growling? You're gonna make people nervous."

I blinked and cleared my throat. I'd been growling? Really? What the hell? I took a sip of my water.

"Sorry about that," she said. "You'd think in a town this big, something like that wouldn't be likely to happen."

I shrugged. "You stay in a town long enough and it's bound to happen, no matter the size."

The servers came around again with another round of meat options, cutting more pieces off for the both of us.

"I meant to ask you," Jessica said, once the commotion had calmed down again. "Back when we bared our teeth at the church, Brooks said something about sending someone through a rift when he was talking to Naiya. What was he talking about?"

I finished the bite of chicken I had in my mouth. "Andy. Brooks had her and a couple of others locked inside this facility up near Midlothian."

"That's just outside the Dallas pack's territory," she said.

"That's probably not a coincidence." I cut off another piece of my chicken. "One of the people she was being held with, she'd apparently fallen in love with. Only he was from the other side of those rifts we've been seeing."

Jessica raised her eyebrows. "Really?"

I nodded. "So when she got free, and while she couldn't be sure of how safe either of them would be, she sent him back home."

"Holy shit. What a choice to make."

"She hasn't been alright since," I said. "I'm not even sure what alright looks like for her yet. It's only been a couple of months, though. With any luck, time'll heal the wound."

She nodded then as she took a bite of her pork loin.

The waitress came over again with her jug. "More wa—" Her foot caught on the carpet, or a chair leg, or something, and the jug came free from her hand, dumping its icy contents onto my shirt and into my lap before landing on the floor and rolling under the table. "Oh no! I'm so sorry!"

"It's fine," I said as I wiped at my face and shirt with my napkin. "I'm sure it was an accident."

Apologies still spilling from her mouth—ones that rang of truth, at least—she grabbed a couple of folded napkins from the table next to us and started to pat them along my shirt. It was white linen, and it had gone nearly translucent where the water splashed. I followed along in her trail, dabbing more water from my clothing. And then her hands landed in my lap. And pressed against things she had no business pressing against.

I clasped her hands as gently as I could manage, trying not to scare her with my grip while still halting whatever progress she was trying to make. She froze and looked up at me, her cheeks turning a distinct shade of crimson.

A choked laugh escaped Jessica and I gave her a quick glare before turning my attention back to the unintentionally too-forward waitress.

"I'll take it from here," I said, releasing the girl's hands as she straightened. "Thank you."

"I'm so—"

"Sorry." I nodded and kept my voice level. "Yes, I know. It's fine. Thank you."

I wiped some of the water from my arm as she bent to retrieve the jug from under the table. When she stood up again, she quickly turned away as the other waitress brought two fresh glasses of ice water to the table.

"She's new," the other waitress said.

She was lying. But she was also trying to be polite.

I nodded, keeping my voice level. "It's fine. Accidents happen."

"I'll speak to my manager to see what we can do about comping your meal."

"No no," I said, waving a hand. "There's no need for that. I'll take care of it."

"I'll be right back."

Jessica caught my eye with a smirk. "Told you she was into you." She pointedly took a sip of her own ice water, pinky out like it was a fancy teacup.

I tossed my wet napkin at her, but she batted it away with a laugh before it could hit her.

The rest of the dinner was uneventful, really. And, after paying the check—which had been comped twenty-five percent for the trouble—we got up to leave. Only it had apparently started to rain while we were eating—something I would have likely noticed if not for the music and the bustle of the servers.

"Aww, dammit," Jessica said.

Which was right when I spotted a familiar red motorcycle getting drenched in the rain. She'd ridden here on one of her Ducati's.

"I'll give you a ride back," I said. "Stay here. I'll grab your helmet and gear and bring the truck around."

"You're going to be soaked by then."

I glanced down at my shirt and then back at her.

"Right," she said. "Good point."

I nodded and ducked out into the rain. Her motorcycle was parked at the end of the first row of parking spaces, just a handful of spaces away from my truck. I could've picked it up and put it in the truck bed if I could be sure no one was watching, but I didn't keep any cargo strapping behind the seats in the cab. I'd have to change that. Carting her bike around unsecured could easily lead to damage I was sure she'd rather not chance. So, I grabbed her helmet and vest and tucked them behind the center fold-down console. When I drove around to the front of the restaurant, I made sure the passenger side was closest to the entrance and hopped out to open her door for her.

"Thanks," she said as she ducked inside.

I didn't dawdle coming back around to the driver's side, and started the drive back to her house.

"When the rain clears, I'll come by and pick up your bike for you."

She shook her head. "Nah, I'll get one of the guys to take my truck and get it later on. It's not a problem. That bike's seen worse."

I chuckled. "Alright. Well... you were right about the hostess."

"I know," she said. "Those apologies were true enough, but it sure seemed like she spilled it on purpose."

"And she got a little handsy trying to 'clean it up.'" I put air quotes around the last three words.

Jessica laughed. "Looks like we both had our share of awkward encounters for the week."

I laughed with her then. "I'd say it must be a full moon coming, but that was a week ago."

She nodded. "Must be something in the water."

I met her eyes and we laughed again.

I hadn't realized how nice it would be to be around another alpha I didn't have to tiptoe around. General Buckheim was always little more than a phone call away, but filtering what I said for him kept a wall up between us that was unlikely to ever fall. Jessica, on the other hand, was a breath of fresh air.

Two days later, I walked over to Jessica's main pack house, which was easily as large as two of the homes I now had on the market in Colorado. It was two stories tall, with a natural grey stone facade, a covered porch that ran most of the length of the front of the house, and black trim around the windows. She had a seating area set up on the porch, with a couple of rocking chairs, a porch swing, and a coffee table complete with a little planter full of succulents. Her big red truck was parked outside the garage, and between the wet ground around it and the scent of soap in the air, it was clear it had been freshly washed.

Kristos, Lynn, and Naiya had all chosen to join me, which felt a bit silly, but I suspected it had more to do with them wanting an excuse to leave the house or see the inside of Jessica's place than it did any concern for whatever it was Jessica had in mind for me. Kaylah decided she had meals she'd rather prep than go see whatever molehill it was my fellow alpha was making a mountain of.

I wasn't so sure.

Jessica had been around long enough to understand the nature of trading favors, and she didn't seem the type to take that sort of thing lightly.

When Jessica answered the door in her black Rage Against the Machine shirt and stonewash cutoff shorts, she took in my entourage and raised an eyebrow at me. "Everything alright?"

I smiled at her as her lavender-and-cloves scent wafted out into the heat—though there were any number of other scents as well. "Sure. Just wanted to come chat about your motives for bringing my pack out this way."

"Right to the point, huh?" She leaned a shoulder against the doorframe and folded her arms across her chest. "Are you at least all settled in?"

I shrugged. "As good as we can be. We traveled relatively light, all things considered."

"And you have a lot of practice," Kristos added.

"That too," I agreed.

"Huh." She ran her tongue across her teeth and

pushed off the doorframe. "Well, come on in then, let's have a chat. Jay's making menudo, and you guys are welcome to some if you'd like."

"Thanks," I said.

We followed her across dark hardwood floors with irregular seams into a massive dining room just to the right, off the foyer, where she had an extra long mesquite wood table with raw edges that sat seven each on the long sides and three on the ends. A matching raw-edge credenza spanned the length of the room along the wall under the giant panoramic picture window with gauzy sheer grey curtains overlaid with an intricate bohemian-style black macrame valance.

I guess it's true what they say: everything really *is* bigger in Texas.

"Wow," Lynn said quietly. "I didn't know they *made* raw-edge tables that big."

"It's custom," Jessica said. "There's a guy on the other side of town that makes them, but I don't remember where he said he sourced the wood from."

At the far end of the table, one of her wolves with short dark hair and a beard was getting a touchup on one of the full sleeve tattoos he had by another wolf that *also* had dark hair and a beard. They were built about the same, thickly muscled, though the tattooed guy was a bit more tanned than the other. The one doing the tattoo had a black rolling tool cart set up next to him with all his supplies.

"Are those two related?" I asked.

The tattooed one threw his head back with a sigh. "Why does everyone think that?"

Jessica chuckled. "Not in the slightest."

The one with the tattoo needle lightly smacked the other with his free hand, which held a paper towel half covered in ink. "Sit still!" He wiped at the skin where he was working with the paper towel. "I dunno, man. I don't see it."

The tattooed one's left sleeve had a few blank spots that were like wide, smooth claw marks up near his shoulder, only there was no scarring, and they didn't run parallel.

I jerked my chin toward his shoulder. "What tore into you?"

"What else?" he said. "Vamp."

I nodded.

"Hunter and his crew just got back from Boise," Jessica said.

The tattooed guy, who I assumed was Hunter, puffed out his chest. "We cleared the brood that was there."

I smiled at him. "Glad to hear it."

Off to the left of the dining room was the kitchen, and stairs to the upper floor started in the far corner of the room. Another one of her wolves, a Hispanic guy with dark hair and a closely trimmed chinstrap of a beard, was in the kitchen, stirring a big pot of soup—likely the menudo Jessica mentioned. There were sounds of some kind of sports game coming from the TV in the room beyond the kitchen, but I wasn't familiar enough with the sport to know what it was.

And then three voices, two female and a male, all shouted 'goal' in unison, stretching out the word for longer than necessary before sharing a laugh.

So soccer, then.

"I'm surprised you didn't bring the whole pack," Jessica said, taking a corner seat with her back to the kitchen.

I shrugged as the four of us took up the corner opposite her—Kristos to my left, and Lynn and Naiya to my right—giving the guys involved in the tattoo process plenty of space. "Kaylah's prepping meals, and the rest of the pack are out around the country scouting for our next location." I gestured to the three with me. "This is all that's left."

The Hispanic wolf from the kitchen brought a bowl of tortilla chips with some salsa over to the table, placing the first within easy reach of Jess and I before holding the latter aloft. "Homemade salsa," he said, pride in his voice, as he set the bowl down next to the chips.

Jessica smiled at him. "Thanks, Jay."

"*De nada, mami*," he replied before bustling back off

into the kitchen.

"So," Jessica said, turning to me, "before I get to what I'd like your help with, I should probably let you know exactly what it is I'm working on out here."

"Sure," I nodded.

Lynn held a hand up. "Wait. Sorry. But... how does that work?" She gestured down the table at Hunter and his tattoo artist.

Jess cocked her head to the side as she looked at her. "You've never seen how a tattoo needle works?"

Lynn shook her head. "No, I know how that works. My roommate freshman year was an apprentice. I mean, how does the ink even stay put with how fast we heal?" She narrowed her eyes in confusion. "Is it silver in the ink that makes it work?" She turned sharply to me, her dark hair whipping around. "Does silver hurt us?"

"I know I'm allergic," Naiya said, dipping a chip into the salsa.

I turned to her. "Really?"

She nodded. "It burns, and I get itchy and blotchy." She shoved the salsa-laden chip into her mouth.

"Interesting." I hadn't known a wolf that was allergic. And I doubted the bears were. But perhaps wereleopards were?

"Some people are naturally allergic to metals," the tattoo artist said. "I had a cousin growing up who couldn't wear gold or she'd get a rash."

"Sheppard, Gideon," Jessica said, gesturing to the guy who could have been Hunter's fraternal twin. "Gideon, Sheppard."

I nodded at him. "Nice to meet you."

He paused and nodded back. "Likewise."

"Turning usually stops things like allergies," I said. "That's why you don't see wolves wearing glasses unless they're blending in."

"That's what Shawn, my paperwork guy, does," Jessica said, dipping a chip into the salsa and taking a bite.

"Yeah, but I'm not a wolf," Naiya said.

"Maybe that's why it didn't go away," Kristos said.

Naiya's hands curled into fists. "I bet that asshole,

Brooks, knows."

Kristos leaned forward and met her gaze, dropping his voice to gentle tones. "It is what it is, Kitten."

"To answer your question, Lynn," Jessica said, finishing her chip. "Silver is an old wives' tale. It's wolfsbane in the ink. Slows the healing down enough that the pigment can settle beneath the skin instead of being expelled. Gideon is the one who figured it out after he got turned."

Gideon wiped at the spot he was going over and dropped the paper towel into the small pile he had collecting on top of his tool cart. He reached down with that hand and pulled up the bottom of his sweatpant leg to show a bunch of colored dots on the back of his calf.

"I had to make sure I knew what it did to the colors," he explained. "Those dots are just the ink that stayed. I tried a bunch of other stuff first, including silver. Most of it just healed away with no issue, but some of them burned like fire as they did."

"Huh," I said and turned to Lynn with a shrug. "So yeah. Silver's basically harmless."

"I mean, a blade's a blade," Jessica said as she leaned forward. "But silver's a soft metal and doesn't hold an edge well. And even if it did, it wouldn't do any more damage than any other blade would. It's more about who—or what—is wielding it."

I jerked my chin toward Gideon, who'd gone back to working on Hunter's sleeve. "Why didn't you tell anyone about that? I'd think there'd be a *ton* of packs all over the country who'd want to know the secret."

Jessica gave a wry snort. "How many of my annual newsletters do you even open?"

"Uhh—"

She crossed her arms over her chest. "It was in last year's update. And the year before that. *And* the one before that."

I opened and shut my mouth a few times, though words failed to emerge.

Kristos huffed out a little laugh as he took a bite of his own salsa-laden chip.

Jessica smiled and leaned back in her chair. "Anyway, you came here to find out what you can help me with, but I should probably start with what I'm actually working on. So, the simple version? I'm working out a plan to make our presence known to humanity at large."

The house went quiet as my eyebrows tried to crawl into my hairline. Even the buzz of the tattoo needle paused.

"I'm sorry," I said as I stopped chewing on the chip I'd just popped into my mouth. "You want to what?" There's no way I could have heard her right. Humanity is every single level of 'shoot first, ask questions later.' If enough of them even *thought* we existed—not the conspiracy nuts, but the actual people in power—they'd wipe entire countries off the face of the Earth before they killed all of us. They'd basically be doing the vampires a favor.

She spread her arms wide and her golden gaze held mine without a hint of trepidation. "I want humanity to know that we exist."

Even her heartbeat was steady.

She was serious.

"I have one of the best PR teams in the country helping me to pick the right time, and the right way to do it," she continued. "And I want us wolves to be the ones to tell them."

I blinked at her as she folded her arms across her chest again. The heat of the gaze of everyone who had line of sight on me was palpable.

I tried to keep my voice level, though incredulity seeped into my words anyway. "That's a *terrible* idea. Are you out of your mind?"

She furrowed her brow. "No."

"You want to tell everyone—all of humanity—that werewolves are real. That the things they've made movies about for decades, and written stories about for far longer, are real."

She nodded. "I do. I want to correct their understanding of us. To disprove the fiction they know with the truth of what we are."

"And you want my help doing it."

She rocked her head from side to side. "I want you on board with the idea at least."

I simply watched her, dumbfounded, while refrains of 'that's a terrible idea' warred with 'what the hell are you thinking?' for loudest thought in my head. Memories of the atrocities mankind had visited upon itself throughout history played through my mind: wars fought because people looked or spoke differently, mass genocide committed for following a different faith, lands conquered or completely destroyed simply because they *could*. There was no possible way they'd stomach our presence.

But she was sure of herself... sure of her words, at least. And I got the feeling that she'd had the idea to do this for a *very* long time.

No one in the house moved—not Lynn, or Naiya, or Kristos—not Jay in the kitchen or the guy working on Hunter's tattoo or the folks watching soccer. Even the TV had been muted.

It was like the whole house was holding its breath to watch my reaction.

Jessica had been dismissed out of hand so much in her life that the last thing I wanted to do was belittle her in her own home. She deserved better than that.

I wiped a hand across my face with a deep sigh before looking up at her again. "Walk me through your logic, Jessica."

"The vampires are trying to do it for us," she said, a hint of relief in her voice. "And I want to get ahead of that. If we can watch how humanity talks about the things that go bump in the night—if we track how their natural curiosity leads them—then we can find a time when their language surrounding us is more favorable and use that time to show them the truth."

"There's no way that's going to happen in any kind of reasonable timeframe," I said. "Certainly not in my lifetime, and likely not even yours."

She was younger than me by at least two hundred years, which meant she had at least five hundred to go before she even reached the age of the oldest wolf currently alive that I knew—General George Buckheim. And the longest-lived wolf I'd ever known had been a full two hundred years older still. The last time humanity had even liked *regular* wolves was back when they tamed them to be their companion animals, and that was before they even started counting the years the way they do now.

"It's going to have to happen sooner rather than later," Jessica replied, dipping another chip into the salsa.

The front door opened and I realized the sounds in the house had resumed, however quietly. The house was still listening, but the tension had eased a bit.

A muscular wolf, built a little more thick than Hunter at the end of the table, strolled into the dining room, his black tank top in hand. He wore a black baseball cap and grey sweatpants, and he smelled of body oil and some woman's perfume. He nodded to us and stepped behind Jessica to fist bump Hunter and nod at the guy working on the tattoo.

"Another late night, huh Nate?"

He grabbed a tortilla chip and scooped a heaping helping of salsa onto it as he smiled. "Lemme know when you want a piece, Jess. I gotchu." He winked at her as he shoved the salsa laden chip into his mouth.

Jessica shook her head. "Not gonna happen."

He shrugged. "Your loss."

She rolled her eyes, but smiled at him. "Go get some sleep, horndog."

He kissed her cheek and dropped his voice to a whisper as he reached past her to grab another chip. "Jealousy is sexy."

Jessica shouldered him toward the stairs with a laugh as he shoved the chip into his mouth.

It sounded like a rote routine of theirs. Like she'd had this conversation with him any number of times.

Jay came back out to the table with a bowl of guacamole and another bowl of chips.

"You okay, Shep?" Lynn's voice was quiet in my ear.

I blinked and turned to her. Her blue-grey eyes flicked up to me and then down to my chest. "I'm fine.

Why?"

She leaned closer to me, letting a curtain of her wavy brown hair hide her face and dropped her voice to be barely audible. "You were staring daggers at that guy."

Jay returned to the table with bottles of water for everyone.

"Was I?" I whispered as I blinked again and straightened.

She nodded.

"Thanks, Jay," Jessica said, passing the water bottles along one-by-one.

Huh. I absently took the water bottles Kristos passed and sent them along to Lynn and Naiya.

My fellow alpha met my gaze again as Kristos set my own water bottle in front of me. "Look, if the vampires get their way, they'll make us out to be the terrifying creatures they keep putting in horror movies—like you said. They *will* turn humanity against us. And humans are *very* good at killing things, in case you hadn't noticed."

It was like she'd plucked the thoughts straight from my mind. I unscrewed the cap to my water.

And then I remembered the vampires we'd encountered in Amarillo on our way here. They had big hats, bright suits, and pointy boots that caught the light in the gas station parking lot. I couldn't help but smile at the hilarity of them.

"We did run into some vampires in Amarillo," I said, the amusement unmistakeable in my voice.

Naiya snorted as Lynn let out a little giggle.

"And they *were* recording," Kristos added.

I shook my head with a little laugh as the memory washed through me. "You should've seen it, Jess. The absolute *cheesiest* rhinestone cowboy vampires I had *ever* seen."

She arched an eyebrow at me, but a smile played at her lips. "Jess?"

I sobered and cleared my throat. "Sorry. Jessica." I took a sip of my water.

The smile escaped as she tucked a strand of hair behind her ear and opened her bottle of water. "It's fine,

Sheppard. You can call me Jess if you want. Most of my pack does."

Jess. I liked it. I weighed whether to tell her she could call me by my own first name. But I wasn't even sure it was something I was comfortable with. She'd used it before on that desolate stretch of highway with her pack around her, but that was addressing me in front of the church, who had known me by that name. No one had actually called me that in ages. Not since my parents passed, decades upon... wow, *centuries* ago.

The tension was certainly broken, at least on the bomb she dropped. And the house had gone back to its usual volume—shit. She was still talking.

"Which means we need to get ahead of it before it goes national, because that's only a matter of time," she said. "I mean, you see it, right?"

I blinked and took a sip of water to stall as I forced myself to catch up. She was talking about the vampires and the recordings online. "I'm sure they're *trying* to out us, but humans are very *very* good at finding explanations for things they don't otherwise understand. I mean, look at what they think of aliens."

"Wait," Lynn said. "Aliens are *actually* real?"

I shrugged. "I wouldn't be able to tell you for sure, but that's not the point. Humans have been explaining away the things that go bump in the night since they've had the language to do it. And they've kept violence a close companion since the dawn of time."

Jessica ran a hand through her hair. "Yeah, but their conspiracy theories are worse. They're based on the complete lack of anything even resembling good information." She took a sip of her water. "I've sent wolves across the country to debunk the videos the vampires are releasing when they hit local news stations, and that'll at least ensure that the conspiracy theorists continue to look irrational and erratic for now. But we have *got* to get out in front of this. We can't let them control the narrative."

Debunking? I narrowed my eyes. "I'd like to see how you're going about this."

She pulled her phone out of her back pocket and swiped open the screen. A few more taps and she turned the screen to face me before reaching around and hitting play. It was a news segment where a wolf was debunking the video from a cell phone. The wolf on screen paused the video playing in the corner and gestured to a spot like a weatherman points out a storm system and noted that the blur there is where someone edited out the wires pulling the subjects of the video around. Her voice dripped with the lie.

"I saw her before," Kristos said. "On my drive to Colorado. She was in..." he snapped his fingers. "Sweetwater, Texas."

Jessica—Jess—huffed out a little laugh. "That was almost two years ago now." She raised the phone. "This is from last week."

"It's the same story," he said, reaching for another chip.

She stopped the video and sat back in her chair. "Of course it is. There's not a whole lot that can explain a vampire or a wolf moving too fast for a camera to record reliably. Even the good ones they're putting in phones these days can't catch it clearly. At least, not without a marker like they use in bullet speed tests."

"And thank God for that," Hunter said.

Jessica looked over at him and nodded.

"You're telling people what to see," I said. "You're lying to them."

She looked back at me. "We have to. You know that. And it's not like they aren't being lied to already. Or are you telling me your driver's license still says Tobias Sheppard?"

Something in my brain short-circuited at hearing my name from her lips again. I blinked and shook it off, hoping it came across as me bristling at her nonchalance. "Of course not," I said. "Just like there's no chance in hell yours still says Jessica LaRoux."

Two can play at that game.

But she smiled cooly at me as she cocked her head in a gesture that screamed 'see?'

"This is our best option for what they're posting online," she said.

"Why not just get in touch with the websites and block their access?" I hooked a thumb over my shoulder. "I could lend you Ian. He's great with computers and electronics. I'm sure he could help."

Jessica smiled at me like I was a child.

I pressed my lips into a line and tried not to glower.

"There are too many places they could get those videos out for us to be able to cut them *all* off," she said. "Nevermind that we don't have werewolves in the C-suites of social media. What I *do* have is wolves in hotspots all around the country, like I said. They're watching news sites and preparing to travel wherever they're needed. These guys have a fabricated paper trail that says they're qualified experts, but I have other wolves in journalism and video editing classes right now, learning what they can. And my PR team is monitoring what the public thinks about the videos and the supernatural world at large. They've been working on the optics to make sure we get the message right when we *do* go public. They just need a face, and you're better than anyone I know to help me with that."

"Wait," I said. "Back up. Just how big *is* your pack, Jessica?" I hadn't heard a number in any recent years, but I knew it was easily among the largest in the country, if not *the* largest.

She took a deep breath and let it out slowly as she thought. "I couldn't tell you the exact number off the top of my head. The wolves I send out sometimes drift and join the local pack. You can feel when they're drifting, y'know?"

I nodded. I was quite familiar with the dull ache of the plucked connection. It happened every time I sent a wolf to go be with a pack that was a better fit for them.

She rolled a shoulder. "But sometimes they pick up someone new. So, I'd have to check my records to give you an accurate count. I can tell you it's a lot more than what you saw when we bared our teeth at the church over Naiya."

"And you want me to help you find the right person to tell the humans we're here," I said.

She smiled at me. "Something like that."

There was something she wasn't telling me. I could feel it.

I narrowed my eyes. "I'm going to have to see for myself what exactly you've got your nose in here before I agree to anything." I folded my arms across my chest. "I'm sure you see what you say you're seeing, but I'm not convinced that going public now is the right call."

She held my gaze for a long moment and chewed on the inside of her cheek.

"Fine," she said finally, getting to her feet. "Let's take a drive."

SEVEN

*** (JESSICA) ***

MY HAND WAS ON the latch of the door when it gave and pushed into me, knocking me backwards into Sheppard's brick wall of a chest. Sheppard's arm came up around my waist to steady me, and when my hand brushed his as I got my feet under me again, I felt it.

It was like static from fresh clothes out of the dryer, or the air just before lightning strikes.

Mine, whispered my wolf.

I shook my head. Nope. Not mine. No one is mine but my pack.

Sheppard's heart pounded against my back with a rhythm that was almost the same as mine, and the warmth of his scent was edged with something I couldn't quite name. I could feel him gazing at me.

Shit.

Don't look at him.

I brushed his hand from me with more static as I took a step away from him and sized up who'd just bowled me over coming into the house. The scent of crisp fresh snow told me what I'd find.

Kaanskkairiskollik.

I looked up, and had to keep looking up all six-plus feet of him with his slim-fit white linen shirt with the sleeves rolled up to his forearms and loose grey pants. He was all long limbs and charisma as he bent to steady me.

"Oh wow, sorry Jess," he said. "Were you on your way out?"

I looked over my shoulder at Sheppard and his entourage, purposefully avoiding meeting Sheppard's eyes. Lynn and Naiya were staring.

So was Kristos.

Interesting.

I mean, sure, Kaan was a silver fox with his chiseled features, cropped salt-and-pepper hair, salt-and-pepper scruff, and smile lines around his silvery eyes, but he was still just Kaan.

I smiled at him. "I was, actually, but it's fine." I took a breath and turned to Sheppard. "Sheppard, this is Kaan."

"Kaanskkairiskollik," he corrected, first finger extended.

I just barely managed *not* to roll my eyes, though I did sigh. "Kaanskkairiskollik." I gestured to Sheppard. "Kaanskkairiskollik, this is Sheppard. He and his pack are using the guest house as a home base while they figure out where to go next."

Kaan smiled and extended a hand to Sheppard. "You can call me Kaan."

I *didn't* manage not to roll my eyes that time as I shook my head. Of-fucking-course he wanted to be the one to introduce his nickname.

Sheppard nodded as he shook his hand, but his eyes were narrowed.

He probably couldn't make heads or tails of the not-quite-human Kaan. But that secret wasn't mine to tell.

"Lynn," Lynn said, shaking his hand.

"Naiya."

"Oh!" Kaan said, his smile widening as he took her hand. He cocked his head thoughtfully at her but then he took a deep breath as he caught sight of Kristos, who'd taken a step toward Naiya.

He held out a hand toward Kristos as his smile turned flirtatious. "And who is this?"

Kristos snorted but the corners of his mouth quirked upward as he took Kaan's hand. "Kristos."

Lynn made a face and I met her gaze with a smile. Sheppard raised an eyebrow at her and her gaze flicked to Kristos and then Kaan before she looked back at him with a wry little half smile.

Even more interesting.

Who knew the bear was so open?

I blinked and looked at the silver fox. "What'd you need, Kaan?"

He winked at Kristos and then looked back at me. He was almost lost for a moment. "Oh yes! There was a rift that opened in my ceiling."

My eyes widened. "Did anything come through?"

He shook his head. "Just a couple of odds and ends: a spoon, a stick, someone's dolly. I threw the last one back—it seemed important. But then this came through." He brought a hand from behind his back and held up a music box.

That hand had been empty when he arrived.

"I thought I'd bring it to you," he continued. "It plays a common lullaby from back home."

"I'm surprised it didn't smash to pieces," I said as he wound up the box and opened the lid.

"I caught it before it hit the ground," he said.

A soft tinkling tune played, its melody simple and sweet. I couldn't help but smile at it.

And then I noticed Naiya's face. Her eyes were wide like she'd just had an epiphany.

"Why would I know that tune?" Naiya asked. She hummed along with the next couple of notes to prove her point.

Kaan blinked at her, his brow furrowed. "Because you're from Arcaniss, of course."

Sheppard looked between her and Kaan. "Wait, what?"

"You didn't know?" Kaan cocked his head to the side. "Can't you smell it?" He dropped his voice to a whisper. "Are you not what I think you are?"

I inhaled myself to see what he was talking about, picking through the scents to find the one that could be hers.

"The fresh snow," Kristos said.

There it was. And what an apt description. She still smelled wild, like every wolf I'd ever known, but that wild ran under clear, crisp snow. Take away the wild, and she smelled like Kaan.

Kaan thought for a moment as the music box wound to an end and then smiled at Kristos. "Do you know? That *is* how I'd describe it. I'd certainly not put a name to it before." He shrugged as he turned to me. "Well anyway, Jess, you're welcome to keep it if you'd like. I'm quite familiar with the tune myself."

I smiled. "That's very kind of you, Kaan. Thank you." I took the proffered box and stepped over to put it on one of the shelves in the great room.

"Where are you off to anyway?" Kaan's face was mischievous when I returned, and he waggled his eyebrows at me as he glanced at Sheppard and back.

I sighed again, suppressing yet another eye roll as I gestured to Sheppard. "Just gonna show the visiting alpha the PR offices—let him get a whiff of what I've got my nose in here."

"Uh huh." Kaan smiled knowingly and then abruptly turned to Kristos. "So you're free then?"

Kristos blinked and looked to Lynn and Naiya.

Lynn crossed her arms. "If we aren't safe here, surrounded by a veritable shitpile of wolves, we aren't safe anywhere."

"Pfft," I said. "You won't find a safer place this side of the Atlantic."

Naiya leaned against the doorframe and gave him a level look. "Since when does a grown-ass man of nearly two thousand years need permission from a couple of twenty-somethings to do *anything*?"

I couldn't help but laugh at that, and Shep and Kaan joined me.

"There is this *beautiful* spot in the middle of this city proper, just thirty minutes southwest of here," Kaan said. "And I know a great place for lunch."

Kristos took another long look at Lynn and then Naiya, the latter of which bobbed her head in Kaan's direction before crossing her arms.

Sheppard tossed him his keys, which Kristos caught easily.

He met Kaan's eyes. "Alright then."

"Great!" Kaan's smile was radiant.

"We can fill you in later about what Jess is up to," Lynn said.

I shook my head with a snort. "You're not coming along, you can hear it from your alpha should he choose to share it."

"Jessica..." Sheppard said in a dark tone that made something go instantly molten in me.

Damn.

But still.

I folded my arms across my chest and stood a little straighter as I looked at Sheppard. "No." It was my alpha voice. "Until I know whether I can count you in, the less eyes on what's going on at my PR headquarters, the better."

Sheppard sighed and nodded before turning to Lynn. "I'll see you when I get back."

"You two are welcome to hang out here," I offered. "My pack comes and goes, so you'll get a lot of new faces, but they're all safe."

"I think we'll just head back over to see what Kaylah's up to," Lynn said.

Naiya nodded and the two of them brushed past Kaan to leave through the front door.

Kaan and Kristos followed them, and I took Shep

around to the garage as the Ram beeped open and then roared to life a moment later.

Sheppard and I took my F350 to the PR offices, which were only a ten-minute drive from the house. I shared the building with three other businesses: Shawn's law firm, a real estate office, and a set of those puzzle escape rooms. We all had separate entrances, though, so I didn't have to worry about people just showing up in my office.

"Eclipse Media," Sheppard said, reading the sign on the building. "Cute."

"Better than Full Moon Media," I said. Which was our first idea, and too on-the-nose for my liking.

"I'd say so."

"Hey Paige," I said, greeting the petite blonde admin with big brown eyes sitting behind the front desk. "Is Blair in today?" The head of my PR spent two days a week in my office and three in hers, but I left it up to her to shuffle around which two days would work best.

"She is," Paige said, "but she's finishing up a conference call in her office right now."

"Ask her to come find me when she's done?"

"Sure."

"Thanks, Paige," I said.

I gestured for Sheppard to follow me, ignoring his arched eyebrow. I knew what his question was, and I'd answer it when I was good and ready to.

"Bathroom's over there," I said, gesturing as I walked him through the office. It wasn't small, but it wasn't exactly sprawling either. "Blair's office is there. This is our small conference room; our main one is much larger. That's my office there, and the server room is over there." I definitely wasn't showing him what was behind the door across the hall from the server room. That would only raise questions I had *zero* intention of answering now.

I leaned around the corner and peeked into Eric's office. He was there behind the desk, frowning at something on his screen. He did that a lot these days.

"Knock, knock," I said, rapping lightly on his door.

Eric looked up at me. "Hey Jess."

I stepped into the office, Sheppard in tow. At the sight of the newcomer, Eric turned off the two TV screens on the wall.

"Eric, this is Sheppard—"

"The visiting alpha," Eric said, extending his hand as he stood. "I'm Eric." He raked his other hand through the mop of dark curls atop his head, though the sides and back were all shorn short.

Sheppard shook his hand with a smile. "A pleasure."

"Eric knows the ins and outs of just about any computer you could throw at him," I said. "He codes and knows internet security and can build a PC from scratch without having to reference things to make sure everything's compatible."

"I still doublecheck it, just to be sure," Eric said.

"Even so, that's an impressive list of skills," Sheppard said.

Eric smiled. "Thanks." He looked to me. "I cleared squad three's channels already. Just let me know who to throw in there when you get a chance."

I nodded. "Thanks, Eric. I will. I'll let you get back to your troublesome code."

The corner of his mouth quirked upward. "Thanks."

We left Eric's office and rounded the corner.

"And this is the main conference room," I said, opening the door.

There were two big-screen TVs each on three of the walls with a long thin shelf running along under all of them with a keyboard and mouse for every pair. There were three oval tables with enough seats for eight each arranged around the room, along with a handful of additional chairs along the back wall.

"What the hell is all of this?"

"Well," I started, "those are called conference tables. And we've set computer chairs around them instead of standard ones because the computer chairs are more comfortable."

I gave him a mischievous smirk. I was a smart ass and I knew it.

He actually fucking *glowered* at me, with his arms crossed and everything.

And holy hell if it wasn't fucking hot.

I pulled my bottom lip between my teeth as my cheeks heated. I quickly turned away from him to hide the color on my face as other parts of me responded to him as well.

God, get it together, Jess!

I shook my head and sighed before gesturing to each screen in turn. "This first screen here is our pack's chat server. Eric built it, largely manages the membership, and keeps the data secure. We use it to stay in touch with everyone spread around the country, and it's an easy place for the pack to drop supply requests and IT needs. The second screen there is the latest keyword report from Blair, which is how we track the public opinion of both us and the vampires right now. We currently check it weekly, but once everything goes live, Eric will have a running check in the background that we can look at anytime. That running check will give us in-the-moment data whenever we need it. The third screen there is just a copy of the chat server again, with the police scanners and local emergency channels as the focus. Obviously the fourth is just a map of San Antonio, so we can map out whatever comes up in the emergency channels. The two screens across the way show just the private playlist of our newscast appearances—"

"You're already telling people?!" His voice was incredulous.

I turned to look at him and shook my head. "Hell no! We're just debunking the vamps, like I showed you! But we keep the playlist so we know what we've said already to keep our messaging consistent. Blair calls it 'staying on brand.'"

Sheppard jerked his chin toward the final TV. "And that last screen is just another copy of the chat server, right?"

I nodded. "Yep. That's focused on the general chat for the squads I've got around the country." I pulled my phone from my pocket. "I'm going to go ahead and add you to the chat server, but until you're on board, you'll have limited access." I looked up at Sheppard. "So it'll be just the general chats for you, plus the emergency channels."

He furrowed his brow. "Who all is in this chat server of yours?"

"My whole pack, plus Blair and Paige, and a handful of others. Everyone there is a trusted contact, so if you trust me, you can trust them."

"I trust you more than I trust most, Jess."

Well, that certainly felt good to hear. I smiled at him. "Thanks. There are channels that you can get into that are much more focused than just the general chat, but I'm not putting you in those until I know you're in. But I can tell you this much: I have a plan, and I'm going to do this with or without you. I'm just gathering the data to find the best time." And I'd much rather do it *with* him than without, because I also trusted him more than I trusted most.

"Jess! Good to see you!" Blair breezed into the room looking as put-together as ever in her light blue button down and navy blazer and pencil skirt. Even her peep-toe heels matched her suit. "And who's this handsome wall of muscle?"

I couldn't help but smile. "Blair, this is Sheppard, Alpha of the Colorado Springs pack. Sheppard, this is Blair, the Chief Operations Officer of Eclipse Media."

Blair extended a hand to shake Sheppard's and he shook it, but looked at me.

"She's human too?"

"She is," Blair said. "And she'd rather you not talk about her like she's not here."

"My apologies," Sheppard said, studying her. "I just... wasn't expecting—"

I snorted. "You thought I'd put a wolf in charge of helping me tell humans that werewolves are real?"

Blair gave a little laugh.

"Well, when you put it like that," Sheppard said, "it certainly makes more sense. And it explains your human admin out there."

"Paige is stellar at her job," Blair said. "I'm lucky to have her."

"How many humans have you roped into this, Jessica?"

I thought a moment. "Only a handful, and it's not any different than the humans in the rehab centers or when a pack gets a trusted friend. Besides, do you really think your friend on the army base has only wolves working for him? With how his program works?"

I was careful about my wording on purpose. I wasn't going to out wolves who didn't want it, and Blair had signed a binding non-disclosure agreement long ago, so I didn't have to worry about her. She'd lose more than just the court case if she broke the terms—she'd lose her reputation and half her client base to boot.

Sheppard sighed. "I suppose that's fair. And I am impressed with the level of detail you're going into here. But the problem is that if we go public, the Church is going to act."

I crossed my arms as I leaned my hip on the edge of a conference table. "That's why I've been telling everyone to read their treaties."

"The Church won't do anything," Blair said.

"And they can't," I added. "I've read those treaties line-by-line. I've had a whole team of lawyers comb through them. There is nothing in there that says anything at all about keeping our presence quiet from the humans. There's nothing that could really even be interpreted that way unless they *really* twist the undue pressure clause. But even that would never hold up. And even if they wanted to do something, what could they do? Debunk our debunking? Allow the vampires to control the narrative?"

Sheppard watched me for a moment, the gears turning behind his golden eyes, before running a hand through his hair and shaking his head. "They wouldn't."

"Exactly." I clicked my tongue at him. "And look at what is going on around us with these rifts! Whatever's causing them is bad. The world clearly isn't ready for whatever comes through, which means it'll fall to us to protect everyone from that too. So we *have* to get out in front of the vampires and get humans used to us *now* before whatever's causing the rifts shows its head."

"We need people to trust you *before* the shit hits the fan," Blair said.

Sheppard sat in the nearest chair and was quiet while he thought. Blair and I took up seats at the same table. His jaw worked while he rolled everything around in his head.

"So," he said finally, "what's the plan, exactly?"

I laughed and shook my head. "Oh no. I need you on board before I give you details. I'm not handing *anyone* the tools to stop me." I leaned forward in my chair. "This is what's good for humanity, Shep. We can better protect them if we don't have to hide."

Sheppard held my gaze for a long time. It was eerie, but not uncomfortably so. I just hadn't had a lot of exposure to holding the gazes of other alphas.

"Just tell me you're in," I said quietly.

Blair sighed. "She wants you for the face of the campaign, Sheppard."

His eyebrows skyrocketed. "You *what*?!"

I winced and glared at Blair, who simply shrugged.

"Look," she said. "You have to extend an olive branch, Jess. You haven't told the poor guy a thing about what you want him to blindly agree to."

Sheppard wiped at his face. "The face of the campaign to make humans aware of werewolves."

I folded my arms across my chest and nodded. "You did say you owed me a favor."

He held my gaze again. "I did. But that's a *big* ask." He sighed and shook his head. "I'm going to need to take some time to think about it."

I nodded again and stood as I blew out a breath. "Fine. I'll drive you back. Thanks Blair." I didn't bother to keep the sarcasm from the last words.

She shrugged, ignoring my sarcasm. "Thank me when he says yes."

Sheppard shot her a look and then stood. I led him out of the conference room and back through the office.

The drive back was tense and silent. I didn't like it, but didn't want to chance pushing him to a 'no' by saying anything. He opened the door as soon as the truck rolled to a stop in my garage. I hurried out as he turned toward the guest house.

"Sheppard," I called.

He turned and looked at me.

"Just... don't take too long, okay?"

He nodded and waved a hand as he turned and continued his way back to the guest house.

Knowing so much of my plans rested on him saying 'yes,' I couldn't even enjoy the view of him walking away.

God, I hoped asking him hadn't been a huge mistake.

EIGHT

*** (SHEPPARD) ***

SHE WANTED ME TO be the face of her PR campaign. Me. A five hundred and fifty year old werewolf. Not some new hotshot that wasn't generations upon generations removed from humanity.

Me.

And God did she ever believe in what she was doing! That woman knew exactly what she wanted to do and how she wanted to do it.

I wiped my face. And just what the *hell* was my wolf thinking, calling her 'mine' just because she fell into me? Had she felt that spark too? I shook my head. No. Even if she had, she definitely was *not* mine.

And what was it she'd deliberately omitted from the tour? She'd gestured and named every door but one. I huffed out a sigh. She'd probably show me that one if I told her I was on board and not a moment before.

As I opened the door to the guest house, Ian and Jamie waved at me from the dining table. Ian was in a black t-shirt with green cargo shorts while Jamie wore just a pair of black basketball shorts, his grey shirt slung over the back of the chair. Kaylah, in a pale pink shirt that proclaimed "life is good," placed a foil-covered pan in the oven—a pork roast, by the smell of it—and water was running upstairs in both of the bathrooms. I grabbed a bottle of water from the fridge and joined the two young wolves at the table. Ian had a U.S. map spread across the table with his laptop alongside it. He was marking locations, presumably where he'd found enough evidence online to call it a rift.

Jamie studied the marks as one of the showers turned off. "If you ignore those outliers, it looks like it's all staying along a planned arc from New York City to Corpus Christi."

Ian nodded. "I like that the data points keep to a trend, but what the *hell* is along that line?"

I shook my head as I looked at the map. The marks did make a neat little arc, but I hadn't heard of any kind of lore that could explain it. "It's almost like it's an arc of a crop circle," I said. "But it's so much bigger than any I've heard of. Any chance you could extrapolate the rest of the circle and see if the rifts continue along it?"

Ian thought about it for a moment. "I could, but it'd run into other countries, so I'd have to run the news reports through translators, making it less reliable. It'd be a *really* big circle." He sat down and started typing and clicking on the laptop.

I nodded and turned to Jamie. "What'd you find in New York?"

"It's basically a hotspot for the rifts," he said, raking a hand through his short dark hair. "They happen something like every other day there, but in clusters of three or four."

Ian looked at me with his sapphire eyes. "They spill shadowy creatures into the alleyways before the rift closes and they dissipate. And the creatures don't stay around."

"They run off?" I asked.

Ian shook his head. "No. They just dissipate with the rift."

"Interesting."

"None of the rifts we saw were stable enough to stay open for more than a handful of seconds though," Jamie said.

"And they were all pretty small," Ian added. "The largest creature I saw come through was about the size of a border collie, and I only saw one such creature."

The other shower turned off as Lynn came downstairs, scrunching water out of her hair with a small towel. She had on purple bike shorts and a long loose white t-shirt.

I looked at Ian. "Any vamp activity?"

"Loads of it," he said.

"There's a pack there, though," Jamie said.

"Yeah, but we didn't catch signs of them anywhere outside of Harlem." Ian turned to me. "The vampires are recording down in Hell's Kitchen. We found a small nest with cameras all over, but I didn't find the system they fed to."

"Ian thinks they're using remote monitoring, but the city's just too big—"

"And too jam-packed," Ian said.

Jamie nodded. "It'd take us *ages* to thoroughly scout the area to find it."

"Where's Daredevil when you need him?" Ian gave Jamie a wry grin.

"Who?" Kaylah asked from the kitchen.

I shook my head. "Humans don't need to get in on this fight." Jamie opened his mouth and I put a hand up. "Not even those with super senses." And we'd have to make sure to make that clear when Jess and I told the world about vampires.

Ian looked over at Kaylah. "Daredevil's this comic book hero that lives and operates in Hell's Kitchen."

"Ah," Kaylah said, and busied herself with the dishes again.

Lynn took a seat at the table, a cold water bottle in hand as she took a look at the map.

"I know you said vampires don't trust each other enough to share information between broods," Jamie said.

I shook my head. "They don't."

Ian shrugged. "Well, they sure seem to now."

"Well, shit," Kaylah said. I looked over to her, and her hand was on her hip as she leaned against the back kitchen counter.

I gave a wry snort. "You said it." I turned back to Ian. "Do you think you grab that vamp's laptop and get into his communications? The one from the cave on the reserve."

"Almost certainly," Ian said, nodding. "What am I looking for, exactly?"

"I need to know what they're doing," I said. "If they're coordinating, there's gotta be some kind of hint of that in that vamp's emails."

"You think they've been doing it for years?" Lynn asked.

I shook my head. "If they *are* coordinating, they could have been doing so for centuries and we just never knew. I highly doubt it, but I'm not eliminating it as a possibility. Not when we have a potential way to confirm it."

Lynn pulled a foot into her chair, hugging her knee to her chest.

"Something's brewing, Shep," Jamie said.

I nodded. "I feel it too. I can't put my finger on what, but I feel it." I ran a hand through my hair. "Which means Jessica is probably right." Humanity needed us as protectors. And our time of hiding was coming to a close.

"What's the problem wi' 'at anyway, Shep?" Kaylah came to sit at the table, placing a bottle of water in front of me before opening one of her own.

I opened it and gulped down a third of the bottle.

"Lynn told me 'bout you buttin' heads wi' Jessica over whatever this plan of hers is."

I arched an eyebrow at Lynn, who looked sheepish as

she tried to shrink back behind her raised knee. "I mean, getting out in front of the vamps is a good idea. And she certainly seems organized enough to pull it off, what with her vampire debunkers all around the country."

Kaylah's face lit with understanding. "You don' like not bein' in charge of it!"

I shook my head. "It's not that."

"Well I know it ain't because she's a woman," Kaylah said.

Jamie's eyes went wide. "Or maybe it *is*." He elbowed me lightly.

I folded my arms across my chest and eyed him. "You've known me long enough to know that's more Matt than it is me."

"Unless someone's got a crush," he mumbled, dropping his gaze to his hands in his lap.

A crush? Seriously? I let out a quiet growl and looked to Ian. "Just let me know what you find?"

Ian's face was screwed up with the laugh he was trying to hold in as he nodded. "Sure. Hey Jamie, any idea where I put that thing?"

"Uhh..." Jamie said.

Kaylah sighed. "It's in th' box with th' extra controllers for y'all's game." She pointed toward the stairs. "Upstairs closet. Top shelf."

"Oh yeah!" Ian lit up with recollection, but then deflated. "I'm gonna need your lanky ass to help me get it down off the shelf."

Jamie snorted as he stood. "Sure."

The two of them headed up the stairs as I took another sip from my water bottle.

"Glad we di'n't scrap 'at thing yet," Kaylah said before taking a sip of her water.

I nodded. "Me too."

"Any chance this is comin' from th' vamp elders?"

Shit. The elders? I wiped my face. "I hope not. The last thing we need is them organizing on a global scale." We could probably still win that fight, but holy hell would it be a war. The amount of packs that would get wiped out would be positively dwarfed by the number of humans that would die without ever knowing why.

Maybe Jessica had seen evidence of that too, which was why she wanted to go public. If we could get humanity to trust us, we could work with them to eliminate the vampires.

God, was that ever a lofty goal.

The front door of the house opened and Kristos breezed in, smelling faintly of freshly fallen snow on top of his usual old leather and not-quite-wolf wild.

Naiya came downstairs about that time as well, her wet hair pulled into a bun on top of her head. She'd put on black jean shorts with a loose green top and was barefoot like everyone else in the house.

"We'd have to give the Church the head's up if they were," I said.

"Yeaahhh, I ain't too keen on 'at," Kaylah said, leaning on the table.

"What are we telling the Church?" Kristos folded his arms across his chest as he leaned against the edge of the kitchen counter.

"Nothing yet," I said. "And nothing at all if we don't have to. But the vampires may be coordinating, and if that's coming from their elders, then the Church is gonna need to know."

"Fuck," Kristos said.

Naiya sat at the table with a can of soda. "Do the vampires usually do that?"

"Coordinate?"

She nodded.

Kristos shook his head. "Hell no."

I sighed. "But if Kitashihime and Vsevolod are the ones calling the shots..."

"Then they'll do jus' 'bout anything," Kaylah said.

I nodded.

We sat in silence for a moment while I mulled over which of the alphas I could trust to ally with. It was an extraordinarily short list. Buckheim. Jessica. Charles, out in Boston. Lawrence, in Phoenix—if he could be pried away from his new mate, Anise. William in Tulsa could be trusted as well. And probably Dante in Tijuana. But I couldn't even be sure they'd all agree to work together.

I hoped it wouldn't come to that.

"Hey Naiya," Jamie said. "Any chance that guy told you about why people can stay this side of the rifts when they close, but the creatures can't?"

Naiya shrugged, but her gaze turned distant. "He just called them rift cats and penumbra dogs. I don't remember him mentioning anything else."

"Huh," Ian said. "I wonder what the difference is then."

"Music boxes stay too, apparently," Naiya said. "If it helps."

Ian narrowed his eyes in thought and cocked his head to the side. "It... doesn't, but it... doesn't *not* help either."

Kaylah stood and grabbed her notebook from the kitchen counter and looked at me. "Where d'you wanna send those two off to next?"

"Jamie and Ian?"

She nodded.

I shook my head. "Let's get everyone back here before I send them out again."

Kayla nodded again. "Well, Daniel and Jonathan'll be back Monday, and Matt 'n Chas said they needed an extra day or two so they'll be back..." She flipped through a couple of pages in her notebook. "...on Wednesday."

"Alright," I said. "We'll re-evaluate then."

"I wasn't tattling like a schoolkid," Lynn blurted. "I just asked Kaylah if maybe you and Jessica had some old beef. She seemed friendly enough before, all things considered."

Just the opposite really.

"It's fine, Lynn," I said. "Kaylah just jumps to protecting kinda everyone."

Lynn nodded. "She moms them."

"Huh?" Kaylah said.

Lynn turned in her chair to face her. "You wanna take care of everyone. Sometimes, that probably includes protecting others from those you care about, largely because the stronger ones don't need your protection."

I snorted out a little laugh.

Kaylah put a hand on her hip as she closed her pen in the notebook. "Now wait jus' a sec."

"You know she's right, Kaylah."

"Mom-ing someone, huh?" Kristos said.

"Oh," Naiya said. "Then you'd get along great with Abigail. She does the same thing."

"In any case," Kristos said, "the spitfire next door is right."

"What's she wanna do exactly?" Kaylah asked.

Lynn dropped her leg from the chair. "What'd those PR offices look like?"

I thought about it before answering. Jess had certainly been cagey enough about mentioning anything at the house, but she'd also made it clear that she understood whose choice it was to give my pack information. And she was going to need more than just me anyway, by my calculations, if she wanted to actually have any chance of success.

"They looked like she knows exactly what she's doing," I said finally, running a hand through my hair. "She wants to take the wolves public, which is wild enough, but then she apparently wants *me* to be the face of that PR campaign."

It'd cost me some of my more tenuous connections to do so, but—with any luck at all—I might be able to call in some other not-quite-favors and get more on board.

"But the Church—" Kaylah said.

I held up a hand to stop her. "Jessica seems pretty certain the Church wouldn't be able to come down on us. She says it's not even addressed in the treaties, which means their bureaucracy would keep them from stepping in."

"And you as the face?" Kristos snickered like there was some inside joke I'd missed.

I waited him out, knowing he'd explain.

"She knew what she was doing when she handed you all that paperwork!" He chuckled some more.

I sighed as I gave him a wry smile. He was right. "She was buttering me up."

Lynn cocked her head to the side as she studied me.

"And it apparently worked. It got you here so she could convince you. So, are you gonna do it?"

"I'd like to take a closer look at the treaties myself before I decide," I said.

"I'll call Daniel," Kaylah said. "He'll look at the fine print again."

I nodded. "Thanks, Kaylah. I was just thinking that."

Kaylah fished her phone from her pocket as she walked to the media room down the hall. Ian and Jamie bounced back down the stairs.

"Found it," Ian said, holding the laptop aloft.

Jamie took the seat next to me as Ian plugged the power cord to the stolen laptop into the wall.

"It'll take a minute to get into this thing, assuming he has a password on it." He rubbed at the back of his neck as he sat back down. "I gotta agree with Lynn, Shep." He looked at me. "If we could do it without pissing off the Church, beating the vamps to the punch on telling the world about us would give us a distinct edge."

"I mean, the Church is gonna be pissed either way," I said.

"That's probably the best reason I've heard yet," Kristos said.

Yeah, except making me the face wouldn't just expose me—it'd expose the pack too.

Lynn studied me. "What does it mean exactly to make you the face of what she wants to do?"

I shook my head. "She wouldn't say exactly, but I know she has a plan."

"Smart," Kristos said. "You can't stop her if you don't know."

"That's what she said." I sighed and looked around the table. "If I had to guess, she's asking me, but she'll need the whole pack to really pull it off. One wolf just doesn't cut it, and I don't know how many of her pack she's outing for this. Assuming I'm right, are you all game for that?"

"The Church already wants to cause problems for me," Lynn said. "What's a few more?"

"It could be a lot more," Kristos said. "But it'd be

worth it to watch them scramble."

"Well, I'm in," Ian said. "Assuming what Jessica said about the Church and their bureaucracy is true."

"Me too," Jamie said.

"I know I'm not technically pack," Naiya said. "But, for what it's worth, I agree with Lynn and Ian... and I guess Jessica, too. My parents might not have thrown me into rehab if they knew that werewolves are real. Even if I'm technically a were*leopard*."

She made a face and Kristos rubbed her knee.

"Yeah," Lynn said, "it's something else to get used to calling yourself something like that, isn't it?"

Naiya gave her a wry smile. "It really is."

"Daniel di'n't see anythin' with a quick keyword search," Kaylah said, coming back to the table. "Which means Jessica's prolly not wrong. The Church can't do anything without it falling under that 'unprovoked retaliation' clause. But Daniel said he'd give it a closer read to be sure 'n' call me back. If she's right—and he thinks she is—it sure would feel nice to beat th' vamps at their own game after havin' to dodge all a them wolf huntin' laws 'cross the country."

I nodded. "That, it would."

I'd need to check with Matt and Chastity too.

Lynn cocked her head to the side. "I thought Jonathan said we were basically bulletproof though?"

Jamie's head thunked onto the table. "Bullets still *hurt*, Lynn! Just like road rash and broken bones!"

Ian snorted out a laugh as I stood and pulled my phone from my pocket.

"I'll call Matt and Chastity." I nodded to Kaylah. "You and Daniel agree then?"

Kaylah returned my nod. "Whatever you need, Shep. We're in. You know that."

I smiled at her. She'd been in my corner since the moment she left her old pack. "Did he say anything about what Jonathan thinks? I don't want to throw the pack into this without everyone being on the same page."

"He had Jonathan on speaker," she said. "He's in so long as th' Church don't come at us harder 'n' they already are with Lynn and Kristos."

"And Naiya," Kristos added.

I nodded and scrolled through the contacts on my phone as I turned down the hall to the master suite. Matt answered as I flopped onto the bed. I knew he and Chastity would follow me come hell or high water, but I didn't want to have to pull them along like stubborn mules. They took a little convincing, and they didn't like it, but they weren't going to stand in the way of it either. He was sure the Church would find some way to make our lives harder for it, and he probably wasn't wrong, but that they begrudgingly agreed in the end was all I needed to know.

NINE

*** (JESSICA) ***

I WAS FINISHING UP my third bowl of Jay's menudo when my phone buzzed. It was a text from Sheppard. I stood and rinsed my bowl before putting it in the sink and padding back toward my room.

"You know how I know it's the other alpha?" Imogen asked.

I looked up at her before turning the corner.

"You make a face and leave the room," she said, following me, and then she dropped her voice to conspiratorial tones. "It's like you have a secret crush."

"Or maybe it's like it's alpha business."

"So I'm at least half right," she said.

I rolled my eyes at her. I didn't have a crush. I didn't *do* crushes. Shaking my head, I shut the door to my room as I thumbed open my phone screen.

Sheppard:

I have your decision.

Another declaration. Peachy. But then the typing bubbles showed up only to disappear again and then reappear and then stop again.

Okay great. At least he's trying *not* to just drop a bomb and walk away.

The bubbles popped up and disappeared a few more times.

Sheppard:

Can we just meet up and chat?

I snorted out a laugh.

Me:

Sure. Come on over. Go around back. I'll meet you on the porch.

I padded out to the kitchen, grabbing two big cups and filling them with ice and sweet tea before heading back to my room. I moved the heavy, black velvet curtains out of the way of the sliding glass door to my rear patio and opened the door. On the deck, we had some rocking chairs with side tables and a couple of big fans. Only one of them pointed to the corner where I planned for us to sit, but I turned on both for whatever privacy their noise could offer us.

And then I checked my reflection in the sliding glass door as I put the cups of tea down on one of the side tables.

This was my favorite time of day, that time between when the sun dips *just* below the horizon and full dark. Dark enough that most people didn't even bother with sunglasses anymore, but light enough that you don't need supernatural senses to see everything.

I was glad I had showered after my session today. I had on a black crop top with shredded acid wash shorts and was barefoot. Not the most professional I'd ever looked, but if Sheppard's answer was yes, he was likely to see me a lot more in the coming... well a lot more. And the odds that I'd always be put-together? Well, next to nil, really.

And it wasn't like I had time to change anyway.

And then the wall of muscle that was Tobias Sheppard rounded the corner, his face somber. He had on a white tank that did really nice things for his shoulders paired with brown cargo shorts that had more pockets than anyone really needed. He paused when he saw me, but only for a fraction. Something I couldn't name crossed his face for barely a breath before the somber face was back.

"That's not a good face," I said, handing him one of the sweet teas and gesturing to the chair on the far side of the side table.

He took it, raised it in thanks, took a sip, and sat down in the chair. I followed suit, sitting in the other chair closest to the door to my room. Thankfully, I'd remembered to put the curtain back, so my collection wasn't on display for God and everyone to see.

"It's just... it's a big ask, Jessica," Sheppard said. "It's one that would take a considerable redirection of my pack's resources and attention."

"So... that's a no then?"

Sheppard took a deeper gulp of his tea this time, his throat moving before he licked his lips as he tried not to make a face.

I blinked.

Shit.

I was watching his mouth. I needed to stop that. I took a sip of my own tea.

"It's not a no," he said, and I almost spit my tea out in surprise.

"What?"

"It's not. It'll just cost you both of your favors to get me and my pack involved in this."

"No one said anything about your whole pack." I arched an eyebrow at him. "And, by my count, you owe me *three*, sir. Unless you aren't going to count me keeping the paper trail to Naiya in my pack."

He shook his head. "No, you're right. That's definitely a third."

"So... two of your three then."

He nodded and held up his hand, first finger extended. "One for me." His second finger joined his first. "And one for my pack. One werewolf doesn't protect a whole country, Jess. You're going to need more faces."

I studied his expression, the smile lines at the corners of his eyes, the serious set of his sharp jaw... No no. The pack. His pack. Can he fold them in? *Should* he?

"Well... maybe not Matt." I gave him a wry smile.

He laughed. "Maybe you're right."

"Pretty sure that one can only go public once the movement as a whole is trending positively."

He nodded.

And then I realized something and snapped my fingers. "Oh yeah! And it'll give another layer of protection to your *purgatum*! If she's a public face—"

"Then the church can't make her disappear."

I shook my head. "Not without a *damn* good story as to why."

"So you mind telling me the plan then?"

"I dunno," I hedged. "Are you in?"

"Are you cashing in your two favors?"

"It looks like that's what it takes," I said.

"Then it looks like I'm in."

That's what *he* said.

Shit.

I just had a session, I didn't need to be this thirsty.

"There's no backing out if I tell you my plan."

"There is if there needs to be."

"Shep," I met his gaze and hardened mine. "This is important. I need you to give me your word. I'll work with you to make sure we're not crossing lines, but I need to know that you're not gonna back out on me."

He watched me and took a deep breath. I was glad he wasn't just flippantly agreeing, but the longer he waited, the more nervous I became.

"Fine," he said finally, nodding. "You have my word, Jess. Don't make me regret it."

"I wouldn't," I said, holding his gaze. "I give you mine that I'm not going to push you to cross a line you wouldn't otherwise cross."

"You'll push me a little."

I bobbed my head side to side. "That's fair. I may try to convince you to change your mind, but you'll still get the final say."

He nodded. "Alright. So tell me the plan."

I took a sip of my tea and then pulled my hair into a low ponytail before pulling my legs into the seat to sit cross-legged. "So we'll start with an ad in this year's Super Bowl. Nearly a third of the population of America is tuned in then, it's too good an opportunity to pass up."

"That's got to be expensive," he said, his eyebrows high.

I nodded. "It was. And I had to pay extra for being an otherwise unknown entity. But Blair knows her shit and had us present them with a mock script and tell them it's a trailer for an avant garde indie film. They'll have to see the final ad before it'll air, but the ink's long dry on the contract. The time slot is mine."

Sheppard folded his arms across his chest. "You knew I'd agree."

I pointed at him like I was booping his nose. "I wasn't born yesterday, Shep. I know you well enough to know you hate hiding this fight."

"Lord knows we've been in enough of them."

"Exactly. You were likely to agree once you had it all laid out for you."

He leaned forward, resting an arm on his knee. "So what's the rest of this plan?"

"Step one, we tell them we're real. Then, we tell them we're good; that we're protectors. That's when we show them how many of us end up as firefighters, first responders, and private security. The third step is where we tell them vampires are both real and evil. As you can imagine, these first three steps are going to go by relatively quickly, and kind of overlap with one another.

We'll mention vampires in passing a few times in phase one and two, so they're subconsciously ready for it."

"What if the vamps start their own smear campaign?" He took a sip of his tea.

I shrugged. "Then I'll roll that into our debunking as well."

"What comes after that?"

"Step four is to show them exactly what we're capable of, and what vampires are capable of, which should give them a *very* good understanding of why we're protecting them. That's when we'll tell them we can't help but protect them from the vampires, assuming it hasn't already come to light. I expect some of this will come up in press junkets prior to this step, which is why I've hired Blair."

"She can help with making sure your message doesn't scare people."

I gave him a wry look. "Scaring them is pretty much inevitable. None of this is comfortable information. Blair's gonna help make sure we're doing damage control without stopping our forward momentum. As it all comes to light, it's gonna feel really overwhelming at first—kinda like it does for new wolves. But you and I have seen enough of that initial adjustment to know what it's likely to look like for a person."

"How'd Blair find out?"

"Close encounter with a vamp," I said. "She was already poking around, but she didn't have any real contacts that could or would tell her anything. It was more coincidence than anything that we connected. I filled her in on what her gaps were."

Sheppard nodded approvingly. "You've... really thought this through, Jess. I'm impressed. When do you plan to tell them about crazed wolves?"

I shook my head. "I haven't put that into the plan. We'll have to add in the protecting them from anything else—like the things from the rifts—into the 'this is why we protect you from vampires' phase. But crazed wolves... I mean... that's how most of us came to be. We'll be lucky if we can manage to keep that fact under wraps."

Sheppard nodded. "It's a dangerous thing to keep secret."

"But if we tell them, we risk everything falling to shit," I said. "I've run through with Blair a number of different ideas for how and when to tell them and they pretty much all end with the humans going nuclear."

Sheppard wiped at his face. "We need to see if we can damage control that before it comes to light on its own."

I nodded. "Sure. But the problem is that if they even *think* we could harm them, this is all gonna crumble."

"There'll be detractors," he said.

"Of course there will be." I took a sip of my tea. "I fully expect the vampires to try to out the crazed wolves. And then there'll be the ones who will retaliate by lying to them some more. And you know there's gonna be a whole flock of people who won't believe that vampires are unequivocally evil. But you gotta trust me, Shep. I've had a *lot* of years to put this together. It's time to make our move."

He nodded. "So what's our next step?"

Our next step is you losing that shirt...

Damn.

I took a deep breath and shoved those thoughts away. I was just excited that he'd actually agreed. It helped that he was easy on the eyes. But I didn't need to complicate this by taking someone who would definitely read it as relationship material for a roll in the hay.

"Jess...?"

I shook my head. "The next step for us is to see who we have to be *sure* we don't out. I don't want to make any more enemies than I'm already going to with this." I stood up and stretched. We'd talked for long enough that full dark had fallen. "We can hash out the details tomorrow—maybe over breakfast?"

He took a final sip of his tea and stood. "It's a date."

"No it's not." I snorted out a laugh and levered up on my tiptoes to kiss his cheek. He bent a fraction to accommodate the gesture.

And it was like I'd rubbed fresh socks across the

carpet before doing so. The spark of it tingled through my lips long after the ridiculously brief contact was done.

"I'll... see you in the morning."

He smiled and there was something almost *knowing* about it. "In the morning." He nodded. "'Night, Jessica."

Unff, why'd he have to say it like that?!

I watched him round the corner of the house and listened for his feet on the gravel before darting back into my room.

I had to take care of myself one more time before I could finally relax enough to let myself be around my pack. The last thing I needed was my thirsty brain deciding Nate was the right choice for the night. That horndog had been after me for years, but sleeping with pack was dumb. I didn't need to complicate the power dynamic with something like that.

))))) 🐾 (((((

The next morning I arranged for Sheppard to meet me at Summer's little hole-in-the-wall diner, where the food was always super delicious. She was doing well enough to get a larger place, but she preferred her current location and had enough regulars that she felt like moving would make her start over.

I disagreed with her, but it wasn't my diner.

And I always had a hard time with her anyway. She was one I probably should have sent to Sheppard, but she was so damn damaged when we found her that sending her anywhere would've only traumatized her more.

I hated that I couldn't help but remember her story every time I looked at her. But it wasn't her fault. She got turned and then got turned again before she actually died. It shouldn't have worked but yet there she stood—all wolf, no vamp—with enough of an unsettling vibe that it was hard to trust her.

When Sheppard arrived at the diner, he had practically his entire pack in tow, all in various versions of the tank-and-shorts look. Even in the morning, summer in Texas was hot. I blinked and called Summer over. I had only planned for the two of us, so we needed more tables. She grabbed a table in each hand and scooted them into a line before moving over the chairs.

As Shep's wolves took their seats I gave him a look. "You sure you got everyone here?"

He gave me a knowing smile. "You said it wasn't a date. My pack likes to eat together."

"Minus your brooding beefcake, apparently," I said.

"Who, Kristos?"

I nodded.

"I think he's taken a shine to your friend."

"Or the other way around," Naiya said. "Either way, he smelled like him when he came home yesterday."

Lynn's eyes went wide. "He slept with him?"

Like we didn't all scratch the itch with a no-strings fling every now and again. Kristos probably had hundreds of notches in his bedpost.

"Can't say I'm surprised," I said. "It's not like Kaan is terribly picky."

"Not my business whether he slept with him or not," Naiya said, though she did seem a little more prickly than she had a moment ago. "I just know he smelled like him yesterday."

Hm, was that jealousy? Or just pent up energy?

Maybe I should send her copy of one of my favorite toys, see if it can't help her unwind a little.

Summer came around and got everyone's breakfast orders before bringing pots of coffee and honey to the table.

Lynn shook her head. "It's not a regional thing?"

Shep followed her gaze to the honey pots. "The honey and coffee? Hardly. There have been times in our history that honey was easier to get your hands on than sugar. I'd honestly be surprised to find a wolf older than fifty that *didn't* use honey instead of sugar."

"Plus th' newer sugars all taste chemically," Kaylah said. "Honey's jus' tastier."

I poured some honey into my mug, just a drop or two to take the bite off the edge.

Sheppard stirred his coffee. "Any chance you've got someone tracking the rifts on your server?"

I looked at him and cocked my head to the side. "Probably someone in the storm trackers has been up to something like that. Why?"

"Well, Ian and Jamie just got back from New York, where they found clusters of rifts opening for a handful of seconds at a time."

"We found vampires and a pack there too," Jamie, his tall and lanky wolf said.

"Sure," the far shorter Ian said. "But the rifts in clusters seem new. And that pattern is too specific to not mean something."

"Pattern?" I arched an eyebrow at him.

"They run in an arc from New York to Corpus Christi," he said. "I wish I knew what was on that arc."

I pulled out my phone. "Text me and I'll get you added to the storm tracker channels. I'm willing to bet one of them can help. Just... remember that they're pretty much all human and some are ridiculously gullible."

"Got some that are real conspiracy nuts in there, huh?" Sheppard said.

"Well I didn't put them all in there, and neither did Eric," I said. "It just taps into the public channel." I turned to Ian. "But you'll be able to get to *their* server where you can ask questions from there."

"Thanks." He smiled and pulled out his phone as Summer came around and served everyone their food. She put an extra plate down for herself next to me and sat down just as I finished giving Ian my number.

"Break time," Summer said with a smile.

I returned her smile and then looked around the table. "Guys, this is Summer." I gestured to her and then around the table. "Summer, this is Sheppard's pack."

"Half of it," Sheppard said, his chest puffing a little.

"More than half," Lynn said.

"Just barely," Naiya added. "We're only missing five, and there's six of us here."

"And one of you is technically hers," Sheppard said, eyeing Naiya and jerking his thumb toward me. "Which makes it an even five, and a full half." He smiled as he took a bite of his toast.

Man, his pack was small. Larger than it had been in the past, sure, but still. I had more than that working at Howlers alone. His entire pack was easily less than a quarter the size of mine.

"Sheppard's in for the PR campaign," I told Summer.

"The rest of us, too," Naiya said. "I'd never have gotten sent to rehab if my parents knew. I'd never have had to go through what Brooks..." She got a faraway look on her face and then it fell. She sniffed and blinked back something as Lynn rubbed her back.

"People should know," Lynn said. "It'd be less scary if they knew what to expect."

"I figured since I was in and these guys are with me," Sheppard said, "you could just give them the short version of the plan so I don't get it wrong."

"Just so I can repeat it again for the *other* half of your pack?" I raised an eyebrow at him.

Sheppard shrugged. "It'll stick better with repetition."

I rolled my eyes. "Fine. But I'm keeping it to the super short version."

"Fine by me."

"So we'll start with letting them know we're here and then that we're protectors. Then we'll tell them about the vampires and how we can't help but protect them from the bloodsuckers, among other things. By that time, we should be trending positively enough that we can do some more intense press junkets."

"When do you talk about crazed wolves?" Lynn asked.

I shook my head. "It's not even in the plan. It'll be some time before we can afford to let them know something like that."

She narrowed her eyes at me, but didn't try to hold my gaze. "What's the point of all of this then if we're not preparing people?"

"The point," I said, "is to get them used to the idea that we're here and ready to protect them from the vampires and the things in the rifts. The point is to show them how in over their head they would be to try to do anything against the vamps themselves. The *point* is to get people used to the idea that the things they think go bump in the night are real, but not all of them are as bad as their stories make them out to be."

Maybe I was a little hot about it. It was why Blair said I needed a better public face. I sighed.

"Why Sheppard?" Jamie asked. "Why us?"

I shook my head again. "I hadn't really counted on all of you." I looked at Sheppard before looking back at Jamie. "But your alpha is pretty well-respected around the country, even if the other packs *are* wary of his relationship with the military. But getting Sheppard on board lends me a legitimacy that I couldn't otherwise have." I looked at Sheppard again. "And he's one of the coolest heads I know, which will come in handy when the press gets aggressive."

Sheppard lit with an epiphany. "You're 'we're here' phase includes showing people that we're not exactly rare. You need me to help you convince other packs to show themselves."

"Even if my whole pack and your whole pack go public," I said, nodding, "that's not enough to protect the country, and I'm already going to have to be spread thin once they start knowing."

"You'll send more squads out," Summer said.

"I'll have to," I said. "The campaign will be in full swing by then. That's the other big part of why I wanted *you.*" I thumped Sheppard's solid arm with the back of my hand. "The other alphas *respect* you."

"They respect you too," Sheppard said with a chuckle.

I gave him a wry laugh. "I'm not an idiot. They don't respect *me*, they respect the size of my pack."

He shrugged. "I mean, it's clearly the larg—"

"Largest in the country," I finished for him. "You think

I don't know that? Do you have *any* idea how many wolves have shown up..." My eyes darted around the table at the collected wolves. I shouldn't... fuck it. "I've had any number of wolves just happen to show up on my doorstep to court me because I'm both born wolf *and* an alpha. Hell, my parents brought me *here*, overseas, because the alpha of the pack I was born into wanted to arrange my marriage... when I was *twelve*. Respect is not something people give to *me*, respect is something they fake to gain access to what I *represent*."

Sheppard blinked at me, something shifting in his perspective.

Great. Pity. My favorite.

"It helps that you're hot," Summer said.

I'm sure she meant well. She had to have meant well. She was trying to lighten the situation. She can't help what she is.

I sighed. "It's *insulting*." My gaze flicked around the table and I raked a hand through my hair, putting my alpha face back on. It must've slipped, judging by the faces of the wolves around me. I guess I'd look a little bewildered and unsure what to say too if a relative stranger just word-vomited at me. "It's also not your problem," I said, meeting Sheppard's eyes. "The point is, you helping me with this makes it easier for the other alphas to warm up to the idea."

Sheppard nodded at me as he shoved a bite of his breakfast into his mouth.

It was quiet for a moment around the table, with a slight tinge of that 'mommy and daddy are fighting' awkwardness.

"What are you going to do about the skeptics?" Ian asked around a bite of his food.

I shrugged. "Nothing. The truth is the truth."

"How are you gonna get the word out initially?" Naiya asked.

"I've paid for an ad in next year's Super Bowl."

Lynn nearly choked on her coffee. "I don't think I'll ever get used to the kind of money you guys just throw around."

I shook my head. "It wasn't an easy expense to just 'throw around.' It cost me millions of dollars to make it happen."

"That you had it just lying around, able to move is impressive," Lynn said.

"Thank you," I said.

Sheppard wiped his mouth and pulled his phone from his pocket. "When's a good date for an in-person meeting?"

"With other alphas?" I asked.

Sheppard nodded.

I pulled out my phone again and looked at the calendar. "Let's see. We're right at the beginning of September, so how about the first weekend of October? Call it the second?"

"Let's make it Friday the first so they can get back home without jetlag?"

I shrugged. "Sure."

Sheppard started tapping out a message. "I'll email as many as I have the addresses for and ask for read receipts, but there's gonna be a lot of bouncebacks." He kept tapping while the rest of us finished up our meals. When he put the phone down, he looked at me. "In the unlikely scenario that the entire country's alphas all want to come and meet with you, where are you going to put them all? If you have any more than, say, twenty or twenty-five, you won't be able to fit them in that giant conference room of yours."

I nodded. "Yeah, that'll get cramped pretty quickly, won't it?"

"And they're not going to trust hotel security enough to be willing to rent meeting space."

He was right. Where could we put them? Maybe find a church? Mmmnh hard to find one you could be sure was on holy ground these days. And if the Church wasn't going to join in—which, Lord knows they should but were ridiculously unlikely to—that was going to be a tough obstacle to tackle. And then I remembered Howlers. There was plenty of space there, and it was plenty defensible...

"Well," I said. "I know a place they'll all fit, but you're not gonna like it."

"Try me," Sheppard said.

I gave a wry shake of my head. "Alright. Let's take another drive."

"Oh." Lynn wiped her mouth and reached a hand in my direction. "I know you have a PR lady, but do you have any connections here in town that can help me track down the wolves I've made human again?"

"You want to keep in touch with them?" Sheppard asked.

Lynn got a little sheepish. "Well... I mean... If I'm the reason they have to face being human again after... well... what they were, then I want to make sure they're okay."

Sheppard nodded approvingly, and a pulse of warmth washed through the room. Lynn straightened and looked up at him with a shy smile.

I looked at her and shrugged. "I have a pretty good system here, but it's not really set up for keeping track of individuals. I don't know anyone in town, but I think I have some wolves that are out and about that would be good at something like that. It's gonna be harder if they don't have a social media presence."

"Thankfully practically everyone does these days," Ian said. "And if they're former werewolves, they're probably young enough that they'd fall under that umbrella."

"You know their names?" I asked.

Lynn nodded.

"Then get me a list and what you know and I'll see what I can do."

"I can do that." She smiled. "Thanks, Jess."

I looked to Shep. "It's already too hot out for you to be clinging to me while I drive us there on my bike. Let's load it into the truck and take the vehicle with AC."

Sheppard chuckled and I tried to push the thought of what that rumbly chest would feel like pressed against mine.

"I c'n squeeze in wi' the young'uns," Kaylah said. "It's a short drive back."

Naiya nodded. "I'll drive carefully. I don't remember if there's a seatbelt for the middle of the backseat."

Out in the parking lot, it took some finagling to get my Diavel tied down properly in the back of Shep's Ram, but we managed and were soon on our way to Howlers. It hadn't escaped my notice that his cargo straps were so new he'd had to unwrap them from the packaging. But at least he had some.

"A strip club?!" Sheppard asked as we pulled into the lot of my pack's nightclub.

"It's big, it's only got two entrances, there's no windows, and it has great internet connectivity," I said, counting the points out on my fingers. "It's perfect, really."

"Are we gonna give them a show while we're at it?"

I snorted. "I don't think most of the alphas swing that way. This place is more the Magic Mike style and less the ladies-on-a-pole style." More like *none* of the ladies-on-a-pole. "Come on, lemme show you."

Sheppard pressed his lips into a line and followed me inside. The club smelled of sweat and perfume and alcohol, on top of all of the guys. There were a handful of my pack on the stage with Delilah, running through a dance number in cut up shirts with loose sweatpants or basketball shorts while the music pumped through the speakers.

"That's Delilah," I said loudly, pointing to the blonde in a red tank top and colorful palazzo pants. "The guys on stage there are Elijah, Derek, Bryce, Forest, and Nate."

Not likely he forgot which one Nate was, given that he'd stared daggers at the guy yesterday.

Which was another reason I couldn't let thirsty brain play with Sheppard.

"The club was technically Delilah's idea," I said. "Well... hers and Forrest's. They have an on-again-off-again thing. That's Leo behind the bar."

Leo waved, not looking up from the limes he was prepping for the night.

"Well," Sheppard said, raising his voice to be heard over the music. "You were right. I don't like it."

Then he *really* wouldn't like it if he ever found out what it is I do in my free time.

"But think about it," I said. "Really *think* about it. This place ticks all the boxes. Plenty of space, a stage to speak from, TV monitors all around for those that can't get a good view, security cameras out the wazoo, no windows, and the only ways in or out are through the front door and the back." I pointed at the doors in turn.

Sheppard closed his eyes like he was actually considering it. I hoped he was. Then he looked at me and sighed. "But do you really think the visiting alphas will even take you seriously if they're meeting at a strip club?"

The song ended in the middle of his last line. Everyone heard him question this place.

"Tssh," Nate said, waving a dismissive hand in Sheppard's direction.

I stood straighter and looked the visiting alpha square in the eye. Or rather, as best I could from well over a foot below him. God, Sheppard was tall.

"Is there a problem with my strip club?"

Square up, bucko.

"*My* strip club," Delilah corrected from on stage. Her hands were on her hips.

I turned to her and used my alpha voice. "*The pack* strip club."

Delilah turned back to the guys, running a hand through her hair.

"Jess," Sheppard said, his tone placating. "You know me better than that. It's not something I'm going to have a problem with. It's just that a lot of these guys are old and not nearly as open-minded as I am. This isn't going to create the most upstanding of impressions."

Delilah turned around again, folding her arms across her chest with her eyes narrowed. "Are you calling this place sleazy?"

Sheppard crossed his arms as well. "I'm not, and I wouldn't, but some of the alphas might."

He wouldn't? I was skeptical, but it rang of truth.

"Well," I said, "it's pack-owned, pack-run, and I can

get Eric in here to make sure the tech is secure."

He thought a moment. "The diner's probably too small."

"And too open," I said. "It's in the middle of a shopping center."

Shep cocked his head to the side. "If we met in the middle of the day—"

"We'd still get prying ears and eyes."

"How close is the closest brood?"

I shrugged. "Not sure – there's not one in town or just outside the limits, I can tell you that."

"Let's track that down if we can."

"It might be closer to Austin than us."

"There's no pack in Austin."

I crossed my arms. "There's no vamps in San Antonio."

Sheppard sighed. "Well if this is our best option, we'll make it work."

"Just don't mention the meeting site until they get into town. Tell them we're keeping it under wraps for security purposes. We'll tell them when we meet them at the airport."

"Security purposes," Sheppard mused.

I tapped his chest with the back of my hand as I smiled. "Exactly. Look. We can set up another camera there." I pointed to the corner on the other side of the door from the bar. "It's the only corner without one. And we can put any alphas who want to attend virtually—instead of in person—on the screens." I turned in a slow circle around the club, counting. "There's only four TVs right now, which would basically get us room for sixteen to twenty-four more. But we could set up a desk alongside the stage there for another handful of monitors if we need them." I looked at Sheppard. "I want as many here as I can get, especially in person."

He looked around the club again as the music came back on. "It just might work." He jerked his head toward the door. "Speaking of this plan of yours, let's head back. I have something related to talk with you about."

I waved bye to Delilah and Leo and we headed out

to the truck. Once both doors were shut, I looked at Sheppard expectantly.

He glanced at me as he started the truck and took a deep breath in, letting it out slowly. "I'm gonna have to tell Buckheim about this."

"Sheppard..."

"Not because I think he deserves to know, though I do think that, but because he's gonna want to have as much time as possible to consider what he's going to do with the military and this whole going public thing. He has a vested interest in keeping the wolves quiet. I need to give him the opportunity to opt out."

I shrugged. "So call him. My PR offices have secure lines."

He shook his head.

Oh no.

"This isn't the kind of thing you should call or send an email about," he said. "Not with the U.S. military. You don't want that paper trail, trust me."

"You're telling me we need to go to Colorado."

He nodded. "I'm telling you we need to go to Colorado." He looked over at me before putting his eyes back on the road home. "You want my help? This is what it takes."

I grumbled out a little growl.

"Did you really think all the alphas would just agree to abandon their territory for a day and come to you? There's over two hundred of them."

"I mean, I was sure a few would opt out entirely," I said.

"More than a few, if I had to guess," Sheppard said. "And of those that don't, do you really think I'm so well respected that they'll just mobilize on my word?"

"You're saying we were bound to have to make some trips out to convince them."

"I am," he said simply.

"But what does any of that have to do with the U.S. military? Are you hoping he'll back this?"

"He just might."

Whoa. That was something I hadn't considered.

Having the U.S. military backing us would be something... well, extraordinary. They were well-versed in only telling people what they wanted them to know. We could use experience like that on our side.

"Fine," I said. "Let's go talk to the military." I pointed at him. "But you're buying the plane tickets."

"Then you get the rental car, Miss I-Spent-Millions-On-A-Super-Bowl-Ad."

I snorted. "Like hell I will. This is your crazy idea."

The truck rolled to a stop on the gravel. In one smooth move, he put the truck into park and leaned across the center fold-down console to unlock and open my door, putting his body *entirely* too close to mine for thirsty brain to ignore.

"Fine," he said quietly. "I'll take care of it."

But something about that tone made me want to throw myself at him.

I didn't.

But I wanted to.

Instead, I simply clambered out of the truck and walked across the gravel to my house, the heat of his eyes on me the entire way.

TEN

*** (SHEPPARD) ***

IT WAS ENTIRELY TOO early in the morning when I knocked on Jessica's door so we could make our flight. She'd grumbled yesterday afternoon when I told her over the phone that I managed to get plane tickets for the very next day, but I figured the sooner we got this done, the sooner we'd know what we'd need to do with regards to the military.

A rail-thin blonde with last night's eyeliner on opened the door in her black tank and blue satin shorts.

She drank in the sight of me with an appreciative expression. "I'm guessing you're not here for me."

I smiled and shook my head. "Afraid not."

"That's a shame." She spun on her heel and gestured with a hand for me to follow her. "Come on in. I'll get her."

As I stepped into the house, she gestured to the dining room, and I took that to mean I should wait there.

"I didn't catch your name," I said, the question clear in the tone.

"I didn't give it," she replied.

"That's Imogen," Jess said, coming through the kitchen. She was positively stunning in a lace-trimmed black satin tank top tucked into black skinny jeans with black platform stilettos making her a fair number of inches taller than her otherwise petite self.

God, she was beautiful.

"You look nice," I said.

"Shut it." She tucked a strand of hair behind her ear and looked me up and down. "I'm not the only one dressed to impress."

She was talking about the fact that I'd put on a grey tweed waistcoat over my black button-down shirt. My sleeves were rolled to the forearms, and the shirt was tucked into black slacks. I had on black leather dress shoes that clicked against the hardwood floors of her home, and my hair was pulled back into a low ponytail.

"It's not every day you get to try to convince the US military to give up one of its biggest secrets," I said.

Imogen opened the fridge and grabbed a soda. "You two have a safe flight." She looked at me. "She better come back in one piece, *Sheppard.*"

"She will, *Imogen.*" I matched her tone with a smile.

Jess rolled her eyes as she threw a small black purse over her shoulder. "C'mon, Shep. Don't wanna miss our flight."

"Of course."

She was quiet for most of the drive to the airport, but as I took the ticket for the parking garage, she looked at me. "Do you honestly think this'll work?"

"Honestly? I can't call it." I shrugged. "But it's worth the trip to try."

She snorted. "I'd hoped you'd come to some kind of epiphany overnight."

The only epiphany I'd had was how alluring she was all cleaned up. And that happened this morning, not overnight.

I shook my head. "Sorry to disappoint."

"You?" She shook her head. "Nah."

She lost something like seven inches when she had to take those heels off for airport security, but speared me with a look that dared me to say something about it.

I kept my mouth shut.

By the time we got through security and over to our gate, boarding had already started for our flight. Jess and I filed into line behind the other passengers, and I checked my emails for replies from the alpha's I'd emailed the day before.

"Huh," I said. "Three have already confirmed for the meeting, and there's a fourth that wants to be sure he can attend virtually."

"Let me guess," she said. "Jasper in Chicago, Nicholas from Miami, and Silas in Vegas said yes already."

I nodded. "Good guesses."

She rolled her eyes and dropped her voice to tones only she and I could hear. "Three of the wolves that have shown up to sniff around the single alpha female? Color me surprised that they jumped at the chance to flirt with me again." She jerked her chin at my phone as we waited in the jetway. "Who's the virtual?"

"Wallace, the Seattle alpha," I said, matching her quiet tone. "But I'll see if I can get him to change his mind. I think his problem is that he's superstitious about planes."

"Really?" She narrowed her eyes. "Who'd've guessed."

I bobbed my head side to side. "Kristos hates 'em too. It's the whole reason I didn't try to send him out anywhere like I did the rest of the pack."

"Plus you'd be sending Lynn and Naiya with him," she said.

"And sending them together puts two relatively new... well... wolf and leopard with a very experienced bear. It just got messy in my head. What do you send them on that doesn't leave at least one of them on the sidelines? Nevermind that Naiya isn't pack-bonded. That girl has one singular person she listens to, and it isn't me."

"Whoa." Jess shook her head. "I didn't think she'd straight up *ignore* pack."

"I could probably make her listen to me, but I'd hate to do it." I gave the airline clerk my boarding pass. "Judging by how relieved she was to not have to owe the Church anything, I can only imagine."

I kept my voice low as we stepped onto the plane and made our way to our row. "They experimented on her, Jess. Not with needles... minus sedating her, but they put her through every physical test they could think of. And nearly killed her friend doing it."

The knuckles of Jess' fist popped at her side. "Holy shit."

I nodded. "So I'd rather her come to me on her own."

She nodded too. "She'll come around. It'd just be better if she was at least listening to someone who was pack."

I snorted wryly. "She is."

Jess arched an eyebrow at me as we took our seats. "Kristos is pack? How? The healing thing?"

"I wish I knew for sure." I shook my head as I took my seat. "That daywalker almost killed me, Jess. It's the closest call I've had in a long, *long* time. And I'm pretty sure I'd've lost most of the pack to their injuries if it weren't for Kristos."

She studied me for a long moment, her jaw slack and eyes wide. "I... well... I'm glad you survived," she said finally.

I met her golden eyes and my voice was quiet. "Me too."

Her eyes flicked down to... my mouth? And then flicked back up to mine. I couldn't hear her heart over the noise of the plane and the chatter of the other passengers. I blinked. Her lips... those cherry red lips were parted invitingly.

"Please buckle your seatbelts for departure." The flight attendant said, breaking the spell.

I snapped my attention to her and then looked to my lap, following her instructions. Jessica did the same, only I was pretty sure I saw a flush of color brighten her cheeks.

It was damn cute on her. Not that I'd ever tell her so. I didn't need to complicate things by getting *involved* with her. Not when she needed me like she did. Not with the power out of balance in our working relationship. In the world of what she was looking to do, she had the power, and I was following her lead. It was unfamiliar territory.

We rode the majority of that short flight in silence, minus the drink orders.

On our connected flight, Jess fell asleep with her head on my shoulder, and for well over an hour, my world was filled with lavender and cloves in a way I wouldn't have escaped even if I could have. My inner wolf sighed with a contentment that washed through me.

When the plane touched down, she startled awake and ran a hand through her hair. "Sorry."

I shook my head, trying to clear it. "Don't be."

I couldn't be distracted by her. She didn't want me for anything other than the face of her PR stunt.

We deplaned and picked up the rental car and drove out to the base all without incident. It took a little talking to the guy at the gates to the base to get him to let us in, but we eventually got directions to where we needed to go and parked outside a squat little metal-sided building that was indistinct from the twelve other squat metal-sided buildings around it other than the number on the door.

"Three-oh-one," Jessica said. "This is it."

I nodded and we got out of the car.

Inside, a familiar face greeted me from behind the desk. Valerie had bleached the rainbow out of her hair and it was pulled back into a low bun. She looked up at me with a start.

"Uh, Sheppard... good to... see you?"

"I'm here to see the General."

"Of course," she said. "Let me see if he's available."

She picked up her phone and dialed an extension. There were a few rings before he picked up.

"Yes, Val?"

"The Colorado Springs alpha is here to see you, sir," she said.

"And the San Antonio Basin alpha," I corrected.

She looked up at me and nodded. "He has the San Antonio—"

"I heard him," Buckheim said. "I'll be there in a moment."

"Yes, sir."

There was a click and the line went dead as she turned to me. "He'll—"

"I heard him," I said.

She put the phone down. "Is... is she okay?"

I narrowed my eyes.

"Naiya, I mean," she said.

"Naiya's fine," I said. "Keeps to herself, slow to trust, as I'm sure you can expect."

"I never meant—"

"But you did." My voice was sharp. "Whatever your intentions were is irrelevant. It's your actions she's not likely to ever forget."

She nodded, her chastised expression telling me I'd said enough.

My phone buzzed in my back pocket. I pulled it out and thumbed open the screen to check the message.

Jessica:
Ouch, Shep.

Me:
She played spy for them on Naiya. She helped Brooks.

Jessica's face darkened and I nodded once.

General George Buckheim arrived then in his crisp green camos, his salt-and-pepper hair as close-cropped as ever.

"Ah, Sheppard," he said, reaching for my hand. "What a pleasure." There was a question in his voice.

I shook his hand and gestured toward Jess. "General

Buckheim, this is Jessica, the alpha of the San Antonio basin pack."

If he was surprised to meet a female alpha, he didn't show it.

Jess extended a hand that Buckheim shook.

"A pleasure, Jessica," he said. "I hear yours is the largest pack this side of the Atlantic."

So he wasn't surprised.

Jessica smiled. "Larger than most on the other side as well. Very likely one of the largest in the world, actually."

"Aside from the Church, that is," Buckheim said.

Her eyes narrowed for a fraction of a second before she blinked and plastered a fake smile on her face. "Of course."

Buckheim led us to a private conference room, and I immediately clocked the camera in the corner.

He followed my gaze as he shut and locked the door. "Damn thing just won't turn on." He was lying. "Technical difficulties, if you catch my drift."

Ah. Good. So nothing recording this meeting.

"So what's this about, boy? You don't come onto my playground without good reason."

I nodded and gestured to Jessica. "Go ahead, Jess."

She put her purse down in the chair on the far side of her as she sat in the second seat from the end on the far side. She took a deep breath and folded her hands on the table. "As I'm sure you know, the vampires are now filming their encounters with werewolves these days. They then put these videos on the internet in an effort to instill fear in the very humans we protect."

I sat next to her.

Buckheim nodded as he sat in one of the chairs opposite her. "I've seen the videos."

"Are you aware there is a counter agency acting to debunk those videos as they go public and viral?"

"Miss LaRoux," Buckheim said, arching an eyebrow. "I certainly hope you didn't call in a favor on dear Sheppard here just to give me intel I already have."

Jess' hand fell to her lap and curled into a fist. I placed my hand down atop hers, prying her fingers flat again as

I took a deep breath that she then matched.

"I was the one who insisted upon this meeting, sir," I said. "Hear her out, if you will."

I should have known he'd try to dismiss her out of hand.

He looked back at Jessica. "I do hope you intend to get to your point sooner rather than later?"

"Let me just cut to it." She took another deep breath. "We're taking the werewolves public before the vampires can back us into a corner with irrefutable proof of our existence. They're currently controlling the narrative, and that needs to change. I intend to be the one to put a stop to it."

I nodded and met Buckheim's cool gaze. "We're coming to you so you can decide whether you're going public with us, or whether you're going to stay hidden."

"And to give me a head start on ensuring the program's most sensitive secrets stay secret."

I bobbed my head side-to-side. "If you won't come to light with us, then I suppose that's right. But we could use the military backing the truth."

Jessica pulled a folded bundle of papers from her purse. She flattened it as she fished a pen from the bag as well. She slid both across the table.

I furrowed my brow. What the hell was that?

"I have NDAs prepared," she said. "Should you opt out, I'll be legally bound to *not* out you and yours."

Oh no. God, I wished she had said something about that.

Buckheim threw his head back and laughed. It was a full belly laugh like Jessica had just told one of the funniest jokes he'd heard.

Jessica pulled her hand out from under mine and stood, fury etched in every stiff line of her body. "What's so damn funny?"

God, she was sexy when she was angry.

Buckheim took a moment to sober before looking at her. "Miss LaRoux. There is *nothing* an NDA can do to put the cat back *in* the bag once it's out." He pulled his phone from his back pocket as he stood and unlocked the door. "I wish you had told me this over the *phone*, boy." He waggled his phone at me.

Something dangerous was in his tone, but I couldn't place it. I stood, my brow furrowed. "This isn't the sort of thing one should just call about."

He tapped something out on his phone and opened the door, stepping out into the hallway. He took a step back, in the opposite direction from the exit. "But had you simply *called* me, I wouldn't have to take measures to protect the program and the wolves within it." A few more taps on his phone.

Jessica's hand wrapped around mine with more static. "Time to go."

Mine.

Shut up, wolf. Not now.

I narrowed my eyes at her, but the footsteps behind Buckheim told me the important part.

He'd called the base police force on us.

"Shit," I said, darting for the exit.

They were just humans, but they had guns. Guns hurt.

We easily outran them to the parking lot, but there were more surrounding the rental car.

"Hold it right there!" One of the ones next to the car had his gun raised.

I shook my head and ducked to the left behind a beige Jeep that I recognized. It was Buckheim's. There was a gunshot and Jessica yelped as she skidded under the Jeep to meet me.

She came up on my side with a key in her hand. Buckheim had hidden a key on his Jeep in case he'd have to get to it after shifting. It was standard practice for virtually every werewolf I knew.

I could have kissed her.

I pulled open the driver side door and pushed her up and in before ducking in myself and taking the key from her. I slammed the gas pedal down and wove through the buildings and other cars on the base as I got to the other gate.

"We're gonna have to shift, Jess. I can't take this Jeep

into town."

"Get to the woods first!"

By some miracle, we managed to get through the back gate of the base without wrecking *and* without them closing the gate on us. We simply zipped through and out onto the highway. I counted a full five minutes of pedal-to-the-floor driving before pulling onto the shoulder and then off the highway and into the woods.

I stopped the Jeep, ripping the buttons from the vest and shirt as I opened them to prep to shift. "Buckheim's gonna hate this."

Jess shook her head. "That bridge is ashes anyway, Shep." Her shoulder was a mess of blood, but it was healing—or at least, I hoped it was. She ripped the tank from her body as she dropped her heels to the floorboards.

It took us both a moment more to be free of our clothes, but then we were on four paws running away from the abandoned Jeep. Her wolf was just as beautiful as she was, all deep sable black with dark red-brown highlights around her shoulders and haunches.

It was a long run from where we were to the closest of the houses the pack had, but we'd have to pick a different one just to be on the safe side.

Buckheim may have let us go, but I couldn't be sure how long he would give chase to keep up appearances. He had higher-ups to answer to, after all.

So we'd take an even longer run. Get to one of the furthest houses from the base. Great. I huffed out my frustration.

There was a growl as Jess darted off to the west. She'd found a rabbit and kicked it into high gear in pursuit, a slight limp to her gait. By the time I caught up to her, she had the poor thing torn to shreds. I nudged her to get her to keep moving, but she snapped at me, her teeth bared and a growl rumbling her throat. I matched her growl with one of my own, nudging her again to get her to move, but she pounced on me then and started to bite and scratch at me. But even her wolf was smaller than me, and I soon maneuvered her onto her back and pinned her there.

She growled and snarled uselessly at me, but I could still smell the blood on her. I buried my nose into the fur of her shoulder, inspecting the wound there. It had closed up and the only blood was just what had escaped while it healed. Satisfied that her injury wouldn't slow her down, I stared long and hard at her. Her golden eyes gazed back at me and something I could not name charged the air. I nipped lightly at her nose once, not making contact, and let her up. She followed me the rest of the not insignificant distance to the house I felt was safe enough for us to change at.

At the house, I shifted back to two legs and entered the code to the back door, ushering Jess inside so she could shift in relative privacy. Thirsty from the run, I headed for the fridge and grabbed a couple of the bottles of water we kept in all of the fridges. I tossed one her way.

"Thanks," she said, catching it. "I guess I *am* thirsty."

Making it to one of the houses meant we were safe. Buckheim wouldn't try to pull two alphas whose packs knew where they were from a safe house. And after his barely-more-than-symbolic attempts to stop us on base? I doubted he'd do more than he already had.

I plopped onto the couch and uncapped my water. "I'm glad it was just your shoulder, Jess." I threw my head back and gulped down half the bottle when warm air, like breath, blew across my lap. Hands fell on my thighs, sending a jolt of static through me, and I swallowed the mouthful of water before looking down.

Jess' mouth was inches from my cock.

I arched an eyebrow at her. "What are you doing?"

"I think it's pretty fuckin' obvious what I'm doing. *Water* is not what I'm thirsty for, Tobias."

Something short circuited in my head for a moment. I wasn't sure I'd ever get used to hearing my proper name again. I swallowed thickly.

Mine.

Not fucking now, wolf.

But my body was already responding to her.

"Jess…"

"It's called scratching the itch," she said. "How long has it been?" She inched closer to me and mimed licking me, making my cock twitch.

"Long enough," I said. "But are you sure you even want this?"

She shrugged. "Don't read into it. It's what I want right now."

This was about to get messier than the cleanup after a house fire. But I sure as hell wasn't going to tell her no. It *had* been too long.

She pressed her body against my leg, her mouth hovering just over my tip as more static rushed through me. "Tell me no, Tobias." Her lips barely brushed across me as she spoke, the electricity making me twitch against her lips.

I shook my head and capped my water bottle, dropping it to the floor. "Not a damn chance."

Her mouth closed around my cock as my hand tangled in her hair and I thrust up toward her, my eyes rolling back as I rode the electricity she sent through me. She pumped me hard for a handful of thrusts before circling the tip with her tongue and pulling away. I was good and hard by then and she straddled my lap, guiding me into her with one long stroke. I groaned my appreciation.

God, she was so wet and warm. And so small! My hands nearly touched each other as they gripped her waist so I could thrust harder into her. I was grateful that I did not have to be gentle about it. Her cries of pleasure were positively intoxicating as she rode me closer to the brink. After a moment, she bit her lip and pressed her hips hard against mine, grinding along my length. She repeated the motion over and over, her hips rolling along in time with mine until she came, shuddering with ecstasy as my lap got distinctly wetter. She rode me hard then until I returned the favor, moaning my ecstasy against her dark auburn hair, the scent of lavender and cloves filling my senses.

She traced a finger along my side, brushing past a

particularly ticklish spot that made me jump. I grabbed her hand and she pressed against me, inhaling deeply along my neck and jaw as she ground the last of the aftershocks away.

ELEVEN

*** (JESSICA) ***

AFTER THE QUICKIE ON the couch, Sheppard showed me where the bathroom was so I could clean up. Water ran elsewhere in the house shortly after, so he must've been doing the same.

And then I caught my reflection. I'd forgotten that changing leaves me needing to re-dye my hair. My natural dark auburn looked so out of place against my fair skin. I vastly preferred the vibrant red.

"Ugh," I said aloud.

"Problem?" Sheppard asked through the door.

I opened it and held up a chunk of my hair. "I have all the supplies I need for this back home."

"Sounds like there's a 'but' there."

I nodded. "I'm not going back to the pack like *this*." I gestured to my hair.

He huffed out a little laugh and leaned against the doorframe, crossing his arms across that hard chest of his. "I'm sure they've seen it plenty of times, Jess. Do you really dye it every week or so?"

"What?" I made a face. "No! Why the hell would I do that?"

He blinked at me. "You're telling me a pack as big as yours doesn't need to let off some steam every week or so?"

"Pfft. More like every handful of days."

"You must go through a hell of a lot of bleach and dye."

And then I understood what he was getting at. He thought *I* went running with them every time. He thought *I* shifted something like once a week. Yeah, no. Not at all.

"Less than you'd think," I said.

He reached and ran a hand through my hair, which felt nicer than I think it should have. "There's a lot of hair here." His voice was soft.

I rolled a shoulder. "Sure. But I don't wolf out much."

He dropped his hand and cocked his head to the side. "What's not much?"

Yeah, this was going a direction I had *zero* interest in continuing. I turned my back to him.

"Just... can we please take a trip to the closest beauty supply store? And maybe grab some food?"

He frowned at me in the mirror as he reached for my shoulder. "Jess..."

I sidestepped him and ducked to look under the counter for spare clothes. We usually kept a few sets in the cabinets of the bathrooms, maybe Sheppard did too.

"It's been nearly a year," I mumbled.

"Holy shit," Sheppard breathed. "That would make most wolves a menace to society. What happened?!"

Nothing happened. At least, nothing I have any interest in talking about.

There were only towels under the cabinet and I closed it and straightened, my eyes closed.

"I'm just..." I blew out a breath and looked up at him,

my eyes trailing up his very naked and very attractive form. "*Tell* me you have spare clothes here."

With a sexy little smirk, Shep pushed off the door frame and jerked his head toward the hallway. I followed him. In the bedroom, he opened the bottom drawer of the dresser.

"You're around the same size as Kaylah," he said. "Except she's taller, obviously."

Had he ever slept with Kaylah? I shook my head. It didn't matter.

"Are you seriously calling me short while I stand here naked, asking a fellow alpha for some damn *clothes?*"

He chuckled as he pulled out a black sports bra and handed it to me. "I mean, you said it, not me." He grabbed a white t-shirt and then a black one, handing me the latter after throwing the first onto his shoulder. He then pulled out two pairs of grey sweatpants, one sized significantly larger than the other, and handed me the smaller pair.

"There," he said. "Better?"

"Thanks," I said, pulling on the sports bra. He was a little off on sizing and it was a little tighter than I'd like, but I wasn't going to complain. The shirt fit well and the pants were a little looser, but it probably made for a cute look, so I didn't bother trying to trade it out.

He watched me as he pulled on his clothes, clearly expecting some kind of answer to his previous question.

"As for what happened." I sighed. "It's not that. I'm just... more *animalistic* than I care to be that way. You saw what that looked like afterward." I waited till he finished adjusting the waistband of the sweatpants on his hips. "So can we go?"

He ran a hand through his hair, watching me for a moment as he decided what to say. "I'm not sure off the top of my head which of the pack's cars are in town, let alone which ones might be here, if any. Let's check the garage. Everyone's got sandals in their trunk."

I followed him across the house to the garage. "Is that a euphemism?"

He laughed. "It's literal."

"How come they didn't put the cars in storage?"

"I mean, they *did*," Sheppard said. "But why rent a storage unit when I have houses they can keep them at?"

"I guess that's one way to invest your money."

"It's not my only line of investments, but it's a solid one. People are always going to need places to live."

"Sure." I shrugged. "But I prefer tech. Between startups and innovations and infosec? Tech is where the money is, and tech is where the money is going."

"That explains a lot about you and your pack and this PR stunt."

I'm sure it did.

TWELVE

*** (SHEPPARD) ***

SO WE WERE JUST pretending what happened on the couch had nothing to do with anything. Interesting. I shook my head.

Out in the garage, there was a little purple Honda Del Sol that belonged to Lynn, and then Matt's classic Camaro was covered with a tarp to keep even the dust off the paint.

"Whose is that?" Jess pointed to the Del Sol.

"Lynn's," I said, knowing full well how the rest of this conversation was about to play out. Everyone loved Matt's Camaro.

"I'm not sure you'll fit in that thing," she said, squinting at the little purple car.

I laughed. "I'm not even sure how *she* fits in it. But you look like just the right size." I winked at her.

She punched my shoulder. "Are you calling me little?"

"Are you seriously trying to tell me you're not?"

"Touché." She jerked her chin toward the Camaro. "What's under the tarp?"

I gave her a wry smile and pulled the tarp from the Camaro.

"Holy shit," she breathed, stepping over to run a hand along the cherry red paint. "You didn't tell me you were into classics!"

Everyone loves the Camaro.

"That's because I'm not." I shook my head. "It's Matt's."

She arched a wry eyebrow at me. "He's got good taste." Her expression turned mischievous. "You think your hothead'll blow a gasket if we take it to the store?"

I smiled. "I think what he doesn't know won't hurt him." I bent to grab the hide-a-key from the undercarriage. Unlocking the passenger door, I opened the glovebox and pulled out the copy of the pack's black credit card, tucking it into my pocket. I then went around to the back and popped the trunk.

"What's your shoe size, Jess?"

"Six."

Small feet for a small alpha. Got it. I found a pair of black flip flops in roughly her size, according to the numbers embossed on the sole.

"Never pegged you as the flip-flop type," she said, taking them from me.

I shrugged. "It's not like we're gonna keep ten pairs of tennis shoes in everyone's trunk. This allows us to keep just a handful of pairs."

"That's fair." She nodded.

I opened the passenger side door again for her, closing it gently once she was inside, and went around to get in on the driver's side. Jessica smiled approvingly when the engine roared to life, and I hit the button on the garage door opener for us to get out. I drove for a while, till I hit the gas station closest to the base, where I filled up the tank and got cash from the ATM. We'd be that much harder to track if we weren't using the card all over town, and I didn't need Buckheim breathing down my neck.

Food was definitely at the top of the to-do list, but we'd also need new phones while we were out. I was just glad the pack's daily withdrawal limit was high enough to accommodate everything we'd need to manage. The phones would have to go on the card, though, so we'd have to pick those up last.

Dammit.

We were going to have to road trip home.

Well, I'd focus on how to make that happen *after* I had food in my stomach.

Jessica arched an eyebrow at me as I pulled into the parking spot of the fast food restaurant. "Inside?"

I nodded. "Matt's gonna have a hard enough time knowing I drove his baby. The least I can do is respect the fact that he doesn't let anyone eat in his car—not even his mate."

She frowned and opened up the glove box, moving papers around until she found what she was looking for.

"What are you doing?" I asked as she pulled a pencil from the glovebox.

"Putting my hair up." She twisted the pencil around in her hair and pushed it through until it was just the pencil holding her hair up and off her neck.

It might as well have been magic.

Inside, we ordered two of the largest meals on the menu. Jess asked for directions to the nearest beauty supply store and I grabbed seats in the far corner, where we could still keep an eye on the Camaro. She came over a moment later with the tray laden with food.

"Matt's had some upgrades done to 'his baby,'" Jess said, putting the tray down so she could put air quotes around the last two words.

"Yeah, Jamie's done some work on it in his shop downtown." I took a sip of my soda. "He's selling the shop though, so he can set a new one up wherever we land."

She nodded as she unwrapped her giant burger. "People are always gonna need their cars worked on."

"And Jamie's one of the few who still know how to work on the antiques."

"There's good money in that."

And then it clicked why we weren't talking about our tryst on the couch. The rabbit and our scrabble as we ran should have been a clue. Jessica was wholly wolf when she shifted. It probably took her a moment to come back to herself when she was back on two legs.

And her wolf had simply recognized an equal and tried to claim it like mine's been doing ever since she fell into me the other day.

I dropped my voice low. "So... you wanna tell me about why you don't change?"

Her eyes darted around the room. We were the only ones in here aside from the staff. "I'd really rather not."

I leaned forward and dropped my voice to even quieter tones. "Come on. Alpha to alpha. You know that's why you're all instincts when you finally do change, right?"

She pressed her lips into a line, blowing out a breath through her nose. "The short version?" She sounded hopeful.

"If that's all you'll give me."

She nodded once and stood to throw away our wrappers. "In the car."

I followed her, eyeing her shake as she headed for the door.

"Nuh uh," she said. "It has a lid, and it's too good to waste." She took a sip from the straw to illustrate her point.

I sighed and nodded. I wanted to challenge her on it, but that'd distract from her telling me her story.

Inside the Camaro, she was quiet as she chewed her lip. I kept the car in the parking spot, waiting her out.

"The first time I turned," she said quietly, "I got someone killed. A human." She looked at me then, clearly expecting a reaction.

I gave her none. It was something that happened every now and again. A wild shot of a gun trying to kill the 'monster' that just appeared, a stampede of livestock who just saw a human become a wolf, a nearby friend when the new wolf turned just happened to be unable to make peace. Casualties happened. I hated it, but sometimes it just happened.

She sighed. "It wouldn't have happened if he knew what I was—if I could have told him. If people knew what we were and what happens when we change, no one would have gotten hurt. And the vampires would have had a harder time getting sheep all these years."

Was she holding guilt at all the human lives lost to vampires since her first change? That's something like three hundred years' worth.

"That's the real reason you want to go public," I said.

"It's the reason I've always wanted to. It's just the vamps aren't giving us much of a choice now." She was quiet for another moment. "I know it's not how it is for everyone else. Every wolf I've ever known has a level of chill that I just can't match on four paws."

"So you don't bother."

She nodded. "I'm plenty good at leading and being alpha without having to wolf out."

God, was that ever true, given the size of her pack.

I gave her a wry smile. "That's fair."

When we got to the beauty supply store, I stayed in the car and sent her in with cash. The last stop before heading back to plan how to get back to San Antonio was to pick up new phones. At least I remembered where that store was.

"Looks like I'll have to grab a new phone when we get back," Jessica said. "I'm on a different carrier."

"We can make another stop," I said.

"Nah." She waved a hand. "The pack can live without 24/7 access to me until I get back. It won't be the end of the world."

"Are you sure?" I arched an eyebrow at her.

She met my gaze and held it. "I am."

"Alright." I nodded.

She followed me into the store. The guy at the counter didn't recognize me, but was plenty accommodating when I explained that my wallet and phone had been stolen. He allowed me to use one of the store's tablets so I could access my online storage where I had a picture of my ID. That, coupled with the password I'd set up on the account, made it so I was able to get what I needed without too much hassle.

Jess looked over my shoulder at the ID photo and pitched her voice low enough that only I could hear her. "William Johnson? What'd you do, use a porn name generator?" She spun around and leaned back against the counter next to me, presumably so she could watch me squirm.

"Shush you," I said. "You know yours isn't any better."

Once I was logged into the phone and it was working on setting everything up in the background, I logged into my online storage and set my old phone to erase itself. I didn't need Buckheim to have any more access to me and my pack than he already had. And he *certainly* didn't need all of the information that access to all of my accounts would give him.

"We should have done this first," I said, keeping my voice low as I leaned toward Jess. "No telling how much Buckheim learned between our visit and now."

She nodded. "Mine auto-bricks if you get the password wrong three times."

I snorted. "The General won't like that."

"Maybe he should have thought of that before he had people *shoot me*."

"Touché."

It took another twenty minutes to wrap up at the phone store, and then it was back in the car, and on the way back to the house.

In the garage, I held my new phone out to her. "Lemme see."

"Let you see what?"

"What your name is this century." I waved my phone.

She folded her arms across her chest. "If you must know, it's Jane Smith."

She was lying.

I tsked at her. "You, of all people, are gonna try to pull one over on me?"

With a little growl, she snatched the phone from my hand. She tapped on the screen for a few moments before turning the phone back to me.

"Angelina Wylde," I said. "Pretty..."

She rolled her eyes with a smile. "Tha—"

"... For a porn star."

She snorted and threw my new phone at me with a laugh, but it bounced in between the seat and the center console—the no-man's land where things disappear forever.

"Oh shit," she said, immediately reaching for it.

I did the same and we almost bumped heads. And then I realized that her hands were decidedly smaller than mine, so she had a better chance of rescuing the device. I paused and watched her. When she felt my eyes on her, she paused and looked up at me. The air charged with something I suspect neither of us were prepared to try to name and then she reached just a little further. She came up a moment later with my phone in hand, her face just inches from mine.

"Thanks," I said softly.

She tucked a stray strand of dark auburn hair behind her ear and nodded once. "Lets... get inside so I can take care of this." She gestured to her head.

I nodded, but neither of us moved.

And then my new phone sang a little notification tune. I thumbed open the screen.

> **Gen. Buckheim:**
>
> *Smart play, boy, but this is far from settled.*

I didn't bother with a response. The spell was broken... again, and we went inside.

Jess found an egg timer in the kitchen and took it with her into the bathroom, along with the last of her milkshake, while she worked on re-dying her hair. I didn't see her again for something like two hours. It worked out fine for me, as I spent that time getting everything set up and connected to my new phone.

Jess finally came out of the bathroom right when my email notification dinged, her hair up in a black towel.

"Looks like we have two more confirmed," I said.

"So five altogether plus the one virtual."

I nodded.

"I'm glad you have black towels here," she said. "Otherwise this dye would stain your towels all to hell and I'd have to owe you new ones. As it is, I'm gonna bring this one along with me so we don't leave dirty laundry in a house you may or may not ever be coming back to."

"I'm sure I'll be back when it sells," I said with a chuckle.

"Sure, which will be who knows how long from now." She went over to the couch and grabbed her discarded bottle of water from before. "It's gonna be real hard to fly home without ID."

I nodded. "And even if the DMV was open, we don't have the supporting documents we'd need to get a replacement license."

"Nevermind that mine's from Texas," she said.

"That too." I took a sip from my water bottle. "Looks like we're driving back then."

Jess lit up. "Tell me we can take the Camaro."

I should have seen that coming as soon as I mentioned it.

"Matt'll shit a brick," I said.

She laughed. "Then it's perfect."

I looked up the route on my phone and then checked the internet's best estimate for the miles per gallon on a car like Matt's.

Ten.

Ten miles per gallon on an eighteen gallon gas tank.

Roughly 870 miles between here and San Antonio, with a fillup every 170 miles or so, meant we'd need to stop for gas five or six times to make it. I went back to the route to check to be sure the gas stations were close enough together to accommodate the old muscle car. It was going to be a hassle and a half. Even with the interior upgrades Jamie did, it wasn't going to be the most comfortable ride in the world.

But damn if I didn't love the way she lit up at the thought of it.

I pulled the black card from my pocket. "It's a good thing we have one of these in every glovebox."

"So... yes?"

I laughed. "Yeah, Jess. We can take the Camaro."

THIRTEEN

*** (JESSICA) ***

"C'mon, Shep," I said. "You know he'll never know. What harm could it do?"

We'd made it a little ways into New Mexico and had stopped for our first fill-up.

"He'll shit an entire brickyard if he finds out," Sheppard replied. He'd called to cancel our flights and to get his truck back to the guest house as soon as we cleared Colorado Springs.

I let the mischief show on my face. "He'll only find out if you tell him. Besides, you can't really expect me to believe you're gonna be good to drive the entire distance by yourself, without stopping."

"Who says we're not stopping?"

"Who says we need to if you let me drive some of the way?"

Shep scratched at the back of his head. "We'd have to switch anyway, is your position."

"We'll get there sooner if we do."

He stared at me hard for a long moment, and I was pretty sure he was about to tell me no... again.

But then he tossed me the keys. "In for a penny, in for a pound."

"Fuck yes!"

We got back on the road in relative silence, but for some tapping of texts on Sheppard's phone.

"So," I said, "are we just not gonna talk about what happened back at the base?"

Because we sure as shit aren't gonna talk about what happened on the couch.

"I'm not really sure what there is to talk about that isn't already part of your plan," Sheppard said. "Buckheim's out, which means the US military is likely to actively work against us."

"Which is fucking dumb, because they're basically siding with the vampires, but that's not what I'm talking about."

Sheppard raised a questioning eyebrow at me.

"I thought that guy was your friend! He's been your friend for years!"

He gave me a wry smile. "If he didn't mean for us to get away, he would have sent wolves, not humans."

I gave him an incredulous look before putting my eyes back on the road.

"If he wasn't my friend, we'd be in holding cells right now." He raked a hand through his hair. "And what the hell was that anyway? An NDA? Really? For the United States military?!"

"What else was I supposed to do?" I said. "I wanted to reassure him that I would guard his secret."

He shook his head. "If you'd mentioned it before, I could've saved you the embarrassment of being laughed at. Any non-disclosure agreement is gonna be child's play compared to their security clearance, which is multiple ridiculous layers deep, might I add."

I narrowed my eyes. "I don't need saving. He's just

another in a *long* string of assholes that look down on me both literally *and* figuratively."

"Okay." He nodded and crossed his arms. "But consider this: you've tipped your hand."

"What?"

"Now he knows he doesn't have the time he might think he does. You're prepared—more prepared than he would have guessed. It was that preparation that made him call it in."

"You're saying I was *too* ready?!"

He shrugged. "Basically. We could have played it off as just some idea a couple of alphas were tossing around. Now we can't."

"Well, I wasn't about to walk into the lion's den completely unprepared," I said. "It'd be a waste."

He nodded and pulled the lever to recline the seat as he leaned his head back and closed his eyes. "Yup. Should've been a phone call."

"I told you I could've gotten you a secure line." I looked over at him. "Maybe it's time to let go of a lot of the traditional ways of doing things. Tech has made the world smaller than it used to be."

"All the same," Sheppard said. "His superiors are gonna read him the riot act. He had to make it look like he was at least doing something to protect his secrets."

I thought for a moment. If the General realized I was more ready than he might have guessed I would be, then maybe he'd scramble to retaliate. And he had the resources to make that happen faster than I could react to it. I was about to lose my reach on the debunking videos.

Shit.

"I know we planned to meet with the other alphas on October first," I said. "But we're gonna need to move that up and get people on video calls to get out in front of him. If he called his superiors, how fast do you think they'll move?"

"Well, they have bureaucracy like the Church does, but they can move fast if they need to." He sighed and brought the seat back upright. "I had hoped we could logic him through it, like you did with me. But he's quick to react."

"So who's above him? Can we reach out to them?"

He shook his head. "I wish I knew. The Pentagon and the office of the President is the *top* of that chain of command, but I have no idea how many steps exist between him and them."

"Shit."

"If the PR offices have secure lines, can we use that to meet?"

"The PR offices won't hold everyone if we get to even half my pack size," I said. "But we can definitely get secure lines. That was always the plan anyway. But let's move the meeting up."

"How far?"

"Mid-September? What's that weekend?"

He fished the phone from his pocket and tapped on the screen a few times. "The fifteenth is a... Wednesday, and less than two weeks from now."

"Let's do the weekend before then," I said with a nod.

"The tenth? As in, next Friday? They are not going to appreciate that reschedule."

"Sure," I said. "But the General beating us to the punch is worse. Let's call it Saturday, the eleventh, just to give them an extra day. And keep it easy. We'll do the whole thing virtual from the PR offices so no one has to scramble to get flights, and Eric doesn't have to retrofit Howlers."

Sheppard shook his head. "Here's to hoping they confirm."

"We only had five anyway, and I'm certain three of those five will reconfirm." I shrugged. "Plus, taking it completely virtual will probably make it more likely more will confirm, not less."

"True." He nodded as he tapped out a message. "We should probably let someone in your chat server know what happened."

No, we shouldn't.

I threw a hand out to stop him and shook my head. "That'll just make them worry. It's not unusual for my people to get hung up an extra day or two on their trips. They won't worry until it's been longer."

Sheppard pressed his lips into a line. "I'm still telling my pack."

"Run your pack as you wish, Alpha," I said. "Mine just won't worry. If yours will, then tell 'em."

He snorted. "I wasn't asking your permission, *Alpha*."

Something in that tone made a part of me heat up, and it wasn't my cheeks. A flash of the way he pounded into me relentlessly on the couch, with the force of someone who knew I could handle it, sauntered through my mind and I blinked as I shook my head to clear it.

"Well," I said. "Good."

He smiled as he reclined the seat and put his arm behind his head. His warm scent filled the car, heavy on the air. But I found I didn't mind it. There was a slight tinge of old tobacco at the edges of the warmth, something I'd caught when I had my nose pressed to his neck. It was easy to miss, but it felt like a secret and a part of me puffed its chest at knowing I had a piece of him others never would.

Which was fucking stupid because that was not happening again. Sheppard was the relationship type. That I convinced him at all to have a quickie was surprising. If I let it happen again, we'd have to have a *conversation* about it, and I didn't do conversations. Not about that. I couldn't afford to get entangled with someone that would only really want me because I'm the Hot Alpha. Even if I *did* like the idea of having an equal around.

I shook my head again as his breathing turned slow and deep, turning on the radio to a quiet volume. I needed to stop thinking about that. He felt good, and I needed the release. That was the extent of it.

Transactional.

Like my sessions.

I turned the tuning dial until I found a classic rock station and let the songs of decades past distract me from my thoughts.

At the next fill up spot, a few hours later, Sheppard

took over driving again.

"I meant to ask you," he said as we pulled back onto the highway. "What's going on with the wolf from the diner?"

"The super pale blonde? She put you on edge, didn't she?"

He nodded.

"That's Summer. She does that to everyone. She can't help it."

He furrowed his brow. "What do you mean?"

"Well," I started, "she used to be sheep."

"So did a lot of wolves."

"Yeah, but she's different."

He was quiet a moment, but then rolled his hand in a 'go on' motion.

"Geez," I said. "You're like a dog with a bone. She got turned vamp first."

His eyebrows shot up.

I nodded. "Exactly. Only she got turned the night the pack attacked. She turned wolf before the vamp turning killed her."

"I didn't know that was even possible."

I gave him a wry look. "Yeah, none of us did. But she still has that unsafe vamp feel to her."

"So she can't help it."

"Just like I can't help but remember what she's been through every time I look at her."

Sheppard's voice turned patiently chiding. "That's not fair to her, Jess."

I raked a hand through my hair. "I'm well aware, Tobias."

He blinked at his proper name, and his right shoulder tensed. A smirk pulled at the corner of my mouth.

"I hate that I do that. She deserves better than that. But that unsafe feel sets me off every time. I want to protect pack from the threat, but she's pack."

"And she's no threat."

"No real one, anyway," I agreed with a sigh. "But she puts everyone on edge, and then everyone just forces themselves to stay patient with her. I should have sent her to you when she first turned, but she pack-bonded so quick..."

"She's been lonely her whole life."

I nodded. "She doesn't talk about it, but I think so."

"Lynn was a lot like that too," Sheppard said. "Pack bonding quickly, I mean. And lonely, too, I suppose. If you need me to, I can talk with her."

I shook my head. "I don't." I let the 'she's mine' through in my voice.

He gave me a wry smile. "Let me know if that changes."

We fell into companionable silence then, and I fell asleep until the next pit stop, where we traded driving once again. We traded once more before we hit San Antonio in the late morning of Saturday.

The meeting was in a week. It was virtual, which was better, prep-wise, but it was still in *a week*.

We said our goodbyes in the garage of the guest house and I walked over to mine. Inside, I stopped in the kitchen for a bottle of water on my way back to my room. I may have slept multiple times on the drive, but I was ready for soft blankets and my own damn clothing.

Imogen rounded the corner, heading for the coffee maker when she eyed me.

"Oh ho," she said. "Freshly dyed hair and clothes that aren't yours? What happened?"

"Good morning, Im," I said. "Good to see you, too."

She shook her head as she grabbed a filter and started scooping coffee into the machine. "You're not gettin' off that easy, ma'am. Spill. Did Shep do something?" She arched an eyebrow at me. "Did the military?" Her voice dropped to conspiratorial tones. "Did you sleep with him? Are alphas better in bed?"

I sighed, knowing she wouldn't stop until I gave her answers. "No. Yes. Yes. And *definitely*."

She gasped dramatically. "Deets?"

I shook my head. "Later. I'm gonna nap first."

"You know I meant the last one, right?"

"Mmmnh," I said. "Then no way in hell."

Mine, whispered my wolf.

I quietly growled back at it.

In my room, I took off the borrowed clothes, took care of myself to the thought of Sheppard pounding into me, put on my favorite pair of panties—black satin with red lace trim—all before setting an alarm for two hours and taking a nap.

When my alarm went off, I cursed its existence, but got up anyway and put on a proper bra and tank top with my borrowed sweats. I found my paperwork for my identity this century, and took the Diavel to the DMV to replace my license. They managed to print me one on the spot... well, as on the spot as the DMV can manage. The whole visit still took me just over two and a half hours. I took my newly minted ID, along with my paperwork, with me to get a replacement phone before grabbing a bag full of tacos on my way to my studio. I couldn't get the thought of Sheppard's hands on my body out of my mind, but I knew something that could.

It's funny how many people will pay to watch a webcam feed of a naked lady eating tacos.

Or doing other things.

I went home a couple hours later, after a check in with Blair. Jay had barbacoa and Spanish rice ready by the time I got home, and most of the pack—at least, most of those that lived at the house—were gathered around the dining room table with half-eaten plates. But I was still tired from the cross-country trek in a car that was not built for long-hauls like that. I grabbed a plate and ate at the table with the pack's calm pervading my senses. I avoided the insistent glances from Imogen and dodged around Alayna, who would likely *also* want the details about my Colorado trip with the visiting alpha, and went to bed.

As I plugged my phone in for the night, I realized I'd never taken it back off silent mode after my studio session. I had a message from the chatty alpha next door.

Sheppard:

I meant to tell you before: it's kinda nice having another alpha around.

I squinted at the screen before giving a huff.

> **Me:**
> *Only kinda? I'm slipping.*

> **Sheppard:**
> *Not at all! You've been a great host.*

I thought a moment before tapping out a reply.

> **Me:**
> *You'll have to show me you mean that.*

The typing bubble came up and disappeared a few times before a message finally came through.

> **Sheppard:**
> *Pretty sure I made that clear in Colorado.*

My cheeks heated, along with other parts of me, at the reminder of Colorado.

And then I huffed at myself. It was one fucking fuck on the couch, for God's sake. I'd had more involved nights ten times over and then some. I didn't do anything more than one night. I didn't do flings. I didn't do 'it's complicated.' I didn't get involved. And I sure as shit didn't do *relationships*.

> **Me:**
> *I thought that was me showing you I appreciated your help.*

> **Sheppard:**
> *So it WAS more than just two alphas...*
> *How'd you say it?... Scratching the itch?*

> **Me:**
> *Shut it.*

> **Sheppard:**
> *Alright, hahaha, but then you won't know what we're up to for confirmations.*

I stared at the phone for a long moment, debating whether to take the bait. Finally, I sighed and tapped out a reply.

> **Me:**
> *Tell me?*

The reply was quick, like he'd had it typed out already and was just waiting for me to ask.

> **Sheppard:**
> *It's like the date change made more people able to come. We're up to a full twenty-three.*

> **Me:**
> *That's… actually really great news. Thanks Shep!*

> **Sheppard:**
> *You're welcome. Now get some sleep already. You must be tired to both ask for more info after telling me to shut up and then thank me for it once it's given.*

Was I really such a hardass? I stared at the screen and read the message another two or three times before the typing bubbles popped up again.

I blinked at the screen, debating which name to use. Did I call him Sheppard like everyone else did? Did I call him Tobias, knowing full well how he'd basically short-circuit at the name? Did I just leave it at good night and pretend I hadn't had one of the best Oh's I'd had in a while thanks to him?

Fuck. I needed to clear my head of him. Leave it at good night, Jess. He's a long-hauler, and you're definitely not that. Don't leave an opening you're not sure you want.

My phone didn't light up again. The typing bubbles didn't pop up.

And why should they? We literally just said good night. He doesn't want *you*, Jess. Don't be stupid. He likes that you're an alpha, and you like that he's an alpha. He likes that you're attractive, just like you like that *he's* attractive. There's no need for all this damn overthinking. Especially when you know he'd drop you like a bad habit if he ever saw your studio.

God, the studio. Even if I *was* the relationship type, that thing would be a deal-breaker for anyone.

I sighed and thumbed open my phone again. I must've watched an hour's worth of tiny little thirst trap videos, most of them featuring sport bikes or muscle cars, before I finally fell asleep.

The next day, I had a keyword update meeting with Blair and then set Eric to prepping the PR offices for the meeting. I needed to make sure we had secure lines and the computers and monitors ready for the kind of workload we'd need. After a studio session, I popped into the server room to help him as best I could, and we worked side-by-side for hours, until rumbly stomachs said it was time to call it for the night.

We hit twenty-nine confirmations by the time I went to bed.

This was actually happening. I was actually going to have an entire chatroom full of alphas hanging on my every word. Finally, they were going to listen to *me*.

In the morning, I had a meeting set to check in with the squads around the country. So, I threw on a black tank top with some skinny jeans and my boots and set out on the Super Chief for the PR office. I didn't usually take the hog of a bike, but it had a cupholder, and I was going to need caffeine to make it through the meeting without grumping at my people. I made a stop at the local coffee shop on the way, but something hit my shoulder as I headed back out to my bike.

The world went fuzzy and my coffee hit the ground at just the right angle to make the lid pop off, exploding the liquid gold all over the sidewalk. No less than three sets of boots came into my field of view as my world went black.

What a fuckin' waste of good coffee.

FOURTEEN

*** (SHEPPARD) ***

BY THE TIME I got up, it was nearly lunchtime. The smell of lunch meat and bread wafted through my door. I threw on a pair of shorts and padded out to the dining room, tugging a shirt on as I did. The two *consanguinea* were at the table already, along with Ian and Jamie. Our resident grump of a bear was nowhere in sight as Kaylah brought out the last of the lunch meat. There was already a bowl of cut-up melon with grapes and a plate full of lettuce, tomato slices, pickles, and sliced onions on the table.

"Where's Kristos?" I asked.

Lynn shrugged.

"He came home late last night," Naiya said.

I nodded as I took a seat at the table. She would know; I'd seen her go up on the roof again after dark, as she did every now and again even when we were back in

Colorado.

"Want some coffee, Shep?" Kaylah put a hand on my shoulder.

I smiled at her. "That'd be great, thanks." She went back to the kitchen as I looked at Ian. "Did you find anything useful in that vamp's emails?"

Ian nodded. "Most interesting is that they haven't taken him off the email lists, so he's still getting a *lot* of the information he would if he were still kicking."

"That's good news," I said. "I'm surprised they haven't figured out he's dead yet."

"I get the feeling he didn't have much in the way of friends," Ian said. "All of these emails have the tone of a courtesy call from a customer service agent reading from a script."

"So, what'd you find?"

Kaylah brought a mug of coffee out, along with the milk and honey, and set it down next to me before taking up one of the empty seats.

I reached for some of the bread and started to make my sandwich, cuing the rest of them to do the same.

"Well," Ian said, "not anything good, of course. The most interesting thing is that the vamps seem to think we're causing the rifts somehow. Not our pack, specifically, but werewolves as a whole."

Lynn made a face. "But that doesn't make any sense. What benefit would that give us?"

I shook my head. "It's not about the benefit—it's that they're quick to assume we had something to do with anything that could potentially be harmful to them."

"Most of the time," Jamie said, "they're right."

Ian swallowed a bite of his sandwich. "He also definitely shared how to track *consanguinea*, and that information is spreading."

A low growl rumbled in my chest for a breath before I sighed it away. Lynn and Naiya were safe here with pack. Even though Naiya wasn't bonded—and even though her paperwork put her with Jess—I'd named her pack, and the pack would protect her and fight for her all the same.

"I can't tell for sure," Ian said. "But I think I know

where he got the bloodline from. Or, at least, *who*."

I raised an eyebrow at him.

"The daywalking vampire we took out. There's enough of a trail back to him that it's feasible."

"Okay," I said around a bite of my sandwich. "But where would *he* have gotten it?"

"Zacchaeus used to be an acolyte before he was turned," Kristos grumbled, padding out to the table in nothing but a pair of flannel pants.

Kaylah stood and went to the kitchen as Kristos took up a chair next to Naiya, who rubbed his shoulder.

"He knew how the Church operated." Kristos' voice was rough. "It wouldn't have been hard for him to charm the right person, and he was old enough that he didn't smell of rot and dead things anymore."

"I don't like the thought of the Church and vampires working together," Lynn said.

"I don't either," I said. "But I don't think they are."

Kristos shook his head. "I can't see that being possible with the wolves the Church is turning out these days."

"Well, the vamps are planning to out us as a distraction so they can kill—or turn, I can't be sure which—all the *consanguinea* they can get their hands on."

The growl that ran through the room wasn't just mine. Turning *consanguinea* usually resulted in a dead human, not a live vampire, and Kristos knew it just as well as I did.

Kaylah set a mug of coffee next to Kristos, and I passed the milk and honey his way.

"Something else I'm working on," Ian said, "is tracking down this group called '2 Points 4 Lyfe.' I can't tell if it's connected to anything, or if it's just... like a hype group for vampires."

"A hype group?" Kristos raised an eyebrow over the rim of his coffee mug.

Ian nodded. "A hype group would be like... a band's street team?" At Kristos' blank expression, he added, "They're basically superfans. They talk them up and try to get others to buy into their fandom."

"And it's for vampires?" Lynn asked.

"Yep," Ian said. "Only I can't tell if it's vampires hyping each other up or if it's humans hyping them up. I still need to do more research." He took a bite of his sandwich. "*Oh!* I almost forgot. I found some interesting things talking with the storm trackers Jessica got me in touch with! It turns out all of the rifts run along magnetic ley lines."

"Ley lines?" Kaylah asked.

Ian nodded. "I don't know exactly what they do, but I suspect the magnetic ones have to do with the metals in the ground and magnetic resonance through them. I really don't understand it." His face turned apologetic.

"Something for Chastity to chase down when she gets back," I said. "She'll be glad for it, I think."

Ian finished the last bite of his sandwich. "Well, the *really* interesting thing is that one of the real spiritual types came into the chat yesterday and mentioned that the rifts *also* align with the widely accepted spiritual ley lines as well."

I cocked my head at him.

"I know," he said. "And I'd've thrown it out as unreliable data, except there is nothing scientific about the rifts themselves that I can find—"

Thunk. Thunk. Thunk.

I stood and went to the door. Those knocks weren't the polite knocks of a solicitor, they were the insistent—perhaps even angry—knocks of someone who'd rather break the door down than simply knock.

A mop of dark curls and a scowling wolf greeted me as I opened the door, along with four others: Imogen, a curly-haired blonde I hadn't met yet, and two other curly haired women whom I'd also not met yet.

I furrowed my brow. "It's... Eric, right? Jess' IT guy?"

Eric's fists popped at his side as he nodded once. "What did you do to her?!"

I looked at him through my eyebrows as I released a pulse of energy that had everyone turning their heads down and away from me.

Don't come at an alpha with aggression.

But my voice was calm and collected. "I assume you mean Jessica?"

Eric nodded once, still not looking me in the face.

"Why on Earth would you think I'd *ever* do *anything* to hurt her?"

The tall woman with the dark curly hair spoke up, though she, too, did not look at me. "Just... Help us find her? Please?"

My eyebrows shot up. "Find her?"

Eric chanced looking up at me. "She didn't show for her meeting with the remote crews. She *never* misses one of those."

"Any chance she's simply running late?" I asked.

"I wouldn't be here if she was just half an hour behind." Eric's voice was half growl. "I waited over an hour before I started calling her—"

"Y'know," Imogen said, looking me up and down appreciatively. "In case she was *busy*."

I pressed my lips into a line.

"Her calls are going straight to voicemail," Eric said. "And her phone's not acknowledging texts—which means it's either off, or she's in a dead zone. And she took the wrong bike today to be joyriding on the back roads."

"Anything in the server?" I asked.

Eric ran a hand through his mop of curls with a growl. "Yes, I turned it all off and back on again, Sheppard. I *know* all the obvious places to look. There's no sign of her. Now would you *please* stop wasting time with the basics?!"

I furrowed my brow as I let another pulse flow from me, this one more calming than the last. "What's the last thing you've seen from her?"

The other blonde with long curly hair pulled her phone from her pocket. "Let me see." She tapped the screen a few times. "The last thing was just her confirming the meeting with all the crews this morning."

I nodded. "Any of the crews find anything coming this way?"

"Not likely," Eric said. "They'd've given a warning in

the server."

The curly blonde shook her head as she swiped across her screen. "Nothing."

"Anything notable going on in town?" I asked.

"I don't think so," Imogen replied. She pulled out her phone and tapped a few things, all of which elicited static from her phone's speaker. "Wait, what?"

"What was that?" Eric asked.

She tapped her phone again, and a different frequency of static spilled out of the speaker. "The feeds are just static!"

The shorter brunette spoke up. "I've only ever heard of that happening when someone like the president or the vice president is in town. Their motorcade jams all the signals in the area."

I nodded again. "Any chance that's what's going on right now?"

The curly haired blonde's thumbs were dancing across her screen. After a moment, she shook her head. "Doesn't look like there's anyone in town. That'd definitely make the news."

Imogen looked at Eric. "Any chance someone changed the settings? Maybe when they couldn't get into today's meeting?"

Eric shook his head. "Not likely, but I'll check." He pulled his phone from his pocket.

The shorter brunette grasped the hand of the taller one, and they both visibly relaxed.

"Maybe someone deliberately sabotaged the feed," Kristos said, stepping over to the conversation.

Imogen's expression turned fierce and she snapped her attention to Kristos like it was a whip that could physically hurt him. "No one here would do that to Jessica—or the rest of us, for that matter. This pack may be huge, but *no one* would hobble the rest of us like that."

I met her gaze and she softened a fraction before dropping her eyes to my chest. "What if some of the pack didn't want to be outed?"

She shook her head. "We all agree with her. We didn't at first, but she listened and worked with all of us to get us on the same page."

"It was no small feat," the taller brunette said.

Dread wormed through me. "Then the simplest solution is the most likely. Vampires." I spit the last word with enough vitriol that Matt would be proud.

The curly blonde shook her head. "The San Antonio basin—and most of central Texas, really—has been clear of vamps for years."

"Dammit." I shook my head with a sigh as the dread pooled in my stomach. "That just leaves Buckheim. Or someone working for him."

Guilt drew a cold finger down my spine, spreading through all of me as I realized that the military wouldn't want Jessica if I hadn't told them what she was doing.

"We need to move," I said. "Now. If the military gets Jessica to an airstrip, we'll never see her again."

There was a growl from the other side of the room. I hazarded a glance that way only to see Naiya on her feet moving toward us. My eyes flicked to the group in front of me and back to her. She nodded.

I pulled out my phone and thumbed open the maps, zooming out a little on the area where we were. "It looks like... there's two airstrips in this immediate area. San Antonio International is too far. But there's one to the northwest in Bulverde, and then there's the Twin Oaks airstrip to the southwest. The latter butts right up against a whole neighborhood of backyards, which means it's too exposed."

"So," Imogen said, "Bulverde is our target."

I nodded and pointed at the two blondes in turn. "You and you come with me. We'll run as the crow flies and head them off before they get the plane off the ground. There's a neighborhood between us and them but it's pretty spread out. Be careful." I looked to Kristos. "I don't recall. Can you keep up with wolves at full speed?"

Kristos shook his head. "I'm not quite as fast, but I can track."

I nodded again. "Then you follow after us—"

"I'm not leaving Naiya here," he said.

Naiya's low growl finally became words. "I'm coming along. They won't take her like that asshole Brooks took me."

Kristos smiled at her.

"I hoped that was the case," I said. "They won't be expecting you. Keep up with Kristos. You're likely faster, but stick together."

I looked to the taller brunette. Her grip with the other woman was white-knuckled, but she otherwise seemed calm. She needed something to do.

I met her gaze and looked down at her hand before looking back up at her. "Gather who you can and get to the airstrip in cars."

She nodded vacantly, but pulled out her phone and started tapping out a message.

"We'll have clothes in the cars," the shorter brunette said.

My phone buzzed with an alert from the server.

> **Kathryn:**
>
> *EMERGENCY!*
>
> *JESS IS MISSING!*
>
> *CONVERGE ON THE BULVERDE AIRSTRIP!*
>
> *FOUR LEGS BETTER THAN TWO!*

"I'll get Levi," the shorter brunette continued. "I think he's off rounds this week."

I blinked at her. "Who?"

"Our EMT," the taller brunette, Kathryn, said. "His mate's an ER nurse, but she's working right now."

"Thanks." I squeezed her shoulder as I released another pulse of calming energy, even though I needed it just as much as they did. "Let's go."

FIFTEEN

*** (JESSICA) ***

MY HEAD POUNDED, BUT at least the fogginess was clearing. I kept my eyes shut to the high-pitched whine in my ears. But I could push thoughts into order now. I'd gone for a coffee, and then... I dropped it when something hit my shoulder on that side. Something must have knocked me out. I didn't know there was anything that had that capability.

And I was restrained. There was something binding my wrists together as well as my ankles. Adrenaline poured through me, clearing the last of the fog and the whine.

There was a lot of commotion nearby—snarls and barks and yelling and pops of silenced weapons. I gingerly opened my eyes and found I was on the floor of... a plane? Probably a private puddle-jumper, really.

I was face down with my head turned to the door, but—in the interest of learning more information before I could be sure I wanted to jump into any more danger than I was currently in—I stayed still. The door was open, and outside the plane was sheer chaos. There were wolves fighting other wolves out on the tarmac, and a bear and a leopard too, and some people had weapons that they were trying to train on the wolves, but it was clear they were either having trouble getting a clean shot, or they couldn't tell for certain which were allies and which were foes.

Some of the wolves I recognized, one of them a timber wolf who'd recently pinned me to the ground in Colorado.

I lifted my head. "Sheppard...?"

There was a soft pop from behind me and something hit the back of my thigh.

If Sheppard was in wolf form, and so was the rest of his pack and much of mine, then it was time to suck it up and ruin the dye job I'd just done.

With a snarl, I shifted, tearing from my clothes and slipping easily from the locked leather bindings that had been used to hold my human form. Batting the little fluff-tipped dart from my leg as more adrenaline flooded my system, I spun to face the guy who shot me. Another soft pop, and another dart sank into my shoulder.

As I lunged at him, a third dart hit my belly and my limbs turned to lead weights. I landed gracelessly on top of him as the world went fuzzy. My head thunked to the carpeted floor of the jet and blackness took my vision from me.

"Restart the clock on red," the man under me said. "Level three."

SIXTEEN

*** (SHEPPARD) ***

WATCHING JESS BONELESSLY HIT the floor of the plane under the influence of three tranquilizer darts sent red through my vision. It spurred me to end the fight even faster than I'd first intended, and with decidedly less mercy than I'd had to start. I snapped at one of Jessica's wolves, and we brought a couple more from our respective packs to rush the plane, easily taking out the three men inside. A part of me hoped I hadn't killed them, but a much larger part of me was too concerned with my fellow alpha's wellbeing to care. All told, it was thirty wolves plus a bear and a leopard versus the military's six-wolf strike team. They'd gone running with their tail between their legs as soon as we'd gotten Jess off that plane.

From there, it took some maneuvering—and more

than one trip to a pack car for bundles of clothing—but eventually, we got the relevant folks back to two legs and loaded the still-unconscious and still-in-her-wolf-form Jess into the bed of her red truck. I hopped in the back with Levi and Naiya as we rushed back to the house, the former because... well... he was an EMT and the latter simply because she insisted on making sure Jess was okay. And because arguing with her would have only wasted time.

I hated that every time I'd seen Jessica's stunningly beautiful wolf, it'd been because she was in danger. She had rich black fur with deep red-amber highlights that blended along her shoulders and feathered through her tail. She should have been able to enjoy letting loose twice within the same week.

"She seems stable," Levi said over the wind. "Just unconscious."

"They drugged her," Naiya said. "I heard the pop of a tranq gun."

"I saw her fall," I growled out. "What the hell works on wolves?!"

She gave me a level look. "Likely the same stuff that works on leopards."

Dammit. "Any idea how long she'll be out?"

"Uh..." Naiya ran a hand through her hair. "Not really. I.. don't remember a lot of the details about my... captivity."

I swallowed the lump in my throat that was definitely trying to be another menacing growl. "I'm so sorry you had to go through that, Naiya. I didn't mean—"

"It's fine," she said, waving me off. "I just don't like trying to remember it."

When the truck stopped at the house, I gingerly picked up Jessica and let Levi lead me to her room, which was filled with the scent of her—lavender and cloves. I placed her on the black sheets of her bed, her head on the plush black pillows, and pulled the heavy grey comforter back toward the foot of the bed. There was no way warmth was an issue, and I didn't feel comfortable allowing a weighted blanket on her when I didn't know what exactly had knocked her unconscious.

But I also didn't know how her pack felt about skin. Mine had long since gotten used to it, minus Lynn, who was still learning, and Naiya, whose change worked completely differently. So, I pulled the flat sheet over her body so that when she shifted back, she would at least be covered.

I raked a hand through my hair and pulled the stool from the end of the bed over to the side. "I'll stay and watch her."

"We can—"

"I said I'll stay." I didn't bother to keep the alpha from my tone.

Levi turned his head down and away from me, but Naiya held my gaze.

"I'll go, but text me when she's up?" Her tone was firm at first, but lightened considerably as she reached the end of her words.

I was growling. I blinked and stopped myself. With a heavy sigh, I nodded.

Finally, she turned away and left the room, following where Levi had gone.

As I sat down, I noticed a display case on the other side of the room filled with... well... dildos. Lots of them. In all different shapes and sizes and colors. I'd only ever seen a collection that large in a sex shop, though even most of those didn't have dildos shaped like *that*.

Perhaps covering her wouldn't have been necessary. *Someone* had likely seen their fair share of her skin.

Mine.

Except she wasn't. Not yet, at least. And maybe not ever.

I pushed thoughts of a relationship with Jessica from my mind. She didn't need another alpha sniffing her tail.

I could ask her about her collection when she woke up. Not if. *When.*

I stared at her for the better part of an hour before the curly-haired blonde from my doorstep came in with barely a knock to preface her presence. She had a lunch meat sandwich in one hand and a glass of water in the other.

"For you," she said, handing me both. "If you want it. Or just leave it for her if you don't."

I nodded my thanks, not trusting my voice around a wolf that'd never met me before today. And what a damn way to meet a wolf.

"I'm Alayna," she said. "Eric... thought you should know we tracked her Super Chief and got it back here."

I nodded again.

Eric. Who thought I had done something to land her in trouble.

Well... I had, hadn't I? Those were military wolves who'd grabbed her, that much I was certain of. Buckheim might as well have pulled the trigger himself.

"It was at a coffee shop on the way to the PR offices," she continued. "Jess probably stopped for coffee, and that's when they kidnapped her."

I put the plate and glass on the nightstand to keep myself from breaking them and checked the time on my phone. She'd probably been out for closer to two hours, if she first got knocked out on her way to the PR offices. The airport was thirty minutes in the other direction.

"I'm... just gonna go." She ducked her head and stepped from the room, shutting the door behind her.

Jess' heart rate was too slow. Levi had said it was fine, but I didn't like it. It sounded flat and dull, a sharp contrast to the vibrant and bright beat it should have had.

What the hell kind of thing knocks out a damn alpha for that long without killing them?!

Likely the same stuff that works on leopards.

Naiya's words echoed in my head as my wolf gave a whine of worry.

I steepled my hands in front of me and placed my elbows on my knees as I watched her, my heart aching with the same concern.

My phone had been randomly buzzing as emails came in, but since none of the buzzes were notifications from the pack trying to reach me, I simply put the phone back into my pocket. After the fifth one, I left it sitting on my thigh.

And when my thoughts turned to how Buckheim could do something like this to someone like her, I had to move my phone to the bedside table to keep from crushing it. I then ignored the buzzing altogether, knowing that if my pack needed me, I would get a call that would do more than a single buzz.

I watched her steady breathing for hours, dozing lightly before snapping myself back awake. None of her pack bothered us; likely none of them dared.

And then she shifted on the bed and came back to her two-legged form, the room filling with more of her lavender-and-cloves scent. My chest clenched for the briefest of moments until I heard her heartbeat again. She hadn't died. She didn't wake, but she hadn't died. At least her heart rate seemed more normal then.

I stood and repositioned the sheets, tucking them around her then to make sure she was covered. The door opened and the rail thin blonde, Imogen, popped her head in.

"Any progre— Oh."

My growl cut her off, but she'd seen Jess in the bed.

"I can take it from here, Alpha."

I don't know what look was on my face, but it couldn't have been good.

She paled and her hands came up. "Okay. Or not. Sure. That's fine too." She backed her head out of the door and shut it with a quiet little click.

I shouldn't have done that. She didn't deserve it. Jess' pack was just worried about her, and rightfully so. I wasn't pack. I wasn't her mate.

Mine.

Shut up, wolf. No, she's not.

I couldn't not stay and keep vigil over her, but her pack also had a right to do the same. They didn't deserve me—a growly alpha keeping watch over their alpha—snarling and snapping at them as if they were unruly pups. Hell, for all I knew, maybe they were. But they were *Jessica's* potentially-unruly pups, not mine.

One thing was certain: I was done with Buckheim. As soon as Jess was up and moving again, the General would be getting an earful. I shouldn't have let him get so close. I shouldn't have allowed myself to keep him so close. Of course his years in the American military had changed the wolf that took me in when my parents were killed. Of course he had seen Jessica's plan as a threat.

Too long had he gone without consequences to his actions. Till this, nothing had been so blatantly over the line. But attacking Jessica—attempting to kidnap her to silence her—was simply a bridge too far.

SEVENTEEN

*** (JESSICA) ***

I WOKE UP *THIRSTY*. It wasn't new, but waking up to stunningly golden eyes watching me was. Simple warmth danced in the air, mingling pleasantly with the scent of my own space.

Sheppard breathed a sigh of relief as his eyes met mine. "Thank God." He was in a white t-shirt that clung to his chest and biceps, and his light wash jeans only barely contained those powerful thighs. His elbows were on his knees, his hands steepled. His chin had been resting atop them, but it didn't matter now. He'd never looked sexier.

Or maybe I was just that thirsty.

On the bedside table was a lunch meat and cheese sandwich along with a glass of water, but neither of those things were what was making my mouth water.

"You're a lot farther away than I'd like you to be." It came out a little slurred, likely from the last of whatever I'd been shot with clearing my system. But at least there was no whine in my ears like there had been on the floor of the plane.

He raised an eyebrow as his eyes flicked to my collection. I looked over my shoulder to follow his gaze, knowing full well what he saw. I somehow doubted he'd be the type to want to make use of any of that. Not that he'd need to, really, he had more than enough stamina to keep up with me.

"See something you like?" I asked him.

His intense eyes refocused on mine. "Are you...? Do... you cam girl as a side hustle?"

I couldn't help but laugh. "I'm legit surprised you know what any of those terms mean."

"I'm old," Sheppard said, "not out of the loop." He sounded entirely unamused.

My face fell. It was likely as I suspected then. He could never handle knowing all of me.

"And... if I said yes?" My voice was quiet.

"It would explain a few things, Ms. Wylde." His expression was wholly unreadable, and I hated it.

But I was pretty sure I knew how to change it. I sat up and let the sheet fall from my body. His eyes followed the movement, but then flicked dutifully back up to mine.

"Would it make you turn me down?" I pulled the sheet to the side, exposing the rest of my body. My skin was flawless, my body shapely, and I knew it. I made bank on stream, and I'd be damned if none of it mattered in that fucking moment.

His answer did.

"Of course not," he said.

Relief washed through me, along with a not-insignificant amount of warmth.

"Then stop pretending you don't want me, Tobias." I let my voice drop to sultry tones.

Something crossed his face and his heartbeat did that little *tha-thump* it did any time I used his proper name. It sent more warmth through me, and my upper thighs slickened to know I had such a profound effect on him. It was clear no one called him that in his day-to-day life, and the way his vision refocused on me afterward gave me every indication that he liked it.

I moved toward him on the bed, swinging my legs over the edge. "You want me, yes?"

He gave a single slow nod, his Adam's apple bobbing as he swallowed.

It made me want to lick it.

"And I want you." I stood. "So let's get this out of our systems."

He gave me a wry smile. "There is no getting *you* out of my system, Jess. Every touch of your skin makes me want *more*, not less."

"Well, I don't hate the sound of that," I said, stepping closer to him. I used my foot to push his legs to either side of my body as I took another step closer.

"Jess...."

I ran a hand along his arm, electricity practically crackling along the touch as goosebumps washed across him and he closed his eyes.

"You're turning me down?" I arched an eyebrow at him. "Really?"

His eyes met mine once again. "I'm not saying *that*."

I reached for his shirt and peeled it off him, his movements accommodating.

"Then this is just two alphas getting their needs met." I opened the fly of his jeans. He hadn't bothered with underwear when he shifted back and put clothes on. And he was at full attention. I ran a hand along his length, watching as more goosebumps washed across his skin.

He let out a quietly throaty growl as he stood and pushed his pants to his feet. Stepping out of them, he reached a hand around my waist and lifted me from the floor as he gently but firmly bit my shoulder. I moaned my appreciation as I pulled him to me and he plopped me unceremoniously down on the bed.

"You should be careful what you awaken, Miss LaRoux."

"Call me that again and I'll... oh god..."

He'd dropped to his knees and pressed his mouth against the spot where my legs met, interrupting my threat in the most sensual way he possibly could have.

"You were saying?"

I shook my head as he lapped hungrily at the juices and circled the pearl with his tongue before pressing it into me and repeating the motions over and over until my hand tangled in his hair and I ground my hips against his face. Toys were great for all sorts of things, but nothing could replace a warm mouth and hands on my body. And those hands held me firmly against him as I came, pouring more of myself all over his face. He wiped it off with a sexy smirk and gently flicked the pearl with a single finger. I jumped at the sudden contact and he gave me a sensual, deep-throated chuckle.

Fuck, I loved that sound.

He flipped me over then, those big warm hands of his wrapping around my waist as he lifted my hips to line up with his. He pressed into me with one long stroke and I moaned my appreciation as he thrust into me a few times, filling me in a way the dildos and vibrators simply hadn't. Sometimes, there was just no replacement for actual, proper dick.

He managed to thrust in time with the waves of aftershocks dancing through me, enhancing my ecstasy in ways I'd only had with toys before. And when those had subsided, he pounded hard into me, pulling my hands behind my back and lifting me for a better angle, his free hand spreading along my belly. After a few thrusts, I broke free of his grip and reached over my shoulder and behind his neck as I rolled my hips in rhythm with his until his hand came up, settling around my throat.

It was not an entirely unpleasant sensation.

He pulled me hard against him then, need feeding his movements as I continued to complement his thrusts with my own. When he came, his grip firmed around my neck and he growled my name into my ear.

It pulled another wave of ecstasy from me, and I was going to need to change the sheets after this one.

Fuck, there was nothing like his hands on my body, his voice in my ear. And suddenly, I wasn't sure I could ever get enough.

EIGHTEEN

*** (SHEPPARD) ***

I WAS JUST SO damn happy she was alive. And what a way to celebrate it. When I released her, I pressed a kiss to the spot where her neck met her shoulder, the same spot I'd bitten before, and smiled at the goosebumps that washed across her skin.

She pulled away from me then, reaching for the sandwich on the side table. She handed me half and we ate in silence.

We weren't going to talk about this one either, apparently.

I traced a finger along her leg. "We should probably let the other alphas know that the U.S. military tried to kidnap you. Alert them that they may try again, and it could happen at the meeting."

She shook her head. "If they hear that, it'll keep any

who might be on the fence from logging in, and it might even make some of the confirmed cancel."

"They deserve to know what they're getting into, Jess."

"And I'm happy to tell them once they're all *online*." I scowled at her.

She sighed. "It's more secure this way too. If we tell them all piecemeal, they'll have a chance to chit chat with each other and their packs about it. Someone'll mention it to the wrong person, and boom." She mimicked an explosion with her hand. "The military blocks my internet access, traces all the alphas as they're trying to log in and doses them all and their packs with whatever bullshit they jammed into me, leaving humanity high and fucking dry to deal with vamps until they decide to release them again."

I looked down at my hands—my *empty* hands. "I didn't expect Buckheim to go that far." I never meant to place her in so much danger.

Jessica stilled, the glass of water in her hand.

"I knew he'd be reluctant," I continued. "But I expected him to see the logic of it, like you showed me. I didn't think he'd try to kidnap you." I sat up and met her gaze as I took a deep breath. "I'm sorry, Jessica. I misjudged him."

She studied me for a long moment, searching my face for something before huffing out a breath. "You don't owe me an apology because some asshole alpha decided he wanted to silence me. It's not like it's the first time it's ever happened, just the first time anyone's actually managed to drug me into unconsciousness."

My eyebrows shot up. "Not the first time?!"

"You think the other alphas like how big my pack is? You think they appreciate that they keep hemorrhaging members to my pack?"

I raked a hand through my hair. "They probably appreciate it about as much as they appreciate me being so close with the military."

"Try considerably less," she said. "You, at least, speak to them first and arrange for members to go wherever is good for them. I appear to just hoard new members for myself."

I nodded.

She tucked herself into my side, and it was like she'd always belonged there. "How soon can we be on the air?"

"On the air? As in, telling the world?" I blinked my thoughts clear and arched an eyebrow at her as I wrapped my arm around her, resting my hand on her knee.

She shrugged and snuggled closer. "I mean, no time like the present, right? Beat the military to the punch?"

I gave her a chiding look, not that she could see it very well from her angle, but still. "How do you expect the other alphas to take us seriously if we keep changing the plan on them?"

"Hmmm. Maybe you're right. Well... maybe I can make some calls and we can start trickling the ad out just after the meeting."

"The ad we haven't even filmed?" I arched an eyebrow at her.

"We can film it right after the meeting," she said. "It shouldn't take long to get it edited up and ready to go."

"Sounds like the kind of thing your PR lady should be looped in on."

"Obviously." She rolled her eyes. "Blair'd lose her shit if I went off half-cocked like that." She playfully bit my forearm, but then her expression instantly sobered, her posture stiffening, like she realized the casual intimacy of the gesture. "In any case, I plan to have NDAs ready for virtual signing for packs or even individual wolves that don't want to be outed. I think the paperwork will be redundant, but I want them to have concrete assurance."

"Well, we won't be lying to them when we tell them we'll keep them out of it," I said.

"Exactly." She nodded. "And they'll know it." She sat up and away from me before taking a big gulp of the water. "How many are we up to now anyway?"

I reached across her for my phone on the bedside table and thumbed it open, forcefully ignoring the way her nose brushed along my jaw as I returned to my place on the bed. A couple taps later, and I was into my emails. "Looks like..." It took me a moment to read the new messages and add to the running count in my head. "...We're up to forty-two."

"I expect a number of the undecided to wait until the very last minute." She looked at me through her lashes. "Because it's me, I mean."

I sighed. "They should have more respect for you than that."

"They should," she agreed. "But they don't. I've raised too many hackles."

I kissed the top of her head, ignoring the part of me that wanted more of this more often. "You don't deserve the rough road you've had to travel to be alpha."

She finished the water and placed it back on the bedside table.

Silence stretched for a long moment, and she pulled her knees to her chest, resting her chin on them.

"Hey, Tobias?" Her voice was soft, almost meek.

I blinked again at the use of my proper name. It sounded so damn good coming from her mouth, but it had been so long since someone had so casually used it that it took me a moment to reply to her.

"Yes?" I said finally.

"Thanks," she said. "For rescuing me."

I stilled.

She snuggled into me then, the lavender and cloves scent of her wrapping around me like a blanket. "I'm glad it was you."

Mine.

Shut it.

But my heart pounded and felt entirely too large for my chest as I wrapped an arm around her again.

"Anytime," I said, hoping it sounded more casual than it felt. I placed a soft kiss to the top of her head as my hand found her scalp through her hair and started to gently rub. She leaned into the sensation and—despite her forced unconsciousness—she dozed lightly against me. The peacefulness overtook me and I, too, fell asleep with her still wrapped in my arms.

NINETEEN

*** (JESSICA) ***

I WOKE STILL TUCKED into Sheppard's side, the warm scent of him enveloping me. It was not entirely unpleasant. In fact, I couldn't help but notice how relaxed and... well... *safe* it made me feel.

But he was also naked. And he was hard. I walked fingers along his stomach as I shifted on the bed.

"Keep that up," he said groggily, "and you might need to do something else with those hands."

I hooked a leg over his and wrapped a hand around his morning wood. "It's like you read my mind."

He blinked and was suddenly quite awake, twitching in my hand no less. "Wait, Jess."

I pumped my hand along his length a couple of times and gave him a sultry look through my lashes. "Wait?"

"Just..." He sighed and covered my hand with his,

gently pulling it from his dick. "What is this really?"

"I mean, it's pretty obvious what this is, isn't it?" I raised an eyebrow at him.

"No." His eyes flicked to my dildo collection before coming back to meet mine. "No, it's not."

I sat up with a huff, my mouth pulled to the side as I ran a hand through my hair. "Why does it have to be anything?"

Why should I have to name something that is supposed to be just a casual thing?

"I just want to know what we're doing here," he said. "One's a fluke, two's a coincidence, three's a pattern." He counted them out on his fingers as he said it. "Patterns mean things, Jess. So what is it you actually want?" His gaze was intense.

I gave him a wry smile. "*Technically*, this is still two. We haven't even left the bedroom." I gestured around.

"Jessica..." He used that voice again that was chiding, but still sexy.

Fuck, he made me so damn *thirsty*.

I met his eyes, matching his intensity with my own. "What we're doing is *not* asking that question."

He arched an eyebrow at me.

I held his gaze. "Because if we *ask* that question, we have to *answer* that question. And I have less than zero interest in *that*. So could we please just *not* put a label on this?"

And could you *please* not make me have to examine these stupid feelings I keep having every time you're around? I'm not a damn teenager anymore. I don't *do* labels.

He was quiet for a long moment, searching my face as his cycled through a few expressions before he finally nodded with a sigh. "Alright."

"I told you not to think too much about it."

He nodded again. "You did."

"So don't."

He put his hands up. "Alright, alright."

I kissed his cheek. "I'll be right back."

I grabbed the shirt next to the bed and pulled it on as

I reached for the plate and glass. As I headed out of the room, I caught my reflection in the full-length mirror on the back of the door. My hair was a mess, and the wrong color, but the shirt fell down to my mid-thigh, and it was early enough that not many would be up, so it was fine if any one or two wolves saw me. At least the pack would know I was awake and alive.

Out in the kitchen, Alayna was making coffee. She had on loose grey sweatpants with a red tank top, her hot pink bra straps showing. She took a bite of an apple as she leaned against the counter. I paused and looked at the clock: it was about a quarter past nine in the morning. I blinked at her.

"Early morning, Aly."

She smiled. "Journalism final, and tomorrow's my editing final."

"Ah." I nodded, putting my plate and glass in the sink.

Alayna put a hand on mine. "Glad you're okay, Jess." She squeezed my hand.

I smiled and nodded again. "Me too." When she released me, I turned to the fridge and grabbed a couple of bottles of water. And then I leaned against the door. "How'd you guys manage to pull that off anyway?"

"Rescuing you?"

I nodded once more, trying my damndest not to feel like a bobblehead.

"It was Shep," she said.

I narrowed my eyes and furrowed my brow. "Not you or Im?"

She shook her head. "No, no. That's beyond my pay grade." She shrugged. "I dunno, Jess, he just jumped right in and knew what to do. He didn't hesitate for even a second. And he stuck around watching you all night." She smirked then. "At least, until he didn't need to and y'all did other things."

I rolled my eyes. "Why did you guys even follow him?"

"What else were we gonna do?" She shrugged again. "He asserted himself. I guess we always understood what it meant for *you* to be our alpha, because, y'know, it's how alphas do. But he's an alpha too. I mean, hell, even Eric listened to him. It was pretty impressive actually."

"That's fuckin' *bullshit*, actually," I said, my eyebrows shooting up. "This isn't his pack."

"Yeah," Aly said. "But you weren't here, so it kinda worked out. Would you rather we all just sat around and waited for you to rescue yourself?"

Water ran from the direction of my room and Aly's eyes went wide as she dropped her voice to a whisper. "Oh my god, he's still here?!"

"Shut it," I hissed, turning back to my room.

"I bet he heard you," she whisper-shouted after me.

I turned and threw a water bottle at her, but she caught it with a wink. My cheeks were hot as I ducked back into my room, pressing my back to the door as I opened the other water bottle.

Since when did I care what Aly or anyone thought about what I did in my bedroom?

Then Sheppard—still fully naked Sheppard—plodded out of my bathroom with my mouthwash bottle in his hand. "You know that's my shirt, right?" He unscrewed the cap to the mouthwash and gestured toward me with the bottle. "You didn't have clothes when I brought you back here."

My cheeks got several degrees warmer as I ducked past him into the bathroom to brush my teeth. If he was going to take care of his morning breath, why shouldn't I?

He followed me in, taking a swig of the mouthwash straight from the bottle.

"By all means, help yourself," I said before furiously shoving the toothbrush across my teeth.

He paused making faces to smile at me. He stepped in to spit into the sink and turned on the water, sipping some from his hand and swishing it around in his mouth before spitting it out too. He then splashed some water on his face and grabbed a hand towel from my counter to dry it.

But I wasn't looking at his face. I was tracing the lines of his body. Because Sheppard was one well-put-together wolf. From his toes to his dick to his chin to his—

Oh god, he was watching me size him up! My cheeks, which had managed to cool while I was brushing my teeth, heated once again and I moved to rush past him.

His hand thunked against the doorframe, his arm in my way. His golden eyes met mine when I drew up short.

"Tell me I can kiss you," he said, his tone so deliciously dark that it felt like a caress across my body.

I rolled a shoulder with a slow blink and forced nonchalance into my tone. "Fine. You can kiss me." I tilted my chin up, ready for said kiss.

He slowly brought his face to mine, the fingertips of his other hand coming up to brush along my chin, static in their wake. And just as I leaned closer to meet him, he redirected to whisper into my ear, his lips brushing the outer edge. "Now tell me you *want* me to kiss you."

He dropped his hand, but I swear I could still feel it on my skin. I stiffened anyway and folded my arms across my chest, ignoring the last of the goosebumps that washed across me at his touch.

"Never gonna happen," I said firmly.

I was lying, of course, and there's no way he didn't know it. But if he kept at this game, I'd end up practically begging him for more than just a simple kiss.

And his smirk told me he knew it.

"You're lying, Jessica." That dark tone was still there, making parts of me go absolutely molten.

And his mouth was still *right there*—temptation just a simple taste away.

I leaned toward him to take what he clearly was offering, but the smirk grew and he trailed a lock of my hair through his fingers as he straightened out of my reach. And then he bent down, wrapped an arm around my waist and threw me over his shoulder.

"*Hey!* Put me down!"

His laugh was rich and full. "Not until you admit it."

"Bite me," I huffed.

And then that asshole *actually bit me*, right on the ass. Not hard enough to draw blood, but still a proper *bite* that elicited a surprised squeak from me. And a not-insignificant amount of warmth and wetness between my thighs.

"Careful what you wish for."

And then I saw my door frame. There were four indentations on the right side, and an indent in the woodwork where his thumb would have been. I didn't have time to marvel or wonder at it. He plopped me onto the bed again and peeled his shirt from me before crawling atop me, leaning into me to inhale deeply along my shoulder and neck.

I couldn't help but do the same to him as well, sucking in lungfuls of his patient and comfortable warmth, though it set me alight to do so. My scent mingling with his was positively intoxicating.

This damn wolf was going to be the end of me.

And then he moved my knee to the side and pressed into me, pumping in and out until he could bury himself to the hilt against my body. And fuck if it didn't feel so damn good.

I arched up to meet him, rolling my hips in time with his thrusts until he sat back on his heels and pulled my hips to him. I sat up then and ground my hips into his lap until he hooked an arm under my leg and practically lifted me onto and off of his dick over and over and over. I threw my head back as every thrust felt deeper than the last, moaning my appreciation and giving not a single shit who heard.

But—as good as this felt—it wasn't getting me closer to the release I wanted, the release I ached for. So I reached for the drawer of my nightstand, where I knew I had just the thing.

Sheppard paused thrusting, an eyebrow raised as he saw my reach. It was enough that I could actually gather the toy I was looking for from the three in the drawer.

I thumbed the switch of the vibrating wand and waved it. "This should help things along."

He gave a dark little chuckle. "In a rush, are we?"

"I just know what I want," I said.

He nodded and thrust into me again, pulling my hips

hard against his. "Then by all means."

He thrust hard into me then as I pressed the vibrator against my body, rolling my hips some more until I could get it into *just* the right position to get it to do its job. And in no time flat I was cumming all over him again, making even more of a mess of the sheets I'd forgotten needed changing until just that moment.

He came as the vibrator tore aftershock after aftershock from me with delicious relentlessness. And when I tried to pull it from my body, Sheppard's hand covered my own, pressing it harder against me until a second wave of ecstasy ripped through me.

"That's my girl," he said as I writhed against him, pouring myself all over the sheets.

He released me a moment later and I thumbed the vibrator back off, tossing it to the side like it was anathema.

He chuckled again and pulled me against him. I tucked into his side, ignoring how nicely our bodies seemed to fit together, despite the size difference.

What the hell *were* we doing? I sure as shit didn't like to try to have a label with anyone, certainly not with someone that I'd wrangled into being the face of the PR campaign, but then again—

I shook my head.

No.

I don't do labels.

I don't do 'it's complicated.'

I don't do relationships.

Sheppard had dozed off in the afterglow. Well, good.

With a huff I got up and pulled an old black shirt from the bottom drawer of my dresser, underwear from the top, and a pair of shorts from the chair in the corner. I quietly snuck into the bathroom, shutting the door with a barely audible click so I could re-dye my hair. Lord knows the smell would probably wake him in a few minutes, but that was a problem for not-right-now-Jess.

As I wrapped my hair up into the shower cap to let the bleach process, Sheppard—now in his white t-shirt and stonewash jeans—padded into the bathroom with two toasted egg and avocado sandwiches.

As I took the proffered sandwich, he jerked his chin toward my hair. "Any chance you're willing to give me the long version about why you don't change?"

He flipped the switch for the fan, but whether it was for the noise cover or for the smell, I'd never know for sure.

I set the timer on my phone and sat on the edge of my giant black claw foot tub to take a bite. "Holy shit, this is a good sandwich."

He smiled and sat on the bathroom floor across from me, leaning against the cabinets under the sink. "Yeah, there's something about the avocado that really does it for me."

I nodded.

"Avoiding the question won't make it go away, Jess."

"Yeah..." I took another bite and was quiet for a long moment.

"You'll get no judgment from me," he said. "I just think maybe I can help. Mistakes happen all the time with our line of work, so there's practically nothing you could tell me that I'd be shocked by."

"This is my skeptical face," I said.

He shrugged. "Try me?"

I stared at him for a long moment, searching his face for something I couldn't name. And then, I took a breath and nodded. "I was twelve years old when the alpha of the pack I was born into tried to arrange my marriage and mate, giving my family little say in the matter. Rather than conceding my fate to his alpha's judgment, my father took us and his four best horses from France and brought us to the new world. It only took him a year to get back to breeding horses like he did back home. His line had a reputation, and he was eager to ensure the line continued despite our move."

I was stalling getting to the point and I knew it. But Sheppard just watched me and waited. I took a breath and barrelled on.

"It was two weeks before I turned sixteen when my first change hit. My family had taken the latest yearlings to auction, and brought our stallion to stud. My parents were made wolves, as were all of the wolves we'd met up with this side of the ocean. Our pack was small. Only five or six wolves, my parents included. They never had to learn about when or how the first change happens for a born wolf, so none of them were really prepared for what would happen to me."

Sheppard nodded along like it was a story he'd heard before. It probably was. I couldn't be the only one to have bad memories from a first change.

"Which meant I had nothing to cling to when it happened." I stared at the tile lines as the scent of horses and hay whispered through me for a breath.

"I was mucking out the stalls the night before the auction, when Samuel decided to come and harass me. Samuel was Samantha's lover, and Samantha—my pack mate—was my best friend. She called him her mate, even though he was human. Anyway, I knew the real reason Samuel was in the stables. He and Samantha were meeting up for an after-dark tryst. I simply had to wait out his barbs, and Samantha would come and sweep him away somewhere."

God, I couldn't stand him. Samuel was probably the worst person Samantha could have chosen, but she loved him, so I had put up with him.

"But he had a lot to say about my mucking out of the stables. He was sure I should be quilting or doing embroidery or something else equally feminine, which he definitely used as an insult. Only my parents had no other children. I was the only one to do it. Which he also seemed to find fault with. His barbs about why Johnny didn't like me were particularly hurtful."

Sheppard took a breath to speak, probably to ask who Johnny was. So, I answered the unasked question, still visually tracing the tile lines.

"Johnny was a human, and he could never understand me fully. He liked me plenty, but didn't like being kept at arms length from me." I shook my head, pushing out the memory of his bright and inquisitive blue eyes and the way his strawberry blond hair always seemed to get in front of them.

"I'd finished the first stall and had the yearling tied out in the aisle for the next one when the first cramps hit. I didn't know what was happening when the first set doubled me over. Samuel thought I was being dramatic and mocked my senses, telling me that the smell is why girls are too weak to be the ones to muck out stables. But then I saw my hand as my fingers bent at wrong angles and the skin darken some. I was sure this was my first change. I couldn't be sure how I knew it, but I knew it was coming."

I looked down at my hand and flexed my fingers, blinking to get back on track.

"The horses were getting agitated with the noises of my body and my groans. Samuel, who had been nothing but a tormenter until that point, tried to help me, probably so he could look good to Samantha. But he couldn't do anything, and I curled into the fetal position."

"You killed him." Sheppard said, interrupting my story.

I shook my head. "Not the way you might think. I tried to save him. As the change started to force my face into shape and my ribs started to shift, I yelled for him to run. He was in more danger from the horses than me, even in that state. A single rope at the front of each makeshift stall wasn't going to keep the horses in when they bolted. And bolt they very much would once a giant wolf appeared in their midst."

Samuel's expression of sheer horror when he came around the half-wall that marked one stall from the next was seared into my mind's eye. I'd never forget it, as long as I lived. I squeezed my eyes shut, like that could make it go away.

"I don't know what Samuel saw, but it was enough that he stumbled back into the horse I'd tied out. The horse reared up and clipped his head on the way down. He dropped like a sack of potatoes, blood pouring from his head, but he was still breathing. And I was in a pack of made wolves who would understand if I could save him. By that time, the change had fully transformed me, and I kicked out of my clothes to get to him. I'd clamped down onto his ankle as the first person came to check on the noises. Of course, it was one of the auction attendants, fully human, who was making rounds to ensure none of the horses got out or got stolen. He made a big hubbub about there being a wolf, and I got shot at as I was trying to save Samuel."

I could still see his misshapen head against the dirt, could still taste the metal of his blood in my mouth. I pressed my lips in a line and swallowed thickly, trying not to make a sour face.

"I bit my best friend's so-called mate once more, despite the bullets flying, as he convulsed on the ground. And then, I bolted for the back wall of the stables. Surely, my full force would simply bust through the temporary wooden structure. I was stronger than people should be, but just as strong as my packmates. I was right. The wall gave way, boards snapping as I crashed into them. Samantha was the first of our pack to arrive. She wailed as I ran."

It had been such a broken noise. She must've known from the moment she saw him that he wouldn't make it. That I had failed.

"My parents found me eventually, but Samuel was long dead by then." I took a deep breath. "Samantha stopped talking to me, as did Johnny, and the two of them hooked up soon after. Last I heard, she was calling him mate as well, but things just weren't the same afterward. I stayed with my pack and didn't try to talk to regular humans much unless we were saving them from vampires."

I hazarded a glance up at Sheppard. His face was shrouded with empathy. It made me uncomfortable. I blinked and looked back to the tile lines as I shifted my weight where I sat.

"My parents urged me not to change much after that. They reminded me of what happened often and were concerned it might happen again. I tried to make sure that when I *did* change, I did it somewhere secluded."

God, I was *still* talking, wasn't I? I needed to wrap it

up or we'd be here all day.

"When my parents passed, I fell in with a Church pack. We only ever wolfed out when it was time to kill vampires. And we did that often enough that there was no need to go on runs or let off some steam. Even when I left that pack for being too dominant and headstrong, I fell in with others whose alphas reinforced my understanding that being wolf meant violence and death. I always ended up fighting with someone in the pack when I changed. So I tried not to change. And I worked hard to not pass that internalized misbelief on to my own pack members. I've built a pack now who joyfully wolf out and play and run and hunt and everything, but I don't."

"Jess..." Sheppard placed a hand on my knee.

"It's not just the guilt of killing that guy," I met his gaze. "It's that nothing in my life has ever shown me that being in my wolf form was good for something other than violence."

"Maybe we'll have to change that."

TWENTY

*** (SHEPPARD) ***

I WANTED TO WRAP her in my arms and tell her it was alright. I wanted to take her on runs and let her howl at the moonlight and just *revel* in the joy of her beautiful wolf.

I wanted to show her... the world.

She turned on the faucet of the tub and flipped her head over toward it, pulling the wrap from her hair. "Also, I'm pretty sure mate is just a word wolves use to describe their partners. It's not anything more than that." She put her head under the water.

The declaration dropped like a lead weight in my heart. I sighed and then wished I hadn't. The bleach in the air was strong enough to sting at my eyes.

"The violence thing is why you fought me in the woods in Colorado," I said.

She continued rinsing her hair. "It had more to do with the fact that I got shot because you had to go and try and do the honorable thing." She pulled her head from the water and grabbed a towel. "But look. Our wolf form is designed for destruction. Samuel was in danger because he didn't know what I was. He *died* because he couldn't know. If he'd known, he would have lived a full life with Samantha, who loved the whole Sam-Sam thing from their names."

"Sure," I said. "But our wolf form can do more than just destroy. We can run, and play, and—"

"And *hunt*," she said. "And whether it's truly meant for destruction or not is irrelevant. Our presence in the world with the humans' ignorance is more dangerous for them."

She grabbed the bowl of hair dye and put on a pair of black rubber gloves. She had the first section of hair in her hand and was taking the dye to it when my phone buzzed from the nightstand. I went to grab it and thumbed open the screen.

I checked my emails on my way back to the bathroom, where Jess was finishing up with the dye in the bowl.

"Three more confirmed," I said as she worked the dye into her hair. "Apparently Daniel and Jonathan got back from Kalispell yesterday. I should go and meet with them—see what they found."

"Sure," she said, nodding as she pulled the gloves from her hands.

I grabbed the empty plates. "I'll take these to the kitchen on my way out."

"Thanks." She smiled.

"I'm... glad you're okay."

"Me too."

I wanted to kiss her, at least on the cheek, but that sort of thing did not exactly seem welcome, despite the sex and the story. So, I squeezed her shoulder and left.

TWENTY-ONE

*** (JESSICA) ***

SHEPPARD'S WORDS RANG IN my head. *Maybe we'll have to change that.*

Yeah, and crown me the queen of all idiots for thinking he could possibly have anything useful to say after hearing my story.

My timer dinged, and I ducked my head under the faucet of the bathtub to rinse the dye out of my hair.

Lord knows he only wants me because I'm a fellow alpha. Not because of me. I mean, an alpha has to have standards, right?

I wrapped a towel around my head as I fished the hair dryer out from under the cabinet.

And what the hell did I care anyway? It's not like I wanted anything more from him than to scratch the itch now and again. Who cared if he was sometimes the cause of that itch? Why shouldn't he then be the way I scratch it?

Fuck, but his hand around my throat felt so... good. No one dared touch me like that, not even my one-night flings.

That's my girl, he'd growled into my ear. And there was a not-insignificant part of me that wanted to hear it again.

I shook my head. It didn't matter, entangling myself with him was a bad idea.

I don't do labels.

I don't do 'it's complicated.'

I don't do *relationships*.

Certainly not relationships with hot ass alphas who I needed to have a clean working relationship with.

Fuck.

I needed to clear my head.

I changed into some jeans and a tank top, pulled my hair back, and headed out to the garage. Alayna pulled up just as the garage door finished opening.

She pulled off her helmet.

"How'd the final go?" I asked her.

"I either know it or I don't," she said with a shrug. "Heading out?"

I pulled on my vest. "Nah, just wanna make sure it all still fits."

She snorted out a little laugh. "Will you at least turn on your 'find my phone' feature? In case those assholes are still lurking about?"

I looked at the Super Chief and back at her. She was right to ask for it. If I'd had it on, the pack might have had an easier time getting to me. With a sigh, I pulled my phone from my back pocket and started digging through the settings to find it. And then a thought occurred to me.

"Why don't you just come with me?" I tapped my phone against my other hand. "I could use the company."

She nodded with a smile and pulled her hair out of her ponytail just to redo it again before pulling on her helmet.

I took the Diavel out. I suspected it would be a bit

before I'd want to go out on the Super Chief again.

Alayna at least had the decency to wait until we were well away from the house before chirping into the mic. "So... You and their alpha, huh?"

"No."

"Jess..." Her tone was chiding.

"No! I mean, look. I can't. Not with him especially. He's just..."

"A tool you're using? Like a living version of your collection?"

"No!" I shook my head. "I just... I can't get involved like that. Not with him. Not with anyone. Not now."

"We all see how you two look at each other, Jess. He clearly adores you. And it was his quick thinking that got you back home instead of... well... wherever the military would have taken you." There was a smile in her voice. "That one's mate material for sure."

I rolled my eyes. "Mates aren't real, Aly."

"Don't let Kat and Liz hear that. Or Levi and Emma. Or Mason and Nikki for that matter."

"Come on, they're different and you know it," I said. "And that's not what I mean anyway. Mate is just a word wolves use when they're in love. It's like how people call each other soulmates. But it's not this mystical connection or anything. Yeah, their pack bonds are stronger with each other than with the others in the pack, but that just makes sense. Levi and Em's connection with Oliver is practically just as strong."

"Sounds like someone trying to convince themselves more than convincing me," she said.

Convincing mys—

"What do you think he's gonna do when he learns about my studio? You think he'll just be all giddy and excited to learn what I do there?"

"You could just show him."

Show hi—

"And lose my best bet for a face for this PR shit? Hell no!"

"Still sounds like you're just making excuses to me."

"Shut it."

We rode in silence for a while then, weaving through some of the lunch rush traffic.

"So," she said, breaking the silence. "Sheppard's hot and all—"

"*Super* easy on the eyes," I agreed.

"And clearly he's good in bed."

"I mean, practice will do that."

"Well that's kind of my point," she said. "What's wrong with him that he's still single? He's what, three hundred plus years old?"

I laughed. "He's got two hundred years on me easy."

"So five hundred and fifty then. That's *worse*! And why's his pack so damn small?!"

"I... dunno really," I admitted. "I know they've taken out more vamp nests than any other non-Church pack, ours included. They may be a small pack, but they're fucking *effective.*"

"Well, it can't help that he moves around so much."

I nodded. "Yeah."

Her voice turned wistful. "Too bad the one with all the scars has a mate. Umnff. That one could break me and I'd fucking *let him.*"

"Don't let Chastity hear you say that. She's got a territorial streak a mile wide when it comes to him."

"Well, it's too bad all the same," she said. "The other beefcake with the long hair would be a nice backup if he weren't so utterly consumed by Lynn and Naiya."

"You wouldn't want him anyway," I said. "He's kind of a grump. Besides, I think he's mostly into dudes. And he's older than dirt. By a *lot.*"

"Like older than Kaan, older than dirt? Or just *regular* older than dirt?"

"I wouldn't know for sure. Kaan says time works differently where he's from, and I have *no* idea how long that bear has been around."

"Is it true he used to be a Church assassin?"

I furrowed my brow. "Where'd you hear that?"

"I dug around," she said. "His paper trail disappears long before the one you created starts. And the last one has him being officially excommunicated. It didn't have a date on it, but it was old, I know that."

"I dunno," I said. "I know he fights like an absolute *beast*. But you gotta get him angry enough to fight first. Mostly he'd rather not care."

We rode in silence for a while more.

Alayna's voice was quiet enough that I almost didn't hear her over the road noise. "We were really worried when you went missing."

"I bet," I said.

"We were!"

"It wasn't sarcasm, Aly. I know you must have been to send Sheppard."

"Eric thought he'd done something." Her voice was sheepish. "To you, I mean."

"He wouldn't," I said.

"Well, we know that now. But... we didn't want to lose you... We still don't."

I heard what she wasn't saying. "I'll turn on the 'find my phone' feature as soon as we get back to the house."

"Promise?"

I smiled gently within my helmet. "I promise."

TWENTY-TWO

*** (SHEPPARD) ***

COMING BACK TO THE pack house was like trying to step back into normality after a vacation. Only that vacation had been rescuing the local alpha and making sure she wasn't dead followed by... well... some damn good sex. It was a little bit surreal and a lot a bit mundane to return to my pack.

But I could use some mundane.

Kaylah winked at me as I came in the door. Jonathan and Lynn were on the couch, the former in his skull-and-crossbones t-shirt with green cargo shorts, and the latter in a flowy grey tank top with tight black shorts. Her legs were across his lap and they were watching some kind of home improvement show.

Daniel had a laptop in front of him and was typing out something or another.

Jonathan's nose went into the air as the blast of summer heat invaded the space. "Well, now I get what had you tied up last night."

Kaylah threw her kitchen towel at him.

"I'm sure I'd have heard something if it was urgent," I said, heading to the fridge for a bottle of water. I looked pointedly at Kaylah as I did.

"Kalispell, Montana ain't urgent," she said with a shrug. "An' these two ain't hurtin' for something to fill the time."

Kristos—in a black tank and grey sweats—gave a snort from where he sat at the far end of the couch. I hadn't noticed he was there, but then, I hadn't noticed Naiya sitting there either, and she was leaning against him with her legs crossed over the ottoman. She had on a sleeveless grey crop top with denim shorts. The shirt said 'Bite me' in bold black letters.

Given her general casual defiance of me, it seemed appropriate.

I shook my head. I needed a nap. Something to clear my head of the image of Jess just lying there as she shifted back to two legs. Something to clear my head of the way she said my name during the activities to follow.

Kaylah got to busying herself in the kitchen, the scent of Mexican spices dancing in the air.

I looked at Daniel. "What did you find, then?"

Daniel shook his head. "A whole lot of nothing. There's a ton of wide open space that would make for easy hiding from the humans. But everything is still really spread out, so there's not a lot of reason for us to go."

"No vampire activity?"

Jonathan piped up from the couch. "Not unless the vampires there are *very* old."

"So, not likely," Daniel said. "Because old vamps usually also means young vamps."

"And sheep," Jonathan added.

"See?" Kaylah said from the kitchen. "Nuthin' urgent. Plenty of space for us to be if we wanna hole up for a while and relax, but not a whole lot of anything else worth us being there."

I nodded. So Kalispell was full of space, and New York already had one pack, though they also still had a vamp problem. Now to just wait and see what New Orleans has to offer when Chastity and Matt get back.

But there was something I could do. I pulled my phone from my pocket, thumbed it open, and scrolled through my contacts until I reached the one I was looking for and hit the call button.

He answered on the first ring. "Tell me you've managed to talk some sense into that alpha friend of yours."

I sucked on my teeth. "Nice try, General, but trying to kidnap Jessica to silence her is only going to make her dig her heels in. And you lost whatever chance you might have had to have a rational discussion with her about it when your people *shot her* in Colorado."

"Oh please, it was just a scratch! You're lettin' this she wolf twist you all to hell, boy. Nevermind that it'll ruin my project—what she's talkin' about is suicide. It'll make 'em turn on us. There's just no way they'll ever accept us as their protectors. Humanity has it in their head they don't need savin'."

"I guess we'll just have to see how that all plays out now, won't we? Either way," I said. "You leave *her* the hell alone."

"Are you *threatening* me?"

I gave the phone a feral grin. "Wouldn't dream of it. Of course, I wouldn't want to see what happens if you tried to cross me on this either."

His voice turned to cold, hard steel. "You'd better think long and hard before you burn that bridge, boy."

"Way ahead of you, *sir*." And I ended the call.

I'd thought on it plenty while watching Jess' unconscious form on her bed. I didn't want to be allied with someone who would go to that kind of length to shut down something that would be inconvenient, but better for the world. Buckheim was on the wrong side of history here, and I wasn't about to stay behind with him.

Kaylah brought out all the best fixings for fajitas: limes, pico de gallo, cheese, sour cream, and tortillas, all before bringing the meat out to the table in two huge bowls. The four couch potatoes joined Daniel and I at the table almost immediately, and I had my first fajita down and was working on the second when Kaylah caught my gaze.

"C'n I chat with you?" Her eyes darted around the table. "Privately?"

"Pack doesn't keep secrets, Kaylah."

"Oh I know." She shook her head. "I jus' don' think you're gonna wanna share this wi' th' rest of 'em jus' yet."

I paused mid-bite and looked at her. "Now?"

"No time like th' present."

I sighed and took another large bite of my fajita before following her down the hall to the media room.

She dropped her voice, but it still wouldn't be enough if the others decided to be nosy. "Burnin' a bridge 'at's been standin' longer 'n I've been alive?" She poked me in the chest. "You got it *bad* for her, Shep."

I raked a hand through my hair. "I know." I huffed out a breath, relieved to say so out loud. "Believe me, I know. But that bridge needed to fall anyway. He's not the same wolf that helped a scared, suddenly orphaned wolf all those years ago."

She whistled. "I din't know it went back 'at far."

"And Jess? She... well... sometimes I think she's on the same page as me, but then the walls go up and I can't tell anymore."

"Well c'n you blame 'er? You said yourself she's had a hard road t' alpha."

I nodded. "Yeah."

... mate is just a word...

I shook Jessica's voice from my mind. I wanted to show her that was wrong, too.

Kaylah watched me for a long moment. "You... know she ain't ever gon' wanna give you kids, right?"

"You don't know that." I probably said it too quickly.

She gave me a disapproving look. "Shep..."

I slumped onto the sectional. "No no. You're right. And I know that. And I'm not sure I'd ever want her to change her mind."

She took a deep breath and sat down next to me. She placed her hand on my knee. "There's more 'n one type of fam'ly, Shep. An' I'm not sure you'll ever find another that's as good a match for you."

That was... a lot coming from Kaylah. She'd held a candle for me for a long time before Daniel joined the pack. To hear her so willingly push me toward another wolf? It really meant something.

"Jess really is a piece of work, isn't she?"

Kaylah nodded. "You should talk to her, Shep. Actually get on the same page together. Before she decides to go write her story with someone else."

And if I didn't already know I wanted her for my own, that last sentence would've done it for me. I couldn't stand the thought of her writing that story with someone other than me.

Mine.

I rolled my eyes at myself.

Not yet, she wasn't.

But she maybe could be, one day.

TWENTY-THREE

*** (JESSICA) ***

My phone buzzed on the table as Alayna and I were finishing up lunch at a local barbecue joint. Of course that would happen while my fingers were covered in sauce.

I made a face as I wiped my hands on multiple napkins.

"Sheppard?"

I shrugged. "It's not like I have a special alert for him, Aly."

"If a guy held a vigil over me while I was unconscious for hours, I probably would," she said.

"Yeah, yeah." I thumbed open my phone.

Kaanskkairiskollik:

If you wanna see what's on the other side

"It's Kaan," I said. "He's got a rift open in his cave."

She jerked her head toward her phone. Her fingers were covered in sauce too. "At least let the server know?"

"You're not coming?"

"Mmmnh, think I'll pass," she said. "Don't need a reminder of the monster in our backyard."

"He's not a monster," I said.

"He would be to anyone who threatened you or the pack, I think."

"That's fair."

"Anyway, I just think you should also let someone know where you're off to—someone who's not just me—since you haven't gotten back home yet and turned on 'find my phone.'"

She knew me too well. I wasn't going to do that until I absolutely had to, even if it *was* the smart call given what the military just tried.

I tapped out a message in the chat server as well, letting them know where I was going and why. I felt like a modern teenager having to keep my parents in the loop on what I was up to. It's not like I didn't want the pack to know, it's that I was the Alpha—the parent, if you will. I was the one *they* should be reporting to, not the other way around.

I sighed. I'd turn on the tracker as soon as I got *home*. But not a moment sooner.

It was a short ride to Kaan's cave, though I had to cross some off-road dirt and scrub to get there. Inside, it was clear the rift was in the cave ceiling. Iridescent purple-green-gold energy warbled around a differently colored scene, but I couldn't quite make out what was on the other side... maybe a city?

Kaan, of course, was already in his dragon form, his

giant silver body eating up something approaching half of the space in this cave. And I was barely as tall as his smallest toe, or perhaps one of his teeth. It was... humbling, to say the least.

"How're we doing this, Kaan?" I tried to play it cool like I was just asking Kaan, the guy, and not Kaan, the giant ass dragon that could swallow me whole.

Kaan gave a deep chuckle that rumbled through the cave... and through my chest. It was an intoxicating kind of laugh really, and I caught myself smiling as well.

"I'll pick you up," he said, his voice sonorous and melodic. He laid a foretalon down in front of me, 'palm' up, like he intended for me to climb onto it.

He could fucking crush me that way. But I also didn't exactly see an easier way to get up to that rift short of me climbing all over him to make it happen. And since that was not the proffered method, and since his claw was *right there*, I figured I could stand to spare a little trust for the dragon I'd known for years.

I gingerly clambered into his palm. It was warmer than I expected.

"Okay," he said. "I'm gonna wrap my claws around you so you don't get pulled through." He closed his talons around me, and I shifted around in his grip until I felt more secure. "Tap twice for down, three times for too tight, four for tighter."

I nodded and tapped once on the silvery scales. They were hard, like I would expect a steel shield to be. "You actually feel that?"

"I do," he said. "Dragon scales are far more sensitive than you might think. Now, hold on tight!"

TWENTY-FOUR

*** (SHEPPARD) ***

"Where's Kaan's cave?" I asked, more to myself than anything, as I came back to the dining room.

"I can show you," Kristos said.

"Jess said she's checking out a rift?" I looked up at him and he nodded as he stood.

"Let me grab my shoes." He looked to Naiya, and then at Lynn. "Pretty sure you two are both gonna wanna see this."

"Well, I'm coming too, then," Jonathan said.

"Naiya can drive," Lynn said.

She gave Lynn a look. "I can? I don't think everyone will fit in the Mini."

"You three in the Mini," I said. "You can follow Kristos and I."

A few moments later, after everyone grabbed shoes,

we were on our way.

Following Kristos' directions, we were soon off the roads and driving across red clay sand and tenacious scrub. And then I could see into a cave where a mass of shining silver took up the back half, but glinted the light back at me nonetheless.

"This is it," Kristos said.

I pulled the truck to a stop and hopped out. Naiya's Mini was a ways behind still, as she had to pick her way more carefully across the off-road terrain than my truck did.

I could smell that the guy from before, Kaan-something, was here, but all I could see was that mass of shining silver... Holy shit, is that a *dragon*? And is that Jess in its claw, half jammed through the rift?!

I peeled off my shirt. "I'm coming, Jess! Just hold on!"

Kristos grabbed my shoulder, stopping me as the Mini rolled up. The doors opened and Lynn's voice echoed my thoughts.

"Holy shit," she said.

"Holy shit is right," Jonathan replied.

"It's like something straight out of a book," Naiya breathed.

"An actual, honest-to-God *dragon*," Lynn said, awestruck.

I looked at Kristos, who smiled. "She's fine."

The dragon gave a rather human sounding laugh, if not for the fact that it came from a chest the size of a cargo container, and brought Jessica back down out of the rift. "Your friend has a short fuse, Jess." His sonorous voice was amused.

Jessica tossed her braid back over her shoulder and brushed wayward strands of bright red hair from her face as she rolled her eyes. "I don't need saving, hothead. Just having a look through a rift." She gestured to the purple-green iridescent ring around a scene that appeared to have an overcast sky, though I was too far to see clearly what was on the other side.

The dragon gently lowered her to the ground so she could climb down onto the cave floor as I pulled my shirt back on.

Lynn's face was scrunched in frustrated confusion. "Sheppard is *not* hot-headed. If anything, *that's* hot-headed." She gestured to Jessica and I couldn't help but laugh.

"Hey," Jess said.

Jonathan joined me in laughter.

"She's not wrong, though," I said.

"She's not hot-headed," the dragon said. "She's just... driven."

"That's what you're calling it, huh?" Kristos raised an eyebrow.

The dragon simply laughed.

Both Jessica and Kristos were completely calm around this absolutely enormous creature, and though it seemed somehow familiar, I couldn't put my finger on it. It smelled like that Kaan guy she'd introduced me to nearly a week ago. Perhaps it, too, was from the other side of the rifts, like he'd said Naiya was.

Jess gestured to the colossal silver dragon as she looked at me. "You remember Kaan, don't you? You two met when he brought me the music box."

That was Kaan?!

"Kaanskkairiskollik," the dragon said.

"Well, that explains a few things," I said. Like how something about him felt like a lie. And like how he liked the sound of his full name. "Wait, this is your natural form, isn't it? The human one is a disguise."

"Well, I don't exactly fit at dinner tables like this," Kaan said, gesturing at himself.

"Wow," Jonathan said.

Lynn had been simply staring, awestruck, at the dragon, but she blinked just then and pointed at the rift as she leaned toward Jonathan. "That's what they're like up close."

"Usually with a few more rift creatures," Kaan said, rolling a shoulder in a very human-like shrug. "But I took care of those when this one opened."

I gestured to the rift as I looked at Jessica. "What's there?"

"It's a city." She shrugged. "But like out of medieval times."

"That's where I came from," Kaan said. "That's Arcaniss. The city of Virilisz, to be exact."

Naiya took a few steps forward, her eyes glued to the rift.

"Why not... go back home while you have the chance?" Kristos sounded almost like he dreaded the answer.

Kaan cocked his giant dragon head in an almost chiding manner. "I like it better here." He actually *winked* at him. "And I've seen virtually everything there."

Lynn leaned close to Jonathan, her voice low. "Pay up, they're sleeping together."

Kaan laughed as Jonathan pulled the wallet from his back pocket and handed a twenty to Lynn.

"Can I see it?" Naiya's voice was barely more than a whisper, and she took a couple more steps toward the rift.

"Of course," Kaan said, reaching a claw toward her.

Kristos rushed to interpose himself. He gave Kaan a look and then turned to Naiya. "I can't let you get yourself killed, Kitten. You've seen the things that come through those."

The look on Kaan's face, despite it being a dragon's face full of scales and ridges and teeth, screamed 'I'd like to see you try to stop me.'

But Naiya's voice was full of tears as she shook her head. "What if I poke my head through and Andy is *right there?*"

"Kitten..." Kristos reached for her.

She shook her head again and sidestepped him, stepping closer to Kaan's outstretched claw. "I know it's not likely. But it is *possible.*"

Kristos looked to me and I nodded at him. She deserved the opportunity to see it, if that's truly where she's from. He looked to Jessica, who gave him a nod as well. He then met Naiya's gaze and held it for a long moment, his heart in his eyes, before he sighed and drooped.

"I won't be the reason you forever wonder," he said, stepping aside.

The dragon nodded approvingly. "I won't let her get hurt."

Naiya carefully clambered into the dragon's claw, and my chest tightened as his claws curled around her. She might not call herself pack, but I did, and I disliked the idea of her being in danger probably about as much as Kristos did.

She re-situated herself once the talons were firmly around her and then Kaan started to lift her up just as droplets of rain started to drip through the rift.

As soon as her head disappeared across the rift, the exposed bits of Naiya's skin lit up with iridescent leopard spots that pulsed through their colors, likely in time with her heartbeat, though she was far enough away that it was hard to discern hers from the ones I was already hearing—nevermind that the dragon's gigantic heart drowned out most of the others' present.

"Isn't that interesting," Kaan said.

"What is that?" Lynn asked. She looked like she was listening to something. "What's happening to her?"

Kristos narrowed his eyes. "I can't be sure. It's... not hurting her..."

"Arcaniss is a world of magic," Kaan said. "It must be responding to her, as a native of that plane."

"Well that about confirms it," I said. "If she wasn't sure before, I bet she is now."

More rain splattered against the dragon's scales and the cave floor, but no sooner had their rhythm started to increase that it then became more sporadic again. And the edges of the rift were silently crackling, their energy almost flickering.

"Hmm," Kaan said, pulling Naiya back from the rift.

But as soon as some of her reemerged on this side of the rift, the speed of the pulse on her spots increased, and she struggled against his grip hard enough that he reached his other claw up to stop her from slipping through his talons as the rift grew smaller and then sealed shut.

"*Bivai, moxt pidas*," he said. "I'm sorry. I'm not sure what happens to things caught across the boundary of a closing rift."

Tears were streaming down her face and when he gently placed her back down, she crumpled to the ground, sobbing. The spots on her skin still pulsed with what was presumably her heartbeat, her hair was limp and wet, and her shirt was sticking to her body, showing the black bra beneath it.

Kristos rushed to comfort her, and both Lynn and I stepped closer as well.

Then I *could* hear her heartbeat, and it matched perfectly with the beautiful iridescence pulsing across her skin.

"It was so right," she wailed. "I was so *whole*."

Kaan shifted to his human form, fully clothed in grey and white linen with close-cropped salt and pepper hair and just barely a scruff of a beard on his chin. "That... makes a lot of sense. I don't know how you got to be here, Naiya, but Arcaniss is certainly where you're from." He traced a finger on her shoulder where a spot pulsed once more before going out entirely.

All of her spots ceased pulsing and faded to nothing. But still she sobbed.

Kaan made a little twisting gesture with his wrist, and a white towel appeared in his hands. He wrapped it around Naiya's shoulders.

"I'd have let the rift close with you on the other side if I hadn't told someone I wouldn't let you get hurt," he said, exchanging a meaningful look with Kristos, who gave him a soft smile and nodded.

"And here I thought watching you dust a vamp was gonna be the wildest thing I've ever seen," Jonathan said to Lynn, his hand squeezing hers.

"Well," Jessica said. "If that's really where you're from, Naiya, then it looks like you have a decision to make." She met Kaan's gaze as she pressed her lips into a line.

Boy, did she ever.

I nodded. "It most certainly does."

Kaan shook his head. "It's unlikely you're from *there* specifically." He pointed at the spot where the rift had been. "They are not particularly welcoming of lycanthropes in Virilisz. But, should you decide to venture through a rift in the future, I am certain I could give you what you'd need to find your friend relatively safely."

"I..." Naiya blinked at him. "I just..."

Kristos pulled her closer. "You don't have to make that decision right now, Kitten." He gently guided her to her feet.

"He's right." I nodded. "Give yourself some time to digest it."

Kristos carefully fished the car keys from Naiya's pocket and tossed them to Lynn, who caught them with a nod.

"We'll see you back at the house," Lynn said, looking to me. She then flicked her eyes to Jess and back at me before winking and turning to the Mini.

I gave Naiya a warm hug, placing a gentle kiss against the top of her wet head as I did so.

Kaan smiled knowingly at me and then nodded once before he simply ceased to be in the cave with us.

The Mini drove off a breath later.

TWENTY-FIVE

*** (JESSICA) ***

AND THEN IT WAS just us in the cave. Two alphas who had no idea what they were doing with each other, while clearly everyone else had a plan.

I took a deep breath full of the fading scents of those from the cave, but mostly of Sheppard's warmth, and chose a path to my bike that did not involve coming face-to-face with him.

He put a hand out to stop me, but I dodged around it, sure he was going to ask me questions I didn't have the answer to. Questions I didn't even want to *consider* having the answer to, really.

As I passed his hand, he balled it into a fist and raised it up like he was pulling it from a fire.

What's wrong with him that he's still sing—

"Jess, wait," he said.

I stopped and turned to look at him.

"Let me take you to dinner? Tonight?" His voice was likely more pleading than he meant for it to be, not that he'd likely ever admit to such a thing.

I shook the braid from my hair and pulled it back into a low ponytail as I thought.

There wasn't anything wrong with him. He just... definitely wanted something more serious than I did. Nevermind that there was a snowball's chance in hell he wouldn't lose his shit if he ever saw my studio.

Dinner with him would likely just end in my bed again. Or maybe his.

Would that be so bad?

I eyed him.

His body language screamed confidence, but his eyes gave him away. He wanted me bad.

"Uh, sure... okay," I said with a shrug before I even realized I was saying anything at all.

It was probably better that way.

"Great," he said, beaming. "Pick you up at six?"

I pulled my armored vest back on. This was probably a mistake.

"Don't be late," I said, throwing my leg over the Diavel.

He put a hand on one of the handlebars as I moved to pull on my helmet. "Hey Jess?"

I paused and met his gaze.

"What you said earlier, about the first time you changed... and about mates..."

Shit. This is *not* a conversation I want to have. Especially not right now. Not here.

He cleared his throat. "I think you're punishing yourself. You blame your friend for moving on, and you blame yourself for letting yourself believe in something as hopelessly romantic as mates. Because if mates aren't real, then you don't have to feel so much guilt about that kid because then he was just a guy. He was a human, sure." He shrugged. "And we're supposed to protect them, but he was just a guy. And I think the reason you *still* struggle is because there's a part of you that knows better. I think if you were ever brave enough to forgive yourself even a little bit, to give yourself even half the grace you deserve, you'd find there's a part of you that knows that all that guilt is just not right."

I ran my tongue along my teeth as I digested that. Forgive myself? For what? Killing that kid? For letting myself think that he could actually have been a proper mate to my friend? Or for letting myself think—even for a few hopelessly romantic years—that mates could have ever possibly been a real thing?

"... Right." I jammed my helmet on as I sighed. He meant every damn word of what he just said too. I flipped the visor down, started the bike and sped off without even so much as looking back at him.

Mates weren't real. That kid was just in the wrong place at the wrong time. Love is fucking stupid like that. And let's just assume, for the sake of argument, that he's right and I just need to forgive myself. How does that make mates real? Even if they were, I wouldn't have time for one. I certainly couldn't afford to lose focus by having an actual freaking partner. No one really wanted me for *me* anyway. I was just a status symbol.

Besides, no one—not even Mister Nothing-Would-Shock-Me—would *actually* want to be with me after finding out what I do when I get bored. Or lonely. Or thirsty.

Sounds like someone trying to convince themselves.
Shut it.

TWENTY-SIX

*** (SHEPPARD) ***

I TOOK JESS OUT to dinner that night. I treated it like a proper date—I got her flowers, took her to the nicest place I could find, opened doors for her, pulled her chair out for her, bought her half the menu and dessert—and yet still it was clear we were *both* avoiding the elephant in the room.

Neither of us were ready to talk about what was very clearly becoming a pattern.

The food was good, but the conversation was all business. I filled her in on what was in Kalispell, and she filled me in on what Blair had to say. Aside from the obvious 'don't leak the ad early' warning, apparently people sitting in living rooms were seen as more trustworthy than guys in suits, so we figured that'd be a good opening for the ad.

And confirmations for the meeting had reached fifty-eight.

To make matters worse, somehow some of her pack ended up at the same place that night. It turned out her paperwork guy, whose name was Shawn, and his assistant were taking a client out to dinner.

Well, she did say I couldn't go anywhere without running into the pack.

When dinner was over, the ride back home was silent, but for the stilted goodnight without even so much as a hand squeeze.

And not a single one of the buzzes of my phone the rest of the night were her.

At least, not until I texted her the final attendance tally for the day. Two more confirmed, bringing the total number of wolves to sixty.

But all I got in return was a simple thanks. Just the one word with a period after it.

Mate is just a word...

I couldn't get her out of my mind. The scent of her, the way her skin felt against mine, the way electricity followed in the wake of her touch, the way her voice sounded when she moaned my name.

My actual name.

The last time someone had so casually called me that, it was a gruff wolf who'd recently come to my rescue when the local vampire brood tore through my family, killing my parents. Except the only name George Buckheim had since been able to get me to answer to reliably was Sheppard.

That same wolf had tried to kidnap her—to silence her. That same wolf had tried to claim Lynn as his when she turned. I should have burned the bridge then, but Lynn had done some real good since then. She'd saved wolves that couldn't be saved, brought them back to their humanity so they didn't have to die.

And she'd claimed Jonathan as her mate. Or he'd claimed her as his. It was mere semantics to try to sort out which way it happened. It didn't matter. Those two were as closely tied as Matt and Chastity or Kaylah and

Daniel.

How could Jess not see that mates were real? Her pack was huge. Did she truly have a pack that large without even a single mated pair amongst them? It seemed unlikely.

At some point during my musings, I dozed off, though I only knew it because I'd awakened to the sound of Kristos coming home. A glance at the clock before I rolled over to go back to sleep told me it was three in the morning.

)))) 🐾 (((((

We were all seated at the table with the morning meal spread before us when Kristos, in just a pair of black sweatpants, came out to join us. He grunted a greeting before slumping into a chair. He still smelled like Kaan. He must've taken quite a liking to the dragon.

Matt came in the door a few moments later wearing a black t-shirt and blue jeans. Chastity, in a blue floral sundress and wedge sandals, followed directly behind him.

He hooked a thumb over his shoulder as the door closed. "Why's the Camaro here?"

"Welcome back, you two," Kaylah said, her voice cheery.

Matt nodded at her. "Thanks." He looked at me. "Why's the Camaro here?"

"Jess and I took a trip to Colorado to talk to Buckheim," I said around a bite of pancake. "It went poorly."

"Yeah," he said. "Color me surprised. But why's the *Camaro* here?"

I sighed. This was where he was going to lose his shit. "Jess... insisted that we take that back to Texas instead of Lynn's Del Sol. Given our options, I couldn't help but agree with her."

Lynn stood to take her plate into the kitchen. "Not sure you'd fit in my car anyway."

I huffed out a laugh. "That's what she said too."

Matt just came over and hugged me. Didn't even bother to wait till I stood up or anything—he just leaned down and hugged me. "Thanks, Shep."

"You're welcome?"

Matt released me and stepped back, looking a little sheepish. "I wanted to bring her when we came out this way, but I couldn't justify it. She sucks gas like a hooker sucks dick."

Naiya coughed out some of her water into her napkin.

"*MATTHEW*!" Kaylah swatted at his bicep.

Matt laughed. "Yeah, but you knew what I meant!"

Kaylah just shook her head as she stood and took her plate to the kitchen. Chastity sat down where she'd been, while Matt took up the seat Lynn had vacated and they both dug in on breakfast as soon as Kaylah had brought them plates.

"So," Matt said around a bite of sausage. "You and the other alpha, huh?"

I sighed and shook my head. I didn't want to talk about it, but I wasn't about to try to hide things from the pack.

"I don't even know," I said.

"Well you're at least holding a candle for her if you let her talk you into something as impractical as taking the Camaro on a long-haul road trip." He took a sip from the orange juice Kaylah left. "I think I get why you worked so hard to convince me to go along with her plan."

I wiped my face with my hand. "Just... tell me what you found in New Orleans?"

"It's pretty well overrun by vamps," Matt said with a growl. "And we didn't smell even a single wolf anywhere near the city. We offed some of the younger vamps, but they hadn't even *seen* a werewolf before they met us, so it was easier to get them out on their own."

"Which means we can learn more if we go there," Chastity said. "The bloodsuckers are organizing like we've never seen. I didn't think you could get them to work together, but something's got them driven. I can't tell what their aim is other than killing people and taking sheep and claiming territory, but they definitely have one."

"The city needs cleansing," Matt said. "Badly. We'd be in over our heads, and it wouldn't be the first time, but Lord knows the city is worth it."

We couldn't let the vampires get an entire city as a stronghold. It was bad enough they'd managed to get a nightclub all to their own in Colorado Springs.

"Any chance you've heard mention of Vsevolod or Kitashihime?" I met Matt's gaze.

He glanced down at his plate and then back up at me as he shook his head.

"Best we can tell," Chastity said, "no one's heard anything about any of the elders in a long while."

"That can't be good," I said. "It means there's either a power vacuum, or something very big is coming."

Matt looked across the table at Naiya, who had more just moved around the food on her plate than actually eaten any of it. "What pissed in your Cheerios?"

She looked up through her eyebrows at him. "I told him I didn't belong there." Her voice was barely more than breath.

Kristos rubbed her shoulder.

"Turns out she's from the other side of the rifts," I said.

"Not taking it well that she's stuck here, huh?"

Kristos looked at him. "Would you?"

Matt shrugged. "I've got a cure for that."

Kristos eyed him, a low growl rumbling in his chest.

"Matt..." My voice held all the warning it needed to. I stood to take my plate to the kitchen.

He stretched his back, cracking his neck once. "Oh please, I can't do anything she can't heal like that." He snapped his fingers.

Naiya put her fork down. "What'd you have in mind?"

He stood and jerked his head toward the back window. "Let's polish up those combat skills."

When Naiya hesitated, Kristos stood.

Matt rolled his eyes. "Oh, come *on*. We haven't had a chance to see what she can really do, and she's been too busy licking the wound of losing her mate to even think about it."

Chastity put a hand on his arm. "Matt. I know you're pent up from New Orleans..."

But there was fire in Naiya's glare at Matt.

"See?" he said, pointing at her face and swirling his finger in the air. "You've got it all pent up in there with nowhere to go. Head full of noise makes it hard to do anything." He jerked his head toward the back door. "Let's clear that out."

Kristos stood with a sigh, pinching the bridge of his nose. "I can't believe I'm about to say this, but three hundred years and you *still* haven't figured out how to think straight." He looked up at Matt. "She's *consanguinea*, Matt. When she hurts you, you'll heal—"

"But it'll be slow," I said.

"Exactly," Kristos said.

"Wait," Lynn said from the kitchen, where she was leaning against the counter. "It didn't heal slowly when I fought him."

"Sparred," Matt corrected. "And she's right. Her wolf bit right through my ankle and I was right as rain by dinner."

Kristos' face turned contemplative.

"But then..." Lynn looked at me. "Remember when I landed on you after dusting Frederick? Why did those scratches take so long to heal?"

Everyone was quiet. I didn't have a sure answer for that.

"Maybe because I'm alpha?"

Kristos shook his head. "Intent."

And then I got it. That was the connection. Or rather, the disconnect.

"Of course," I said looking at Lynn. "Did you want to hurt Matt?"

Lynn shook her head. "No."

"But you *did* want to kill Frederick."

She pressed her lips into a line and sighed. "I did in the moment."

I nodded. "I just happened to be under him when he dusted."

"And you got hurt before I realized it was you," Lynn said, understanding in her tone.

"Exactly," Kristos said.

"Great," Matt said impatiently as he threw his hands out to the sides. "So she's not gonna kill me, okay?" He hooked a thumb toward the door as he looked at Naiya. "So put on something you don't mind getting dirty—or potentially destroying, should you decide to change—and meet me out back."

Naiya, who was still in her black satin pajamas, narrowed her eyes and pushed herself to her feet with a huff.

Kristos grabbed her hand as she turned to head to the stairs. "You don't have to do what he says just because he's older than you, Kitten."

She raked a hand through her long black hair. "No, but he's right. Getting some of this energy out is probably good for me. Maybe I'll sleep better."

She went upstairs and came back down a few moments later in black bike shorts and a tight grey tank, as Chastity was helping Kaylah clear the rest of the plates from breakfast.

"I'll keep an eye on them," Kristos said to me as Matt and Naiya stepped out the back door.

I nodded. "Thanks, Kristos."

He mirrored my nod and followed the other two out into the backyard.

I turned to Kaylah. "What do you think about New Orleans?"

She shrugged. "Like he said, it wouldn't be the firs' time we'd been in o'er our heads. But I don't much care for it."

"I don't think I'm ready to be somewhere there's just non-stop fighting," Lynn said. "Even if I *do* only need to touch them to dust them."

"And Ian's still new enough that he'd have trouble too," Chastity said. "I told him if we went there'd be a good chance we'd lose our two youngest pack members."

"I'm glad Kristos is out of earshot—he'd forbid it entirely," I said.

"I'd like to see him try to stop me from doing something I truly wanted to do," Lynn said.

Jonathan rubbed her arm. "He's stronger than all of us, stronger even than a bunch of us put together. I don't doubt he could stop you. But I also don't doubt you'd make him hate every moment of it."

Lynn shrugged. "It's not like I relish the thought of potentially sacrificing myself to help cleanse a city. Even if something in me is surging to do just that."

"Not something," I said. "Your wol—"

Something twanged through the pack bonds. An intense fear flooded along behind it. And it came from Matt.

My attention snapped to the backyard. Matt didn't *get* scared. The last time he'd even come close was when Kristos gave him the scar on his face. And even that had been tempered with anger.

This was just raw fear.

I was out the back door in a flash, and saw what the hell had him terrified.

Naiya had gotten into some kind of half-form between human and leopard. At least, I think that was Naiya, she was wearing the same black bike shorts she'd come outside in, and the tank top she'd had on was now straining at the seams around this thing that practically towered over Matt on digitigrade legs. Her head was large as a person's, but with the build of a leopard, and her skin was covered in black fur with blacker spots that held a dash of iridescence.

Minus the spots, she looked exactly like what the humans would immediately assume werewolves look like. She looked like something straight out of a horror movie.

And she was stalking Matt, her eyes focused on

him, her movements steady and smooth. Even her ears were pointed directly at him, though one had flicked my direction as the backdoor shut behind me.

My eyes were wide. "What the hell is that?!"

Kristos shook his head. "That's Naiya. Beyond that, your guess is as good as mine."

She backed into the shade of the giant oak tree in the backyard and then simply ceased to be there. Even her scent had vanished.

She reappeared less than half a breath later, coalescing from out of the shadow of the house—fifty feet from where she disappeared—as she slashed at Matt. Luckily, Matt managed to move quickly enough to dodge the blow, or else she'd have torn open his guts.

I pulled my phone from my back pocket and opened my text conversation with Jessica.

TWENTY-SEVEN

*** (JESSICA) ***

I WAS ON MY way home from a morning session at the studio when my helmet dinged.

"New text message from Tobias Sheppard," my comm system narrated. "You're gonna wanna see this. Out back behind the guest house. Matt and Naiya are sparring."

I dictated a reply. "Why is that noteworthy, question mark. Send."

Another turn or two later. "New text message from Tobias Sheppard. Come and see for yourself."

I rolled my eyes. Cagey bastard.

A moment later, I pulled my bike around the back of the guest house. Utter confusion greeted me. Kristos was restraining something that came straight out of a horror film, Sheppard stood with his arms out between the thing Kristos restrained and Matt, who was on the ground. Matt had blood dripping down his chest from a series of parallel scratches, Kaylah was rushing out to him with bandages in hand, Matt's mate hot on her heels.

Holy fucking shit.

And no sooner had I shown up than the ground erupted into shadowy tendrils that grew from the shadows created by the blades of grass. They wrapped around the feet and ankles of all of Sheppard's people, minus the thing in Kristos' grip, and stopped just short of me.

But the leopard-spotted thing from a horror film was still struggling against Kristos' calm restraint, looking for all the world like she wanted to actually kill Matt. She wasn't exactly winning against Kristos' strength, but he was having a harder time now that his feet were planted. So, I launched myself at the thing, knocking it to the ground.

It smelled like Naiya.

It had leopard spots.

Holy fucking shit, it was Naiya!

"Naiya, knock it off!" I yelled as she struggled against my grip. "Come on! I know you can't actually want to hurt any of these people!"

The shadowy tendrils dissipated as Naiya's hand came free and came arcing toward me. Kristos' hand intervened and he gripped her wrist. She struggled and brought her other hand full of claws to bear and Kristos gathered that hand too, holding it alongside the other in a single-handed, but firm grip. She tried to kick at him, but I helped him pin her legs down.

That horror movie creature turned into a toddler throwing a tantrum for a moment before smoothly shrinking back into a human shape.

"I don't belong here," Naiya sobbed. "I don't belong here."

Kristos scooped her into his arms, his face somber. "I know, Kitten. I know." He picked her up and took her inside.

I looked over at Matt. Kaylah was working at dressing his wound, while Chastity knelt next to him.

"Why isn't that healing?" I asked.

"*Consanguinea* wound," Sheppard said.

"What?"

"Apparently she actually *did* want to hurt me," Matt said, a wry grin on his face.

Chastity swatted at him. "It's not funny, Matt."

"It is, though," he said. "She got so mad!"

"She could have killed you!"

I looked at Sheppard. "*Consanguinea* wound?"

He nodded. "If you get hurt by a *consanguinea*, and they actually mean to hurt you, then the wound doesn't heal like we usually do. It takes longer."

"Not human long," Kaylah said, not looking up from her work. "But longer'n a wolf is used to."

"She's going to be incredible at fighting vampires," Matt chortled. "They won't know what to do with something that towers over them and tears them apart."

My heart panged at the thought of the pack going elsewhere.

Of Sheppard going elsewhere.

Because elsewhere they would have to go to continue that fight. San Antonio had been clear of vampires for decades by now. I had wolves in my pack who hadn't even *seen* a vampire in person.

Ugh.

I shook my head.

"She's not as strong as a wolf though," Sheppard said.

"Well," I said. "Should she be? She's not a werewolf."

Sheppard rocked his head side to side. "That's a fair point."

"What the hell was that thing that planted you all in place?" I asked.

"Dunno," Sheppard said. "But it was something Naiya did. It started from her and she was the only one free."

"Minus myself," I said.

Sheppard nodded. "Minus yourself."

"You think she's gonna decide to go across the rifts?"

He pressed his lips into a line. "I think she's already decided, but hasn't put the words to it. Not that Kristos will appreciate it much."

"He's taken quite the shining to her," I said.

"He has," Sheppard agreed. "But that's not why. He's basically her bodyguard. Hers and Lynn's. It'll be hard for him to do that if she's in another world."

"One might even call such an endeavor impossible."

"One might indeed."

"That's some kind of special problem you've got on your hands there," I said. "I don't envy you."

"It's not... Okay, so maybe it is," Sheppard replied. "But... I know we'll find a solution."

"You have so far. I'd hate for this to ruin your record. Thanks for including me in this, though. Good to know what I'd be getting myself into, should she both stay and decide your pack isn't the right place for her."

Sheppard nodded. "Of course."

If he was my partner... my lover... if we had a *label*, I'd stay and support him as he figured this all out. And a part of me ached to do just that.

But I didn't do labels.

I turned back to my bike. I'd just walk it back to the house, it wasn't like it was far.

"Hey, Jess, wait." Sheppard jogged around in front of me.

I paused and raised an eyebrow at him.

"Look." He raked a hand through his hair. "None of this is going at all how I planned." He gestured between him and I. "I think... I think maybe we could both use a sort of reset. Why don't we go somewhere tomorrow? Just you and me, no business talk. Just two alphas spending time together. Show me your favorite place in town?"

A... reset? Really? Fat lot of good it's gonna do.

I studied his face. He seemed so earnest. Would it really be so terrible to have something a little more...?

No.

I didn't do relationships.

He and I didn't want the same things anyway. I'm just the Hot Alpha.

And he'd *never* be okay with the things I did in my studio.

But that didn't mean I couldn't have some fun anyway, did it? I mean, Lord knew his hands felt so good on my skin. And his throaty growls as the ecstasy took him were fucking hot. So maybe I could have my cake and eat it too.

Like a living version of your collection?

Shut it.

"I'll think about it," I said.

TWENTY-EIGHT

*** (SHEPPARD) ***

JESSICA DIDN'T TEXT ME for the rest of the day, and Kristos and Naiya didn't come down for dinner. I went to bed with an unfamiliar loneliness pooling in my stomach. The closest thing to connection that I got was a single word of thanks when I gave Jess the updated attendance numbers. And since Kristos and Naiya hadn't shown their faces, I sent out a group text to the whole pack to let them know we'd be discussing the next steps tomorrow. We had to go somewhere, because I wasn't about to stay here if Jess was so intent on not wanting anything but business between us. I couldn't keep scratching the itch with her, because every time I did, I wanted more.

But damn if her body didn't feel good pressed against mine, her voice ringing in my ears as ecstasy took her. Images of her breasts bouncing in time with my hips slammed into my mind's eye, and the remembered sensation of her hips rolling along my length brought me to full attention beneath the sheets.

Mine, whispered my wolf.

No.

She'd all but decided she didn't want that.

And why should she? I'd become yet another alpha sniffing at her door.

The thought was poor company for sleep, and yet sleep took me all the same.

In the morning, after breakfast, I had Ian hook Daniel's laptop up to the TV in the living room. I gave the pack the most salient points of what Ian had found in the emails of the dead vamp—the supposition that us wolves must somehow be the cause of the rifts, and the knowledge of the lineage of *consanguinea* being released.

"So they're working together now," Matt said.

"It would appear so," Ian replied. "There's also this '2 Points 4 Lyfe' movement going on, but I still can't tell if they're just a whole bunch of humans pretending to be vampires, or if it's an actual group of vampires. It's all text-based with avatars, like an old-school message board from the early days of the internet, so it's hard to tell for sure."

"When was the last post?" I asked him.

He shook his head. "It's super active, so people are probably posting there now. I tried hacking into it to get the IPs of the people posting so we could know where to go to try to verify, but I couldn't get through the site security. I asked Jess' IT guy—Eric—for help, but he hasn't gotten back to me yet."

I nodded. "So, that's tabled until we can manage to track down a location. Let me know when you find something?"

"Of course," Ian said.

"Jamie, give us the short version of what you found in New York," I said, pulling up a map of the city on the laptop.

He nodded. "There're vamps in Hell's Kitchen.

There's a pack in the city proper, but they're in a different area. They may eventually end up cleaning up the vamps we found. There's not a lot of space to wolf out and run in the city unless we take a trip out past the suburbs or scare people in Central Park."

I found a more generalized map of the city, with areas of town marked more clearly and pointed to Central Park and Hell's Kitchen.

"Nevermind that it's stupid expensive to live in New York City," Lynn said.

"We could manage the expense," Daniel said. "But we're used to having space to wolf out, so I don't much like the idea of eliminating that."

"Where would we play woofball?" Jonathan asked.

Jamie shrugged. "We'd have to pick a roof to play it on, I think."

"Ew," Jonathan replied.

"Speaking of space to wolf out," I said, "Jonathan, why don't you tell us what you found in Kalispell."

Daniel scooted over to the laptop to put Kalispell up on the screen.

"There's not much to tell," Jonathan said. "Not really anyway. There's a whole lot of space and not a whole lot of anything else." He thought for a moment. "But it *is* relatively close to tribal lands, so we *could* potentially connect with any of the packs there."

"No vampires?" Mat asked.

Jonathan shook his head. "None that we could find."

"So jus' miles 'n' miles of jus' miles 'n' miles," Kaylah said.

"Pretty much," Daniel replied.

"Great for woofball," Lynn said.

"But not much else," Matt said.

"And what about New Orleans?" I asked, looking at Matt.

"Like I said yesterday, the town's overrun." He shrugged. "We could do the most good there, but it would be nonstop fighting."

"With a new wolf." I nodded at Lynn. "And a young wolf." I nodded at Ian. "We've been in hairy situations before, but I'm not sure those two are ready for that."

"I was afraid you'd feel that way," Matt said. "But there is green space there, so woofball is doable. And there's a lot of new vamps there."

"Plus, with Lynn's ability to dust vamps with a touch," Chastity said, "I think things would be less hairy than they normally would be."

"Yeah, but you're talking about putting my charges in very real mortal danger," Kristos said, his voice rumbling on the edge of threat. "And don't forget about Naiya, who has never been in a real fight with a real vampire."

"They had me fight them at the facility," she interjected. "It was awful. The leopard came out and just eliminated them with ruthless efficiency."

"And you've got a fair number more abilities than you seem to have had at your beck and call in that facility," Matt said.

"I do," she agreed. "But I also don't have any real control over them."

"Yet," Matt pointed out.

Kristos growled. "You're not putting her in danger so she can find the triggers out in the field."

Matt took a breath to retort to that, but I held a hand out to stop him.

"And I don't like the thought of putting Lynn in that kind of learn-on-the-fly situation either," Jonathan said.

"No one likes the thought of their mate in that kind of danger," I said.

Matt opened his mouth again, but I speared him with a look.

"Even you, Matt," I said. "You lost your shit when you couldn't find Chastity at the house fire in the Springs, and she wasn't even in any real danger. She'd just taken a walk around the perimeter to watch how the flames spread."

"And to watch how unsalvageable everything there was." Chastity cuddled into Matt's side. "I shouldn't have done it. At least, not without telling him."

Matt kissed the top of her head. "I forgave you already."

Jonathan rolled his eyes.

"In any case," Matt said. "I can't think of anywhere else we'd be more needed than someplace like New Orleans."

"Yeah," I said. "But with this PR campaign Jess is doing, it might not be the best idea to be somewhere that we have to be fighting all the time."

"Actually," Lynn said, "as much as I hate the idea of being in constant danger, we could potentially be a big help to her campaign if we are seen fighting the vampires and getting the sheep help."

"We'd look like heroes to all of them," Jamie said.

Lynn nodded. "We would."

"But it's still a lot of danger for a chancy payoff," Ian said.

"Why the big rush t' leave?" Kaylah asked.

I gave her a gentle smile. "No real rush. We just aren't Jessica's pack, is all. We don't need to impose on her any more than necessary."

Naiya met my gaze. "She's the one that offered, isn't she?"

I sighed. "Yes, but we're not doing anyone any good here."

"Maybe we should check some other spots 'fore we try an' make a decision," Kaylah said.

Lynn leaned forward onto her knees. "What about crazed wolves?"

Matt arched an eyebrow at her. "What?"

"What about them?" Jonathan rubbed her arm.

"Well," she said. "Couldn't we track them down and save them?"

"Pfft, good fuckin' luck," Matt said. "Crazed wolves aren't predictable enough to track."

"They aren't like regular wolves," I said gently. "There's still a human intelligence there, except it's coupled with the instincts of a wild animal."

"Closer to something rabid than wild," Kristos said.

I nodded.

"But," Lynn said, "aren't there packs all over the country?"

"The sane kind?" I asked.

She nodded.

"Sure." I shrugged. "There's something like two hundred or so."

"Then how do the crazed ones even happen?" she asked. "How do they get away and just *not* get found?"

I furrowed my brow. I thought I'd explained this to her already. Had she forgotten? "Sometimes, when a wolf doesn't mesh well with a pack, or they lose a mate—"

"Or their entire pack," Chastity said.

I nodded. "Instead of finding or building a new pack, some wolves will go off on their own and become a lone wolf. Only we're not built for that."

"They should know better," Kristos said.

"Yeah," Matt said. "But most of them aren't thinking clearly."

"They're convinced they'll be the exception," Daniel said.

"Or they're too grief-struck to 'member why they need a pack," Kaylah added.

I nodded. "And that's just the ones that come from sane wolves to start, some of them are just crazed from the turn."

"Okay," Lynn said. "But how does not meshing with the pack or grief turn a sane wolf crazed? How does being a lone wolf do that?"

"Without a pack," I explained, "your wolf itches to make one of its own. Usually, someone turns someone, thinking they'll be fine. Only that person loses control at the moon. Maybe they kill the one that turned them, maybe their unhinging makes the other one lose it." I shrugged. "It's hard to say exactly. If it happens in a pack, it's just a newly turned pup who can't make peace with their other half when the moon calls."

Lynn looked down at her hands. "So there could be any number of crazed wolves out there."

Matt nodded. "Yep."

She looked up at him, her head cocked to the side. "Well, can't we at least *try* to help them?" She turned to me.

I took a breath and let it out slowly as I put a hand on

her shoulder. "We're spread a little thin right now with the rifts to worry about on top of the usual vampires and this whole 'going public' thing."

Lynn's face fell. "Couldn't we do that instead of fight—?" She blinked and waved a hand. "Nevermind, even *I* don't like thinking of it as 'instead.'"

Jonathan put an arm around her and pressed a kiss to her shoulder.

"Time, Lynn," I said. "We have lots of it."

She sighed. "You know, you—I mean, *we* have an odd relationship with time."

"How so?" Jonathan asked.

She frowned. "Some things, like the crazed wolves, you're in no real hurry to do anything about. But others, like this PR thing with Jessica, you're in a real rush to accomplish. You're driven." She looked at Matt. "And you're practically buzzing in your seat at the thought of going to a city where you can have your fill of fights with vampires."

"Never gonna get my fill of that," Matt said.

Chastity smiled at him and brought the back of his hand to her lips for a kiss.

I cocked my head at Lynn. How far do *consanguinea* stray from the fundamental truths of being a werewolf? It was really something to learn about Naiya's allergy to silver.

"You're not driven?" I asked Lynn.

She ran a hand through her hair. "No, I am. But for *both*." She met my gaze for a moment, her heart pounding. "Crazed wolves kill people too. Maybe not as much as vampires do, but not everyone survives a crazed wolf attack."

"Sure," I nodded. "But we just can't split our focus like that right now. The PR stuff is adjacent to our vampire fight anyway, and even that's only happening now because they're forcing our hand."

Lynn sighed and looked down at her hands again. "After the rifts then?"

"We can add it to the list of options then," I agreed.

She looked up at me before pressing her lips into a

line and nodding, her gaze returning to her lap.

Jonathan kissed her temple and a small smile took her features.

"Were there rifts in New York?" Naiya asked.

Jamie nodded. "There were. They didn't stay open long, but there were lots of them."

"New York is where my parents found me," she said. "Maybe if we went there, I could potentially find my actual parents."

"Kitten..." Kristos said.

"No," she said. "Stop it. I'm from there. There isn't a doubt in my mind. You have to stop treating that knowledge like anything that could possibly follow from it is silly!"

"That's not what I'm doing," he said, his hands going up in a placating gesture. "I'm just saying that even if the world there is half as large as this one is, the odds you find *anything* or *anyone* even remotely familiar on the other side of a random rift is abysmally small."

"But not zero," she insisted.

He shook his head. "Not zero, no. But how many times are you going to ask me to watch your heart break?"

She turned a blazing green gaze to him before abruptly pushing herself to her feet and storming up the stairs.

"You know she's going to figure out a way to go there, right?" Lynn said softly, looking at Kristos.

He met her gaze, his heart in his eyes.

Lynn swallowed. "It's what I would do. It's what you would do. It's what any of us would do. She's got to go where she feels she belongs."

Kristos just held her gaze for a long moment and then pushed off the couch to go upstairs after Naiya.

I let the silence fill the room for a moment before looking at the screen. I went to the laptop and put three windows up on the TV, one with each of the locations I'd sent scouts to.

"Let me see where the votes land right now," I said. "Who's for Kalispell?"

Kaylah and Jonathan raised their hands.

"Why?" I asked.

"The space," Jonathan said.

"We deserve a li'l rest," Kaylah said.

I nodded. "And New York?"

Ian and Daniel raised their hands.

I nodded at Ian.

"I like the tech there," he said. "And it'd be interesting to cohabitate a city with a pack that wasn't military."

"I like the idea of being closer to the people I network with on the regular," Daniel added.

"And New Orleans?" I asked.

Matt and Chastity both raised their hands.

Of course they did.

"We'd do the most good there," Matt said.

"It's what we're supposed to be doing anyway," Chastity added.

But it hadn't escaped my notice that two pack members hadn't voted. I knew Kristos would go wherever Lynn and Naiya went, and Naiya's vote was clearly New York.

"Lynn, Jamie, what are your thoughts?" I asked.

Lynn looked at Jamie before looking at me. "I don't really know that I have a preference, other than just *not* New Orleans. Lots of city and lots of nothing appeal to me in different ways. And I'd like to see both, eventually."

I nodded and looked at Jamie, who shrugged.

"I also am mostly just *not* New Orleans," he said. "I'm not exactly the fightiest of us, but I'm not the least fight-y either, and I don't like the idea of non-stop aggression."

Jonathan stood. "Do we need a decision right right now?"

I shook my head. "No."

"Good," he said. "Because it sounds like a round of woofball might be a good idea." He stood and picked up the ball from the side table next to the back door. "Let us digest all the information while getting some of the energy out."

I huffed out a little laugh, the corner of my mouth turning up.

And so, despite the heat, what was left of the pack

downstairs went outside to play woofball. Eventually, Naiya and Kristos joined us, and we learned that Naiya could take the ball with her when she jumped from one shadow to another. The game was eventually called on account of heat, and we retreated to the sanctuary of the air conditioning.

Everyone was drenched in sweat. Everyone was in less clothes than they went outside in. And everyone needed a shower.

We eventually came back together for dinner that night, but any conversation about where to go next ended in the same result: no clear consensus.

It meant we'd have to stay here a while longer and do another round of scouting. Which meant more time in Jessica's backyard.

Mine.

Nope. She wasn't. And if I didn't chill the hell out, she never would be.

And in five hundred and forty three years, not *once* had my wolf tried to claim anyone or anything beyond my pack, and *now* it spoke up? I didn't even know I *had* an instinct to find a mate, I just always assumed that would have worked itself out earlier.

Now that instinct was trying to claim someone who didn't want to be claimed. Only she had a hard time keeping her hands off me. Both the times we'd been together had been things she had started. So, clearly some part of her wanted me.

Just apparently not enough to overcome her hesitation about mates.

She hadn't even texted me once the whole day, despite seeing the weirdness that was Naiya's abilities. I went to bed with that same unfamiliar loneliness. And her only reply to an update on the attendance numbers was, again, a simple *thanks*.

The number of wolves who were 'trying to make it' was growing. Which reminded me why I hated emails. It was easier to lie in text. Or rather, it was harder to tell if someone was lying in text. But no alpha worth their salt would lie to another alpha, would they?

I'd find out when the meeting happened.

I rolled onto my side. Was Jess really just avoiding me because she'd been vulnerable around me? Or was I just way off about why she felt the way she did about mates? Was there someone else that she'd rather spend her time with? Why was I trying to complicate something so much when all she asked for from me was to be the face of her PR stunt and to help her get her needs met every once in a while. That it'd happened twice in a single week didn't mean anything... Did it?

I shook my head and growled into my pillow.

I needed to clear my head. I remembered the streets and turns we'd taken to get to where she'd shown me she went for open space and privacy. I pulled it up on my phone and mapped out a path I could take on four legs. And then I opened a window, shifted, and darted away from the house as fast as my feet would take me.

I hunted some of the ground animals I came across, and even startled a sleeping coyote, but it didn't clear my head of her. I wanted to be running in the night air with Jessica, to show her the exhilaration of running with nothing to tell you where to go or why but your instincts. I wanted to show her the night sky through her wolf's eyes. I wanted her to hear the silence of the dead of night with her wolf's ears.

I wanted to share a night with her that wasn't just scratching an itch, and it was clear taking her to dinner wasn't cutting it. I'd have to come up with something else.

Or... I could just leave the ball in her court, like it was.

That she hadn't answered was answer enough, really. I needed to let it go.

I headed back to the house.

When I got back to my room, it was nearly three in the morning. There was a mug on my nightstand, filled with Kaylah's sleepy-time tea, along with a note in her handwriting. It could have passed for schoolhouse cursive.

If you were gone long enough for it to get cold, 30sec in the microwave will fix it. Drink up and get some sleep,

Shep.

I couldn't help but smile at her thoughtfulness. The tea had indeed gotten cold, so I padded into the kitchen, microwaved it for 30 seconds, and drank it down right there. I put the empty mug in the sink and padded back to bed.

I hadn't bothered to turn on a light or put on even a scrap of clothing.

TWENTY-NINE

*** (JESSICA) ***

So Naiya was able to break reality. Cool. I was kinda glad that wasn't my problem, really. I felt bad that it meant Sheppard had to figure it out, but I was mostly able to put it out of my mind.

Instead, I had this outstanding nebulous *thing* that was whatever was between Sheppard and I. I raked a hand through my hair. I wanted it to be simple. It was supposed to be simple. Instead, it was complicated.

I didn't *do* complicated.

I should never have slept with him. It just made me want him more.

Mine.

Jesus fucking hell. No, he wasn't.

He was, at best, a friend with benefits. But until and unless we actually laid out that boundary, he wasn't even that. And that would definitely fall deeper into the 'it's complicated' territory when I would really rather avoid it altogether, thank you very much.

But he was making a real effort. And he genuinely gave a shit about me. Because no one sits in vigil over your unconscious frame for hours upon hours without actually caring about you. And he wanted to see my favorite spot in town. He wanted to take me somewhere he knew I would love.

But when he found out what that place was, he'd laugh at me.

Fuck, that rich laugh of his rumbled through me every time. I loved seeing him smile, and I loved the feel of his big, warm hands on my body.

I spent the rest of the day with my pack, watching shows and laughing at jokes and eating dinner. But a part of me wished I was sharing that with Sheppard too.

The next day, I was slated to meet with Blair in the morning. She warned me again not to leak the ad early, reminding me that people watch the Super Bowl commercials for new things, not for repeats of the same thing. We briefly tossed around the idea of moving up the plan so that I could leak the ad this year and then go to phase two or even three with the Super Bowl ad, but that got kinda messy, and phase two—where we show them we're protectors—was not as strong a candidate for that as phase three—where we show them vampires are real.

And all of it kind of hinged on what kind of support I could get anyway from the meeting we had planned. I'd move forward whether I had any other wolves on board or not, but the more support I could get from the werewolf community, the smoother this was all going to run.

I didn't trust the military not to run a counter message, after taking a swing at me like they did. Blair didn't either and suggested that we start putting together some ideas to debunk things the military will say to keep the public complacent and unaware. I set her on keyword research for that as well and then we broke for the day.

After that, I checked in on Eric's progress with getting our network secure enough and with enough bandwidth to support nearly a hundred attendees.

"You're up that high?"

"Nah," I said. "We're still at only seventy-three, but the number grows daily, so I wouldn't be surprised to see it hit one hundred or more by the time the meeting happens."

"Well, then everything here is mostly good to go," he said. "I'm just troubleshooting a couple of the VPNs here. They keep throwing an invalid IP. I'll get it sorted today and do a dry run tomorrow with Blair and Sheppard's computer guy, Ian."

"Great," I said, smiling at him. "Lemme know how it goes?"

"Nah," he said. "Think I'll keep that bit to myself."

Sarcastic fuck.

"Thanks, Eric."

He waved me off as he went back to work.

From there, I headed over to Shawn's office to check on the NDAs I had him working on. He had everything in order for the meeting, including NDAs for entire packs as a whole as well as individual NDAs. His assistant, Mikaela, had copies of the treaties ready to go with the relevant bits highlighted. I intended to show the packs exactly where they could see that the Church wouldn't be able to retaliate, at least, not in any meaningful way without meeting with a metric fuck-ton of resistance.

And the Church didn't dare risk the exposure.

I had plenty of time until dinner, so I made a stop at the post office on my way to the studio. Apparently CrimsonMoonrise87 liked my stream enough to send me a gift to use on air. I bungeed the box to the back of my Diavel and took it back to the studio with me, stopping on the way for tacos once again.

Thank god my patron hadn't sent me another realistic animal penis. Those never made it to the private collection, just one time use on stream and then into the trash. CrimsonMoonrise87 even remembered my favorite color was red, and what a fine shade he'd sent me too. Or she. I had my fair share of both on stream. And I didn't much care one way or the other so long as they were respectful... and paying.

Anyway, I ended up having to call the stream early and send the guy—who confirmed himself a guy on stream—a voucher for a private session. My thoughts were too wound up in the upcoming meeting to get anywhere with my stream, which was frustrating. I always had a little trouble when I knew the username—I got off on the anonymity—but it was never this bad.

I tried again in the shower I had afterward, filming it just in case, but for all the good the twisted forked tongues felt, they just couldn't get me where I needed to go. So, I deleted the video, finished my shower and got dressed.

Fuck, did I ever need to get my damn head clear.

Back at the house, I traded the Diavel for my little DesertX and took it to the dirt hills between the house and Kaan's cave. I got myself good and covered in red clay and dirt and sweat before I started to run out of daylight. With one last jump and skid down the hill, I shook some of the dirt off me, wiped my visor clean... well... mostly clean, and turned the bike back toward the house.

I took off most of the worst of the dirty stuff in the garage, but it still left a bunch of red clay and dirt stuck to my skin. It was probably streaked all through my hair too, despite my helmet. Which meant another shower.

But a relaxing bubble bath after a quick rinse might actually be just what the doctor ordered. I grabbed the bottle of tequila and cut up a lime into fourths with some salt and headed back to my bedroom.

I put the tequila and limes on the bathroom counter while I rinsed off, but brought it to rest on the stepstool before I sat down in my giant-ass black clawfoot bathtub. This thing could easily fit two, and it wasn't a stretch to think of who might make a nice addition. A certain wolf's big warm hands on my hips as he thrust into me came instantly to mind. I couldn't see the hurt in enjoying myself to the thought of his hands on my body, so I took a pull from the tequila—knowing full well it'd take the whole bottle before I'd even feel anything, if I felt anything at all—before sucking a little on a salt-covered lime to get the taste out of my mouth. I then grabbed one of my toys from the little cabinet I had next to the tub and checked that the batteries were still good.

My phone buzzed right as I started to get worked up. I'd forgotten to put the damn thing on 'do not disturb.' I rolled my eyes and turned off the toy for a moment as I reached to remedy my mistake.

Only the buzz was a text from Sheppard.

"Speak of the devil, and he shall appear," I said wryly, my voice quiet as I thumbed open my phone.

Sheppard:

Three Church alphas confirmed today.

"Holy shit," I said.

Me:

I didn't know you had Church alphas on your list.

The typing bubbles appeared and disappeared a few times.

Sheppard:

Pretty sure they just happened to be in my contacts. It certainly wasn't a conscious inclusion.

Me:

I hope that doesn't mean you sent an invite to that asshole General of yours.

His reply came quick.

Sheppard:

That bridge is ashes.

"Holy *shit,*" I said, my eyes wide as I read the text again. Then another came in.

> **Sheppard:**
> I've blocked him every feasible way I can.

> **Me:**
> I feel like I owe you a thank you for that.

> **Sheppard:**
> You don't. Not after what he did to you.
>
> He might not have been the one kidnapping you directly, but those were his wolves, which meant he signed the orders.
>
> These are the consequences of his actions.

I blinked at that and didn't reply for a moment. He burned a bridge for me. A bridge that was old, sure, but it should have been solid and hard to burn. He talked about it like it was simply a matter of course.

> **Sheppard:**
> I told you. You deserve better than that.

> **Me:**
> Well... Thank you anyway.

> **Sheppard:**
> You're welcome.

I tapped the back of my phone against my hand while I thought. There were Church alphas coming to the meeting. And not just one... *three* of them. Shit. We'd have to watch what we said even more than I thought.

Me:
Those Church alphas probably just want to spy on what I'm doing.

Sheppard:
Maybe. But if we can convince them too, it might sway some of those who might otherwise be on the fence.

Me:
Or it'll push them away.

Sheppard:
True. I guess we'll have to just see how it plays out.

I nodded at the screen. And then his offer to take me to my favorite place popped into my head. I'd almost forgotten about it.

Me:
When you said you wanted to see my favorite place in town, you meant for dinner, right?

Sheppard:
I meant for anything. But if your favorite happens to be a restaurant, I'd only be a little surprised.

I narrowed my eyes at my phone and started to type

a message. I deleted that one and started to type out exactly what we were going to do. But I deleted that one too. Finally, I just sent one.

> **Me:**
> You're gonna think it's dumb.

> **Sheppard:**
> I promise I won't.

> **Me:**
> Pretty sure you will, but fine. I'll pick you up at ten? Wear comfy shoes and make sure you have a pocket your phone won't easily fall from.

> **Sheppard:**
> You're not gonna tell me where we're going?

I couldn't help but laugh at that. Of course I wouldn't give him the opportunity to laugh at me ahead of time. He was going to laugh, and he was going to have to see the consequences of that in real time. But a part of me wanted to be wrong.

> **Me:**
> Where's the fun in that?
> See you tomorrow, Tobias.

I then actually turned on the do not disturb and got back to work taking care of myself. It was easier to envision his hands on my body when I'd just spoken to him, easier to hear his rumbling laugh in my head, easier to pretend the toy pressing into me was him when I'd just...

And then my ecstasy ripped through me.
Mine, growled my wolf.
"Holy shit." Damn, have I got it bad for him.

THIRTY

*** (SHEPPARD) ***

JESSICA KNOCKED ON MY door right at ten, wearing a white tank top that you could see her black bra through with faded black cutoff shorts and black combat boots. I'd taken her advice and worn khaki cargo shorts with a black t-shirt and tennis shoes.

"You're gonna wish you hadn't worn black," she said. "But you do you, boo."

"Gonna be outdoors all day are we?" I said with a chuckle.

"You'll see."

We hopped into her truck a moment later and drove. I couldn't help but laugh when I finally saw the rollercoasters.

"I told you you'd think it's silly," Jessica said, her tone sour. She crossed her arms over her chest.

"Not at all," I said, patting her leg. "I just should have known. Let me guess, it's all about the 'coasters?'"

"There's a total of eleven of them here, though one of them's more for kids, and another is a super short ride, but there's a handful of other fun rides too." She smiled up at me. "Am I that easy to read?"

I returned the smile and shrugged. "I'm just saying it comes as no surprise that the motorcycle enthusiast happens to be an adrenaline junkie."

She snorted out a laugh. "Maybe not so much a *junkie* as an aficionado."

I nodded along with her laughter. "Sure, Jess, we'll call it that."

When they'd first come around, I'd hated roller coasters, with their jolts and bumpy rides, but—according to Jessica, who'd been much younger than I when they first started showing up—the rides had become much smoother and more complex since their inception.

Turned out she was right. Modern-day roller coasters were actually *enjoyable* and I found myself yelling and laughing alongside her through some of the more thrilling rides. The park wasn't terribly busy, so we got to ride nearly half the coasters in the park before stopping for lunch.

We shared a funnel cake for dessert, which—of course—got powdered sugar all over my shirt. I peeled the shirt off to shake it out and caught her studying me again. Appreciating me, really. Desire was written in every line of her body, though she tried to hide it.

She was easier to read than she thought.

So, I took my time putting the shirt back on, until her eyes met mine and a flush took her cheeks.

I wanted to kiss her.

Hell, I wanted to do more than that.

But that was *not* what today was about. We were resetting. She hired me to be the face of her PR campaign. Recruited me, really. We were colleagues. Equals.

With a laugh, she wadded up her napkin and threw it

at me. She didn't know she still had powdered sugar on her lip, so I reached out to wipe it for her, but as I went to lick the sugar off my thumb, she grabbed my hand with a spark of that same electricity that seemed ever present between us and licked it clean with a wink.

Mine.

Dammit, wolf.

No, she wasn't.

She grabbed my hand, the electric current running between us again as she tugged me to my feet and off we went to another ride's line.

By the end of the day, we'd ridden every coaster at least once, and her favorites two or three times. We didn't close down the park, but we did stay till after sunset. I'd won her one of the stuffed unicorns from one of the just-this-side-of-rigged games, which was hard thanks to the control I had to use not to destroy the damn game in the process, and we'd managed to avoid talking business nearly the entire day.

Well, almost. Her IT guy confirmed the PR offices were good to go for the alpha meeting and Blair tried to call her, but she sent her to voicemail.

She pulled me down to place an electric kiss on my cheek when we got back to the house.

"Thanks, Tobias," she said. "I had fun today."

I blinked and smiled at her. "My pleasure, Jess. Thanks for sharing the fun with me."

She tucked a strand of hair behind her ear and gently closed the door as I turned to walk the gravel drive back to the house my pack was using.

She was positively incredible. If she ever did decide she was ready for something more serious with someone, they'd be one hell of a lucky guy.

Mine.

Shut up, wolf.

But I took care of myself in the shower to the thought of her. She was too beautiful, too smart, too *Jessica* to not.

I shouldn't have given my wolf the fuel.

My phone buzzed as I was toweling off.

Jessica:

Blair left me a voicemail. She wants to go over PR tactics with you before the big meeting.

Me:

Sure. When and where?

Jessica:

10am. The conference room of the PR offices. I'll pick you up.

I stared at the phone, debating. Do I let her pick me up and let whatever is between us start to escalate again like it was likely to do? Or did I try to give her the space she clearly needed?

I sighed. The latter was the better call.

Me:

No need. I remember how to get there. See you at ten.

I waited a few moments, debating whether to state the obvious again, but the day had truly been one of the best I'd had in a while, and it was all thanks to the alpha just next door.

Me:

I had a really great time today, Jess. Thank you.

Jessica:

You're welcome.
'Night Tobias.

I blinked at my phone before taking a deep breath. I couldn't deny that—as strange as it was to have someone using my proper name again—it was really nice that it was coming from her.

THIRTY-ONE

*** (JESSICA) ***

SHEPPARD ARRIVED RIGHT ON time for our ten AM meeting with Blair. He was in a white button-down shirt, the sleeves rolled up his muscular forearms, and it was tucked into his dark jeans. It was a sexy look for him. Something ruggedly casual and yet still put-together enough for a meeting like this.

Blair, on the other hand, was in a navy pencil skirt with a pale blue blouse—wrinkle-free, of course—tucked in. She wore her hair up in a neat bun today, and her demeanor was all business.

She smiled at my fellow alpha. "This'll be a trial by fire, Sheppard. Here's to hoping you're as cool-headed as Jess says you are." She adjusted the glasses on her face as she forcefully redirected her gaze to her clipboard for the fourth time since Sheppard had arrived. "The alphas are likely to ask you the same questions an investigative journalist would, though theirs at least will be from the perspective of someone who wants the secret to stay hidden."

"The journalists are gonna wanna blow it wide open," I said.

Sheppard shrugged. "Sure, that's their job."

"So, I'm gonna play the role of an investigative journalist." Blair sat down at the conference table and crossed one leg over the other, gesturing for Sheppard to sit across from her. "My job is to get you to tell me things you don't want to."

"Sure," Sheppard said, sitting down.

I stayed leaning against the wall of the small conference room. I had a better view of the both of them that way.

"Your job is to stick to only what you intend to tell me," Blair continued. "You want to keep your answers short and succinct. The more you give them, the more they will question. More questions mean more answers that you have to give them."

"And we aren't looking to answer all of them yet," I said. "We simply can't."

Sheppard nodded. "Got it."

Blair forcefully redirected her gaze again. "Where do werewolves come from?"

"We were created sometime around 335 AD," Sheppard replied.

"Created?"

He nodded. "Yes. We were created with a mixture of human and wolf blood, among other things."

"Too much," Blair said. "Created?"

He sighed. "Yes."

"Who created you?"

He raised a questioning eyebrow at me, but I knew he already knew this answer. I shook my head.

"That is a secret that is not ours to tell," he said.

Blair pressed her lips into a line. "They won't like that."

"It's the only answer we can give them without the

Church signing on," I said.

She shook her head and sighed. "...Alright. *Why* were you created?"

Shep's answer was automatic. "To protect humanity."

"From what?"

He smiled, a tinge of something uncomfortable in the expression. "The evils that bump in the night."

"Stop that," Blair said. "Regular smile, or straight face. You want allies here. Don't remind them that you're just as scary as the vampires are."

"But we're not," Sheppard said.

"To them you are," she replied. "Try again."

Sheppard took a breath and smoothed his face.

"You were created to protect humanity?"

"We were, yes."

"From what?"

He didn't smile this time, he just calmly met her gaze. "The evils that lurk in the darkness."

"So... like rapists and murderers?"

Sheppard rocked his head side-to-side. "Those too."

"Leads to more questions," Blair said. "Try again. So... like rapists and murderers?"

"Yes."

"Good," Blair said. "Where were you created?"

"Somewhere in Europe."

"Where?"

Sheppard folded his arms across his chest. "That is not our secret to tell."

Blair shook her head, but continued. "How many of you are there?"

"I am not at liberty to disclose that number."

"Keep your posture open," Blair said. "Crossed arms looks closed off. Why not?"

Sheppard blinked and dropped his arms. "It is not my secret to tell."

"Would you say that the wolves who show their faces on werewolvesarereal.org represent more than half the population of the world?"

"Werewolves are real dot org?" Sheppard raised an eyebrow and looked pointedly at me.

I shrugged. "We're going to put up a website that has the faces of some of the wolves that opt in. That's what we're going to point people to at the end of the ad."

Sheppard blinked at me. "So when you mean go public, you really mean it. And you're making it specific."

I nodded. "They won't believe it otherwise. I plan to put up a video of our shift too, once we figure out how to keep the nudity down. Im's been practicing shifting in an oversized shirt. She can get out of it okay when she goes to four legs, but she's struggling shifting *into* it so she ends up covered when she comes up on two."

"How about a blanket, or a poncho?" Sheppard asked. "That'd do the trick and should be much easier."

"Because the larger the cloth," I said, "the more likely they'll think it's a trick with a trap door or something."

"Why not just use censor bars?" Sheppard asked. "Or blur the important parts?"

"Because I want to keep it as unedited as possible. The more raw the footage, the more believable it is."

He nodded, clearly impressed.

"Paige has most of the site built, with placeholder images if you want to check it out," Blair said. "The link works if you type it in."

He pulled his phone from his pocket and thumbed open his screen. He opened up his browser and typed in the address. A familiar black and yellow website popped up, the slideshow starting immediately.

"Huh," he said. He tapped on the 'want proof?' button and got to the artist sketch renditions of a person changing to a wolf and a wolf changing back to a person. "Well, okay then. Could you repeat the question please, Miss...?"

"Jacobs," Blair reminded him. "But please, just call me Blair." There was a little too much flirt in her tone.

Sheppard simply smiled at her like he hadn't even heard it. "Blair then. Could you please repeat the question, Blair?"

She looked back down at her clipboard, but it was for show. "Would you say that the wolves who show their faces on werewolvesarereal.org represent more than half the population of the world?"

Sheppard snorted. "No."

"Don't," she said. "The snort gives more away than you think. Keep your answers flat or friendly, but professional."

Sheppard nodded.

"Would you say that the wolves who show their faces on werewolvesarereal.org represent more than half the population of the world?"

"No."

"So the total number of werewolves in the world is more than double what's on werewolvesarereal.org?" She arched an eyebrow at him.

"Yes," he replied.

"But you are not at liberty to disclose the actual number?"

"Even if I had that number, that's correct. I would not be at liberty to disclose."

"Says who?"

Sheppard cocked his head to the side at her. "I'm sorry?"

"Who made the decision about how many wolves stay secret?" Blair flashed him a radiant smile.

Sheppard was unfazed. "The wolves who do not wish to disclose their identities did."

"Individually?"

"Yes."

"So... my next door neighbor could be a werewolf and I'd never know it."

"It's unlikely, but correct."

Blair clucked her tongue at him. "That leads to more questions."

"I'd rather be honest about that."

"Alright," she said wryly. "Why is it unlikely?"

Sheppard leaned forward, resting his forearms on the table. "Because it wouldn't just be your next door neighbor."

She shrugged. "Why not?"

"Because lone wolves don't—" He stopped himself. "Oh. I see. That question leads to discussing crazed wolves."

I nodded at him, smiling.

Blair pointed at him with the eraser end of her pencil. "Exactly. So let's rewind. So... my next door neighbor could be a werewolf and I'd never know it?"

"Unlikely, but correct."

"Why?" Blair cocked her head at him.

Sheppard shrugged. "Wolves are pack animals. We stick together."

"So you're animals?" She narrowed her eyes.

"We're more in touch with nature than most humans are."

I ran a hand through my hair. "You're going down a rabbit hole, Shep."

Blair clicked her tongue. "She's got a point."

Sheppard gave me a wry smile and nodded. "How far back do we rewind?"

Blair huffed out a little laugh, but her voice was flirty. "So... my next door neighbor could be a werewolf and I'd never know it."

"Correct."

Blair checked her clipboard again. "What do werewolves want?"

"To keep humanity safe."

"What else?"

"It's our driving force. Why does a painter want to paint? Why does a writer want to write? What keeps a journalist asking questions?" He arched an eyebrow at her.

She clucked her tongue again. "Don't get combative. Try again. What do werewolves want?"

He shrugged. "We have families and lives, just as humans do. But our driving force, our reason for living, is to keep humanity safe."

"How do werewolves reproduce? Is it like the movies?"

He scoffed but then stopped himself as soon as Blair took a breath. "No, it's not like the movies."

She gestured to keep going.

Sheppard sighed and deflated a little. "We can have

children, but it is hard, and our women often miscarry."

"Good," Blair said, smiling. "Play the sympathetic angle. So then... a bite or a scratch will not make someone a werewolf?"

Sheppard paused, thinking.

She shook her head. "Answer the question that was asked—not the question you know they meant."

"They didn't ask if an attack is what makes a werewolf," I said. "The question is will a single bite or scratch turn a human?"

Sheppard nodded his understanding and sighed. "No."

She gave him a chastising look. "Make me believe it, Shep. Will a bite or a scratch make someone a werewolf?"

Sheppard looked her in the eyes. "No, a bite or a scratch won't make someone a werewolf."

She looked down at her clipboard. Smart. "So we're safe from werewolf attacks?"

"As safe as we can possibly make you."

"What does that mean? Are you saying we're NOT safe from werewolf attacks? Are werewolves a danger to humans?" Blair went into rapid fire mode in no time flat, her tone aggressive.

"No—"

I growled. "Look, we're just trying to keep you safe. There are way bigger things out there trying to eat your face, and we're trying—"

Blair waved her clipboard. "Whoa, whoa, whoa. White flag! I'm not the enemy! This is why you couldn't be the face of this, Jessica! Breathe." She turned to Sheppard. "Look, you're a likeable guy. You've got plenty of charisma, and that whole dad-like thing going for you. Jess had the right idea picking you. Just keep the answers short and sweet and you'll be fine." She put the clipboard down. "You already know what lines you don't want to cross, what things you don't want to tell them. So make sure you're only answering the question that was asked and don't take the bait when they try to lead you."

Sheppard nodded with a wry smile. "Alright."

Blair held up a finger. "One more."

Sheppard nodded again.

"Why now?"

He answered slowly, watching me as he picked his words. "Because the internet and cell phones are making the world much smaller than it used to be." I nodded for him to keep going. "We would rather come to you than you find us accidentally."

"Good," Blair said. "Stick to that. While it's true the vampires are forcing your hand, they're doing it because the internet and cell phones have made it easy for them." She stood and extended her hand. "Well done, Shep. You made it through your first press conference. A few more of these and you'll be ready for the five o'clock news."

Sheppard stood and shook her hand. "Thanks."

Here's hoping the meeting would go as smoothly. I wasn't holding my breath.

THIRTY-TWO

*** (SHEPPARD) ***

JESS HAD CHANGED INTO an outfit similar to the one she wore when we went to meet Buckheim. She looked great for the meeting. I, on the other hand, hadn't changed and almost felt like I should have when I saw her.

But it was too late for that. Eric had the feeds going live to the screens in the big conference room of the PR offices, and though our camera and mic were off, the other alphas were chatting with one another while they waited. Eric was organizing the feeds on screens as best he could as the alphas connected. I stuffed my hands in my pockets as I waited. The other alphas I knew I trusted—Charles, William, Lawrence, and Dante—were scattered across three of the screens, and I couldn't help but smile as I saw Anise bring her mate a plate of ribs before sitting beside him in plain view of the camera.

"Those three are the Church alphas," Eric said, pointing to a screen on Jessica's left where three video feeds were situated by themselves, the wolves on screen sitting patiently motionless. I'd have thought the screen was frozen, if it weren't for the slow rise and fall of their shoulders as they breathed.

Jess nodded at Eric, her body tense as she focused on one of the other screens.

"Thanks," I said. Despite the camera not being on, I turned my back to it anyway and leaned down to Jess' ear. "You're gonna do great, Jess."

Her golden eyes met mine. "You didn't tell me my former alpha was among the confirmations."

"Which one?"

She gestured to the screen that had held her attention. "Paul from Portland."

I shrugged. "He should be used to you, then."

"He's not gonna be swayed."

"Maybe not," I said. "But it's worth the shot."

She took a deep breath and shook out the tension, replacing it with cool confidence as she surveyed the other screens.

She was amazing.

Eric showed us where the controls were, and we started the meeting just a couple of minutes past seven.

Jessica gave them the rundown on things she'd included in recent emails: wolfsbane in tattoo ink will make the color stay for werewolves, one of the three oldest vamps was killed in Colorado two years ago and the other two haven't been heard from since.

That's when I jumped in and informed them that not only did the vampires think werewolves were causing the rifts somehow—which meant *they* weren't—they also knew how to track the *consanguinea* bloodline. I watched the church alphas' screen as I shared that last part. If they knew about that already, they didn't show it. They did, however, frown at the revelation. Whether they knew or not, they weren't happy with the knowledge being so widespread. They started to say something, but Jess held her hand up and took over again.

She nodded to Eric, who put the highlighted sections of the Church treaties up on the screen—the ones that forbade the Church from putting undue pressure on non-Church packs. She pointed out that the treaties we signed in 1770 protected the werewolves far more than they protected the Church.

The Church alphas didn't like that bit either.

But she bulldozed past their next attempt to interrupt her, informing the wolves present that the vampires were doing all they could to push the werewolves public. She mentioned that—as some of the alphas were aware, thanks to her informing them when wolves were passing through their territories—she had teams spread across the US working to debunk the videos being posted online.

She then had Eric pull up her latest keyword report from Blair and started pointing out that search histories were showing that more and more people were looking up information about werewolves, and a not-insignificant amount of that was clearly curiosity based as opposed to fear-based, judging by the keywords and clicks afterward.

"The internet makes the world smaller and more accessible," she said, "which the vamps are taking full advantage of, likely thanks to the fact that so many of them are so much younger than the majority of us. A large percentage of them *grew up* with this tech heavily integrated into their day to day life, while we stand on traditions and the hopes that humanity chooses blissful ignorance. But blissful ignorance is *killing them*. And it doesn't have to. They could be our *allies* in this fight—helping us find vamps before the bodies pile up enough for us to take notice. So I'm going to show them the truth. *We're* going to show them the truth."

Mine.

I stopped myself from shaking my head, not wanting to send the wrong signal to the watching alphas. But she wasn't.

We were just two alphas working together to try to beat the vamps at their own game.

Bruce from Tallahassee popped onto the main screen. "What happens when they want to be turned too?"

Jess shrugged. "Would that be so bad?"

Isaac from San Francisco chimed in. "Who's going to turn them? Which of us is willing to ignore the part of us that says to protect them for long enough to kill them so they can *maybe* revive as one of us?"

I put a hand on Jess' shoulder. "Far be it from either of us to tell you how to run your pack—or how to recruit members. The point is Jessica is right. These vampires are going to expose us whether we're ready for it or not. Now is not the time for inaction."

"Besides," she added, "do you really want their voice to be the one humans hear first?"

"Easy," Cornelius from Cleveland said. "We just kill the vamps with cameras any time we see them."

Jess shook her head with a sigh. "They're live streaming—broadcasting our fights in real time, as it happens, for all of humanity to see. There is only so long the humans are going to buy the debunking that my teams are doing."

Alejandro from Monterrey, Mexico piped up. "So we shut down their access."

"That's not going to work," said Phillip from Raleigh.

I nodded. "He's right. The internet is too big for something like that to be possible." I shared a knowing smile with Jess, who smiled back at me.

God, she was beautiful.

One of the Church alphas, Marshall from Detroit, spoke up. "Since we've clearly reached the Q&A section, we'd like to know how you plan to introduce the werewolves to the humans."

I nodded and glanced at Jessica, who gestured for me to continue. "We'll happily loop you in on details once we know you're in, but it's better that we keep the specifics on a need-to-know, opt-in basis."

"Which brings me to the million-dollar question," she said. "How many of you would be willing to opt-in to going public, with your face, as I roll out my plan for showing the humans we're here?"

Chaos exploded across the monitors, the alphas all talking at once. I pinched the bridge of my nose and took a deep breath. I then looked directly at the camera.

"Now is not the time or place to try to debate out whether this is a good idea," I said. "The military knows, and the military is going to take action. We don't have time for maybes. If you're not sure, you're a no for now, and we can loop you in if you change your mind. If you're smart enough to see the writing on the wall now, then you're in. The rest of you will see in time that this is the best thing we can do to continue to keep humanity protected. What we're looking for right now is a simple show of hands please."

Only about a third of those present, maybe as many as twenty, raised their hands.

Jess nodded, her posture deflating a little before she straightened again. "I understand. I've prepared NDAs for all of the rest of you." She nodded to Eric, who put an email address up on the screen. "Please send an email to this address, and I'll make sure you are protected. In the meantime, you have my word that we won't out *anyone* who doesn't expressly give us permission to do so. Additionally, we'll make sure you all have access to the recording of this meeting in perpetuity—"

All the feeds went down at once.

I looked over to Eric, whose brow furrowed. "What?" He tapped a couple of keys. "The internet went out."

"It doesn't go out here," Jessica said.

And then the door to our left flew open, pouring vampires into the space.

Jess dodged out of the way of the first few, putting the conference room table between us and them so she could assess.

"Eric," she called. "Get Blair and Paige out, now!"

Eric was already moving toward the other door.

The vamps menacing us all had machetes in hand, but there were only ten of them. They poured in around us and Jess and I moved to be back-to-back to ensure each other's safety. As they attacked, we made quick work of them—divesting the first attackers of their machetes as we snapped their necks into misshapen angles. From there, we bashed in skulls, amputated limbs, and even beheaded a few until there were none left. Strewn around us were ten vampire bodies, more or less, and we carried our bloody machetes in hand as we ran to follow Eric.

We found him in a standoff with two vampires, Blair cowering behind him. She was white as a sheet and her eyes were wide. One of the vampires—a thin brunette—was behind the assistant, Paige, holding her by the throat as tears streamed down her face. The other vampire—a stocky blond guy—stood closer to Eric.

"Let us leave," said the brunette, "or I kill her and at least one of us gets away anyway."

"Please," Paige whispered. "I don't want to be one of them."

That's when I saw the pinprick wounds on her neck.

"She bit her," Blair said shakily.

Paige made a choking sound and her eyes rolled back into her head as her body started to shake.

"Paige!" Blair exclaimed. "Oh no..."

The vamp had already turned her. She was dying now, but she would reawaken in moments.

Jess nodded to the vamp closest to Eric. He was inching his way toward the door.

"That one's yours," she said as she dashed toward Paige and the brunette.

In one smooth move, Jess swung her machete, cleanly beheading both Paige and the vampire holding her.

Blair screamed as the vampire near Eric made a dash for the door. But Eric grabbed his head before he made it, wrenching it around to an unnatural angle as the bones cracked. The body fell to the floor like a sack of potatoes.

I reached for Blair and pulled her into me as the scream turned to sobs. "Paige!" Her knees buckled, but I held her up.

"Eric," Jess said, her voice tight. "Tell me you can get the feeds back up."

Eric looked between all of us. "Jess..."

"Eric." She gave him a look that dared him to defy her.

He pressed his lips into a line and nodded as he turned to the hallway.

My phone buzzed in my back pocket.

"Jess," I said. "Take Blair."

Blair was a sobbing mess. Jess came and steadied her as I pulled my phone from my back pocket. It was Germaine, the alpha from Des Moines. I shook my head at my phone.

"I can't start fielding calls or it'll never stop."

"They cut the telco lines," Eric called from the server room. "There's no connectivity to the building. I can get a mobile hotspot up and run comms through that. We can get the feeds up that way, but they'll be spotty. It might still work though if you can get everyone to turn off their screens."

My phone buzzed again, this time it was Paul, Jessica's former alpha.

"Answer it," she said, hugging the sobbing Blair tighter. "This'll take long enough that if you can at least tell one, they can tell the rest."

I tapped the button on my screen.

"What happened?" Paul asked.

"Vamps attacked and took out our comms," I said. "Tell everyone that can stick around to do so and tell them to turn their cameras off. We'll be back on soon, but it's going to be a spotty connection."

Jess took Blair over to her office. "Just sit here, Blair. I've got to finish what we were in the middle of wrapping up." Her voice was tight with restrained emotion.

Jessica was not okay.

I reached to give her a hug as she passed me, but she speared me with a look and shook her head.

"We have to finish this," she said. "Help me get the bodies out of the conference room."

I nodded and followed her. "Where do you want them?"

She sighed. "In the hall for now. Once we're done,

we'll load them into the back of your truck and take them out to the backroads to dust in the morning sun."

It didn't take long to get the conference room clear, though we'd be finishing what we could of the meeting surrounded by bloodstains.

Eric came in a moment later. "Okay. I think I've got it set up for right now." He nodded toward the screens. "Let's see who's still here."

It turned out, almost all of them stuck around. Or at least, they were there when we got reconnected.

"What happened? Is everyone okay?" Silas from Las Vegas was the first one to get anything intelligible out.

"We were attacked by vampires," Jessica said. "Thankfully, none of them were recording, but they took down one of my assistants."

"I'm sorry for your pack's loss," Paul from Portland said.

"I'll be on the next flight out," Jasper from Chicago said.

Jess shook her head. "No, you won't. You'll stay there—"

"Bloodsuckers can't be allowed to do something like this without retaliation, Jess," Nicholas from Miami said.

"Jessica," she corrected. "And they won't—"

"We might not agree that going public is a good choice," Paul said as Jess curled her hands into white knuckled fists. "But we'll help you with tracking the roots of this attack."

A barely restrained growl rumbled in Jessica's chest. "I—"

I reached over and muted the mic, turning my back to the camera to face her.

Her blazing golden eyes met mine. "What the hell—"

"You need them, Jess," I said, putting a hand on her shoulder. "Let them help you."

She pulled her shoulder away from my hand. "I don't need saving, Sheppard."

"No," I agreed. "But if you let them help, you might get the chance to change their minds."

She narrowed her eyes at me for a long moment

before reaching around me to turn the mic back on. She kept her eyes on me as she said, "I'll forward along anything that looks like a lead to anyone who'd like to help track down where these vamps came from."

"How big is the brood there?" Paul asked.

Jess shook her head. "San Antonio's been free of vampires for nearly two decades." She brushed a hand through her hair. "Look, guys, I'd love to stay and chat more, but I have bodies I need to dispose of and cleanup to arrange for. Thank you very much to those of you who stuck around. Please, let me know if you're in. This attack only goes to show me that I'm on the right track. It's too coincidental that they'd attack here now. Send me an email to the address from before—"

"It's on the screen now," Eric said.

She nodded. "Send me an email to let me know if you're in or you're out. I'll get the requisite paperwork to you. And let me know if you need a copy of the treaties. I'll happily send those along."

"Thank you for your time, everyone," I said.

"Thanks," Jess added, and hit the button to mute the mic before turning off the camera.

"I'll leave the email address on screen for a little longer," Eric said. "I'll cut it off in a few minutes."

Jess nodded and looked at me. "Help me with the bodies?"

I gave her a gentle smile. "Of course."

I pulled my truck into the alleyway between buildings so we could take the bodies out the side door instead of the front. It was darker there, and there was less chance of people seeing a pile of bodies getting thrown into the back of a truck that way. Thankfully, I kept a tarp behind the passenger seat, and once all the bodies were loaded, Jess helped me tie down the tarp over them all.

And as we turned to head back inside, we saw the fresh graffiti on the side of the building. "2 Points 4 Lyfe" was sprayed in dripping red paint along with big black splotches with white vampire fangs stenciled over them, some of the paint dripping from the tips of the elongated teeth.

"What the shit is that?" Jess asked, walking around toward the front of the building.

I tilted my head to the side before following her. "It looks like that's the group Ian found online." I pulled the phone from my back pocket and thumbed it open as we rounded the corner.

The graffiti was repeated on the front of the building.

Ian answered on the second ring. "Yeah Shep?"

"Looks like that '2 Points 4 Lyfe' group actually contains vampires," I said. "We just got attacked."

"Everyone okay?"

I looked at Jessica. "We lost the assistant to her head of PR."

"Shit," Ian said. "Is Jessica okay?"

Jessica paused taking pictures with her phone to give me a look that positively dared me to say something.

I nodded once. "She's fine."

Jessica nodded her approval and returned to taking pictures, walking around to the side of the building where the truck was to photograph that side as well.

"I'm helping her clean up before I head back," I said.

"Roger that," Ian replied. "I'll let everyone know."

"Thanks." I ended the call and shoved the phone back in my pocket.

"Looks like you'll need a new shirt," Jess said, jerking her chin toward my chest as I came around the side of the building after her.

I looked down. There was blood splattered all over my shirt.

"There are worse things." I sighed. "Like having to hire a cleaner who won't ask questions."

Jess tossed her hair over her shoulder. "No need. We just need to get someone to pressure wash the graffiti off, and then borrow one of the UV room sanitizers from the hospital. The latter should dust the blood and then we just need a good vacuum."

"How're you gonna manage the sanitizer?"

"Emma's an ER nurse." She shrugged. "She can make it happen."

"I take it Emma's a packmate?"

"Handsome *and* smart? How do you manage to still be single, Tobias Sheppard?"

I couldn't decide whether the first half of it was sarcasm or not, which might be the short circuiting from the name drop, but I at least had an answer for the second half.

"It's hard to settle down when you can't find a true equal that even your wolf will acknowledge," I said.

Mine.

Except she'd be the one to decide that, not me.

THIRTY-THREE

*** (JESSICA) ***

"You told me there weren't any vampires in San Antonio!" Blair was frantic. We'd gotten her home the night before—before we took the bodies out past the city limits to dust—but she hadn't had much to say. Apparently, that had all changed. It was mid-afternoon when I got her call, and I paced around my bedroom as we talked.

"There haven't been for over twenty years," I said. "I don't know where those guys came from, but I will find out."

"Finding out won't help me if I'm dead," Blair said, her voice cracking on the last word. "I can't do this, Jess. I'm out."

Oh no. No no no no no.

"You can't be out, Blair," I said. "I need you. Attacks

like this are why we need to go public. Don't you see? If we didn't have to try to hide this shit, we could focus our energy more on eliminating them altogether!"

"No Jess, that could have been me last night. Paige didn't deserve to have to die like that."

"You're right," I said. "It could have been you. Just like it could have been you three years ago in Dallas." Pushing on her past run-in with a vampire was dangerous, but I needed her with me. "But it wasn't. Maybe that's for a reason Blair. Don't let Paige's death be for nothing."

She sniffled and a quiet sob escaped her. "No Jess. I'm out."

I couldn't let her be out. I needed her.

"Please Blair," I said. "Don't do this to me. Not now. I need you." My voice might have cracked a little too. It might have even been real.

She was quiet for a long moment. "You bitch."

I had her.

"You were the first person I thought to protect when those vampires showed up," I told her, my voice still thick. "Eric was already on the move. You've got a whole pack that'll throw themselves between you and a vamp."

"Fat lot of good that'll do me if they try to get me when no one's at the office."

"Then I'll get one to be your full-time bodyguard," I said. "Pretty sure I can get Leo to agree without hesitation."

She and Leo had a thing before, and they still sometimes hooked up, so I knew he'd be a perfect choice.

"You *bitch*."

"That's 'you *savvy* bitch,' thank you very much," I said with a little smile. "And you're welcome."

"I could kiss you."

"Save it for Leo," I said. "Just stick with me, Blair. Please. I'm begging you."

She was quiet for a long moment. "Howlers is gonna need a new bartender."

"Or you get a lot of free shows."

"I get that anyway," she said.

"Touché." I clicked my tongue. "Does that mean you'll stay?"

"Yeah, Jess." She sighed. "I'll stay."

"Good," I said. "Because there's no one better at this than you."

"Don't blow smoke up my ass," she said. "I'm not the top game in the country, I'm just good at my job."

"I couldn't do this without you," I said.

"Now *that* is true," she said. "You'd be fucked and have to pay someone ten times what you pay me to get half-assed results."

"Alright, I hear you. I'll throw in a raise too."

"Your stream is really poppin', huh?"

I laughed. "It is, but don't think I'm the only cam girl in this pack who makes bank."

"Oh, I don't doubt it." She was quiet for another long moment. Then she sniffled and her voice was tight again. "Thanks for not letting her become one of them."

I froze in my pacing. I hadn't really been close with Paige, but she'd done a great job with everything the pack had needed from her. She was going to be hard to replace, if not impossible. And I hated that it had happened on my watch. In my PR offices. Paige was supposed to have been safe with us. We'd failed her.

"I couldn't have even if I wanted to," I said, my voice tight. "None of them were leaving that office alive."

"She'd have given away practically everything," Blair said. "She knew my schedule like the back of her hand, and she had access to all of the plans."

I fell back into step around my room. "We'd have shut down her access, but that would have only bought us some time."

Blair was quiet. "I'm sad to have to replace her." Her voice cracked again.

"I'll talk to the pack, see if any of them want the job," I said.

"Better to keep it in the family than try to pull in someone new," she said. "Better do more than just see if they want it, try to convince them."

"Same thing," I said.

"If you say so."

"What are you going to tell Paige's parents?"

Blair sighed, swallowing audibly. "I haven't figured that out yet. I keep seeing her crying face every time I think about it."

"You could try the truth," I said.

"And when they don't believe it?"

I ran a hand through my hair and shook my head. "We'll have to have something plausible lined up."

"She deserves better than whatever bullshit story you guys usually use," she said. "You know, the one about some animal attack or another."

I huffed out a wry laugh. "Animal attacks don't result in clean beheadings."

"Touché."

"I'll come up with something," I said. "And we'll have her cremated so we can ship the remains to..."

"Michigan," Blair said. "She was planning a trip there later this year."

I nodded and swallowed. "Let's make arrangements to cremate right away so there's less chance for questions."

"Okay," Blair said with a sniffle.

"I'll get you the number for someone who won't ask too many questions," I said, glancing at the clock. "Assuming he's still in the business."

"That'd be great," she said.

"I gotta go meet up with the pressure washers," I said. "I'll text you."

"Okay," she repeated. "Thanks."

"Of course." And I ended the call.

Because the paint was fresh, it didn't take the pressure washers long to get the graffiti off my building. It left me with patches that I needed to repaint, but at least that could wait a little. Emma came by with the UV sanitizer while I was waiting on the guys to finish, and we set it up to do its thing in the conference room. Every thirty minutes, we moved it somewhere else, so the whole process took something like three hours.

By the time I got home, it was after dark. Imogen met

me at the door wearing her Stormsworn band shirt with cutoff shorts. She had glitter on her cheekbones, and her sleek blonde hair was freshly straightened.

"There you are! Are you going like that?!"

I looked down at my own cutoff shorts and white loose-fit shirt. "What's wrong with what I'm wearing? And go where?"

"You forgot?! Stormsworn!"

"Is that tonight?"

"It has been for weeks now," she said, exasperated. "Hurry up and change so we can go!"

"What's wrong with what I'm wearing?!"

She speared me with a look. "You mean besides the fact that shirt hides all your best assets?" She pushed me toward my room. "It also looks like you don't give a shit how you look, and I know that's not true."

A few minutes later, I came back out of my room in a schoolgirl-style skirt with a black tank top, my spiked choker, and black block-heeled boots.

"*That's* more like it!" She hooked her arm in mine. "Let's go!"

She rode behind me on the Diavel as we sped over to the Aztec Theatre. We didn't manage to get there in time to be at the front rail, but we weren't far. I put in my high fidelity earplugs and waited through the opening band—some no-name group of guys from Allen. Im did the same, but she cheered for the openers like they'd really made a name for themselves.

Either she really liked the music, or she was hoping for a hookup tonight.

And then Stormsworn took the stage. Up until this point, I'd only seen their music videos with funky angles and mood lighting, so I guess it had never really hit me like it did when the lead singer stepped up to the mic.

He was a werewolf.

I looked at the others in the band.

The bassist. The guitarist. The drummer.

They were all werewolves.

Holy shit. Why didn't anyone tell me? Who's their alpha?

"They're all wolves, Im!"

"I know, isn't it great?!" she said, yelling her excitement along with the rest of the crowd.

She must've thought I meant they were all hot. And they were, for sure, but that wasn't at all what I meant.

"No, Imogen, *look*," I said, leaning close to her ear. "They're werewolves!"

She stopped and looked and then leaned toward me. "*Holy shit.*"

I nodded. "I'm gonna figure out a way to talk to them!"

"Good luck!"

We sang along and cheered and yelled through most of their set, but I was watching the crew. I was pretty sure I knew who the manager was, and—between songs—I searched their social media for a name: Vince Scagliotti. He wore a black long sleeve shirt with loose, worn blue jeans. He was a skinny guy—a human—with a shaved head, but he had a hint of a goatee going to offset his shiny head and he carried an air of no-nonsense everywhere he went.

The next song they played was my favorite, so of course I took a video of the bridge and last chorus.

By then, I'd made it to the far side of the audience. Im had come with me.

"I'll meet you back at my bike," I told Imogen. "I'm gonna see if I can get backstage."

"You're out of your mind!"

"And if it works," I said, "I'll be lucky as hell. So, cross your fingers for me."

She held up both hands, her fingers crossed.

A few moments, a few lies, and a borrowed All Access pass later—a prime bit of luck that a complete newbie to the tour scene would be in the ladies' room toward the end of the set—and I was backstage and on my way to the dressing rooms.

A hand curled around my bicep.

Human, by the smell of it.

I froze. Damn. Should've taken out the earplugs.

I turned as I remedied my mistake, wincing at the

sudden noise as I tucked the silicone plugs into a tiny pocket on the waistband of my skirt. The tall guy with the shaved head—Stormsworn's manager, Vince Scagliotti—was the one with his hand on me.

Well. He was someone I could talk to anyway, even if I would rather get the guys directly.

He leaned to the radio clipped to his shirt. "Keep Stormsworn from heading back to the dressing room. We have a security breach."

I frowned.

A voice on the other end of the radio crackled out, "Do you need backup?"

Vince looked hard at me as he turned me around and steered me back the way I came. "Negative. Keep eyes on the boys."

"Roger that. Give us the all clear when they can move."

"10-4," Vince said. "Keep this channel clear in the meantime."

"10-4," the disembodied voice replied.

A few moments later, we got to a dressing room, or maybe a lounge room, which was in the opposite direction from where I'd been going, so Vince was doing me a favor anyway. But he shut and locked the door as soon as he released my arm. The room held a cacophony of scents, but I could connect the ones with the wild underpinnings: cool and crisp edged ozone, mint-tinged sage, lavender, bright lime, and some kind of earthy cologne. There were only four guys in the band. Who was number five?

Vince put his back to the door as I surveyed the room—he blocked the only exit. Not that he'd be hard to get past; he was just a human, after all. There was a brown leather couch along the far wall with three black leather armchairs spread around the room at odd angles. There were empty cans of soda, along with candy wrappers and balled up napkins on the side tables next to the chairs and couch. A handful of folding chairs leaned against the wall next to a table that was covered in food: ribs, chips, salsa, guacamole, a bowl of snack packs of M&Ms and

Skittles, and rows of bottled water. Under the table was a cooler. There was a full length mirror leaned against one of the corners adjacent to the door, and five duffle bags littered the floor, along with one of those heavy duty camera storage boxes. Cameraman must be the fifth in their pack.

"I suppose I should thank you for not harming my crew," Vince said, crossing his arms.

I waved a hand. "No need. I wouldn't hurt them."

He held out a hand for the badge. "Whose did you lift?"

I pulled it over my head and handed it to him as I shrugged. "Some girl in the ladies' room. Clearly new."

He nodded. "And what is it you want?"

"You've got a special group of guys there, Vince," I said, stepping over to the table of snacks.

Vince watched me, his expression hard as he nodded. "More than you know." He was playing it cool, but his heart rate pounded.

I think he knew what he'd run into. Or at least had an inkling.

I winked at him as I dipped a chip in the guacamole. "I think I have an idea." I popped the chip into my mouth and sat in the closest armchair, crossing my legs in a well-practiced flirty display.

Vince's Adam's apple bobbed.

"Lemme level with you," I said. "I'm working on bringing awareness of a certain brand of special to the world at large, and I think the guys could be a huge help to my project."

He shook his head. "That's gonna be a hard pass. The guys aren't interested."

"You could convince them."

"But I won't." He shook his head again.

I sighed and reached for my phone. It was tucked into my waistband. Vince's heartbeat kicked into high gear.

"Then I'd like to stay in touch," I said. "If you give me your contact info, I'll send over my signed NDA to protect them from being outed by me or mine."

"You can send that to the fan mail address on their

site."

I narrowed my eyes at the obvious brushoff, and though his heart didn't race any faster, it thumped harder. But you'd never know it just looking at him. Good job, Vince.

"You're not even going to look at it, are you?"

He just stared at me.

"Look," I said. "I'd like to be connected to as many people like those guys as I can. I have resources to help—"

"They don't need or *want* help."

I ran a hand through my hair. I was losing this battle and I didn't like it. "People like them usually tell people like me when they're moving through specific areas, Vince—"

"You're gonna make me activate my insurance, aren't you?" He gestured toward the door. "The tour dates are posted on their website."

"I'm not gonna make problems here," I said, shaking my head. "I'm gonna let this one go. Largely because I'm a fan. But others like me wouldn't be so kind. Whoever's really in charge needs to let someone know when they're moving through, or it'll be taken as an invasion."

Some of his control slipped. "They're a band, for fuck's sake! They go all over!"

"All the same, Vince. All the same."

He steepled his hands in front of him and gestured toward the door. "Look, I'm going to ask you politely to leave—immediately." He clicked his tongue at me. "Tell the merch guy on your way out that Vince owes you a t-shirt. The guys love their fans."

I got up slowly as I took a deep breath.

Vince held my gaze.

"I thank you for your time." I held a hand out to him.

He took it and shook it once before I turned to leave.

I picked up that shirt on the way to meet up with Imogen at my bike. She smelled like she'd had a quickie with Mister Mint-Tinted Sage, but we made it all the way home without conversation.

"So," Imogen asked, shaking her hair free from the

helmet in the garage. "How'd it go?"

"It didn't," I said, pressing my lips into a line as I put my own helmet down on the bike.

"Well, you don't need them anyway." She waved a hand. "You've got Sheppard."

"I just thought they'd make a nice backup plan," I said, resecuring my ponytail.

"Why would you need one? Y'all are great together."

I speared her with a look.

"What?!" She put her hands up in surrender. "We all saw the meeting. Eric ran a feed here so we could cheer you on."

"More like so you'd know whether to give me some space if it all went south."

"Which it did." She rolled her eyes. "But not before everyone saw you two thick as thieves over there."

I looked at her for a long moment, contemplating how much to say. Then I grabbed her by the wrist and pulled her down the hall and into my room, shutting the door behind her.

"Jess..."

"Im, look. I can't with him. He used to talk all the time about how he wants a family like he had growing up. He hasn't mentioned it recently, but I can't decide if that means he's changed his mind, or if he's hoping I will."

"You could just *ask* him," she said.

"Even if he *has* changed his mind, he's *never* gonna be okay with the studio."

She snorted. "You could show it to him and find out."

"You didn't hear what he had to say about Howlers. He said he didn't judge it, and he wasn't lying, but then he *also* thought it a terrible idea to try to have the meeting there when we wanted it in person."

Imogen shrugged. "He was probably right. Most of those alphas are stick-in-the-mud pieces of shit, based on your descriptions."

I smiled at her and sighed.

"I mean... maybe he's just waiting for you to say something."

I nodded and looked at my boots. "He *did* ask what we were doing the other morning."

She shrugged. "We'd all like to know, really. Mostly because you sleeping with the same guy more than once is outside of your MO, and that he's a wolf on top of it? Sheesh. There's a running bet on when you two are gonna make it official."

"Now I don't want to just on principle."

She batted at my bicep. "C'mon, Jess, don't be like that."

"No, I'm serious," I said. "What I want and *who* I want is *my* business!"

"Sure," she said. "But you *also* seem a lot happier when he's around." She moved her head into my field of vision until I looked up at her. "Just talk to him. Because otherwise, you're gonna try to guess his motives, and we're not much better than humans at that. I'll bet you a new bike if you ask him, he'll tell you directly."

"What if that's what I'm scared of?" My voice was quiet. "What if he is *exactly* like every other wolf that's courted me?"

"This isn't the 1800's, Jess. No one 'courts' anyone anymore. And if you ask him, and he is, at least then you'll have your answer and you can decide then what to do with that."

I pressed my lips into a line as a growl quietly rumbled in my chest at the thought that he could possibly be just as arrogant as every other alpha that's shown up on my doorstep.

"Or," Im said. "Here's a thought. Maybe it doesn't fucking matter if he only wants you because you're an alpha. His actions show that he clearly cares about what happens to you. You said yourself he had your back when the vamps attacked."

I nodded. "He did. But it matters, Im."

She held my gaze for a long moment before shaking her head. "Fine. Then it matters. But tell me this. Why would *Sheppard* value you *solely* because you're an alpha?"

"What?"

"The other alphas that've come sniffing around? I get it. Humans? I get it. But you get that his pack works different than those, right? Like you've seen it?"

I didn't say anything, but I thought about it.

She was right. Sheppard's pack *was* different. He treated his wolves like equals, like *family*. He wasn't alpha because he gave orders the rest of them followed, he was alpha because they *trusted* him to lead them, they *trusted* him to get pack input before making a plan of action.

"Look," Im said. "Before Shep agreed to help you, how many of the alphas even bothered to *open* your emails?"

I shook my head. "No one's really opened them in years... so, maybe... one or two?"

"And then Sheppard said he'd help you and sent emails too, right?"

I nodded.

"So how many replied to him? How many *showed up* for your meeting? How many were willing to come *in person* before you moved the date?"

I just gave her a look, but her expression told me she understood it.

"Right," she said. "So do you really think Sheppard needs *your* status?"

I stared at her some more.

She opened the door and booped my nose. "*That's* why he's different, Jess." She turned and sauntered off, leaving me staring after her in my doorframe.

THIRTY-FOUR

*** (SHEPPARD) ***

"Are you sure they're wolves?" I asked Jessica.

She'd come over the next morning, barely after breakfast, in denim cutoff shorts and a black crop top that said 'what doesn't kill me *BETTER RUN*' in white block lettering. We were standing in the open front doorway to the house she'd let us borrow, but I looked over my shoulder at the rest of the pack as I stepped outside. Kaylah winked at me as I shut the door.

Jessica nodded. "I know what I saw."

She pulled her phone from her pocket and thumbed it open. A few taps later and she turned the screen toward me. Sure enough, there were four werewolves right there on stage in front of God and everyone, playing music for the crowd.

"Holy shit," I breathed.

"And their manager knows," she said. "*And* he knows that I know. Believe me, that door is shut."

"Who's their alpha?"

She shook her head. "I couldn't tell. I don't think it's any of them, but I didn't smell any other werewolves around other than one that I'm pretty sure is their tour photographer. It's a damn ballsy play to have such a public face with such a big secret."

I nodded. "It really is, though it's clear they're not telling anyone."

"Yeah, their manager made that *abundantly* clear."

"I don't know of any packs south of yours in Texas," I said. "Not to say that there isn't one, because there clearly is, but they aren't on my radar."

"I was afraid of that," she said. "I didn't recall seeing any alphas at all from south of here at the meeting, let alone ones from Texas."

"There was an alpha from Monterrey," I reminded her. "And my friend Dante from Tijuana."

"Tijuana's south of California," she said.

"But Monterrey is south of Texas."

She nodded, conceding the point.

"Wait," I said, snapping my fingers. "Didn't you mention something about a newish wolf from South Texas before? Any chance they're connected?"

"I'd say it's even likely," she said. "But Anthony just woke up in the woods after his attack and then went on the run after his first change."

"What?" I furrowed my brow. "Why?"

The corner of her mouth pulled outward. "He didn't know anything about what had happened to him. He thought he was a danger to people, so he stayed on the move. I'm just glad we found him before he went crazed."

I wiped at my face. "Jesus, Jess... Every story you tell me shows me why you want to go public so bad."

She shrugged. "The vamps just gave me a good excuse."

She got real still then and quiet. A cicada started up its chatter, probably from the tree in the backyard.

"You look like you've got something on your mind," I

said quietly. "Like telling me about Stormsworn was just an excuse to talk to me."

She looked up at me. "How are you so perceptive?"

I smiled. "Practice."

She nodded once and looked past me.

I looked over my shoulder at the window. My pack was cleaning up after breakfast. Jamie had the football in hand. They were probably about to head out back for some woofball.

I looked down at myself. Blue-grey t-shirt and brown cargo shorts. I was barefoot, but that could be remedied.

"Do we need to take a drive?"

She looked up at me again and was chewing on her lip. I wanted to kiss her to get her to stop it before she chewed it raw. But then her expression changed, like a wall locked into place for her.

"I think we do," she said with a sigh. "But let's take my truck."

I nodded. "Let me grab my shoes."

She drove us to her PR offices, greeted Blair and Leo—Blair's new werewolf bodyguard, a wolf only slightly less musclebound than the bulky Nate—and led me down the hallway the vamps had busted in through. She typed in a code to the last door on the right—the door she'd omitted from our tour before—and it beeped to indicate that it was unlocked.

"I'm the only one with the code to this room," she said, her hand on the latch, "and what happens inside isn't exactly *secret*, so much as it's not exactly advertised."

"Okay," I said slowly.

I was beginning to wonder if perhaps my guess from before had been on the nose.

As she opened the door and flipped the lights on, I was bathed in the lavender and cloves scent that was all Jessica, along with a not-subtle underpinning of arousal.

The room beyond was a lot to take in. It was painted black, and there was a white leather couch angled across the far corner, facing the L-shaped computer desk in the corner adjacent to the door. A red and black leather computer chair faced the desk, which had three large monitors with a ring light between each of them. A strip of lights lined the walls, right where they touched the ceiling, bathing the room in a pale pink glow, and there was a ring light tripod with a camera atop it facing the couch.

But what was a lot was the fact that there was one of those machines with a dildo attached to a jackhammer engine on the floor between the legs of the tripod, the business end pointed toward the couch. On the side table was a bottle of lube, along with a Hitachi wand, a bright pink C-shaped toy, and a bright pink bullet-shaped toy with a tail that widened to a little disk at the end. On the desk was a black vibrator, and a webcam that was pointed at the lap of the chair.

It was a solo porn studio.

Judging by the chair, and the fact that only she had the code to the room, this was *Jessica's* solo porn studio.

She *was* a cam girl.

"So, about my collection."

I turned to look at her as she shut the door behind us, my eyebrow raised.

"They're pretty much all from patrons," she said. "They send them to me, I use them once on stream, and if I like it, I keep it. The rest get tossed."

I nodded.

"I don't know anyone's names, and I try to keep it that way. It's better for me if I don't know. I... uh... get off on the anonymity."

"Okay," I said slowly, nodding.

She pressed her lips into a line as she thought for a moment.

"Even when I've gone to a club," she said slowly, "I usually don't bother with getting someone's name. We just... have a night and that's it."

"Right." I nodded again.

"It's true!"

I put my hands up in a placating gesture. "No no, I believe you. It... makes sense."

"But this?" She gestured to the machine on the floor. "And those?" She gestured to the toys on the side table. "And these?" She gestured for me to follow her and we passed into a bathroom with a giant shower stall with a number of dildos suctioned to the wall and the chair-height ledge. "And that?" She gestured to the camera and ring light up in the top corner of the shower, pointed down to face the spray of water. "This is who I am. It's who I've been for years. When I tried it out, I never guessed I'd like it as much as I do. And now? It's probably my favorite part of the day."

"Okay," I said again, unsure what she was trying to say.

"I'm never going to stop this."

I got it. She thought I was going to judge her for this. And her expression was so damn earnest, breaking through the wall she had tried to put in place.

I could barely keep myself from laughing, and a little chuckle came out. "Of course not."

"What do you mean 'of course not?' This isn't a joke, Tobias." She raked a hand through her hair.

I swallowed, trying to sober as my brain short circuited on my name from her lips again.

"No," I said finally. "I'm honored you'd show it to me. I don't really get why, but it's fine. This is who you are."

"'It's fine?' But... this is yet another in a laundry list of reasons you and I can't... I mean the jealousy alo—"

My hands fell on her shoulders as I held her gaze. "This isn't a dealbreaker for me, Jess." I shrugged. "This is just a modernization of probably the oldest profession in the world."

She blinked at me.

"Do you honestly think I give a shit if some horny asshole with too much money wants to throw some your way while a machine half-asses its way into making you cum?"

She blinked again. "Well... When you say it like that..."

"Exactly." I nodded. "Just tell me you hide your face... for the sake of your PR plans."

I followed her as she went back to the desk. Laying on top of the keyboard was a piece of black lace I hadn't noticed before. She held it up and put it over her face. It was a black lace mask that covered the entire top half of her face.

"Faces make more money, but this is a good compromise," she said. "I'm thirsty, not stupid. It's why I don't have any ink. You couldn't prove anything was me if you tried."

"Tech is getting better these days."

She rocked her head side to side. "True. And they are coming up with voice printing, so that might get me in the end, but the deep fake stuff can manage that too with enough of a sample."

"And you're thirsty," I said. "But not for the muscle-bound walk of shame?"

That may have tipped my hand.

She smiled at me like she knew. "I don't mix business with pleasure."

I nodded. "Reason number two, I take it?"

She gestured between the two of us. "For us? Hah, more like yet another in that laundry list."

"Care to name the others?"

"I don't do relationships. Or it's complicated. Or labels."

I nodded. There it was.

With a hard stance on that, she'd never want more than just the no-strings-attached flings we'd already had.

Kaylah was wrong. She wouldn't write her story with someone else. She'd just write it on her own. She didn't need me, she just clearly *wanted* me, if only sometimes.

And damn if that wasn't hot. Even if it was, on the whole, disappointing.

"Maybe one day, we can both give them a show." I winked at her.

"Hell no!" She shook her head. "I'm not letting them hear that!"

I stepped closer to her. Maybe it was her arousal in the air getting to me. Or maybe it was just her.

"So I was right," I said, pitching my voice low.

She raised an eyebrow at me.

I closed the distance between us, leaning down to

murmur in her ear. "The machines *do* just half-ass it."

She turned to face me then, her eyes locked on my mouth. She leaned closer to me, but I straightened with a smirk, tapping her lips lightly with a pointer finger. She blinked her gaze to mine.

"Four's a choice," I said.

THIRTY-FIVE

*** (JESSICA) ***

FOUR'S A CHOICE. YEAH, well. What if I choose you, you lug?

I shook my head. Nope. Bad idea. Stop thinking with the lady bits.

But would it really be a bad idea?

I mean, sure, if it went all to hell, I'd need a new PR face, but by that time I'd have other wolves on board. I'd been forwarding the emails to Shawn since the meeting, so I didn't have a count, but it was a non-zero number of wolves that were in.

Which was relatively exciting, all told.

"Jess?" Sheppard leaned his head down and was looking at me like he'd asked me a question.

Shit.

I blinked. "What?"

"I asked if you had any leads yet on the vamps that graffitied this place."

"Oh," I said. "Sorry. I... well. Let's find out."

I led Sheppard over to Eric's office. He was wearing the shirt that he'd described to me as his blue screen of death t-shirt. It had white writing on it that started with 'Windows has encountered an error and needs to shut down,' and followed on from there with a whole lot of computer jargon I hadn't managed to pick up on. Anyway, he paired the shirt with black jeans and sneakers. He was finishing up a phone call as I came in.

"Okay," he said. "Let me know if you find anything else. Poke around in the dark web. The last vamp we took down here was using that to find his sheep."

"I'll check it out," came the voice on the other end of the phone.

"Cool," Eric said. "Keep me in the loop?"

"Sure," the other voice said. "I'll call you when I have something."

"Talk to you then," Eric said, ending the call.

"I'm glad Ian can help you," Sheppard said.

So that was the name of the guy on the other end. I knew the voice sounded familiar.

"Any info at all yet on '2 Points 4 Lyfe?'" I put up air quotes around the phrase that had accompanied the vampire fangs on the walls of my building.

Eric shook his head. "According to Ian, it's a vamp organization. Do broods name themselves?"

"Not usually," I said.

Sheppard shook his head. "I've never heard of it. Though, we don't name our packs either."

Eric nodded. "Well, we're still digging. They've hidden themselves pretty well, using VPNs to bounce themselves around. Someone actually cut the telco line into the building for the attack, but I got that replaced now." He ran a hand through the mop of curls on the top of his head, making some of them stand up at odd angles. "But I think we're gonna need to replace the whole backend of the system anyway. We got shut out less than a month ago, and then there was this? After having our system so open with all the wolves dialing in, I think it'd be smart to, just in case."

I nodded. "Do you need more equipment?"

"Yes," he said. "I can repurpose some of what we have so it's not a complete waste. But there is a fair amount that will just need replacing."

"How long?"

He shrugged. "It'll have to be done in pieces if I'm cannibalizing old machines. Maybe a couple of months?"

I nodded again. "Any luck tracking how we got shut out before?"

Eric shook his head. "I know it came in through Paige's computer, but I don't know how. Hers was one of the first we locked down."

"I want the source of that before we trade everything over, or we're just leaving ourselves open to it again."

"Any way I can help?" Sheppard asked.

"Not unless you're better with computers than Ian," Eric said.

Sheppard shook his head. "I'm not."

"Then no," Eric replied. "Your best help is that you've agreed to be the face of this campaign Jess has put together."

"Blair put it—" I stopped myself. "Blair." The word was a growl.

The leak came from Paige's computer, but we couldn't track it. Blair had just tried to quit on me, as soon as we'd started digging into the source of the attack. Blair knew what Eric was capable of, she'd worked with him to ensure the systems were locked down, she'd helped him test it.

"Blair," I said again.

"What about her?" Sheppard asked.

"She wouldn't be the leak," Eric said. "That would show up from her computer, not Paige's."

That was too easy to dismiss. I shook my head. "Not if she did it when Paige was away from her computer." It didn't feel right, but it didn't exactly feel wrong either. I couldn't place it.

"Let's just ask her," Sheppard said. "We'll know if

she's lying."

"If she doesn't quit on the spot for it even being suggested," Eric said.

"If it wasn't her," Sheppard said. "Then it could've been Paige. Or someone in your circle might have helped them."

"Paige wasn't that tech savvy," Eric said. "And if you're trying to say that someone in the pack would have tipped off a vampire, then you're out of your mind."

I growled and he ducked his head.

"No one in the pack would do that," he grumbled, looking at the floor.

Sheppard turned to me. "Anyone in your pack against this whole 'going public' thing?"

I shook my head. "Hell no. A lot of them would have been better off their first time around if they'd known what the hell was going on."

"Then maybe you're right," Sheppard said. "Blair could be the leak."

"I just don't get why she would go through the trouble of setting up all the PR stuff if she was going to do that."

"Any chance she's someone's sheep?"

"I've never smelled vamp on her," I said.

"Neither have I," Eric said. "But I often smell a whole bunch of Leo."

I snorted. "Why do you think I chose him for her bodyguard?"

Eric huffed out a laugh. "At least you know."

Sheppard looked at me. "So we ask her directly then."

I took a deep breath and raked a hand through my hair as I tried to calm down at the thought of someone so close betraying me.

"Okay," I said. "Let's ask her."

Leo was watching a college football game on the sectional in the lounge, a take-out box full of lo mein in front of him. Blair wasn't with him, so we headed to her office.

Blair was at her desk, sushi takeout in front of her. She popped a piece of her roll into her mouth as we walked in. She was wearing skinny black slacks with nude heels and a white sleeveless blouse. Her brown blazer was tossed on the upholstered chair next to the door.

"Hey Jess," Blair said as I poked my head in. When she caught sight of Sheppard, she sat a little straighter. "Hi Shep." She looked between us. "What's up?"

"There's not really a gentle way to ask what we need to ask," Sheppard said.

I didn't hesitate. "Did you know about the attack?"

Blair blinked at me. "No."

She wasn't lying.

I had more. "Did you know Paige's computer was compromised?"

"No."

Also true.

"Did you have anything at all to do with us being shut out of our systems or with the group that graffitied the building?"

She sighed. "No, Jess, I didn't have anything to do with any of that."

That was true, too.

She looked between the two of us. "Why would you think that?"

"Because Paige's machine was the thing that got us shut out of our system a couple weeks ago," I said. "And then you threatened to quit right after the attack."

"I threatened to quit because I thought I might get killed if I stayed," Blair said. "I'm terrified of dying, Jess. If there were any way to guarantee turning me wouldn't kill me, I'd ask to be turned."

"I'm sorry," I said. "I had to ask."

She shrugged. "I get it. It's simpler if the leak was internal." She popped another piece of sushi into her mouth and turned to grab papers off the printer.

"Could it have been Paige, then?" Sheppard asked.

I shrugged, hating the idea that we were questioning the loyalty of someone I'd had to kill. "I never smelled vamp on her, and I passed her desk nearly every day."

"So she probably wasn't someone's sheep."

"She never seemed to be not herself," Blair said, her

voice tight. "If that helps at all. And I trusted her."

I nodded. "I just hate that we can't know for sure."

"Yet," Sheppard said. "Maybe Eric will find something more in her system."

I nodded again.

"While you're here," Blair said, "lemme give you the latest reports."

She spent the next twenty minutes going over some of the latest keywords trending positively. She then showed me a new report she found with test audiences and trustworthiness of the speaker and took another thirty minutes spitballing ideas with me.

Eric knocked on the door, interrupting the latest idea—a fireside chat, like the old presidential speeches.

"Found something," he said. "Nothing concrete, but something you should know."

"What is it?" I asked.

"Someone from outside the building accessed Paige's computer just minutes before the attack. I'm tracking through what I can to see what she was up to just before the attack. Maybe I can get lucky and find an IP address I can trace."

"Stay on it," I said. "Find me an address we can raid."

"You got it." He left, presumably back to his office.

I looked to Blair. "Your sushi's making me hungry. I'm gonna take Shep to grab lunch and then we'll put our heads together over this."

Blair nodded. "Sure. And Jess?"

"Yeah?"

"No hard feelings," she said. "I mean it. I absolutely get why you had to ask me. I'm a human, and I'm not your pack."

I patted the doorframe. "Thanks, Blair."

Shep and I grabbed some quick tacos on the way back to his place. The pack was out back tossing a football around when we got there. We had the house all to ourselves.

No prying ears.

No.

Knock it off thirsty brain. We aren't getting involved.

"When will your commercial air again?" Sheppard asked.

"*Our* commercial will air during the Super Bowl."

Maybe I shouldn't have put so much emphasis on that first word, even if I did like the thought of something being *ours*.

"I know that," he said, tearing open a wrapper. "I mean when during the game."

"Oh," I said around a bite of taco. "It'll be the first commercial to air during the very first commercial break of the game. I figure everyone will already have their snacks and drinks, and no one's going to need to use the bathroom yet."

"Good thought," he said.

"Blair said brand recall from the first quarter commercials is something like twenty percent higher than those in the last quarter, so doing it later is risky. Especially because if the game isn't even close, lots of people won't stay till the end."

Shep jerked his chin toward the backyard. "We could include some of that as part of the ad."

I looked over my shoulder as the pack rammed into the guy who had the ball, tackling him to the ground in a messy—and sweaty—dogpile.

"Blair did say football was one of the things positively trending," he said.

"I like the idea," I said. "But we should probably leave out the chasing and the dogpiling."

"So... not woofball then."

That's when the person at the bottom of the dogpile stood up, shrugging off the attempts of no less than four of the pack trying to pull him back down.

It was Kristos. Holy shit he was strong.

"You can't be serious," I said, turning back to meet his gaze.

"Why not?" He took a bite from his taco.

"I mean, we could include part of it. Maybe one person throwing? And then another shot with someone catching it? But the bigger issue is, you call that 'woofball?'"

He shrugged. "Jonathan started it, but it's growing on me." He eyed the backyard where the game was clearly fizzling out and then leaned close, dropping his voice to a low murmur "Don't tell them I said that last part." He winked at me.

And it made me wet for him.

Fuck.

The pack piled back inside then, everyone spreading around the house to cool off before showering. One of Sheppard's wolves—some tall and lanky kid—laid down flat on his back on the tile floor, his limbs all stretched out like a starfish.

"Jamie," Kaylah huffed. "I'mma hafta mop thanks t' you!" Her pink blouse was sweat-stained, and she had a grass stain on the hip of her jean shorts.

"Just show me where you're keeping the supplies," the one on the floor said, "and I'll do it once everyone's showered."

The wolf with the wavy dark hair to his shoulders peeled his black t-shirt off and wrung it out, the sweat splattering to the floor.

Kaylah spun on her heel. "*JONATHAN!*"

The wolf who'd just wrung out his shirt—Jonathan, I guessed— held up a hand. "Don't worry, Kaylah, I got it!" He stepped over and grabbed the lanky guy's ankle, pulling him through the sweat puddle.

But then the lanky guy broke free of the others' grip and Jonathan's expression turned to one of 'oh shit' before he darted up the stairs. The lanky kid ran after him as a door slammed upstairs. It opened again a split-second later.

"*JAMIE!*" Lynn squealed.

"He dragged me through his sweat!"

"And yours," Jonathan said.

Kaylah stormed over to the bottom of the steps. "I'mma drag you both through a patch 'a brambles if y'don' come down 'n' clean it all up!"

I looked to Sheppard. "What's got them all riled?"

"This is just my pack." He shrugged. "Some days they're calm and relaxed, other days they're like a mischievous litter of puppies."

"Some of us aren't pups," Naiya said, not looking up from her phone.

"No," I said with a sigh. "Some of you definitely aren't."

THIRTY-SIX

*** (SHEPPARD) ***

AS WE FINISHED UP our tacos, there was a knock on the door and I stood to answer it.

It was Kaan, in a grey linen button down shirt that was opened at the neck with the sleeves rolled up to his forearms. He wore slim-fit blue jeans to match it and I mentally stopped myself from readjusting my own pants at the thought of his being that tight.

"Hi Sheppard," he said. "I heard Jessica is here"

Jess stood and came over to the door. "What's up Kaan?"

"Well..." He cocked his head to the side. "I guess—now that I think on it—you're not quite the person I need to see." He craned his neck past me as Naiya turned to the door.

"Kristos is in the shower," she said.

And then a little purple crystalline spider clambered up onto Kaan's shoulder from behind him. A *familiar* little purple crystalline spider. It made an excited little chitter as it clambered back down the front of him and shot across the floor to Naiya.

"What the hell is that?!" Jessica said.

The last time I'd seen that spider, he'd been on the shoulder of a young man on the other side of a closing rift.

Naiya's face scrunched into confusion and she put the phone down on the coffee table. "Chad...?" She bent down to him and her eyes went wide as the little creature chittered again and danced his way onto her hand. "Chad!"

"I, uh... have someone who's looking for you," Kaan said.

It couldn't be.

Naiya stood and took a step toward him. "... Andy?"

Kaan stepped out of the way with a smile to reveal someone who was as tall as Naiya, the guy she'd sent back through a rift nearly six months ago. He had dark eyes and a mess of light brown hair that waved to his ears and he wore a loose, cream-colored shirt with purple and black trim over brown pants that clung to his legs and tucked into his scuffed and worn black boots. His shirt was cinched at the waist with a black leather belt, and a purple pouch hung at his hip. Around his neck was a black leather cord, from which dangled a purple iridescent amulet that pulsed slowly with a pale light. The rhythm of it matched his heartbeat, which was absolutely pounding.

Andrezmes Kjelliho, if I recalled correctly. Though he preferred Andy.

"Naiya!" he exclaimed as she ran to him.

Chad clambered quickly up to her shoulder as she slammed into Andy hard enough that it knocked the breath from him in a whoosh.

Andy pressed a kiss to the side of her head and held her tight to himself for a moment, his eyes closed as she melted against him, before he grabbed her shoulders and pulled back from her.

"Naiya," he said excitedly. "You're *from* Arcaniss!"

"I know," she said, matching his excitement. "Kaan showed me a rift and I got these weird abilities, and—Andy—it was like I'd never even been *breathing* properly until I poked my head through on that side!"

He pulled her tighter to him then as the little crystalline spider skittered over the tops of both their heads, his feet somehow managing *not* to get caught in either one's hair.

Then Naiya pulled away. "Wait. How on Earth did you get here?!"

Andy turned sheepish.

"The rift reopened," Kaan said. "And he fell through."

Naiya narrowed her eyes at Andy. "You *tore* it back open, didn't you?" She smacked his bicep lightly. "I told you not to *do* that!"

He grabbed her hand. "And I told you I wasn't going to listen." He kissed her hand and then her forehead. "Meddling in the boundaries is what I *do*, Ny."

"Okay, smarty," she said. "Then how are you gonna get back home now? There's no magic here."

Andy shrugged and gestured to the door. "I can tear open that rift again. The fabric between my world and yours is weaker there." He turned to Kaan. "I could probably just set up a stable portal there if you want a way to go back and forth?"

Kaan shook his head. "Nah, there's a place down south I can go if I need that. Just close it up tight behind you please, I don't need rift cats tearing up my home."

"Wait," I said. "What's down south?"

"There's someone in..." Kaan thought a moment. "Corpus Christi, I think, that has a portal that goes straight to the Adamo stronghold."

Corpus Christi. I looked at Jess, who was already looking at me.

"*Suiaerl mitne*," Andy said. "That can't be true?"

"He's not lying," Jess said.

Kaan shrugged. "It's been open down there for... at least sixteen years, I think?" He looked at Andy. "And why would I *lie* about something like that?" He pressed a hand to his chest. "I'm a *silver*, Andrezmes. I have more integrity than that."

"No, no." Andy shook his head. "Of course you do. I just... didn't know the Adamos would have something like that."

Naiya picked up his glowing amulet. "What's this?"

"It's kind of like a... battery?" He said. "It absorbs wisps of power and just kinda hangs onto them. It's attuned to me, though, so it allows me to power my magic with it. And then it just reabsorbs the energy once the magic has run its course and I can use it again. It's a little bit of diminishing returns, but there's enough threads of power showing up here with the rifts that I could... theoretically..." His voice dropped to a low mumble as his cheeks colored. "Stay here indefinitely?"

"Andy..." Naiya said.

He looked up then, excitement lighting his face as he bulldozed past what he'd just said. "I did some digging. Do you know wereleopards just skipped generations in your family? Your parents weren't leopards, but your grandfather *was*."

Naiya blinked at him and shook her head. "Why would you... *How* could I possibly know that, Andy?" She smiled. "Are they—?"

He deflated then. "No... they all died in Luca's war." He looked up at her. "I'm sorry Naiya."

What a rollercoaster.

"'At's a lot to be throwin' at a girl all at once," Kaylah said, gesturing to the table. "Sit, y'all. Lemme getcha some food." She looked up at Kaan. "You too, handsome. We got plenty."

As they sat down, Andy leaned close to Naiya's ear. "I still love you, y'know."

Tears filled and immediately spilled from Naiya's eyes as she closed her mouth against his for a long moment.

"I still love you, too," she said when they finally split.

That's when I noticed Jessica. She was staring into space, her mind clearly working overtime. I brushed my fingers against hers, the spark causing her to blink and focus on me. When she did, she gripped my hand and pulled me closer.

"Can we go somewhere and talk? Alpha to alpha?" She gestured between us with her free hand. Her other still held mine like it was the only thing tethering her to her chair.

I gave her a gentle smile. "Sure. Where do you wanna go?"

"Throw some pants on," she said. "Let's go for a ride."

THIRTY-SEVEN

*** (JESSICA) ***

ONE SIMPLE, OTHERWORLDLY ACT. That's what it took. If mates weren't real, then why would he have come back from an *entirely different world* to find Naiya.

Love.

I believed in love, sure. But love doesn't do that. Not *just* love.

Love alone couldn't make you rip holes in reality to get back to someone.

But mates probably did.

I'd always thought of the word as just a bastardization of 'soulmates,' which I *definitely* didn't believe in.

But Andy had come back for Naiya.

And they still loved each other so much that the energy of it filled the room.

"What'd you want to talk about, Jess?" Sheppard's

voice through the helmet comms cut into my train of thought.

It was that time of day photographers call the golden hour—where everything is bathed in this beautiful golden shade thanks to the ongoing sunset—and I'd taken him out to my favorite back roads, letting him borrow the Supersport again.

"I wanted to ask you if you knew yet where you were taking the pack?" I bit my lip inside my helmet as I waited for his reply.

"Well," he said. "I think New York is out. It may be a big city, but there is already a pack there, and they're likely to move around the city once they clear the area they're in."

"Sounds like going there would leave your pack playing second fiddle to the New York alpha," I said. "And he didn't make it to the meeting, I might add."

Sheppard's helmet bobbed as we cruised along the riverbed that I'd raced him on before.

That had been just a couple weeks ago, hadn't it? In just a couple of weeks, he'd gone from a fellow alpha whom I respected to... well... more than that. And it had gotten complicated on me.

"We'd probably bump heads then," Sheppard said, breaking my train of thought again. "But then, there's not a pack in Kalispell, and there is *plenty* of space. So that's definitely an option."

I furrowed my brow. "I know you told me before, but where the hell is Kalispell again?"

"Montana," he said. "The space should help us with privacy for being your public focus."

"Sure," I agreed. "But it's gonna be a hell of a lot harder to schedule flights. Where's the nearest major airport?"

"There's a regional one, but the best option is gonna be flying in and out of Spokane, which is about four and a half hours west. And I can hop a little regional plane and make the trip in like an hour plus airport time."

"You don't exactly sound enthused about that option."

"No vampires there," he said. "Matt'd go stir crazy."

"And that's a logistics nightmare I don't want to have to deal with when I need you and I in the same place for this PR stunt. What else you got?"

He chuckled. "New Orleans. It's overrun by vamps right now. It'll be a hell of a fight, but it'd be worth it. Probably make for great PR, too."

"More like you're gonna get yourselves killed."

He slowed down and his helmet turned my way. "Why are you trying so hard to talk me out of going anywhere? You don't do 'it's complicated,' remember?"

I *don't* do it's complicated.

I don't do labels.

But his question made me realize that... I *didn't* want him to go. And I shouldn't have cared. If he was just like every other alpha, I wouldn't give a shit whether he stayed or went.

But I did.

I cared.

I gave a shit whether he'd leave.

"Jess... ?"

"I— I'm not," I said. "I just... don't think those places are good for you."

Because I can't tell him that maybe I'd changed my mind about things, or that maybe I'd be *open* to changing my mind about things, not when I wasn't even sure he'd want to stay.

"I mean," I hurried to add. "You see it, right?"

"Sure," he said. "But I can't stay here."

"Why not?"

"You know why, Jess. Whatever's between us? You don't want it. And I'm not gonna sit around pining after something I can't have like a lost little puppy. And you don't deserve to have to watch it even if I did." He looked up to the sky and then back to the trail in front of him. "It's gonna be hard enough with this damn PR stunt."

Pine after me? He was pining after me?

I took a deep breath and blew it out slowly.

And then another.

"Why does it explode your brain when I use your

name?"

His helmet turned to me and then back onto the road. "What a non sequitur."

"Does that mean you won't answer the question?"

He shook his head. "I just... no one has used that name in a very long time."

"But it's on the treaties," I said.

"Yeah," he replied, swerving around a boulder in the dried up riverbed. "Because my full name had to be."

I narrowed my eyes, thinking. "How long is a long time?"

He shook his head again. "I haven't counted. Haven't had a reason to. My parents were the last to use it with any regularity."

"Were? How long have they been gone?" I sensed we were digging into a sensitive topic and slowed down. Shep only ever talked about his past as it related to the present.

He sighed into the microphone of his helmet. "They passed something like five hundred years ago, give or take."

My eyebrows shot up. "No one's called you Tobias in five hundred years?!"

"Sheppard was the only name George could get me to reliably respond to when he found me."

"George?"

"Buckheim."

"The General?!"

He clicked his tongue. "That's the one."

"You're telling me that the General—who sent people after me—is the wolf who took you in when your parents died?! How old were you? How did you not end up like him?"

"I was in my late twenties," Sheppard said. "And he wasn't always like he is now. My parents—my pack—we were a Church pack when I was growing up, until the Church sent my pack on a losing mission. We took out most of the vamps in the nest they sent us to, but not enough to keep them from killing nearly everyone. Buckheim had just lost most of his pack to the same brood, so when he found me unconscious among the bodies, he took me in. He wasn't part of the Church then. I don't think he works closely with them even now, but I suspect it's close enough."

"And that was when you turned away from the Church," I guessed. I hadn't known he grew up in a Church pack. He knew the dogma well enough that it certainly made sense.

He nodded. "The Church was responsible for my parents' death—for my pack's death. They knew that brood was too big for one pack, but they wouldn't send a second. Instead, they sent the largest they had."

"Shit, Shep."

"Tobias," he corrected, his voice soft. "At least from you."

I looked over at him, we were barely going twenty miles an hour now. "Tobias."

His bike swerved a little.

My thoughts turned back to my initial question. It was too easy to envision him and his pack caravaning away.

My heart panged at the thought.

I didn't want him to leave.

"Look," I said. "I... I don't..." I sighed. "I don't want you to go. I want you here. And I'm not gonna try to pretend like I don't. And yeah, maybe I feel something for you. How could I not? You're charming, and smart, and a damn great alpha to your pack and there's any *number* of reasons on top of those." I huffed out a breath. "But... one question. Just one."

He nodded. "Shoot."

"Do you only want me because I'm an alpha?"

"Do I...?" He snorted. "Look, Jess. If you don't think you're an equal mate for me, that's all you had to say." He chuckled. "But you're kinda my best option."

Best *option*?!

I pulled my bike around in front of his and broke hard, skidding to a stop as I tore my helmet from my head. Sheppard swerved and nearly laid down the bike trying not to hit me.

"Your best option?!" I didn't bother to keep my voice down, no one was around to hear us. "Who the fuck do you think you are?! I'm *every bit* your equal, and you'd be fucking *lucky* to have me as your mate!"

He took off his helmet as he swung a leg off the Supersport. "I mean... you said it Jess, not me." He was beaming playfully at me.

He was *fucking* with me.

"You absolute—"

He closed the distance to me and wrapped an arm around my waist, pulling me against him as he lifted me to bring me eye level to him.

"Listen here, you little shit," he said. "I'm in love with you, and now I *know* you feel the same."

Warmth spread through me, pooling between my legs, but also spreading through the rest of me.

"Oh do I?" I tried to play it cool, but his face told me he saw through it.

"You do." He shook me gently. "So stop fucking around and just let yourself be happy for once." He sobered. "Or are you gonna tell me you *don't* feel anything when we touch." He raised a hand and brushed the back of his fingers against my cheekbone.

I leaned into his touch, electricity following in its wake.

Mine.

I shook my head and lightly smacked his hand away. "Of course I feel it too, you dolt. But... I... Put me down already!"

He did, but he kept his hand on my hip.

"Look," I said. "You might be okay with what I do in the studio. And you'll probably never challenge me for leadership of my pack—"

"Or I'll challenge you all the time." He rolled a shoulder.

I rolled my eyes. "Until you get tired of losing. But that's not the point. I just... I don't think I'll *ever* want the kind of family you used to talk about. The kids and the white picket fence. That's just not me, Sheppard."

"I know that, Jess." He sighed. "You're probably the

most incredible woman I've met in my entire life. So let me tell you what someone dear to me once said: there's more than one type of family." He ran a hand through his hair. "I've spent my whole *life* building a family of my own. And I thought at first that was just the pack, but the meeting showed me I have family all over this country. You've seen it. Most of the wolves that are in already for your PR stunt are doing it because they trust me enough that if I'm in, they're in." He put his hands on my shoulders. "I wouldn't have seen that if not for you. So maybe we'll have kids—"

I made a face.

"—maybe we won't." He shook my shoulders. "As long as I'm with *you*, and my pack, I'll have all I want."

He... wasn't lying.

"You... actually mean that."

"Of course I do."

And then his mouth was on mine—or mine on his—our tongues dancing. I wasn't sure who started it or who leaned into who, but it didn't matter. The warm scent of him suffused my senses, the faint hint of tobacco lingering on the far edge along with something I couldn't quite name.

It felt like coming home.

The kiss turned darker as the sun sank below the horizon, and I reached for the button and zipper of his jeans. He was rock hard behind them and I broke the kiss to drop to my knees to taste him. I pumped him hard, getting him slick with my own saliva and his precum as he thrust against my mouth and hand. Then I stood and he hurriedly helped me out of my shorts and underwear, lifting me onto the bike so he could thrust into me. I rolled my hips along with his as best I could, trying to be cognizant of the bike's balance point, but it didn't take long for me to lose my concentration on that as I ground my hips against his thrusts. When my ecstasy tore through me, it drenched the space between us and splattered to the cracked earth below us. He kissed me then, and I bit his lip as he thrust harder and faster into me, pumping over and over until the ecstasy took him as well.

But there was nowhere to cuddle or bask in the afterglow here.

I bent to pick up my shorts and underwear as he lifted his jeans back into place.

"You always go commando?" I asked him.

He huffed out a little laugh. "Less to take off, should I need to change."

"Careful, alpha," I said. "You never know what I might do with information like that."

He wrapped an arm around me and pulled me close to him again, closing his mouth against mine for a brief moment before pulling away. "I should hope you'd use it wisely... and often." He winked as he released me again.

"I think it's my turn to buy you dinner," I said.

"I might say no," he replied.

"Like hell you will," I said, levering up onto my tiptoes to nip his lip. I dropped my voice to sultry tones. "You'll say yes, and you'll beg me to stay the night."

He smiled darkly at me. "I don't beg, Jessica."

There was that fucking tone again.

Jesus Christ, I had it bad for him.

I gripped the bulge of his jeans and kissed his chin. "Well, good then." I stepped over to the Diavel and revved the engine as I lifted my helmet from the ground. "First one to the house picks the restaurant!" I shoved on my helmet, jumped on my bike, and dashed off before he'd even gotten a leg over the Supersport.

I beat him back to the house, of course, but only by a handful of seconds.

"I feel like I know that one road," he said, taking off the vest he'd borrowed.

I nodded. "You should. That's where we told the Church they couldn't have Naiya. It's near the spot where a rift tends to open every couple of days. Most of the time, nothing comes out, but sometimes, my packmates have to try to fight things off." I shrugged. "I set Kaan to keep an eye on it. He seems to be able to make it close pretty readily."

"I still can't get over the fact that *that guy* is a dragon that's just walking around in human form like it's not even a thing."

"I don't think it is for him," I said. "He seems to spend more time on two legs than he does on four."

"Kinda like we do."

"Sure. Except this is our base form and we're just sometimes wolves. He's always a dragon and just sometimes a human."

"About that thing we did for Naiya... Or, rather, the thing *you* did... Have I shown you my appreciation for that?" He bent to place a kiss on my neck.

"Mmm, I think you'll have to remind me," I said. "Like tonight, after dinner, when you come back to stay the night."

"Planning on a night of little sleep, are you?"

"Aren't you?"

"Touché," he said, booping my nose.

))))) 🐾 (((((

I think it was the best food I'd ever had at that particular downtown steakhouse, though I'll admit it might've had something to do with the company. He even followed me home and we had a nice romp in the sheets before settling down into each other's arms.

And while I wasn't sure I was ready to call him my mate, I certainly felt more at ease knowing that he simply loved me for *me*. Not because I was an alpha, not because I was some hot girl on a stream, not because I had the largest pack in the country, not because I could give him the family he'd always wanted.

Because I was me.

And maybe because the sex was good. Because *damn* was it good.

But we were two alphas. Two packs.

What did we do about that? I certainly wasn't going to give up mine, and I would expect he'd feel the same.

I could work on integrating them all into my pack. It wouldn't be hard.

"What's the face, Jess?" Sheppard moved his face into my field of view. "You seem a little lost in thought."

"I'm thinking of what to do with your pack."

"What we do with *both* our packs if we're going to be together."

"Exactly." I nodded. "I mean, I could fold your pack into mine pretty readily, it's not like it'd be the first time I've added so many at once."

Something in his posture changed. His chin lifted a fraction of an inch, and he shifted a smidge away so he could turn to face me. "I could fold yours into mine." There was a challenge to his tone.

I waved a hand. "I don't think that would go as well as you think it might. And do you know how to manage that many wolves? The delicate balance between too tight of a hold and just loose enough that they trust you instead of blindly following?"

"I could manage it," Sheppard said.

"Perhaps," I said. "But I bet you'd step on some toes and drive some away unintentionally while you figured it out."

"You could help me."

"That's my pack, Shep."

"And that's mine, Jess."

"You could try handing your pack off to someone," I offered. "Someone in the pack, I mean. Maybe Kaylah?"

"Hand off the pack and just *stop* being alpha?" His eyebrow rose.

I snorted. "There's always gonna be alpha in you, Tobias." I kissed the underside of his chin. "That's probably why I like you."

There was a spark of something mischievous in his eye and he let out a growly little laugh as he pounced on me, rolling me onto my back. "You mean you love me."

I rolled my eyes. "You're gonna make me say it, aren't you?"

He placed a light, spark-laden kiss to my chin. Then another on my collarbone. Another between my breasts. "I highly doubt *anyone* could make you do something you didn't want to." His voice was a low rumble.

It made me hot for another round.

His kisses drifted lower, and he nipped lightly at my hip bone before they drifted even lower, running along my inner thighs. "But I might not give you what you want if you don't." His breath on my already sensitive folds sent a shiver through me.

I squirmed, rolling my hips toward his face to try to get that warm mouth against me, but he moved it away. I squirmed closer and he moved even farther away, a playful smirk on his face. When he did it a third time, I grabbed his face and pulled it up to meet my gaze. He balanced himself with a hand on either side of my hips.

"Yes, *Tobias*," I purred, watching him turn to putty with a sultry smile. "I love you."

MINE.

And something surged within me. It was like a cord got pulled taut between Sheppard and I. My brow furrowed as I sat up and closed my eyes to concentrate, my hands still on Sheppard's face.

There, branching off my subtly sparkling ties to the pack was a bright, iridescent cord that pointed straight at the wolf hovering inches away from me.

How long had that been there?

In any case, I was sure it was the thing that had been pulled taut. It vibrated with the energy between us.

Sheppard shifted on the bed and I opened my eyes as he put his hands over mine. I released his face and he pulled my hands to his chest as he rested his forehead against mine and inhaled deeply. His heart pounded, but its beat matched mine perfectly.

No one's heartbeat ever matched mine.

I matched his deep inhale, closing my eyes again as I whispered, "I love you."

The cord between us thrummed again, shining like a suncatcher crystal. And I could swear I could see the rainbows it cast around my heart like it was a physical space I could exist in.

His mouth closed against mine then and iridescent fire lit the cord as the electricity of the kiss sparked against my lips.

"I love you too, Jessica," he said, and the cord grew somehow even more taut.

Or perhaps it just thickened.

Another kiss sent more iridescent fire along its length, and I hooked a leg over Sheppard's hip, smoothly swapping places with him on the bed as I lowered myself onto his hardened length. I watched the cord as I rolled my hips along his, watching it thrum and pulse with light.

Mates were real.

And this one was *mine*.

THIRTY-EIGHT

*** (SHEPPARD) ***

JESSICA WAS MINE. I was hers as much as she was mine. But she was mine.

Mine.

Yes, yes, wolf. She's ours.

She stirred gently awake in my arms, her leg curling around my thigh as her golden eyes fluttered open.

"Good morning," she said.

I smiled at her. "That, it very much is."

She kissed me then, slow and deep. "I owe someone a private session today."

"And you have to go right now?"

She turned and tapped her phone screen till the clock came on. Nine fifty-seven AM.

"Maybe not *right* right now," she said. "But I do need to prep to head to the studio. I set it for eleven today."

She bit her lip and looked at me, thoughts swirling behind those beautiful golden eyes.

"You could... I mean... If you wanted to come and watch—"

I kissed her forehead. "Next time. When you're sure you want me there."

She let out a small sigh.

"Besides," I said. "I need to have a chat with my pack."

She nodded and stretched and it was so damn sexy that I pulled her onto my lap.

"Hey!" She laughed.

"Don't worry," I said. "I won't keep you from your private session." I lifted her hips and guided her down onto me. "I'm just giving you a reason to come back to me."

She bounced in my lap a few times before she rolled her hips along my length, grinding against me as I thrust into her.

And then, as abruptly as it started, I lifted her off of me and kissed her deep.

"You... unnf."

I pressed my fingers into her, my thumb swirling around her clit a few times.

Mine, whispered my wolf.

I brought her right up to the edge of ecstasy before slowing down and stopping.

"Let your patron finish what I started," I said. "You'll come back to me for more."

"I will, you know," she said, a dark and sultry promise hiding behind her eyes.

"I know," I replied. "I trust you."

She rolled out of bed then with a grump and plodded over to her closet. She came out of it a moment later with a pair of shredded black jeans and an oversized grey shirt. She tossed those on the foot of the bed before going over to her dresser. She picked out some bits of black and red lace from the drawer, and—when she put them on—I twitched to be inside her once again.

But I stayed very still on the bed, watching her cover that deliciously sexy underwear with the jeans that clung to every curve and contour of her legs. She then pulled the grey shirt over her head and tucked the front of it into the waistband of the jeans.

"You can't just hide out here in my bed all day," she said.

"I could."

She shook her head. "No no, come on Alpha. You just said you've got a pack to explain some things to."

"And you don't?"

"Mine have mostly guessed what's going on," she said. "I hear there's a running bet on when and whether we make it official."

I nodded. "Alright, alright."

I got out of bed and pulled my black slacks on, following it with my white button down. As I sat at the foot of the bed to put my socks and shoes back on, Jess bent to zip up her boots, giving me a *fantastic* view of her ass as she did.

I smacked it with maybe a little more force than I intended to, but her yelp was delicious.

And those golden eyes blazed as she spun around and pointed a finger at me.

"You can smack my ass all you want, but I can't smack yours? Hardly seems fair Ms LaRoux."

She narrowed her eyes at me, but dropped her hand. "You're lucky you're so damn sexy."

I laughed and we headed out and down the hall, passing the laundry room, where a lanky kid who was a handful of inches shorter than me was moving clothes from the washer to the dryer. He had dark hair, but the striking bit was his golden eyes. I'd nearly forgotten Jess said she had a kid in her pack.

"Hey, Aunt Jess," he said, waving.

"Hey Oliver," she replied. "Lemme know when Levi and Em clear you for a motorcycle lesson, okay? You'll be legal for it next month."

"I know, right?" He sighed. "But mom's still convinced I'll be an organ donor."

I chuckled. "She underestimates werewolf healing."

Jess looked over her shoulder at me. "She's an ER

nurse." She looked back at Oliver. "I'll talk with her."

"Oh would you?" Oliver's eyes got wide.

"Sure." She nodded. "I can't guarantee she'll say yes when I'm done, but I'll talk with her."

Oliver threw his arms around Jess and hugged her tight. "Thanks, Aunt Jess!"

I waited till we were out in the garage, with the door shut to tell her, "Cute kid."

"Shut it," she said. "I love him to bits, but I'm glad I didn't have to change his diapers or wipe his snotty nose."

I laughed and kissed the top of her head. "See you later, Jess."

She smacked my ass before kicking a leg over her Diavel. "Count on it."

I walked across the gravel driveway to the house we were borrowing. Those who were up just kind of stared at me as I came into the house, grabbed a bottle of water, and headed to my room to shower in my ensuite bath.

I sniffed the collar of my shirt. Lavender and cloves. Of course.

Mine.

I nodded as I pulled my clothes off and showered. I took care of myself to the thought of Jess bouncing on my dick while I was in there, and threw on a pair of grey sweatpants afterward. I headed back out to the living room, still rubbing my hair with a towel. Lynn and Jonathan were on one side of the sectional, while Naiya and Andy were on the other. Matt and Chastity sat between the two couples, filling the last of the available space on the couch. Kristos sat cross legged on the floor, his jewelers tools spread out on the coffee table in front of him. Daniel, Jamie, and Ian all sat at the dining room table, while Kaylah put away the cereal and toast.

I stopped her and grabbed a bowl full of Fruit Loops before heading over to join the three at the table.

Kristos leaned his elbows on his knees as I shoved the first bite of cereal into my mouth. "So, you and the little alpha next door, huh?"

I raised an eyebrow. "You and the dragon she knows, huh?"

"Fair point," he said with a chuckle.

"What does that mean for us?" Ian asked.

I paused in bringing the next spoonful of cereal to my mouth, milk still dripping back to the bowl. I hadn't really had a chance to consider what being mated to another alpha would mean for the pack just yet.

"Well," I said slowly, shoving the bite of cereal into my mouth to stall, "we should probably discuss that."

Kaylah brought me a glass of juice, and I took a swig, thinking quickly before continuing.

"Jessica is... my mate," I said, naming the thing hanging unsaid in the air. "So, the way I see it, there's a couple of options available to us. I could put you all under her leadership..."

The words tasted disgusting as they left my mouth.

The faces around the room of general unease told me that wasn't an option even if I could have stomached it.

"But I like that about as much as the rest of you do, which is to say, not at all. I may be in love with her, but I have a duty to make sure you folks are alright."

"I'd never let anything hurt us," Matt said.

I gave him a gentle smile. "Not everything you face will be fightable, Matt. At least, not in the physical sense."

Kristos snorted.

"Why don'tcha call up one a them alphas from the meetin'?" Kaylah said, coming to sit at the table. "I'm sure some of 'em've seen what happens when two alphas fall in love 'n become mates."

I shook my head. "I'd rather not involve another alpha in our business any more than they already are with this PR stunt with Jessica. I've spent a few of my favors just to get them to meet with her."

Daniel leaned forward on the table. "Are you suggesting instead that you perhaps hand leadership to one of us?"

I paused before answering. I suppose I could try to pass along the leadership of the pack. I didn't really like that idea either, but...

"I think the only one who might be able to manage

that is sitting right there next to you." I nodded at Kaylah, who suddenly looked like a deer in headlights.

She laughed. "You think Matt'd listen to me? Hell no!"

Matt snorted as a relief washed through me.

"B'sides," she continued. "I don't have all the c'nections you got with the packs 'round the country—favors used up or not."

"I think you could get Matt to fall in line just fine," I argued, partially for my own benefit—to reinforce her rejection. "But if you don't want it, you don't want it."

She shook her head. "Maybe ask me again in a hun'red years."

Tension released from my shoulders, and I huffed out a laugh. "Want some more experience, do you?"

"Least 'nuff that I can un'erstan' where the other alphas're comin' from."

I nodded and took another bite of my cereal as I considered the options. What does an alpha do when they fall in love with another alpha? What do the packs do? This couldn't be the first time it'd ever happened.

"You could merge the two packs," Kristos said finally. "You could co-alpha."

I blinked at him. "Co-alpha?"

Kristos nodded. "It's been done before. It used to happen a lot more when there weren't as many wolves in the world. Two packs would come together and the alphas would lead them together. Some of the wolves listened better to one alpha than the other, but the pack still worked as a single unit when it counted."

"That sounds like a pretty good option," Lynn said.

"I agree," Jonathan added, squeezing her hand.

I nodded, pieces locking into place as I considered it.

"And it keeps us all together," Ian said.

"We're a *family*, Sheppard," Daniel said. "Maybe not by blood, but by your leadership and guidance."

Kaylah smiled at him and laid her head on his shoulder.

We were a family. Pack is family. And if marriages could bring two families together, why shouldn't mates do the same with packs?

"*Sarcina eiusdem sanguinis*," I said.

Kaylah nodded. "'Zactly."

I smiled as I polished off the last of my cereal. "I'll talk to Jess about it then, assuming you all agree."

"I assume that means we would stay here?" Matt asked.

I nodded. "As far as I'm aware, yes. Some of you might even be good to join her squads debunking vampire videos around the country." I looked between Ian, Chastity, and Lynn.

"I can keep looking into the wolves I've changed back easily enough from here. Maybe even easier, being so close to Jess. Besides... It'll make it easier for Kristos and his dragon friend," Lynn said.

I looked at Naiya, who shrugged.

"This whole concept of 'pack' is too new for me to have any kind of opinion," she said. "And I'm not even sure whether I'm staying or going to Arcaniss."

Kristos pressed his lips in a line.

Andy kissed her temple. "No telling what the future holds, anyway."

I looked to Kristos. "After what happened in the cave with Kaanskkairiskollik—"

Kristos sighed. "You really can just call him Kaan."

"With Kaan then," I said, looking back to Naiya. "After what happened, I suspected you'd be more intent on getting on the other side of those rifts anyway."

Naiya nodded. "It's not like Andy could stay here forever."

"My amulet will keep me powered for an almost indefinite amount of time, like I said." Andy brought her knuckle to his lips and pressed a kiss to it. "But for you? It'd be worth it, even without magic."

Jamie made a face. "God. Does *everyone* who falls in love turn into a mush brain?"

I laughed. "Falling in love isn't the same as mates, Jamie."

"And 'love makes you do the wacky,' as the great Buffy Summers once said," Lynn added.

"Now there's a show I haven't thought about in a

while," Naiya said.

"Who's Buffy Summers?" Andy asked.

Jamie's head thunked to the table.

Naiya laughed. "She's this superpowered girl from an old TV show. She killed vampires."

"In any case," I said, taking a sip of my juice. "It sounds like there's no real objection to talking with Jess about merging the packs." I looked around at everyone, who all gave me some form of visual agreement, whether it be a thumbs up or a head nod. "Kristos, is there anything you know of that has to be done to facilitate that?"

He shook his head. "I was never privy to pack business before now."

"There's likely paperwork to update the treaties with the Church," Daniel said.

I nodded. "Almost certainly that."

My phone buzzed from my pocket. I pulled it out. It was Jess. I thumbed the call over to voicemail and then tapped out a text to her.

> **Me:**
>
> *Meeting with the pack. Wrapping up now. I'll call you back.*

I tucked the phone back into my pocket. "Well, if anything comes up, for any of you." I looked around the room. "Or if you want to talk about it privately with me, you know I'm here."

"I'm jus' glad you fin'ly listened to the parts a ya that knew it already," Kaylah said.

"Told you you had a crush," Jamie added.

I snorted out a little laugh. "You did, Jamie. You did."

"What are we going to do about those '2 Points 4 Lyfe' jokers?" Matt asked.

"I'm working with Eric from Jess' pack to track down what info we can online," Ian said. "Since the attack started with the video feeds to the other alphas going down, and since none of the vamps were particularly powerful, tracing the online activity back to its source is our best option."

"And when we have something," I said, "we'll make a plan."

"I'm itching for that fight," Matt said.

"I know you are," I replied, standing and taking my bowl to the kitchen.

After depositing it in the sink, I padded back to my room and called Jessica back.

She picked up on the first ring. "Did you know that on the south side of town, there's one neighborhood in the middle of a whole bunch of old construction that's wired for ultra-fast connectivity?"

I smiled. "Sounds like you have a lead."

"I do," she said. "There's a house in that neighborhood with too much power going in. Eric says the IP address coming from that connection point matches a user—" She cut herself off with a growl.

"What is it?"

"CrimsonMoonrise87," she said.

The last time I heard her voice that full of growl was back when we were fighting the Anglican church.

"It's a username connected to a 2 Points 4 Lyfe message board," she said. "Where they last posted minutes before the attack."

"Breathe, Jess," I said gently. "It sounds like there's something else to it. You weren't even this angry that the vamps attacked."

"That asshole has been on my streams for months," she said. "He's the one I owed the private session to today."

A low growl rumbled through me, and the bottle of water in my other hand crumpled, spilling water to the carpet of my room.

Mine, snarled my wolf.

"My thoughts exactly," she said. "I'm going to delete my account and set up a new one on a different site after Eric gets our new network security in place. I'll have to start over, but I'll be more secure."

I dropped the crumpled bottle into the bathroom trash can and grabbed the towel from my shower, dropping it onto the spilled water and stepping on it to soak it up.

"It's always gonna be a risk." I raked a hand through my hair as I blew out a breath. "But I'm not going to stand in the way of what makes you happy, even if I do absolutely *abhor* the idea of a vampire having such intimate access to you."

"You can't hate it any more than I do." She blew out a breath. "When can you be ready to raid the house?"

I looked out the window and checked the time on my phone. It was barely past noon. "We have plenty of daylight left. I'll be ready to go as soon as you get back here."

"Great," Jess said. "See you in fifteen. And Shep, please don't—"

"No one needs to know how close the vamp got to you unless you want to tell them," I said. "I'm certainly not introducing them to your side hustle."

I could hear the smile in her voice as she said, "Thanks," and ended the call.

It was all I could do to keep myself from destroying something bigger than a bottle.

I took a deep breath. I would get my chance. I just needed to be patient.

CrimsonMoonrise87 was done for.

THIRTY-NINE

*** (JESSICA) ***

SHEPPARD'S SCARRED WOLF, MATT, had wanted to come with us, but I told Sheppard to call him off. The pit fighter of a wolf made us promise to call for backup if we needed it...

Well, he made *Sheppard* promise.

I made no such deal.

I had zero interest in anyone potentially finding out the vamp's connection to me. Aly and Im would never let me hear the end of it.

The ride over to the house in Sheppard's truck happened in a seething silence. He gripped the steering wheel tight, took turns just a little too fast, and his jaw muscles worked the whole time. Worked out just fine for me, because I was practically seeing red.

We pulled into the driveway of an old red brick

ranch-style home with white shutters and a shingle roof. The front yard was a little overgrown, the shrubs unkempt. No cars were in the driveway, but every light in the house appeared to be on, based on all the windows, despite it being early afternoon. Coming up to the front door, it smelled of rot and decay, but not the rot and decay of vamp—the rot and decay of multiple dead bodies. Bursting into the house, we found bodies propped up on chairs and couches like an entire house party had been invaded and slaughtered. A banner hung across the room, the words 'see you in hell, WHORE' spelled out in what I was sure was blood.

And we couldn't smell anything beyond the rot.

When we finally did find the office, and the computers, I was so angry I could have burned the whole place to the ground and torn the vampire there limb from limb. The same graffiti that had been on the outside of my PR office was repeated here along three of the four walls of the room.

But there was no vampire in the office. Nor in any of the bedrooms. And there wasn't a basement to the house.

A monitor flickered on as we came back to the office, and words spelled themselves out on the screen.

Congratulations, whore!
You found NOTHING!

The computers immediately started to smoke, and then, with quiet little pops, they burst into flames. Sheppard had the forethought to grab the computers on our way out, but—by the time we got them disconnected—the flames had already started to spread up the walls and along the carpet.

We got out of there before the smoke was too bad—before any of the neighbors would have called any emergency services.

We got the computers back to the house and Ian met up with Eric to head over to the PR offices to see what they could manage to pull from what was left. We suspected we wouldn't find anything.

And with nothing else to go on, we had nothing else we could do about 2 Points 4 Lyfe. At least, not yet.

I hated that he'd gotten the better of us. That he was still out there. And all signs pointed to him being the coordinator of the attack that brought ten to fifteen vampires to my town under the radar and then threw them at my door at perhaps the most inopportune of times. And he was still out there. I'd tear him apart when I found him.

))))) 🐾 (((((

"What do you know about co-alpha's?" Sheppard asked, apropos of nothing.

"Never heard of such a thing," I said.

We'd gone for another ride out to the empty roads and the riverbed. The mid-September sun was still hot, baking the already baked clay where the barely-better-than-a-creek used to run, so we were again in just the armored vests with helmets. Some light clouds dotted the sky, but none of it was cover enough to provide any real relief from the heat.

"Kristos said it'd been done in the past," Sheppard said. "He said we could basically merge the two packs and co-alpha."

"Co-alpha?"

"Well," he hedged. "You'd have a hell of a time getting Matt to follow your orders if you tried to be his alpha."

I shrugged. "It might be worth giving it a shot at least."

"It'd likely make us the largest pack in the world," he said.

"I kinda like the sound of that."

"Of course, we should probably have some kind of

barbeque or party to see how the packs mix before making a final decision."

"Smart," I said. "I can make sure my pack is free for something like that tomorrow."

He pulled in front of me and rolled to a stop before taking off his helmet. I did the same, pulling out my hair tie and shaking my hair free in the evening breeze.

"In a hurry, are you?" He raised an eyebrow at me.

I simply met his gaze, my expression flat as I stepped over to him. "When you finally figure out what it is you want for the rest of your life, dicking around about it seems kind of pointless."

"I like the sound of that," he said.

He leaned down then to press a static-lined kiss to my neck, nipping playfully at the tender skin there as he came back up to meet my eyes.

"You know I am so completely yours, don't you?"

I smiled. "I do indeed." I beckoned him closer with a curled finger. When he bent down, I whispered in his ear. "Do you know the same is true for me?"

He beamed at me. "I suspected as much, but I'm glad for the confirmation."

Mine.

Yes, wolf. Yes he was.

FORTY

*** (SHEPPARD) ***

THE MIXER WAS A hit. My pack was co-mingling with everyone, and they all seemed to be making new friends. The mid-afternoon sun was still much hotter than our pack was used to for September, and practically everyone was either shirtless or in a sports bra and tank top. Jess was in blue jean cutoff shorts with black boots and a sleeveless black crop top that tied across her back with little more than string.

I sidled up to her. "How'd you get your whole pack to show? It's hard sometimes to wrangle even just my ten."

She shrugged. "I just told them all to call in sick for a pack-bonding day. We do that every now and then. I can't get the traveling members here that quick, obviously, but those guys are all super flexible and are used to coming back to new pack members. And this isn't even all of them, a few couldn't move things around on short notice. It was Levi's turn on call, for example, and Shawn had a client meeting that he needed Mikaela for as well."

"I hope to one day be as familiar with these guys as you are," I said.

"You will be," she replied. "Everyone seems to be getting along, so this co-alpha thing may just work. We'll do something more official next week, and have a couple more of these after."

"That sounds great," I said.

A large silvery shadow passed overhead, flying through the clouds before there was a small burst of iridescence and then a much more human-shaped Kaan appeared next to Kristos, fully-clothed in pale linen. They exchanged a greeting before Naiya and Andy pulled Kristos aside for a chat.

"Kaan," Jess started, stepping over to lightly backhand his bicep. "I told you people will see you!"

Kaan shook his head. "I don't fly over any houses on the way here." He angled his head and studied her. "I have been in this world quite some time, you know. I've kept my presence hidden for this long."

"Yeah, Jess," Imogen said, bending to bump her hip against Jess. "Besides, what are they gonna do? Send cops to look for a private jet that doesn't exist?" She huffed out a little laugh as she gestured around the area. "You don't even have a shed that could maybe possibly be mistaken for a hangar."

"And I am silent as the grave while flying," Kaan said. "Certainly, far quieter than even the quietest plane."

Jess crossed her arms. "I still wish you'd be more careful, Kaan."

He winked at her. "Do not worry for me, *moxt daariv*."

Before Jess could respond, Naiya and Andy came up to me and Jess, Kristos in tow. The couple's excitement was a sharp contrast to the morose and somber Kristos, which told me just about all I needed to know about what was coming. Kaan read the incoming situation and, with a nod of his head, made himself scarce, pulling Imogen along with him.

Naiya watched the two of them make their way over to the coolers full of beverages before turning to me. "There's no gentle way to say this, but—"

"You're going to Arcaniss with Andy," I said.

She nodded.

"I can't protect you there, Kitten," Kristos said, his voice rough. "I don't belong there."

"I know," Naiya said. "But I don't belong *here*."

"I know." Kristos blew out a breath and ran a hand through his long dark hair.

"I won't let the Church know you've gone," Jess said. "They'll figure it out eventually, but I'll keep them in the dark as long as I possibly can."

"Hopefully our outing the werewolves will keep them busy enough that they don't have the time to notice," I said.

"Fingers crossed," Andy said, doing just that with a lifted hand.

I pulled Naiya into a hug and dropped my voice so low I was relatively sure only she could hear it. "*Sarcina eiusdem sanguinis*, Naiya. You will always have a pack here."

And then I caught sight of Lynn. Jonathan was holding her as she cried.

I didn't know she and Naiya had gotten close enough for that.

"It's because of me," Kristos said, catching my gaze. "She can feel it."

"He hates it," Naiya said, tears filling her eyes. Andy squeezed her hand and she looked at him. A single tear rolled down her cheek, but she smiled at him with a radiance the sadness couldn't touch as she blinked her watery eyes clear with a sniffle.

Andy wiped a thumb across her cheek and kissed her temple.

I nodded. "You belong with your mate though." I looked at Andy and held a hand out. "Promise me you'll keep her safe."

"On my life," Andy said, clasping my wrist with a

surprisingly tight grip.

He meant it. I nodded once as I returned the grip on his wrist.

"Take the truck," I said, tossing Kristos the keys from my pocket.

He caught them in midair and nodded.

"You take care, Naiya," I said. "Remember what I told you."

"I will, Shep," she said. "And thank you. For everything. You too, Jess."

"Of course," Jess said. "I'm not letting the Church just have their way whenever they want simply because they think they're entitled to it."

Naiya smiled before hooking her arm in Andy's. The two of them turned toward my truck, Kristos following along behind them.

Ian brought a couple of beers over to Jess and I, keeping a third for himself.

"*Sarcina eiusdem sanguinis*," he said, quietly.

I smiled and tipped my beer toward him. "Sure."

Jess looked between us. "What?"

"*Sarcina eiusdem sanguinis*," I said. "The blood and the pack are one."

"Oh wow," she said. "I haven't heard that since before my parents passed."

I put an arm around her waist and pulled her close. "Some things are worth keeping around that long." I clinked my beer bottle against hers and took a swig.

She followed suit and then levered up on her tiptoes to kiss me. I returned the kiss, and our tongues danced long enough that when we came up for air, Ian had wandered off.

I huffed out a little laugh.

"Whoops," she said. She watched as Jonathan pulled out the football and gathered our pack together with some of Jess' to teach them woofball.

"Oh no," I said. "Looks like you're never going to be free of the silliness of that name."

She rolled her eyes. "It's not that bad." She took a sip of her beer. "Oh! I meant to tell you. I don't care if your pack finds out about my stream. I just didn't want—"

"Their intro to it to be because of a vampire?"

She smiled and her shoulders relaxed. "Yeah."

"I get that," I kissed her forehead.

The flash of a camera went off and Imogen, in a purple sports bra and black bike shorts, started to practically cackle.

"Proof!" She laughed some more and turned the phone around.

Jess' smile in the picture was probably the softest and gentlest thing I'd ever seen. Certainly the softest I'd seen from her.

"*Proof* that our spitfire alpha is just a big softie," Imogen crowed.

Murder crossed Jessica's face and Imogen took off at a run, Jessica hot on her heels.

"You delete that right now, Imogen!"

"What was that?" Imogen feigned ignorance. "'Post it to the pack's chat server?' If you insist!"

It took her a second, but Jess caught up to Imogen and wrestled the phone from her hands just as my own phone buzzed with a notification.

There it was, the pic Im had just taken, right there in the general chat for the whole pack to see. She even tagged everyone so you couldn't miss it.

I couldn't help but laugh.

FORTY-ONE

*** (JESSICA) ***

THREE MONTHS LATER, WE sat in the big conference room, my feet propped onto Sheppard's lap. Blair had the final cut of the Super Bowl ad for us to go over, and both Sheppard and I were eager to put eyes on it.

"This'll be the final cut and then we'll send it in for their ad team to review," Blair said, hitting the lights. She pointed her remote at the screen and started the ad playing.

It opened on Sheppard, sitting in a comfy leather chair in an all-American living room, complete with hardwood floors and Americana decor. Next to him, a fire crackled in the hearth. The camera pushed in on him as he leaned forward to rest his elbows on his knees.

"What if I told you that everything you think you know about vampires and werewolves is nothing more than propaganda?" He held eye contact with the viewer for a moment and nodded before sitting back in the chair. "My name is Tobias Sheppard. I'm five hundred and forty-four years old. And I am a werewolf."

The commercial then cut to Lynn in a spacious backyard. A golden retriever ran through the frame as she tossed a football toward a group of guys that were out of focus.

"My name is Lynn Cartwright," she said. "I'm twenty-five years old. And I am a werewolf."

The commercial cut again to a clean and crisp kitchen, where a bowl of granny smith apples sat on the counter. The camera panned over to Kaylah, who was putting an apple pie into the oven.

"My name's Kaylah Abernathy," she said with a smile. "I'm a hundred an' fifty-six years old. And I am a werewolf.

The commercial then cut yet again to Daniel, who sat behind an ornate wooden desk in his office as his assistant handed him a file of paperwork.

"My name is Daniel Chapman..."

The camera cut to Jonathan, who caught the football Lynn had thrown in the earlier shot.

"Jonathan Holt," he said.

The camera then cut to Chastity, who was in a different kitchen, kneading dough with flour-covered hands. Her curly auburn hair was pulled back in a look that was both effortless and elegant. She tossed a stray curl out of her face as she smiled at the camera.

"Chastity McAllister..."

The commercial cut to Ian then, who turned away from the laptop sitting open on the desk alongside a computer monitor. There's a document open on the laptop screen, and the computer monitor had a black screen with white code on it.

"Ian Peterson..."

And then the commercial cut to a stretch of Route 66, where three motorcycles approached the camera. The front bike came to a halt, and the two behind followed suit. The front driver pulled her helmet off to reveal a shock of maroon hair that shook loose from her ponytail. The other two drivers also removed their helmets to reveal a blonde with long, curly hair and a rail thin blonde with hair to her shoulder blades and an intense gaze. The Route 66 sign was visible in the background.

The camera focused on the curly haired blonde.

"Alayna Powell..."

The camera panned to the blonde with the intense gaze.

"Imogen Stiles..."

The camera then focused on me.

"Jessica LaRoux."

The camera cut back to Daniel at his desk.

"I'm one hundred and five..."

A quick cut to Jonathan, still holding the football.

"Seventy-five..."

The commercial then cut to Chastity, placing a tea towel over the bowl of kneaded dough.

"One hundred and one..."

Another quick cut, this one to Ian, still sitting in front of the computer code.

"Forty..."

Yet another quick cut to a close-up of Aly.

"One hundred and forty-two..."

And a quick cut to a close-up of Im.

"Eighty-five..."

And finally, it cut back to me. I leaned forward onto the handlebars of my Diavel.

"... Three hundred and fifteen years old."

Quick cut back to Daniel.

"And I—"

Quick cut to Jonathan.

"I—"

Quick cut to Chastity.

"I—"

Quick cut to Ian.

"I—"

Quick cut to Aly.

"I—"

Quick cut to Im.

"I—"

And finally, a quick cut to me.

"*I* am a werewolf," I said. "There are more of us than you think." And then I winked at the camera.

The screen then faded to black and simple white text faded in that read

find out more at WerewolvesAreReal.org

The text stayed on the screen for a handful of seconds before fading back to black.

"Oh wow," Sheppard said.

I nodded. "No kidding."

"You like it?" Blair asked.

"That's absolutely fantastic," I told her. "I can't believe you managed to make us all look so..."

"Believable?" Blair supplied. "It's not like it's hard. You're all telling the truth."

"Trustworthy," Sheppard said. "You made us all look like we were the kind of safe people you want to have around when the shit really hits the fan."

"That's not exactly hard to do either," Blair said. "I'm glad you like it. We have until next week to get it sent in, but I'm going to send it off in the morning—just to be sure they have the time they need to review it."

"It looks really great," I said as Blair stood to turn on the light. I squinted at the sudden brightness.

"Oh look," Sheppard said, looking at his phone. "You have just enough time to get a good session in before dinner."

"Come and watch?" I offered.

His golden eyes glittered hungrily. "Gladly."

EPILOGUE

*** (ETHAN) ***

"*I* AM A WEREWOLF. There are more of us than you think." The redhead on the screen—Jessica LaRoux, co-alpha of the San Antonio Basin pack—shoves her helmet on and zooms away on her motorcycle.

The next commercial starts up, but I turn the TV off and look at you.

How you're standing here is beyond me, but there you are nonetheless.

My voice is mocking as I press a hand to my chest and bat my eyelashes. "I'm Ethan Prescott, and I'm a *vampire*." I drop the mocking voice and my hand. "Can you believe that fucking *whore* beat me to it?! And all because these fucking bloodsuckers would rather slit each others' throats than work together!"

There is a wall of nine computer monitors behind

me, with three computers—which were all top of the line when they were rebuilt a month ago—running three of the screens each. The top row has various threads from the 2 Points 4 Lyfe message board. The second row has a screen with that whore's pack chat server on it, a screen with a live feed of her office security cameras, and a screen with the replays from her new cam girl stream. It was hell breaking into their new systems, but I'm too good for that whore to keep me out for long.

"Oh, you think changing sites and screen names would keep me from fucking with her? She's a two-bit whore, but she's also a squirter." I don't bother to hold in my sly smile. "And she's one of the few whose orgasms are as real as the heartbeat I get when I feed." I shrug. "I could find my entertainment elsewhere, but—of course—you aren't the type that could really understand why continuing to use her streams to get my jollies off appeals to me."

I consider your face.

"Then again, perhaps you could... It's about power, you see. She doesn't know how much of it I have over her. And it'll stay that way until my plans are all in place."

The bottom left screen blinks with a message, and you point at it, drawing my attention to it. It's in Japanese. Or at least, that's what Google translate tells me when I shove the nonsense into a search bar.

My printer prints a flight itinerary with a confirmation number as my eyes scan the words.

Your flight leaves in the morning.
You'll get your boarding pass at the
airport.
Don't miss it.

I grab the paper from the printer and wave the itinerary at you. It's a flight to Tokyo that leaves in a little over six hours.

"Kitashihime," I spit the name like an expletive. "Now

that's a flight I won't be on. Meeting with her will only end with me in ashes." I shake my head. "No fucking thank you. If that bitch or the Russian prick wanted different results, they should have listened to Frederick or Zacchaeus." I tear the paper in half and then in half again, tearing it further into smaller and smaller bits of confetti. "Fuck that whole 'don't mess with the alpha's' bullshit and their old world rules." I throw the confetti in the air. "You don't win a war without taking down the leaders." I smile at you. "Just you wait. It will be glorious. Maybe you'll even get to live to see it."

AUTHOR'S NOTE

You can actually visit
www.WerewolvesAreReal.org
to view a facsimile
of the site
that Jessica sets up
in the story!

ABOUT THE AUTHOR

Born and raised in Texas, Becca Lynn Mathis has been writing stories and daydreaming about other worlds since she was a little girl reading books in the branches of the tree in her front yard. As she grew, so did her love of stories, so much so that she often got in trouble at school for writing them, even if her other work was already done.

Today, she is a graduate of Lynn University in Boca Raton, FL with her B.S. in psychology. She is a dreamer of the highest order, involving herself in as much storytelling and geekery as she can manage, whether that's playing Dungeons & Dragons (or Pathfinder), prepping a musical performance for the next local renaissance or pirate faire, or simply getting lost for hours playing video games like Beat Saber or World of Warcraft. She lives in sunny South Florida with her amazingly supportive husband and their awesome blended family.

Be sure to visit her website and sign up for her newsletter to keep up to date about the rest of the Trials of the Blood series!

www.beccalynnmathis.com